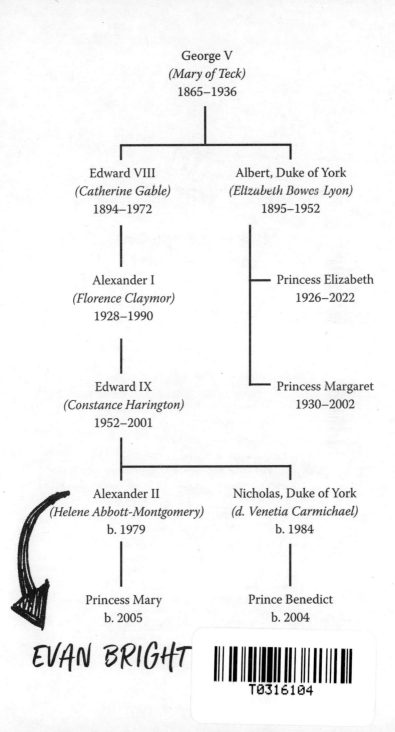

George V
(Mary of Teck)
1865–1936

Edward VIII
(Catherine Gable)
1894–1972

Albert, Duke of York
(Elizabeth Bowes Lyon)
1895–1952

Alexander I
(Florence Claymor)
1928–1990

Princess Elizabeth
1926–2022

Edward IX
(Constance Harington)
1952–2001

Princess Margaret
1930–2002

Alexander II
(Helene Abbott-Montgomery)
b. 1979

Nicholas, Duke of York
(d. Venetia Carmichael)
b. 1984

Princess Mary
b. 2005

Prince Benedict
b. 2004

EVAN BRIGHT

T0316104

For Ro and Allison

First published in the UK in 2023 by Usborne Publishing Limited, Usborne House, 83-85 Saffron Hill, London EC1N 8RT, England, usborne.com

Published by arrangement with Rights People, London

Usborne Verlag, Usborne Publishing Limited, Prüfeninger Str. 20, 93049 Regensburg, Deutschland, VK Nr. 17560

Text copyright © Aimée Carter, 2023

Author photo © Taylor Lee

Cover images: woman © Shutterstock / Dean Drobot; crown © Shutterstock / Subbotina Anna; ripped paper © Shutterstock / AVS-Images

A CIP catalogue record for this book is available from the British Library.

ISBN 9781803701721   7847/1   J MAMJJASOND/23

Printed and bound using 100% renewable energy at CPI Group (UK) Ltd, Croydon, CR0 4YY.

AIMÉE CARTER

ROYAL BLOOD

USBORNE

Content note

ROYAL BLOOD is a work of fiction but deals with many real issues including mental illness, abandonment, classism, sexual assault and murder

Chapter One

To be a king and wear a crown is a thing more glorious to them that see it than it is pleasant to them that bear it.

—Queen Elizabeth (b. 1533, r. 1558–1603)

Breaking into the academic wing of St Edith's Academy for Girls isn't the most reckless thing I've ever done, but it definitely comes close.

What makes the whole thing exceptionally irresponsible is the fact that I have only one week to go until graduation. In one week, this nightmare that has been the past six years of my life will end, and I'll never have to set foot in a boarding school again. I should do the smart thing and stay in my dormitory, where my roommate is crying into her pillow and thinks I can't hear her. But I've built my reputation on never doing the smart thing, and there's no point in subverting royal expectations now. And so, at ten o'clock on a Monday night, I creep down the windowless corridor in complete darkness, my fingers brushing against each door handle as I pass. Though it's almost impossible to navigate without banging into something, the lack of light also works in my favour. I've already disconnected the sole ancient security camera – the only piece of technology allowed in St Edith's hallowed halls – but there's always a chance a custodian might be lurking, and all the careful planning in the world won't hold up against someone else's outrageously good luck.

I stop in front of the fifth door on the right and dig through my pocket. The lockpicks were a Christmas gift to myself last year, and while I've practised on my dormitory door, I haven't had the chance for real-world application until now. A thrill runs through me as I hold the lock taut with the tension wrench, nudging each tiny pin one by one with the pick in my other hand. Headmistress Thompson would spontaneously combust if she knew what sort of education I've been giving myself while everyone else has been vying for acceptance into Harvard and Yale, but this is quickly becoming the most worthwhile thing I've learned since arriving at St Edith's in January.

The lock gives way before I expect it to, and I almost drop my tools in surprise. I've done it – I've actually picked a lock. Pretty sure it won't win me an award anytime soon, but it feels like a superpower, and adrenaline courses through me as I push open the door.

Creak.

The hinges complain loudly, and I freeze. As my heart pounds, I remain perfectly still, listening for any sign that someone's on their way to investigate.

Nothing.

With a renewed sense of urgency, I slip into the classroom. Calculus. Not my favourite. When you start trying to apply logic to the imaginary and infinitesimal, the rules get murky, and I

6

like knowing the rules. I read the code of conduct for St Edith's – along with the eight other boarding schools I've attended since the age of eleven – cover to cover, and I can quote whole sections in a pinch. Knowing the rules, after all, makes it easier to manipulate them. And to break them in spectacular fashion.

Moonlight shines through the stained-glass windows, offering a kaleidoscope of relief from the oppressive darkness, and I hurry on silent feet to the teacher's desk. Mr Clark isn't a bad person. He's just stuck teaching in an archaic system that values test performance above learning, the same way I've been stuck in a Vermont forest for the past five months thanks to an archaic system that values image above family. We're both victims of circumstance, and I already feel a hefty dose of guilt for what I'm about to do. If there was a better way to handle this, I would, but there isn't. So here we are.

The single drawer in his wooden desk is also locked, but I have it open in under thirty seconds. And there, nestled between stray pencils and paper clips in all its hunter-green glory, is my holy grail.

The grade book.

It doesn't take me long to find the right page, and I tear it out with a single satisfying *rip* before pulling a lighter from my pocket. While St Edith's draconian ban on technology makes life infinitely more difficult than it has to be, this is the one time it works in my favour.

The paper browns and shrivels as the flames devour it, leaving behind curls of grey ash. I'm not a pyromaniac, but there's something poetic about all that hard work disappearing in seconds. Everything is temporary. Even permanent records.

"*Evangeline Bright!* What on earth do you think you're doing?" The overhead lights buzz to life, and I wince. Headmistress Thompson stands in the doorway, her hair in curlers and her face purple. I've never seen her in anything other than a matching tweed skirt and blazer, and I'm so transfixed by her shabby pink robe that for a moment, I forget what I'm doing.

"Put that out," she demands, her voice shaking. "At *once*, Evangeline!"

"I would," I say slowly. "But I'm sort of all in on this now, you know? And it's only one page. Mr Clark will barely even miss – *ow!*"

The flames reach my fingertips, and I hiss in pain, dropping what's left of the burning paper. As Headmistress Thompson and I both watch, it floats down onto the desk – and lands right in the middle of the grade book.

Within seconds, the entire school's math grades go up in flames.

Headmistress Thompson gasps, her face now a sickly mottled colour. "The fire extinguisher! Where—"

But as she darts back into the hallway, clutching her curlers, I'm rooted to the spot – by shock or disbelief or dissociation, I don't know. All I can do is stare as the hungry flames grow bigger and brighter, until they spread to the pile of dry timber that is Mr Clark's desk.

Shit. *Shit.*

I rip off my cardigan and try to smother the flames, but they're too strong, and all I accomplish is setting my school-issued sweater on fire. A spark jumps onto my skirt, threatening to catch, and I bat it away, my pulse racing.

It was only supposed to be a page.

"Evangeline!" booms Headmistress Thompson from the doorway. "Get away from there!"

"I—" I begin, not sure if I'm about to apologize or insist that I can put it out with my smouldering cardigan, but it doesn't matter. Headmistress Thompson surges through the thickening smoke and seizes my elbow, yanking me away from the blaze.

There's a dull roar in my ears, drowning out whatever it is she's shouting at me, and as she drags me into the dark hallway and towards the nearest exit two corridors down, I glance back at the classroom. The fire is spreading, faster than the single missing fire extinguisher could handle, and I'm dimly aware that the anaemic alarm going off is identical to the bell that rings when class begins. I don't know much about buildings, but I'm pretty damn sure that none of this is up to code.

At last, as Headmistress Thompson shoves me through the side door and into the cool night air, I take a deep gulp and stumble across the grass, my lungs burning and my eyes streaming. We turn back towards the school, and our mouths hang open as flames shatter the stained-glass windows of Mr Clark's classroom in an explosion of rainbow shards.

Well. At least it's spectacular.

Chapter Two

Watch out, Britain! We're less than a month away from Princess Mary's eighteenth birthday, when the traditional media coverage restrictions on underage royals are lifted, and the world is champing at the bit. What kind of juicy gossip will rise to the surface? After a lifetime of private tutelage and being sheltered from the limelight, is our enigmatic future queen ready for the scrutiny she'll face now that the silk gloves are coming off?

We'll certainly see plenty of her in the weeks to come, as Her Royal Highness has reportedly already sat her A levels and is expected to make a splash during the jam-packed social season this summer. Trooping the Colour, Royal Ascot, Wimbledon – according to our royal sources, she'll be there for them all.

What will she wear? Will she have a date? And most important, how long will it take for our beloved princess to headline her first royal scandal?

—*The Regal Record*, 6 June 2023

I'm sitting inside an interview room at the police station, staring at my haggard reflection in what must be a two-way mirror, when the door opens for the first time in hours.

A brawny officer stands on the threshold, a deep frown etched onto his bulldog face. We lock eyes, and even though I'm nauseated from exhaustion and the fear that's been simmering in the pit of my stomach all night, I keep my expression painfully neutral. I know better than to say a word without a lawyer present, but it also means that he and the rest of what passes for a police force in the tiny town near St Edith's all believe Headmistress Thompson's *highly* dramatized story about what went down in Mr Clark's classroom. And while I haven't had the pleasure of hearing the entire scintillating tale, judging by her wails the night before as another officer took her statement, it doesn't exactly paint me in the best light.

I brace myself, expecting yet another round of questions I won't answer, but instead the officer crosses his arms over his broad chest. "Evangeline Bright," he says gruffly, "you're free to go." I stare at him, not sure I've heard right. After nearly ten hours in this room with only a plastic water cup and a ticking clock for company, I'm expecting handcuffs and a court date, not freedom. But before I manage to form a question I shouldn't be asking, the officer steps aside, revealing a balding Englishman with a trimmed salt-and-pepper beard. And suddenly I understand.

"Jenkins!" I leap to my feet, even though my whole body aches after spending all night in an agonizingly uncomfortable chair. "The police said they couldn't get ahold of you—"

"Your headmistress contacted me first," he says, stepping past the officer as if he isn't even there. "I was already on the plane when they called. Are you hurt? When is the last time you had anything to eat or drink?"

I shake my head, suddenly aware of the fact that my mouth

11

tastes like a dirty sock. "I don't know. It doesn't matter. What happ—"

"You left a minor alone in an interrogation room overnight without proper bedding or sustenance?" says Jenkins, rounding on the officer. "Has a doctor examined her? Or have you neglected to even consider the harm smoke inhalation may have caused?"

While Jenkins has roughly the same muscle definition as a newborn kitten and is hardly what anyone would call physically intimidating, I swear the officer flinches. "Wasn't my shift," he grunts. "Take it up with the sergeant."

Jenkins gives him a look so searingly English that, despite everything that's happened, I have to bite my tongue to keep from grinning. "I most certainly will," he says imperiously. "Unlike you and your co-workers, *I* do not neglect my duties."

The station is bustling now that it's morning, and as Jenkins leads me to the exit at a pace that makes it clear anyone in our way will be bowled over without a second thought, I can feel every pair of eyes on us. On me. And I know exactly what they're thinking.

Who the hell am I?

There's a black SUV idling at the kerb, and a chauffeur wearing a holster and a plastic earpiece greets us with a nod as we step into the bright morning sun. Once we've both settled into the bucket seats that make up the middle row, the chauffeur closes the door firmly behind us, and Jenkins sighs.

"A felony this time. Impressive, Evan."

"I try to exceed your expectations every chance I get," I say, but one stern look from Jenkins, and I bite the inside of my cheek. "I'm sorry. It was only supposed to be a single page out of the grade book, but Headmistress Thompson—"

"Do you understand what will happen if the police decide to charge you?" says Jenkins, and while he doesn't raise his voice, his tone sends a chill through me. "Five years. That is the sentence here for arson in the second degree. Five years of your life, down the drain, all because of a single choice you made without considering the ramifications."

"But – it was an accident," I say, my voice breaking. "I never meant—"

"A judge will not care about your intentions, only the outcome of your actions." Jenkins shakes his head. "I've always feared that you would eventually find yourself in the kind of trouble I cannot get you out of, and it seems that day has finally come."

I stare at the ragged ends of my bleached hair, which, despite my best efforts, are still tinted green from dye that hasn't fully washed out in a year. "If I were Mary, no judge in the world would convict me," I mumble.

"Perhaps not," says Jenkins, gentler now. "However, you are not Her Royal Highness. You are you, and that is the life you must live."

"But – I'm his daughter, too," I say, hating the way my voice hitches. "Not that he cares."

A beat passes, and I can feel Jenkins's eyes on me as I pick at a split end. "I sent a courier to retrieve your things from St Edith's," he says at last. "It seems your roommate was exceptionally helpful."

"Prisha's one of the nice ones," I say quietly. No matter how much distance I've tried to keep between us, she's never held it against me.

"The courier met us at the airport," says Jenkins, and he pulls something from the inner pocket of his suit. "According to him, Miss Kapoor insisted I deliver this to you post-haste."

I look up, and Jenkins offers me an envelope with my name written in Prisha's flowing cursive – mostly a lost art form, but a requirement at St Edith's. I take it suspiciously, and as I do, I realize there's something inside other than paper.

Frowning, I peel open the flap, and a platinum bracelet slides into my palm, complete with a single charm in the shape of a music note. I recognize it instantly. In the five months we've slept in the same room, Prisha's never taken it off.

"This isn't mine," I say, confused, and I fish around for the piece of folded notebook paper inside. Instead of the letter I expect, Prisha's only written two words.

Thank you.

That's it. No greeting, no signature – nothing. Just her gratitude.

I stare at her swooping script for longer than I should as something in my chest tightens. Prisha and I aren't exactly close. We're on decent terms – I long ago learned my lesson about antagonizing the people who have unfettered access to everything I own – and we've occasionally helped each other with homework. But we've never sat together during meals or spent any of our free time together, and we never swapped numbers or addresses or social media handles – none of which I have anyway – because we were never friends in the first place. We simply exist in the same space, and that's how it has to be. That's how it always has to be.

But as I gently refold the note and tuck it back into the

envelope, I let myself wonder what it'd be like if things were different for once. If I accepted Prisha's invitations to spend time with her and her friends, or if we talked about more than essays and homework assignments. It wouldn't change anything, though, and I force myself to let those thoughts go. There's no point inviting that kind of hurt when there's no cure.

Instead, I focus on the bracelet and latch it around my wrist. I can't remember the last time someone gave me a gift – a *real* gift, not something picked out by an employee. My father likes to send me expensive jewellery and cashmere sweaters, and for my twelfth birthday, he even bought me a tiger that lives in the London Zoo. But considering I've never met His Majesty, they feel more like bribes than presents. Bribes to keep my mouth shut. To behave. To not embarrass him more than I already do by existing. "I spoke with your mathematics instructor, Mr Clark, this morning," says Jenkins as we pull out of the parking lot and onto the highway. "He told me that you missed only one question on your final exam, and you were at the top of your class."

"Of course I was. I paid good money for that grade," I quip. Jenkins ignores me. "He also mentioned that your roommate failed the exam, and she was dangerously close to losing her place at Dartmouth next year."

I shrug, running my fingertip along the sharp tail of the eighth note. "Guess that explains what all the crying was about." Jenkins pats my knee the way a doting grandfather would.

Or at least the way I imagine a doting grandfather would. "You're a good person, Evan. It's a shame you don't believe it."

"You're the only one who does," I say, so softly I'm not sure he hears me.

We're both quiet for a minute. He doesn't feel the need to fill the silence, and neither do I. But his presence is reassuring, and despite everything that happened last night, I feel like I can exhale for the first time since arriving at St Edith's. He knows this, I think. He could easily send someone else to pick me up, someone who doesn't live an ocean away, but no matter what kind of chaos I cause – or, apparently, how much bail money is involved – he's always there.

"I don't have to repeat my senior year, do I?" I say, almost too afraid to ask.

Jenkins raises an eyebrow. "Considering you spent the night in a police interrogation room, that ought to be the least of your worries. However," he adds, drawing the word out, "given your stellar academic performance, with a bit of blackmail and financial incentive, I'm cautiously optimistic I'll be able to convince your headmistress to allow you to graduate."

"Blackmail?" I say warily. Jenkins may be willing to do damn near anything for his king, but I can't picture him leaping over that line for me.

"Of a sort," he says. "From what I understand, only a single classroom suffered any significant damage – damage that could have been prevented, had there been a working fire extinguisher on hand. Not to mention any lingering effects you may have suffered due to the smoke. I'll have a doctor meet us at the airport," he adds. "Just in case."

"I'm fine," I insist, but he waves off my protest.

"Any injury will only help our case, both against the school and those incompetent buffoons who call themselves officers of the law."

After seeing the look on Headmistress Thompson's face as we watched Mr Clark's classroom burn, I highly doubt any amount of evidence will ever convince her to let me graduate. "I'm not going back to boarding school, no matter what she decides," I say. "I'll get my GED if I have to. But I'm done."

"You've just committed a felony, darling," says Jenkins pointedly. "I would be hard-pressed to find another boarding school in the country willing to take you, regardless of your feelings on the matter."

Relief floods through me, chasing away the last of the tension in my muscles, and I rest my head against the cool leather seat. "Does that mean I get to go home?"

Jenkins is quiet for a beat too long, and the small flicker of hope inside me dies instantly. No matter the reason, the answer is always no. In the six and a half years His Majesty has had custody of me, he's never given me a single ounce of control over my own life, and I have no reason to think it'll be any different now. "Do I at least get to know where Alexander's sending me this time?" I say, resigned.

"Wherever it is, I expect it will be better than prison," says Jenkins.

"Dunno," I mumble. "I can think of worse places."

He shifts in his seat, and I think he might reach for me, but he doesn't. "I cannot pretend to know how difficult this has all been for you over the years, Evan, but rest assured that His Majesty only ever wants what is best for you."

Yesterday, I would have laughed at that. Bitterly. But after last night, all I can muster up is an exhausted sigh. "How can he know what's best for me when we've never even met? I could walk right past him, and he wouldn't recognize me. I'm no one to him, Jenkins. Just an inconvenient cheque he doesn't even write himself."

"Evan…" begins Jenkins, and I can already hear the protest in his voice.

"Don't," I say quietly. "Please. He's had plenty of chances to show me he cares, and he doesn't. I'm not Mary. I'm not his *heir*. He doesn't want me, and I don't want a constant reminder of that. As soon as I turn eighteen, we're done, and he won't have to pretend to be my father any more." And maybe I can finally stop hoping that one day he'll decide he really does love me after all. "It'll be better that way."

"For whom?" says Jenkins. "If the police decide to pursue the case against you, we have the resources to protect you."

"But you won't be protecting me," I say. "You'll be protecting *him*, in case anyone ever finds out who I am. So I don't humiliate him and the crown."

Jenkins regards me for a long moment, and instead of meeting his gaze, I stare at the chipped purple polish on my nails. "You would rather go to prison than accept our help?" he says at last.

I nod. "Unlike him, I'm not afraid of facing the consequences of my actions."

"Very well," says Jenkins, so softly that I barely hear him. He doesn't say anything else, and neither do I. Instead, I close my eyes and rest my forehead against the window, toying with the music note dangling from my wrist.

Twenty-five days. That's how long His Majesty has left to control my life, and no matter which gilded cage he stuffs me into this time, once those days are up, he'll finally be rid of me – one way or the other.

Chapter Three

Alexander II

From Wikipedia, the free encyclopedia

For other uses, see Alexander II (disambiguation).

King of the United Kingdom and the other Commonwealth realms

Reign:	14 May 2001–present
Coronation:	7 June 2002
Predecessor:	Edward IX
Heir apparent:	Princess Mary
Born:	18 February 1979, Windsor, UK
Spouse:	Queen Consort Helene (m. 2003)
Issue:	Princess Mary Victoria Alexandra Elizabeth
Full name:	Alexander Edward George Henry
House:	Windsor
Father:	Edward IX
Mother:	Constance Harington

Alexander II (Alexander Edward George Henry, born 18 February 1979) is King of the United Kingdom and a further fourteen Commonwealth realms.

Alexander was born at Windsor Castle in Windsor, the first son of the Prince and Princess of Wales (later King Edward IX and

Queen Constance). His grandfather, Alexander I, had ascended the throne seven years prior, making the young Alexander second in line at the time of his birth. He was educated at Eton and deferred a military career to accept a place at Oxford during his university years. Upon the sudden and unexpected death of Edward IX in 2001, Alexander became king at age twenty-two. In 2003, he married Lady Helene Abbott-Montgomery, with whom he has one daughter, Mary (b. 1 July 2005).

When Jenkins and I arrive at a tiny private airport, the royal family's jet is waiting for us on the runway, regal and glimmering in the morning sun. I submit to a mercifully brief examination from a doctor Jenkins has managed to summon, and as soon as she gives me and my raspy voice the all-clear, Jenkins and I board.

I immediately head for my favourite seat – one of four reclining leather armchairs with AIIR embroidered on the headrest, all gathered around a sizable tabletop that extends from the wall of the plane – and as I approach, I spot a slim package wrapped in silver paper resting on the gleaming surface.

"What's this?" I say, knowing better than to assume anything on this plane is mine, but it's excruciatingly conspicuous.

"A graduation gift you do not deserve," says Jenkins, even as the corners of his eyes crinkle with a smile. "I thought you might find it useful."

I sit down in my usual seat and pick up the present, testing its weight. There's heft to it, and while there's no bow, it's expertly wrapped. Confused, I peel the tape back and reveal the box underneath, nearly dropping it in surprise.

"A laptop?" I gasp. "But I thought—"

"Now that St Edith has had her Luddite way with you, it is my hope you will use it for schoolwork come autumn, rather than wreaking havoc on Columbia's internal network," says Jenkins, still lingering in the aisle. "Assuming, of course, you're not rotting in a prison cell."

I run my fingers along the edge of the box. After months without a single electronic device, I'm practically choking on joy. "Thank you," I manage. "I almost forgive you for sending me to that place. *Almost*."

"You did it to yourself, sweetheart," says Jenkins kindly. "Do try to stick to essays and research at university. For the sake of my nerves, if nothing else."

I hesitate. "I, uh…I turned down my acceptance to Columbia."

While Jenkins is usually unflappable, this seems to catch him off guard. "Oh? Have you decided to take a gap year?"

"No," I say. "When I turn eighteen, I'm going to live with my mom."

Jenkins watches me, his gaze piercing. I try to ignore him, but for a split second, our eyes meet, and I hastily look away. I can't take his sympathy right now. Not when I know he sees me – *really* sees me – for everything I am, and everything I'm not. "You're a smart girl," he says at last. "You shouldn't throw away your education like this."

"There's a community college fifteen minutes from her house. They have a good computer science programme."

His expression grows pinched, and I know exactly what he's thinking. The daughter of a king going to community college

21

is so laughable it's practically a sitcom. "Evan," says Jenkins. "Your father—"

"—has had six years to destroy everything that was good about my life, and he's done an excellent job. Now it's my turn. And don't worry," I add as I set the box aside, "I'm going to pay my way through school on my own. I won't ask him for a dime."

Instead of trying to argue, Jenkins simply nods and makes his way towards the back of the plane, which is always stocked with enough refreshments to keep a small country going for a week. While he makes himself tea – possibly coffee, considering the night we've both had – I unbox and power on the laptop. Jenkins has already set it up for me, and rather than clicking the browser or seeing what I've missed on Netflix over the past five months, I open VidChat instead.

My mother's icon greets me, a circle with her smiling face that she hasn't changed in years. Thanks to St Edith's ban on technology and my mom's aversion to talking on the phone, we haven't spoken since New Year's, and I take a deep breath before starting a call. My stomach is in knots at the thought of explaining my arrest to her, and I've already decided it isn't necessary to catch her up on every little detail when a message pops up.

No Wi-Fi networks available.

I curse. As the plane rolls down the runway, I try again, but still nothing happens. After ten thousand feet and several more attempts to connect, I finally close my laptop and curl up in my seat instead. Disappointment gives way to exhaustion, and I decide my mom will still be there after I nap. It's been five months, after all. Another hour or two won't hurt.

When I wake up, groggy and feeling like my mouth is stuffed

with cotton, we're still almost forty thousand feet in the air. I blink and rub the sleep from my eyes. "What time is it?"

"Shortly after nine o'clock," says Jenkins, not looking up from his crossword puzzle. There are more than a dozen seats and sofas to choose from on the plane, but he sits in the chair opposite mine.

"Nine?" I say, confused, and I glance out the window. The sun is rising. Or setting. I don't know which, and a fist of anxiety wraps around my insides. "Wait – are we actually fleeing the country?"

"That is something you and I must still discuss," says Jenkins, and my stomach contracts so hard I think I might be sick. "I can't leave my mother," I say, the words spilling out of me. "Please, Jenkins – I'm sorry, I really am, but I don't care what the police do to me, all right? Just don't put an ocean between me and my mom. I don't want to live in New Zealand or – or Malaysia or—"

"Evan, darling, do you really think your father would send you to the other side of the world?" says Jenkins, clearly taken aback.

"I have no idea," I mumble. After all, I've never even spoken to him.

Jenkins sets his crossword puzzle down. "How many close friends do you have?"

"What does that have to do with—"

"Answer the question," he says gently. "You've been to nine boarding schools in six years. How many friends have you made?"

"Plenty," I lie. Jenkins watches me silently, and I trace the polished wood grain of the tabletop with my finger. "You're my

23

friend, aren't you? And apparently Prisha doesn't hate me, so that's two."

Instead of giving me the withering look I expect, his expression grows grim. "I am sorry," he says. "I've failed you."

"What? No, you haven't." Sometimes I think he's the only person who hasn't. "But – what did you expect me to say? That I've left behind a trail of heartbroken classmates each time I've been expelled? I'm never in one place long enough to get to know anyone that well. Besides, how am I supposed to make friends – *real* friends – when I can't tell anyone who I am? When I have to keep everything about myself secret so no one ever finds out that *His Majesty* isn't the paragon of virtue he wants everyone to think he is?"

"It isn't that simple," says Jenkins. "If things were different—"

"But they aren't," I say, my throat tightening. "And they're never going to be. I know that, and I'm not asking for anything to change, or for Alexander to protect me. All I want is—"

"To go home," he finishes. "Yes, I know. And home is where I am taking you."

I open my mouth, but for a moment, nothing comes out. I haven't been home – *really* home, with my mom in our blue house outside of Arlington, Virginia – since I was four. My grandmother's nearby condo was my home for seven years after that, until she died of a stroke and my royally inaccessible father took full custody. Ever since, home has been nothing more than a pipe dream. Until now.

"I get to see my mom?" I launch myself out of my seat and wrap my arms around Jenkins. It feels about as awkward as I expect, considering I can't remember the last time I hugged anyone, but I don't care. I'm finally going home.

After a beat, however, I realize Jenkins isn't hugging me back. I let go, taking in his stiff posture and the deep furrow between his brows. He doesn't meet my eye.

"I'm not going home," I say, all of the excitement draining out of me, and I sit back down heavily.

"You are," he says, and for the first time in all the years I've known him, he sounds uncertain of himself. "Just…perhaps not the home you're expecting."

"Not the—?" A wave of horror hits me, and I look out the airplane window. The sun is definitely sinking into the horizon. We've been in the air all day. Except we haven't – it's been six hours at most, and a glance at the digital clock above the cockpit confirms my theory. It's only four o'clock in Vermont.

But we're flying over water. Lots and lots of water.

"No." I stand with such force that I bang my leg against the table. "Jenkins—"

"Evan, please sit," he says. I can't, though, and I pace the length of the aisle, my heart beating so rapidly that I think it might break my ribs.

"He can't do this," I blurt as panic spreads through me, seizing every one of my senses. "This – I – he can't *do* this, Jenkins. *Please*. I don't—"

"*Evangeline*." His voice is sharper now, and he catches me as I pass. Holding my shoulders, he stares down at me, his nose an inch from mine. "You know the reality of your situation as well as I do. If you remain in the States and the police decide to charge you with a crime, you'll be completely alone. You have no friends, no close family—"

"I have my mom," I say, and my voice breaks. "He can't keep me from her for ever."

"He isn't trying to keep you from her," says Jenkins. "Her doctors are adjusting her medication at the moment, and she simply isn't fit to care for you right now, especially given your potential legal situation. The stress would be too much."

My eyes well up. Alexander always has an excuse. "He's never given her a chance," I manage thickly. "She's a good mom. She's always been a good mom, and I'm old enough to take care of myself now. She wouldn't have to worry."

"She is a wonderful mother," agrees Jenkins. "Which is exactly why she would worry. And even if you hadn't been arrested, your presence…"

He trails off, but I know exactly what he's going to say. My presence throws her off-balance. I haven't been a regular part of her life since my grandmother took custody of me, and I'm only a reminder of the things she's lost.

"I am very sorry," says Jenkins quietly. "As much as I wish to reunite you, now is not the time for it. And you have nowhere else to go."

His last sentence hits me like a semitruck, and his words seem to echo endlessly between us. He's right – I know he's right. But I don't want him to be.

"Then send me to the Maldives. Or – or New Zealand, or Malaysia. I don't care. Just not there, Jenkins. Okay? Anywhere else in the world, I'll go. But not there."

"This is the best place for you right now, Evan," he says. "You may not believe it, but there are people here who will love you very much, if you let them."

"Who?" I choke out. "*Him?* He doesn't love me, Jenkins. You know he doesn't. He wasn't there when my mom got sick. He wasn't there when my grandma died. All he's ever done is keep me as far away from his life as possible, and – I can't. *Please.*"

Jenkins brushes his thumb against my wet cheek. "I am not asking you to stay for ever, darling. Once we've untangled your legal woes, I will give you your passports, a credit card and a ticket to any city in the world – including Arlington, if you wish. When you turn eighteen, you can live anywhere you choose, any *life* you choose, and you will never have to set foot in the country again. In the meantime, however, you've been alone long enough. It's time to get to know your family."

"But they're not my family," I say thickly. "You think the Queen will bake me cookies? You think Mary will braid my hair and tell me stories about growing up in a palace?"

"I think you need something to hold on to," says Jenkins. "And I fear this may be your last chance."

He lets me go, and I stumble towards the bathroom and lock myself inside. Easing onto the tiled floor, I bury my face in my hands, and as I finally break down and sob, the plane begins its descent into the one place I thought I could never go:

London.

Chapter Four

No one puts an outfit together like Queen Helene.

I'm waiting for Her Majesty in Sapphire, a chic tearoom nestled on a quiet corner in Mayfair, one of London's most exclusive neighbourhoods, when every head turns towards the door. You might think that's artistic embellishment, but when it comes to Helene, Queen of the United Kingdom and the most recognizable woman in the world, there is no such thing as exaggeration.

The first thing I notice is her famous pink sundress from Alexander McQueen's summer 2021 collection, paired with a cream Whistles cardigan Her Majesty confirms is off the rack from Selfridges.

"I don't believe in wearing an outfit once and discarding it," she says in her soft voice after I've enquired about her ensemble – the same one she wore to Royal Ascot two summers ago. "The fashion industry's negative impact on the environment cannot be overstated, and my family have all taken steps to lessen our carbon footprint over the past several years. We only have one Planet Earth, after all," she adds, squaring her shoulders as if she's used to receiving opposition for her humanitarian efforts. "We must show it the same respect regardless of our privilege."

Her sincerity is magnetic, and I feel the eyes of the other patrons upon us. Hovering protectively nearby are the four personal protection officers who remain with her in public at all times – a necessity after the infamous paparazzo attack that saw Her Majesty's nose broken during her pregnancy with Princess Mary – but she remains undaunted. She's a far cry from the timid animal shelter volunteer who married King Alexander at age twenty-one, and as we shift to discussing her outfits for the upcoming social season in London, she lights up.

"Each designer was chosen for their commitment to sustainable fashion," she says, brushing back the new curtain bangs that blend seamlessly into her wavy blond lob, which has become the sensational overnight style of the season. "I'm delighted to have the opportunity to showcase up-and-coming fashion houses from the kingdom and Commonwealth, and each design will be available from their labels for twenty-four hours, with all proceeds going to charity."

Helene may be Queen of the United Kingdom, but her concern doesn't stop at her nation's borders, an endearing attribute that has seen her popularity soar worldwide since her showstopping wedding twenty years ago.

—"The Queen of Fashion", *Vanity Fair*, June 2023

As our car winds through a village fifteen minutes from Heathrow Airport, I think I'm going to throw up.

It would serve Jenkins right if I ruined his shoes, but I keep my mouth clamped shut. I haven't said a word to him since the plane landed. It's the first time in my life I haven't wanted to talk to him, and no matter how many times he insists it'll only be a month, or that it won't be so bad, or that he'll give me everything I ask for when it's over, I still want to scream until my throat is raw and my voice is gone.

No one has ever told me the details of how I came into being, but I'm not an unfortunate accident that happened before Alexander met his wildly popular queen consort, Helene. I was born two years after they married, and it's not hard to do the math on that one. My mom had an affair with the King of the United Kingdom, and I arrived nine months later – on the very same day as the heir to the throne and my only half-sibling, Princess Mary.

I know it's not my fault. It probably isn't even my mom's fault, considering the serious power imbalance between her and Alexander. But I'm the one who's had to suffer the consequences. No one but Jenkins and my parents even knows who I really am, and while I wasn't raised in the royal family, I've done enough late-night Googling to understand exactly how big of a problem my existence is for the monarchy. The people love Helene. She's been on the cover of virtually every magazine in Europe, and I've read more than one headline calling her the beating heart of Britain. If the world ever found out that Alexander cheated on her, it would be the scandal of the century and the defining moment of his reign. Which is why, as the car drives through a gate that leads into the enclosed grounds of Windsor Castle, I have absolutely no idea what I'm doing here.

"This is the preferred residence of the royal family for most of the year," says Jenkins, as if I'm not currently giving him the silent treatment. "Late summers are spent at Balmoral, of course, and Sandringham for the holidays. His Majesty will often stay at Buckingham Palace during the working week, for the sake of convenience, but the royal family considers Windsor to be their true home."

The chauffeur opens the door, and I reluctantly climb out. Jenkins follows, and after a brief word with the pair of staff members waiting to take my luggage from the trunk, he leads me through a side door and into a brightly lit corridor.

It's much plainer than I expect, and I frown, glancing around at the white walls and worn carpet. I'm still furious with Jenkins, but silence doesn't always work in my favour, and this is one of those times.

"This is the castle?" I say at last. "It looks more like one of my old dorms."

"This is a service entrance," he explains as we turn a corner. "The grandeur is mostly reserved for the state apartments."

"So…you're sneaking me in the back," I say. Somehow I'm not surprised.

"Well, you are a common criminal," he says with a glimmer of his usual humour, and I huff.

He guides me through the maze of corridors with ease. Most of the doors we pass are shut, but the few that are open seem to lead into storage rooms or offices. It's nothing remarkable, but my nausea only gets worse the deeper into the castle we go.

It's just another temporary place to stay, I tell myself. No different from the blur of boarding schools and summer camps I've lived in over the years. With any luck, the King will be too busy to bother with me, and if I keep my head down, no one else has to know I'm here. I can do this – I *have* to do this. And as long as no one tries to arrest me again, in twenty-five days, I'll be gone.

As we pass a room full of cloth napkins in every imaginable colour, a middle-aged man with blond hair and no chin stops us. "Jenkins," he says with a respectful dip of his head. "Louis is waiting for you in his office."

"Lovely," says Jenkins, and for once he sounds pleased. "I, er, noticed the royal standard as we drove in. His Majesty is in residence?"

"Just returned an hour ago. It seems His Majesty has decided to spend the rest of the week at Windsor." The blond man glances at me, and when our eyes meet, he hastily looks away.

He knows, I realize. I don't know how, but he does. "Should I inform him of your arrival?"

It might be a trick of the light, but I think I see Jenkins gulp. "If it isn't an inconvenience," he says, and as the man bobs his head again, we continue on.

"Who was that?" I say, glancing backward. The man has already disappeared down another hallway.

"A discreet member of His Majesty's personal staff, and someone you will likely never meet again," says Jenkins. "Now come – there's no time to waste."

I follow him at my own pace, in no hurry to get any closer to the royal family. "Where am I staying? Next to the septic tank or behind the dumpster?"

Jenkins chuckles. "I'm pleased your sense of humour is returning."

But he doesn't give me an answer, and as he ushers me up a narrow staircase, I have to fight the sudden urge to run in the opposite direction. Strange places are nothing new to me, but there's something foreboding about walking through a thousand-year-old castle, knowing my absent father is somewhere inside. My absent father who happens to be the monarch of an entire kingdom and commonwealth.

Two floors later, as we step into a sparsely decorated corridor, I'm about to ask Jenkins if the Tower of London is where the royals still send prisoners when I notice a slim Black man in a navy suit waiting in a doorway. Before I can say a word, he hurries towards us.

"Harry! There you are," he admonishes, though he kisses Jenkins's cheek in greeting. "You didn't leave a note."

"It was urgent," says Jenkins apologetically. "The police were involved this time."

"I see," says the man, and I feel myself flush as his focus slides to me. "You must be Evan. I'm Louis Jenkins."

His dark eyes twinkle with an affection I don't expect, and I blink. "There's another Jenkins?" I say, and Louis chuckles.

"There's only one Jenkins," he says fondly, touching the gold band on his left ring finger. "But we do share a name."

Oh. *Oh.* "You never mentioned you're married, Jenkins."

"You never asked," he says, but the coolness is missing, and the corners of his lips twitch into a smile as he gestures to a nearby door. "Shall we?"

Louis leads us into his office, which is bigger than I expect, with a long desk in one corner, a rack of gowns in another, and several armchairs and love seats scattered about. As I look around, he openly studies me, his gaze moving up and down as he takes in every detail.

"You're a slip of a thing, aren't you? And your hair is more colourful than I was led to believe."

"I trust you can fix that," says Jenkins, eyeing me critically now, too. "She'll need a polish before we present her to His Majesty."

"A polish?" Louis's eyebrows shoot up. "That's putting it mildly."

"I'm right here," I say, flopping onto a sofa beside the door. "And the dye was supposed to be temporary. I didn't know it would turn green and stick around."

"It isn't just the hair, love, though that will certainly be our first priority," says Louis. "The royal family's style is very... *particular*. There are rules, written and unwritten, and if you're going to participate—"

"I'm not," I say. "I'm here for a month, and that's it."

A shadow passes over Jenkins's face. "That is still a month we must make sure you're presentable. Louis is Her Royal Highness's personal stylist, and he can guide you towards the appropriate—" Suddenly heavy footsteps echo in the hallway, and a sandy-haired man strides into the office. The open door blocks me from his view, but from where I sit, I can see him shaking with fury.

"Jenkins," he says, his voice low despite his obvious anger. "What on earth do you think you're playing at?"

Both Jenkins and Louis immediately stand at attention. "Your Majesty," says Jenkins with a bow of his head, and bile rises in my throat. "Perhaps we might speak in private—"

"I need you to explain to me why you thought bringing her here was acceptable, let alone necessary," says the man with sandy hair. Alexander. *King* Alexander II, monarch of the United Kingdom and the other Commonwealth realms, and my supposed

34

father. Who, I realize, most definitely did not know I was coming.

I pull my knees to my chest and open my mouth, but nothing comes out. It's impossible not to know what he looks like – I exist, after all, and I don't live under a rock. But there's something wholly unsettling about being in the presence of someone I've seen in pictures my entire life, and as I stare at the back of his head, all I can think about is that he's shorter than I thought. Not by a lot – a few inches, maybe – but he isn't the towering giant that's lived in my imagination for almost seven years. He's just an average-sized man. And a slightly balding one at that.

"Sir," says Jenkins imploringly, and his gaze flickers towards me, but Alexander doesn't take the hint. "Perhaps there is another place we could discuss—"

"Answer me, Jenkins," he says with sharp, unwavering authority. It's the voice of a man who's never been told no.

Jenkins presses his lips together. "She has nowhere else to go, sir," he says at last, clearly giving up on any semblance of discretion. "And given the, er, incident this morning, there's a strong chance the police will press charges. By keeping her close, it will be easier to protect her, and—" He hesitates. "If I may be frank, it is my strong opinion that this is the best place for her."

"Your opinion has no merit here," snaps Alexander. "*I* am her father. It is up to me to decide where she would be better off, and that place is nowhere near Helene and Maisie."

Maisie. It takes me a moment to realize he's talking about Princess Mary, his *real* daughter, and the queasy feeling in my stomach turns hot with shame and devastation as something inside me shatters. Maybe it's the hope I've clung to all these years that he might secretly love me after all, or maybe it's every lie I've told myself about happy endings. But whatever it is, it's in pieces now, and I'm left aching in its wake.

Before I can stop myself, I sit up straighter, my fingers digging into my shins so hard that I wouldn't be surprised if I have bruises tomorrow. "If you don't want me here, then send me home," I say, cutting Jenkins off as he starts to respond. "It's obvious you'd be doing both of us a favour."

The King jerks around, and I see my father's face in person for the first time. His eyes are blue, his brows bushy, and as his otherwise unremarkable features go slack at the sight of me, I feel like someone's plunged a knife into my gut. At one point in my life, before my grandmother died, I desperately wanted to meet him – to talk to him, to hear his voice, to know that despite the distance between us, I actually did matter to him. But now I would give almost anything to never see his face again.

"Your Majesty," says Jenkins, and there's no mistaking the quaver in his voice this time. "May I present Miss Evangeline Bright. Evangeline—"

"I know who he is," I say, forcing the words out. "I mean it. Send me home. You don't want me here, and I don't want to be here, so let's just move on and forget this ever happened. We both know you're good at that."

The room is deadly quiet, but after several long seconds, Alexander manages to speak. "E-Evangeline." He wheezes my name like he's never said it before in his life. "I...of course I want you here—"

"No you don't. You just said you don't," I say, and although my eyes prickle, I refuse to let him see me cry. "Please. Let me go home."

Alexander looks stricken, and Jenkins takes a half step forward. "Sir, if you truly think it best, I will escort Evangeline back to the States in the morning," he says quietly. "But...if you do wish for her to stay, Louis and I have arranged an apartment for her in the staff quarters. She will remain out of your hair, and we will keep her occupied until you are – able to spend time with her."

I can hear his hesitation on *able*, and I know that's not what he wanted to say. *Until you're ready*, more than likely. I'll never be ready, but Jenkins isn't asking me. I stare openly at Alexander, and he stares back, his throat contracting as he swallows.

"No," he says, and I hold my breath, bracing myself for that final swing of the axe that'll sever this so-called relationship permanently.

Good. All he wants is his legitimate family, and all I want is to go home. At least now we'll both walk away satisfied.

"Her presence will put the staff on edge," he continues. "She will stay in the private wing with us."

At once, all the air seems to leave the office, taking what little self-control I have left with it. "Wait – *what?*" I gasp. Louis's mouth falls open, and even Jenkins looks shocked. "I don't want to be anywhere near you. Or your real family."

A flicker of hurt passes over Alexander's face so quickly that it's possible I imagine it. "Though your visit is...unexpected, you are a welcomed guest, and our guests stay in the private wing with us. Unless you wish to be awoken at five o'clock every morning with members of the staff," he adds, "I suggest you accept my generous offer."

My eyes narrow, and I let my feet fall to the floor with a thud.

37

"Your *generous* offer? Do you have any idea what I've had to go through because of your *generosity*?"

"Thank you, sir," says Jenkins in a rush. "I will make sure she is settled in."

"Please do," says Alexander. "And see to it that she does not cause a scandal. Her hair alone…"

"Already being handled, sir," says Louis.

As the King's gaze lingers on me, I feel more like my tiger in the zoo than a human being. But he looks away suddenly, and as he steps towards the door once more, I have an overwhelming urge to say something – anything, so long as Alexander and his judgmental stare don't get the last word.

"If you're going to force me to stay, then you should probably let my mother know I'm here," I blurt, and to my deep satisfaction, the King falters. "You *do* remember her, right? Laura Bright? Because she remembers you."

His lips thin into a grimace, but with his eyes fixed on the floor, he strides out of the room as if I haven't said anything at all.

Chapter Five

Maisie:

Mummy's just texted. Something's happening at Windsor.

Kit:

Has someone broken onto the grounds again?

Maisie:

She didn't say.

Kit:

I'll send for the car.

Ben:

Security isn't swooping in to save us, so it can't be that bad. Let me finish my drink.

Maisie:

You have thirty seconds, and then we're leaving.

Ben:

Someone's prickly tonight.

Maisie:

The last time I received a text directly from Mummy instead of her staff was in 2019. Whatever's happened, it must be serious.

—Text message exchange between Her Royal Highness the Princess Mary, His Royal Highness Prince Benedict of York, and Christopher Abbott-Montgomery, Earl of Clarence

The divide between the hallways lined with staff offices and the palace corridors meant for the royal family is painfully clear, like a dark slash of classism on stark white paper.

The grandiose staterooms are full of hundreds of paintings, glitzy antique furniture, and priceless trinkets that decorate every surface. It's an explosion of mind-boggling wealth, and even though I've spent the past six and a half years surrounded by millionaires' daughters, my mouth still goes dry at the sight of it. One wrong step, and I could knock over a vase older than Elizabethan times.

"I can't believe you didn't ask *His Majesty's* permission before bringing me here," I say as I follow Jenkins through a gilded dining room with an elaborately moulded ceiling and a table big enough to seat at least two dozen. "Isn't that like adopting a stray dog without telling your partner first?"

"Do you have any fleas or worms I ought to know about?" says Jenkins. I shrug.

"Wouldn't matter if I did. This place is already full of leeches." We step inside an extravagant drawing room with crimson walls, and I try to convince myself that the tightness in my chest and the tension in my muscles is just exhaustion. "What exactly do you do for him, anyway? I'm pretty sure *royal bastard wrangler* isn't an official job title."

"I have been His Majesty's private secretary for twenty-five years," says Jenkins, and the pride in his voice is unmistakable. "It is my job to support the King in his role as head of state, and I assist with many of his day-to-day duties. I would go further into detail," he adds, "but I fear your eyes would glaze over."

"Probably," I agree as we enter a second drawing room, this one emerald green with an astounding number of gold panels and fixtures. I try not to stare, but it's a losing battle, and by the time we pass into a third, which is decorated in white and gilded furnishings, my jaw is practically hanging open. It's absurd how much wealth those three rooms alone hold, and I'm relieved when we finally step into a long hallway. It isn't any less fancy, but at least it's functional.

"These are the royal family's private apartments," says Jenkins as we pass a number of doors on the left, all interspersed with a seemingly endless series of marble busts and gold-framed portraits. "You mustn't go anywhere you are not invited."

I shift my gaze to the right side of the hall, where tall windows draped in red velvet curtains look out onto a courtyard. "Exactly how much space do three people need?"

Jenkins clears his throat. "Several relatives of the royal family also keep rooms here," he says, and I stop in the middle of the hallway.

"Which ones?" I say, and he hesitates. "*Jenkins.* Who else is here?"

He sighs. "The Queen Mother resides at Windsor for most of the year, as well as the Duke of York and his son," he admits. "Though I'm afraid I can't begin to guess how they might react to your unexpected visit."

I take a deep breath and release it slowly. Even though I'm not a royal expert – not when a single Google search is enough to wreck my mental health for a week – I know enough to recognize those titles. "My grandmother lives here? And my

41

uncle? And cousin?" But when Jenkins's mouth forms a thin line, I add, "Don't worry. I won't call them that to their faces."

"You have as much of a right to call them family as Princess Mary does," he says. "But perhaps it would be best to allow everyone time to...adjust to your presence first."

He's not wrong, and I nod, my mind racing as I trail after him once more. It's a long shot, but while Alexander and I are a lost cause, maybe someone else in the family won't hate me on sight. "Is it Mary or Maisie?" I say as we round a corner into another long hallway nearly identical to the first.

"Coming from you," says Jenkins, "I am certain Her Royal Highness will happily take offence to both."

That's not exactly a surprise. "Which one is less likely to get me locked in the Tower?"

"She prefers Maisie in her social circles," says Jenkins, "but perhaps when it comes to the royal family, one might consider sticking to titles and a curtsy for now."

I snort. "I'm American, Jenkins. We don't curtsy."

"Your dual citizenship says otherwise," he corrects. "I will have someone teach you in the morning."

"I'm not doing it," I say as what little humour I have left evaporates. "They haven't done anything to earn my respect."

"Nor have you done anything to earn theirs," he says. "Now, if you will, your suite."

He stops at a door halfway down the wing and turns the knob. I'm expecting a broom closet with a cot shoved in a corner, but as I follow Jenkins into a sitting room, my mouth drops open, and my vow to remain unimpressed is sorely tested.

It's cosy, but every bit as opulent as the rooms we've passed through, with creamy white walls, gilded panels and oil paintings of people and landscapes I don't recognize. Curved lounges and chairs with velvet cushions fill the carpeted space, and near a tall window is a table made of dark wood that's big enough to seat eight.

My hopes curdle. It's a room fit for Maisie or my stepmother. There's no way anyone would let me stay here. "This isn't funny."

"I assure you, I am not trying to be," says Jenkins, and there's a strange tone to his voice. "Evan, life has not been terribly kind to you. But whether you wish to acknowledge him or not, you are still the daughter of a king, and His Majesty has made it clear that while you remain here, you are to be treated as such."

"That's rich coming from the guy who wanted to put me in the staff quarters half an hour ago," I say. He smiles faintly.

"We both know you would be more comfortable there. We do not live in squalor, after all."

Yet again, he's right. All this expensive stuff makes me nervous, and there's nothing protecting the priceless oil paintings from an errant hair tie or a flying cup of coffee. And as I look around, my hands clasped tightly behind my back, Jenkins crosses the room and pushes open a door near the ornate fireplace. It leads into a matching bedroom, with golds and creams everywhere and a canopy bed that looks like it was made in the eighteenth century.

"How many people have died in here?" I say warily as I join him. "If this room is haunted—"

"It is not," he promises. "At least not on any regular basis. Anne Boleyn reportedly haunts the Dean's Cloister, and Henry

VIII often roams the halls bemoaning her and his other five wives, but he undoubtedly has better things to do than to bother you."

"Dunno. I heard he liked teenagers," I say, not at all reassured. But then I spot my new laptop resting on an old-fashioned desk in the corner, and I make a beeline for it. "Please tell me this place has Wi-Fi."

"You are already connected," says Jenkins. "The en suite bath is to your left, and should you need anything, simply press the silver button on your nightstand. I will have dinner sent up for you shortly."

"Thanks," I say, sitting down at the desk, "but I'm not hungry."

"You didn't eat anything on the plane, and the police hardly offered up a buffet this morning."

I shrug. "Still not hungry."

He sighs. "Very well, then. Should you change your mind—"

"Press the button. Got it," I say. "You should get some sleep, Jenkins. I could fit my entire wardrobe in the bags under your eyes."

"And who do you think put them there?" He smiles tiredly. "Don't stay up too late, Evan. Tomorrow will be a very busy day."

"Ominous," I say, but he's already gone, and the door closes softly behind him. Now that I'm alone, I notice the shadows lurking in the corners of the room, and a shiver runs through me. No matter what Jenkins said, someone has definitely died in here.

I try to focus on unpacking the few things that haven't already been taken care of for me – apparently no one in the palace knows what to do with a lopsided ceramic mug full of small rocks, a collection of photos from my childhood that I'm admittedly relieved to find, and a stack of fantasy novels that were, technically speaking, considered contraband at St Edith's. But before I can finish arranging the books in any coherent order, my stomach gurgles. Loudly.

Jenkins is right – I haven't eaten anything today, and food sounds like a decent distraction. I eye the silver button embedded into my nightstand, but no matter how hungry I am, I can't make myself push it. The thought of forcing someone to walk those long corridors to get me a cheeseburger is absurd, and so, even though I know Jenkins will have my head for it, I slip out through the sitting room and into the main hallway. The lights are on – I have a feeling they always are – and thankfully Jenkins hasn't had the chance to station anyone outside my room yet. A matter of timing instead of oversight, no doubt. I'm simply breaking the rules faster than he expects.

I'm not sure what I'm looking for. A kitchenette nestled between drawing rooms? A staircase that leads to a dungeon filled with pots and pans? There's a smaller dining room set within the sharp angle where the two corridors meet, which means there has to be a secret entrance to the kitchen somewhere nearby.

As soon as I think it, I notice a door that's cracked open and spilling soft yellow light into the hall. Enormously pleased with my own powers of deduction, I stick my head inside. But unlike the stairwell or narrow hallway I expect, it opens into a sitting room even more luxurious than mine, with a crystal chandelier hanging from the ceiling and gold-framed pictures decorating the mantel.

There's no way the staff would risk carrying trays of food through a room that looks like it belongs in Versailles. Before I can back away, however, I hear murmurs of tense conversation.

"...can't believe you're allowing this," says a woman, her voice soft but vicious. "Think of Maisie. Think of *our* daughter, not just your bas—"

"I have thought of only Maisie for far too long. Now I am thinking of both my daughters."

The second voice is thin, but unmistakably Alexander's. Hearing him call me his daughter makes my body go cold, and the woman – his queen consort, Helene – scoffs. "Since when have you ever wanted to be a father to that insubordinate parasite?"

"That is none of your concern," he says, so low now I can barely understand him.

"Isn't it? Have you any idea what you are doing to Maisie? How do you think she'll feel, knowing her father is an adulterer who is flaunting his indiscretion right under the public's nose?"

"She knows about Evangeline," says Alexander tiredly. "I told her ages ago."

"You told – are you *mad*?" gasps Helene, while my eyes widen. "You had no right to do so without my permission."

"Evangeline is her sister," he says, "and she has every right to know the truth about her family."

"The American is inconsequential," snarls Helene. "A footnote in history. A mistake that should have been corrected in the womb."

I inhale sharply, feeling like she's slapped me across the face. I never imagined she would like me, but her sheer loathing is staggering.

"Evangeline is of royal blood," says Alexander, and he sounds more solid now. Like he did with Jenkins and Louis. "And you *will* be civil to her. Is that understood?"

"The only thing I understand is that you are refusing to do the right thing and send her back to the States, where she belongs."

"She belongs where I say she belongs," he says. "I have spent a very long time doing all I can to earn your forgiveness. I have apologized again and again, and I have kept her out of our lives. But she is nearly eighteen now, and I have a right to know my own—"

"Pardon me," says a voice inches from my ear. "But who the hell are you?"

I whirl around. Standing behind me, with two teen boys flanking her, is the last person I want to see right now. Or ever.

Maisie.

Chapter Six

The important thing is not what they think of me, but what I think of them.

—Queen Victoria (b. 1819, r. 1837–1901)

We look nothing alike.

I know that's a ridiculous thing to contemplate as Maisie and I stare at each other, me shocked into silence and her waiting for my reply. But we don't. She has wavy strawberry-blond hair that makes her look like she's just stepped out of a world-class salon, and her eyes aren't icy, like they seem in some photos, but a vivid ocean blue. She's taller than me, too, by a good four inches, which makes it easy for her to look down her button nose at me. "Are you deaf?" she says in a honeyed voice that sounds almost exactly like her mother's. "Or simply stupid?"

"Maisie," says one of the boys behind her, and there's no mistaking the gentle warning in his tone. He has dark hair that's a touch too shaggy for royalty, and he meets my gaze, his expression sombre. I look away.

"What? It's a fair question," says Maisie, and she refocuses on me. "You have one more chance before we call security. What are you doing in my—"

"Maisie?" The door I'm leaning against flies open, and I lose my balance, nearly stumbling directly into the Queen. Helene gasps, and I manage to avoid her by an inch, grabbing the doorway instead.

"I'm sorry," I croak, desperately wishing the ground would open up and I could disappear. "I was looking for – for the kitchen."

"The kitchens?" Maisie glances at her mother, seemingly bewildered. "Are you a maid?"

I consider lying and saying yes – anything to get out of here – but before I can come up with a coherent reply, Alexander appears behind his wife. "Evangeline?" he says, his face draining of colour. "What are you doing here?"

"*Evangeline?*" The Queen instantly goes cold, and her eyes narrow into slits. "Alexander—"

"It's Evan," I say, my voice shaking, "and I'm leaving. I just wanted a sandwich, all right? And there aren't exactly any signs in this place."

"There's no need for you to leave," says Alexander, but he's wrong. As I try to escape this sudden nightmare, however, Maisie blocks my way.

"Is someone going to tell me what's going on?" she says. "Or am I supposed to guess?"

The silence that follows is profound. Helene looks to Alexander, and he looks to the floor as if he's also waiting for it to swallow him whole. Neither of them says a word, and I can feel Maisie's frustration building.

49

"Fine," I say. I already know hell will freeze before I win Helene over, and I doubt it'll be any better with Maisie. I have nothing to lose, except the chance to get out of here with any shred of dignity I have left intact. I turn to Maisie and stick out my hand. "I'm Evan Bright, the royal bastard. From what I hear, we're half-sisters."

She recoils like I've offered her a rotting limb. "Is this true?" she demands, speaking past me to her parents. "*This* is your illegitimate issue, Father?"

"This isn't how I'd hoped you would meet," says Alexander stiffly. "If we could all sit down…"

But I have no desire to stick around and hear him apologize for allowing a stain onto their impeccable family tree. "Excuse me," I mumble, forcing my way past Maisie and the two boys who stand behind her. The shorter one – a blond with glasses who looks unnervingly familiar – gapes at me, while the dark-haired boy with a solemn gaze simply watches. I don't know who they are, and I don't care. All I want is to get as far away from this circus as possible.

My range is limited, though, and so I race down the corridor until I reach my sitting room. Bolting inside, I slam the door hard enough to wake the corpse of Henry VIII, and as the reverberation gives way to silence, I slide to the floor and press my knees against my chest, burying my face in my trembling arms.

I don't cry. Even though Helene's words echo endlessly in my mind, and even though the disgust on Maisie's face is etched onto the back of my eyelids, I swallow the lump in my throat, refusing to give them the satisfaction. I'm nothing to them, and there's some small amount of comfort in that.

Twenty-five days, and I'll be gone. And after I leave, I will never, ever come back.

I'm not sure how long I sit there, taking deep, slow breaths and trying to calm my racing heart. When a soft knock sounds on the door I'm leaning against, I freeze.

"Jenkins?" I say hoarsely. "Is that "

"Miss?" says an unfamiliar female voice. "I have your dinner." My dinner? I scramble to my feet, tugging the door open right as the woman on the other side is turning the knob. She jumps in surprise and takes an automatic step back, nearly running into a footman carrying a tray covered in a silver dome.

"I think you have the wrong room," I say. "I didn't ask for anything."

"The order came from the King," she says as the footman enters and sets the tray down on the dining table. "There is a variety of sandwiches for you to enjoy, as His Majesty was unsure of your preferences."

I open and shut my mouth, not knowing what to make of that – of Alexander going out of his way for me, even if it probably only took a phone call. "Thank you," I finally manage.

"You're very welcome," says the woman kindly, and once she and the footman excuse themselves, I inspect the meal. Half a dozen sandwiches are artfully arranged on a plate, complete with a side of neatly stacked French fries.

I blink. French fries. In Windsor Castle. Something about that breaks my brain, and I sit down at the table in a daze. I'm strangely numb now, but it's better than feeling like my entire world is collapsing around me.

Even though my appetite is gone, I force myself to eat, managing most of the fries and three-quarters of a sandwich before I lose the will to finish. I don't know what I'm supposed to do with the tray, so I slide it into the hallway outside my door before returning to my bedroom, where I should've stayed in the first place, safely ensconced with my laptop.

Lesson learned. Desperate for familiarity and a reminder that not everyone hates my guts, I open VidChat and click my mother's icon. The ringing echoes through the high-ceilinged chamber, and I hastily turn down the volume as my face appears on-screen. In the glow of the laptop, my skin is so pale it's practically translucent, which only makes the purple smudges beneath my brown eyes more pronounced than usual. This is definitely not a good look.

"Hello?"

Her voice arrives before her image, and my stomach flip-flops. "Mom?" I say, instantly perking up. "Can you—"

"Alex?" The hope in her voice is unmistakable. "Alex, I can't hear you."

My heart sinks. "No – it's me, Mom. It's Evan."

"Evan?" Finally the video appears, and I see her for the first time since our call in January. My mom leans towards her computer, her glasses askew and her curly auburn hair wild and frizzy. She's wearing a smock stained with a rainbow palette of paints, and on the easel behind her, I spot an impressionistic blend of bright spring colours in what must be her current piece.

"Hi, Mom," I say, forcing myself to keep my tone light. She's every bit as beautiful as she's always been, but her cheekbones are sharp, and she's lost weight. Too much weight, I think.

"Evie? It's you?"

"It's me," I say, a genuine smile tugging at the corners of my mouth. She hasn't called me Evie in years. "I miss you. I'm sorry I haven't been able to call. Did you get my letters?"

She doesn't answer. Instead, she disappears for a moment, and I worry she's wandered off. It wouldn't be the first time. But a few seconds later, she reappears, holding a large canvas covered in blues and greens and accented with strokes of pinks and violets. It's always hard to tell exactly what she's painting, but I recognize this instantly. My grandmother's garden.

"I wanted to send this, but I don't have your address," she says anxiously. "Did I miss your birthday?"

"Not yet," I say. "It's only early June."

"June," she murmurs, as if reminding herself. "Right. I still have time."

"You still have time," I assure her, and as my vision blurs, I hastily wipe my eyes. "How are you feeling? Jenkins said you're on new meds. Are they working?"

She waves one hand dismissively, her body mostly off-screen now. "The new nurse hates me. Caught her trying to steal my brushes. Has he called? He said he would call."

He is Alexander, and whenever my mom and I speak, our conversation inevitably ends up here. She's always waiting for him to call, and he never does. It's a delusion, a symptom of the schizophrenia diagnosis she received when I was four years old, and this particular manifestation of her illness is undoubtedly fuelled by the short-lived relationship she had with him before I was born. But even though I know this, it's never easy to hear her talk about him as if he's an integral part of our family.

53

Especially when he couldn't care less about us.

"Actually, I, uh…have some news," I say slowly, not sure how to tell her without feeding her delusion. "I'm in London."

"London?" Suddenly I have her full attention, and she leans towards the screen again. "Are you with him?"

"Um – sort of," I say. "I'm staying at Windsor Castle until my birthday."

"He didn't tell me," she says, frowning. "He should have told me."

"Alexander didn't know, Mom. *I* didn't even know until—" The video screen goes blank, and the call disconnects. Muttering a curse, I check the Wi-Fi connection and try again. I don't want to end the conversation like this, not when she's so confused. But the laptop rings – and rings, and rings, until my chest is heavy with an ache I can't name, and I have no choice but to give up. I'll call her again in the morning, I promise myself. Maybe by then Jenkins will have explained everything, and I won't feel so helpless and adrift any more.

THE KING TO HONOUR CITIZENS, CELEBRITIES AT WINDSOR

The stars will be out for this afternoon's investiture ceremony at Windsor Castle, as the King is set to honour some of Britain's stand-out citizens and biggest celebrities.

His Majesty will be joined by the Duke of York as he hands out knighthoods, OBEs, MBEs and other awards to deserving Britons. Among those expected to be honoured are film star Tom Holland, Olympic gold medallist Duffy Goodrey, and media mogul Robert Cunningham, owner of the *Daily Sun*. We congratulate Mr Cunningham and all the honorees on this magnificent achievement.

—*The Daily Sun*, 8 June 2023

I'm beating Henry VIII in a game of checkers when the sound of bagpipes blares directly outside my window, waking me from my dream with such force that I forget how to breathe. For a moment I don't know where I am, but the memory of the day before quickly rises to the surface, and I mutter a string of curses, burying my face in my pillow.

Bagpipes. Actual *bagpipes*. My head pounds with the need for more sleep, and I will the noise to stop, but of course it doesn't. It keeps playing and playing and playing until I'm ready to rip something to shreds with my bare hands.

"Good morning," says a crisp voice from my bedroom door, and I look up to see a tall woman in her mid-twenties stride towards the window. With a single fluid motion, she pulls a cord, and the heavy gold curtains slide open.

I wince at the sudden burst of sunlight. "Who are you?" I mutter. Henry VIII haunting this room is one thing, but another living human barging in is not okay.

She raises a single eyebrow in a gesture more condescending than any look Headmistress Thompson ever gave me. "I am Lady Tabitha Finch-Parker-Covington-Boyle, descendant of Queen Victoria and fifth cousin to His Majesty," she says primly. "You may call me Tibby. His Majesty has tasked me with looking after you, Miss Bright, and ensuring you remain on schedule."

The way she says *schedule* makes it sound like there's no *c*. "I have a schedule?"

"Indeed." Her black hair is styled in a pixie cut that wouldn't look out of place in the punk scene, but she wears it in a no-nonsense way that zaps all the fun out of it. "It's nine o'clock, and your breakfast is waiting for you in the sitting room."

I groan. "It's four in the morning in Vermont. Wake me up at noon." I pull my pillow over my head, but she snatches it from me. "Your team will arrive in thirty minutes, and you need to be showered and fed by then. Should you prove to be uncooperative," she says over my protests, "I have been instructed to ask His Majesty to join us."

"Go ahead," I say. "If he really has nothing better to do with his time, then he can sit here and stare at me, too. But I'm exhausted, and I didn't agree to any of this, so I'm going back to sleep."

Shockingly, this actually works, and she hands over my pillow with an insulted sniff. I burrow inside my blankets again, and after a moment, the muffled click of her heels fades as she leaves me in peace.

At long last, the bagpipe serenade stops, and I'm almost asleep once more when a soft knock yanks me back from the edge of consciousness. I groan again, my head pounding. "Go *away*."

"Evan," says Jenkins quietly. "May I come in?"

I take a deep breath before muttering, "I guess." All I want to do is sleep and forget where I am, why I'm here, and everything the royal family said last night, but clearly that isn't in the cards. The edge of my mattress dips as Jenkins sits beside me, and after a beat, I pull the pillow from my face. He looks alarmingly well rested, and somehow the bags under his eyes have disappeared.

"His Majesty told me what happened," says Jenkins, and I sigh. Of course he did.

"I didn't mean to—"

"I know," he says. "I am not admonishing you. I'm here to make sure you're all right."

My throat tightens. "Yeah," I mumble. "I've always figured Helene hates me."

To his credit, Jenkins doesn't try to convince me otherwise. "It will get easier," he says. "Perhaps not immediately, but it will. I promise. In the meantime, Louis will be arriving with a style team in twenty minutes, and I would consider it a great favour if you would be willing to indulge them today."

I shake my head. "I'm not playing dress-up with Maisie's hand-me-downs."

"I assure you, none of the outfits are hand-me-downs. Louis has been up all night choosing pieces from Harrods for you – pieces Her Royal Highness has never worn," he adds. "Between you and me, this is the most excited I've seen him in ages."

Something inside me twinges, and my fingers tighten around my pillow. "If you're trying to guilt me, it isn't working."

"Isn't it?" He smiles faintly. "Surely after all I've put you through, the least I can do is help spruce up your wardrobe."

"It won't matter. No one's going to see me," I mumble. "I just want to sleep."

Jenkins frowns, and for a moment I think he's going to keep pushing. But instead he says, "Very well. I will inform Tibby of your decision."

"Thanks," I say quietly. "Tell Louis I'm sorry."

"Louis will understand," says Jenkins, patting my hand. "And I'm the one who should be sorry."

He says this last part so softly that I barely hear him. Before I can come up with a coherent response, however, he stands and heads back into the sitting room, leaving me on my own once more, exhausted and utterly miserable.

I don't remember falling back asleep, but when I wake up, the sunlight has shifted and my headache is gone. The bagpipes are back, though, tinny and distant now, and I mutter a curse as I drag myself into the bathroom. If this is going to be a regular thing, I need to find some earplugs.

Once I brush my teeth and splash some cold water on my face, I pad towards the sitting room, debating whether to order breakfast or try to find the kitchen again. After what happened last night, leaving the relative safety of my suite seems about as appealing as a root canal, but maybe I won't have to. I have five months of Netflix to catch up on, after all, and as long as the Wi-Fi holds

I stop cold on the threshold of my sitting room. Lounging on a sofa, phone in hand, is Lady Tabitha Finch-Parker-Covington-Boyle.

"What are you still doing here?" I blurt. It comes out ruder than I intend, but Tibby doesn't bat an eye.

"It's my job to be here," she says, finishing her text before looking up. "Is there a reason you're still in your pyjamas, or is this a quaint American custom I'm not aware of?"

I ignore her question, which is definitely an insult anyway. "I'm almost eighteen. I don't need a babysitter."

Tibby scowls. "I am not your *babysitter*. His Majesty is a family friend, and he requested I assist you during your stay."

"And keep me out of his hair," I grumble.

"And make sure you stick to your schedule," she corrects. "Though I dare say the morning is a lost cause."

"Did he tell you who I am?" I say, not sure I have the energy to play along with whatever charade Alexander's created to explain away my presence.

"Naturally. I wouldn't be able to do my job if I didn't have all the relevant information." Tibby studies me for a moment. "I didn't see the resemblance at first, but I do now. It's in your eyes, and a bit in your mouth and chin."

I resist the urge to squirm under her scrutiny. Still, it's a relief to know I won't have to tiptoe around the truth in my own sitting room. "Sorry you waited all this time, but the only thing I'm planning to do today is curl up in bed and watch Netflix until my eyes bleed."

Tibby sniffs. "As charming as that sounds, you'll have plenty of time to indulge after the investiture ceremony."

I blink. "The what?"

"Investiture ceremony." She says this slowly, as if enunciation will somehow make me understand. I stare at her blankly, and she sighs. "During which members of the royal family hand out knighthoods and damehoods and various other royal awards to honorees who have benefited the kingdom and Commonwealth. His Majesty has, in all his unquestionable wisdom, invited you to watch this afternoon's ceremony in the Waterloo Chamber, but thanks to your little lie-in, we're already running late, so if you wouldn't mind—"

A knock on the door catches us both off guard, and Tibby hastily stands. I'm quicker than her and her spiked heels, though, and I'm across the room before she can even manoeuvre around the sofa.

"Jenkins?" I say hopefully as I yank open the door, but I'm not greeted by salt-and-pepper hair and an imperious manner. Instead, a young blond man with glasses stands on the other side, and I recognize him as one of the boys who was with Maisie the night before – the one who looked frustratingly familiar. He's wearing a black-and-grey three-piece morning suit, and I notice a matching top hat perched jauntily on the bust beside my door. "Sorry to disappoint," he says with a hint of amusement in his voice. "I heard you hadn't eaten yet, and so I thought I'd take the liberty of bringing you some lunch, in case you were hungry."

Only then do I notice a woman standing off to the side, holding yet another large tray covered in a silver dome. "Thanks," I manage, vaguely stunned, and I step aside to let her into my sitting room. "You didn't have to do that."

"I wanted to," says the boy. "It seemed only right to check in, given all that happened last night. We are family, after all."

It's this reminder that lights a spark in my memory, and I blink. "*Oh*. You're Benedict."

"Prince Benedict, son of Prince Nicholas, the Duke of York, and grandson of the late Edward IX," he says. "And you are Evangeline Florence Phillipa Constance Bright, illegitimate issue of His Majesty King Alexander II."

I scowl. "It's Evan."

"And I'm Ben," he says. I can't tell if he's smirking or smiling. "Rumour has it we're cousins."

Cousins. I've known about him for years, even if he looks significantly older than in the pictures I've seen. But there's something jarring about hearing him say it – about hearing him acknowledge me as family when I'm sure no one else in this castle will.

Behind me, Tibby clears her throat. "As heart-warming as this all is, Evangeline still has to dress," she says pointedly. "We're already running late for the ceremony."

"Ah, right," says Ben, and he takes half a step back. "My apologies for interrupting."

"You didn't interrupt anything," I say to him while glaring at Tibby. Ben is the only member of the royal family to show me any decency, and despite the fact that I don't know what to make of it, I'm not about to let her chase him off. "How bad is it out there? With – Helene and Maisie and everyone, I mean."

Ben hesitates. "It isn't good," he admits. "But it's less because of you on a personal level, and more because – well, we didn't have any warning, did we? No one knew you were coming until you were here."

"If it's any consolation, I didn't know, either," I say. "And I'm not exactly thrilled about the whole thing."

He chuckles, even though I haven't said anything funny. "It could be worse. You could be a simpering sycophant who does nothing but kiss our arses all day. *That* would truly be a nightmare."

I wrinkle my nose. "I'm sure you have plenty of those hanging around already."

"Too many," he agrees. "But while no one's especially happy about this, I suppose we can take some solace in knowing that the party responsible is being dealt with accordingly, and once you've had the time to adjust—"

"What do you mean?" I interrupt, my heart suddenly in my throat. "Who's being dealt with?"

"Jenkins, of course," he says with a frown. "From what I understand, not only did he bring you here without forewarning, but he also explicitly defied Uncle Alexander's orders—"

I don't stick around to hear the rest. Instead, I slip past Ben and storm down the hallway, the carpet rough against my bare feet as I march straight for Alexander's private apartment. Dimly I hear Tibby's muttered curses as she and Ben hurry after me, but I refuse to slow down.

"Evangeline," calls Tibby. "Where on *earth* are you going?"

I don't bother to explain. Once I reach the sharp turn in the corridor, I locate the door that was ajar the night before – the one that led into Alexander's sitting room. It's locked now, and I pound on it with the side of my fist. "Alexander! I need to talk to—"

"He's not here," says Ben as he joins me. "He's preparing for the ceremony."

"Where?" I say tightly.

Ben grimaces. "The state apartments. I'll take you there if you'd like, but we need to be discreet. The crowd is already gathering for the investitures, and—"

"You're not going anywhere dressed like that," says Tibby as she appears on my other side. "Whatever this is about, it can wait."

"No, it can't," I say, my jaw clenched. I slept in all morning – it could already be too late. I turn to Ben. "I won't make a scene. Where is he?"

Despite Tibby's protests, Ben leads me deeper into the castle – through the white, green, and crimson drawing rooms, the ostentatious dining room, and several other state apartments that are filled with a thousand years of expropriated finery. Tibby follows us every step of the way, but she doesn't try to stop me. Physically, at least.

"I don't care how upset you are with His Majesty," she presses. "You cannot simply drop in on him whenever you wish. He's the King—"

"He's going to fire Jenkins," I say as Ben leads me into an empty wood-panelled room with bright blue carpet and portraits of dead monarchs on the walls. The throne room, I remember from my brief tour last night, and I glance at the raised seat at the head of the room. I should be intimidated – I should feel a surge of jealousy, of wistfulness, of *something*, but all I can muster is furious resolve. "I need to talk to him *now*."

"His Majesty has every right to dismiss his own staff for gross misconduct," says Tibby, but she must see the murderous look on my face, because she sighs. "And how exactly do you plan on stopping him?"

"Easy," I say. "I'll make it clear that if he does fire Jenkins, then I'll go straight to the biggest newspaper in London and tell them everything."

Tibby freezes in place. "You can't."

Ben stops as well, so suddenly that I nearly run straight into him. "Tibby's right," he says, his eyes wide behind his glasses. "You can't do that, Evan."

I cross my arms. "Why? Because it'll ruin his life?"

"No," he says. "Because it'll ruin yours."

Tibby steps closer, her face ashen. "If you reveal who you are—" She glances over her shoulder and lowers her voice. "If the press finds out His Majesty was unfaithful and that you're his – his—"

"Bastard?" I supply, and Tibby huffs.

"You will be hounded for the rest of your life. They'll stalk you. They'll take countless photos of you and publish the most unflattering ones for the public to mock. You won't be able to buy a coffee without it becoming front-page news, and no matter what you accomplish in the future, it will always be overshadowed by your paternity."

My skin crawls at the picture she paints, but I shake my head stubbornly. "If he fires Jenkins, then I'll have no choice. And as bad as it'll be for me, it'll probably be a million times worse for Alexander."

"And what about your mother?" says Ben quietly.

This brings me up short. "What did Alexander tell you about her?" I say, my heart hammering as I look between them.

"Nothing," admits Ben. "No one seems to even know her name."

"I assure you someone does," says Tibby. "And it won't stay secret for long."

Her words settle over me like a thousand-pound weight, and I suck in a deep breath. Tibby's right – if I tell the press who I am, they won't rest until they've found my mom. I'm willing to accept the consequences of throwing myself head first into the fire, but the thought of a pack of reporters showing up on her front lawn makes me sick to my stomach.

I can't stand by and do nothing while Jenkins loses his job, though. He may be the one who took the risk of bringing me here, but I'm the one who got arrested. I'm the one who gave him a reason to think this was necessary, and even though he was wrong – even though this is the last place I should be – he still cared enough to try. He's the only person in the world who would put his entire livelihood on the line for me, and I'm not about to leave him high and dry.

And so, even though Ben and Tibby must be able to hear the resignation in my voice, I say, "Just show me where Alexander is. Please."

They exchange a look that's impossible to miss, but reluctantly

Ben leads me to the head of the room. While the throne isn't much more than a cushioned chair, we both eye it for a split second before he steps to the right of the platform, stopping in front of a blank wooden panel. "The antechamber's through here," he says, pressing a dark knot in the wood. "Uncle Alexander should be inside."

The panel swings open, revealing another ornate room with a high ceiling on the other side. I'm not exactly surprised – Windsor is almost a thousand years old, after all, and it probably has more secrets than any one person knows – but my pulse still quickens.

"That's useful," I say, examining the nearly invisible hinges. I'm about to ask how many hidden doors there are in the castle when Ben swears.

"Damn," he says as he steps over the threshold. "I really thought Uncle Alexander would be here by now."

Sure enough, as I follow Ben into the antechamber, our only company is the mauve wallpaper and elegant furnishings that include a bust taller than me. But while the curtains are drawn, the lights are on, and the staff has set out a tray full of bite-sized cakes on a table in the centre of the room, which means Ben must be right about Alexander showing up eventually.

"He's probably just running late," I say, glancing at the double doors across the room.

"His Majesty is never *late*," says Tibby indignantly. "Jenkins may have his faults, but his timekeeping is superb."

And then, as if the universe is determined to prove that Lady Tabitha Finch-Parker-Covington-Boyle is always right, footsteps sound on the other side of the far wall. I square my shoulders as

I prepare to face Alexander, but it isn't his voice that filters in from the next room.

"...*swore* he would never bring her anywhere near Maisie," says a honeyed murmur filled with spite. "It's an insult to our family. To our country. To the institution of the monarchy itself." Before I can move – before I can even think to hide – a second concealed door swings open, and standing in the frame, dressed in pale blue chiffon and the incandescence of her own rage, is Helene.

Chapter Eight

Family is both the bane of the crown's existence and the only thing holding it upright.

—Alexander I (b. 1928, r. 1972–1990)

I freeze, my heart stuttering as I stare directly at the Queen, but my seething stepmother doesn't seem to notice me. Instead, she's looking over her shoulder as another set of footsteps joins her.

"It's an insult to us all," rasps a second voice, and another woman appears – one three decades older than Helene. She's wearing a sapphire dress with her silver hair pulled back in an elegant French twist, and her posture is so perfect that my spine hurts just looking at her.

Constance, the Queen Mother. And my grandmother. "After all the trouble we went to, burying his indiscretions," she continues, her face contorted as if she smells something foul. "Now he's parading around proof like a mangy stray at a dog show. You're certain he won't reconsider?"

"We argued all night after poor Maisie went to bed," says Helene bitterly. "He insists that since *the stray* is already at Windsor, she might as well remain until she's of age. I of course pointed out how cruel it is to keep her here like a pet when he has every intention of washing his hands of her once she turns eighteen, but as always, his selfishness knows no bounds."

Beside me, Ben shifts, as if he wants to put himself between me and the conversation happening right in front of us. His movement catches Helene's attention, however, and she stops cold, her face turning the colour of sour milk as she gapes at us. As she gapes at *me*.

My cheeks grow hot, but I refuse to look away. After years of rejection, I know I'm not wanted, and I can't blame Helene for despising me – I'm living, breathing proof that her husband cheated on her, after all. But even though I've never met the Queen Mother, the fact that I'm somehow not *good enough* for my own grandma burns away at me until my edges are dark and jagged.

"Don't worry," I say with false ease. "I only heard most of that."

While Helene opens and shuts her mouth, seemingly rendered speechless, Constance doesn't flinch. Her stare is white-hot with displeasure, and she regards me with thinly veiled disgust. "May I help you?"

I step forward. "I'm Evan," I say, though I suspect she already knows. "The mangy stray."

"Evangeline Bright," clarifies Helene in a choked voice. "Alexander's...unexpected issue."

"I see." Constance eyes me up and down, and while it wouldn't make a difference to someone like her, I suddenly wish I'd listened to Tibby's advice about changing out of my pyjamas. "This room is for family only."

"I'm not leaving," I say coolly, and behind me, Tibby manages a single squeak of protest. "Listen, it's obvious you all don't want me here – I don't want to be here, either. I'm not interested in following a bunch of archaic traditions that require a dozen forks to eat dinner, and we all know you're not interested in having an *insubordinate parasite* running around uninvited."

Helene blanches, and Constance regards me with the kind of condescending ire that could melt the sun.

"But I am here," I continue. "And thanks to the fact that Alexander couldn't keep it in his pants, I'm part of the family tree now, as much as we all hate it."

Constance stiffens, and she grips the back of a chair so tightly that the tips of her nails disappear into the velvet. "You may feel slighted by the charity we have shown you, but you will not speak of His Majesty in such a crude and disrespectful manner."

"Charity?" I say with a humourless snort. "I'm not some orphan begging for gruel. I'm your *granddaughter*. And all I'm asking is that you not treat me like a *mistake that should've been corrected in the womb* because of something I can't help."

"You *were* a mistake," says Constance, her words ringing through the antechamber. "One that nearly cost my son his birthright. And I will not have you traipsing through our home, calling yourself family when you and that American trollop are nothing more than parasites—"

"What's going on here?"

I whirl around. Alexander stands in the concealed doorway, his forehead furrowed so deeply that his eyebrows practically connect. Beside him is a handsome man in a dark suit – my uncle, Nicholas, the infamous Duke of York, who looks like he's watching a vaguely amusing play. And behind them both, still inside the throne room, is Jenkins.

"Alexander." Somehow Constance manages to stand up even straighter, but she doesn't curtsy to her son. Only a frazzled Tibby does. "Evangeline was just leaving."

"No, I wasn't," I say, and I fix my glower on Alexander. "I need to talk to you."

I expect pushback, or for him to insist that whatever I need to say can be said in front of the rest of our loving family. But instead, he focuses on Helene and Constance in turn, his expression strangely unreadable.

"Leave us."

Helene opens her mouth, but yet again, nothing comes out. She glances at me once more before slipping back out the way she came, and Nicholas crosses the room to join her, though I don't miss the significant look that passes between him and Alexander. And while at first Constance doesn't budge, she seems to think better of it and trails after them, leaving a cloud of royal indignation in her wake.

"Uncle Alexander—" begins Ben, but the King cuts him off.

"I said leave us. Except you, Jenkins."

As Ben and Tibby slink back into the blue-carpeted throne room, Jenkins cautiously steps into the antechamber, clearly not sure what he's doing here. But I know. Even though he's my father, Alexander still can't face me on his own.

71

Once it's only the three of us, my stomach flip-flops, and for a long moment, none of us says a word. I stare at Alexander, Alexander stares at me, and Jenkins stands to the side, his face blank but his hands clasped so tightly that his knuckles are white.

"I am very sorry you had to hear that, Evangeline," says Alexander at last. "I cannot and will not make excuses for my mother's and Helene's poor behaviour, but I hope you will accept my sincerest apologies on their behalf."

"It's Evan," I say. "And don't waste your time. We both know they're not sorry."

He sighs. "No, I suppose they're not. Still, some members of the family take the bloodthirsty lions on our coat of arms more seriously than others, I'm afraid."

I blink. Is he trying to crack a joke? Whenever I've pictured Alexander, I've never imagined him having a sense of humour, and this glimpse of humanity throws me. I want to smile – to offer him some gesture to let him know I appreciate him taking my side on this one, but a little decency doesn't make up for seventeen years of failure. And I'm here for a reason. "Are you really going to fire Jenkins because of me?"

Out of the corner of my eye, I see Jenkins stiffen, while Alexander's face goes slack. "Fire him?" he says, clearly lost.

"Because he brought me here without your permission."

Alexander rubs his jaw. "As you may have noticed, Helene and my mother are deeply upset by the whole situation, and Maisie is still processing—"

"Jenkins was just trying to protect me," I insist. "And if you fire him—"

I stop. Jenkins seems to be bracing himself, and he watches me with a kind of silent pleading I've never seen from him before. I haven't told him my plan, but for a moment I wonder if he knows me well enough to guess.

"Yes?" says Alexander slowly.

I hesitate. Even though I have no actual intention of putting my mother in danger by running to the press, I could still blackmail him. I could still make my cooperation wholly dependent on Jenkins's continued employment. But that's a line in the sand that will never wash away, and Alexander won't forget that I threatened his entire reputation over something he doesn't seem to want to do in the first place.

I dig my toes into the rug, not quite able to look at him. "I'm never going to be a real part of your family," I say at last, "and I get it. I'm not trying to be. Jenkins has always made me feel like part of his, though, and he shouldn't be punished for it, or for being the only person who actually cares about me. I'll stay away from Maisie and Helene and – everyone," I promise. "But don't fire him. Please."

Alexander exhales deeply, and it's the kind of sound that carries impossible burdens with it. "Evangeline – Evan. I owe you an apology for all you overheard last night. I was taken aback, that was all, and I am not used to being surprised."

I bite back a snort of disbelief, but Alexander must be able to see it on my face, because he grimaces. "I mean it," he says quietly. "While the circumstances are far from ideal, I am glad you are here, and I will do all I can to ensure the entire family makes an effort to include you during your stay. You are my blood, and you will be treated as such."

"I don't need their fake decency," I say. "I just need you to promise me nothing's going to happen to Jenkins."

We both glance at him at the same time. Instead of acknowledging our conversation, Jenkins stares resolutely into the empty fireplace, seemingly doing his best to blend in with the wallpaper.

"You have my word," says Alexander solemnly.

My shoulders slump with relief. It doesn't matter how badly the rest of my time here goes, so long as Jenkins is safe. "Thank you. I won't get in your way, I pro—" I begin, but I'm interrupted by a soft knock on a pair of large arched doors – the only actual doors in the room.

Jenkins rushes forward to intercept whoever it is, but he isn't fast enough, and a man wearing military regalia pokes his head inside. "Your Majesty," he says with a bow, and his gaze lingers for a second too long on me and my shabby pyjamas. "The guests are seated, and the honorees are ready for you."

Alexander nods once, his posture straightening. "I will be there in a moment," he says, and the man dips his head again before departing, leaving the doors cracked behind him.

"I, uh – I should get back to my room before anyone else sees me," I say. As I start towards the hidden panel, however, Alexander clears his throat.

"Er, Evan, before you go...I want you to know that Jenkins isn't the only one."

"What?" I say, confused.

"When you said that he is the only person who cares about you," says Alexander in a voice so low it's almost inaudible. "You've always been part of my family. It was simply..." He swallows so tightly I can see his Adam's apple bob. "I was trying to shield you from the consequences of my greatest mistake. And it seems I failed miserably."

Greatest mistake. They're only two words, but they're exactly the wrong ones, and my body goes cold. "Yeah," I manage thickly. "You did. But don't worry – with any luck, in a month I'll be gone, and you'll never have to face the consequences of your *greatest mistake* again."

Alexander winces like I've hit him, and I don't give him a chance to offer me yet another meaningless apology. Before he or Jenkins can muster up a word, I slip back into the throne room and close the panel behind me, wishing I'd never come here in the first place.

Chapter Nine

QUEEN MOTHER TO DEPART
FOR BALMORAL

Windsor Castle has announced that the Queen Mother will depart for Balmoral this evening, nearly two months before her traditional journey to the royal family's Scottish retreat at the end of July.

"It's highly irregular, considering Trooping the Colour is next week, with Royal Ascot following," says Henrietta Smythe, journalist and former member of the Royal Rota who has written best-selling biographies of Queen Constance, Edward IX, and Queen Helene. "The Queen Mother hasn't missed either event since marrying into the royal family in 1974, even in the wake of her husband's death."

Though palace officials have remained mum on the topic, there are whispers that the Queen Mother, 71, is in ill health.

—*The Daily Sun*, 8 June 2023

No one is waiting for me in the throne room.

I don't mind – after my conversation with Alexander, I'm not exactly in the mood for company. But I also don't remember the way back to my suite, and that presents its own set of problems, considering how many guests are allegedly wandering around the state apartments right now.

I pause under a portrait of a man in a ruffled collar. Even if Ben has places to be, Tibby will show up eventually. Probably. Unless she's mad at me, which is likely. I wouldn't blame her – she's only been on the job for four or five hours, and I've already run off and insulted half the royal family in person, mere feet from the press and investiture crowd. It's not a good look for her. Or for me.

Just as I'm about to take my chances in the mazelike halls of Windsor, the opening notes of a familiar song drift in from the next room. Confused, I move to a nearby door and press my ear against the panel. I'm not imagining things. The melody of "My Country, 'Tis of Thee" – an American staple – is playing on the other side.

"I do believe that door opens, if you'd like to watch," says a deep voice behind me.

I straighten so quickly that I throw myself off-balance, and as I stumble, a hand reaches out to steady me. "I'm not—" I begin, but when I look up, the brittle words vanish from the tip of my tongue, and my racing thoughts turn to static.

Standing inches from me, his sun-bleached hair tousled, his palm warm against my bare arm, and his sea-green eyes locked on mine, is the most gorgeous boy I've ever seen.

"My apologies," he says kindly. "I didn't mean to startle you."

"You – you didn't," I manage, my head swimming. His navy suit is impeccably tailored, and his jaw is so sharp that it looks like it was carved from stone. *Why* didn't I listen to Tibby and change, or at the very least brush my hair?

"Good." He grins, and I think my heart actually skips a beat. "I'm Jasper Cunningham."

"I – I'm Evan," I say, biting back my last name. "I was just…" I trail off. I have no good explanation for what I'm doing here in my pyjamas with my ear pressed against a door. The corners of Jasper's eyes crinkle, though, and his hand lingers on my arm a moment longer before letting go, leaving my skin tingling in its wake.

"You don't have to explain," he assures me. "I've no desire to go inside, either. My father's being knighted, and he's thrilled, of course. But he's one of the first up, and I'm not keen on sitting through the rest of the ceremony."

"Did you want to watch?" I say, gesturing clumsily towards the door. Somehow in the past thirty seconds, I've lost full control of my limbs.

He nods. "The anthem's over now, so it shouldn't be long. If you stand just here, we'll both be able to see."

I let him guide me into place. His body is directly behind mine, so near that I soak in his heat like he's the sun, and as he cracks open the door and places his hand on my shoulder, something in my brain short-circuits. I've never been this close to a boy before, let alone one who looks like a cross between a Hollywood star and a literal piece of art, and I have to remind myself to breathe.

Through the narrow opening, I see a crowd of several hundred people seated in a vaulted gallery filled with yet another collection of enormous portraits. But unlike the throne room, these all seem to be of military commanders, and suddenly the name Tibby used – the Waterloo Chamber – makes sense.

At the head of the gallery stands Alexander, with more than half a dozen officials hovering nearby. A man whose face I can't see kneels in front of him, and to my surprise, Alexander raises an actual sword and taps the blade on both of his shoulders, as if we're still in the sixteenth century.

"Just in time," whispers Jasper, his breath tickling my ear. "That's my father. He's going to be insufferable after this, but it's well deserved."

"Congratulations," I manage with considerable effort, and then I mentally kick myself. Jasper isn't the one being honoured, after all. But as I glance up at him, I can see his smile, and his green eyes meet mine once more.

"Where—" he begins, but before he can finish, the door closes with a firm click.

"Dare I even ask?" says a familiar voice, and Jasper shifts, revealing Tibby standing behind us.

"Ah, Tibby," he says. "What a wonderful surprise. We were just watching my father's knighting ceremony."

"Oh? How lovely," she drawls. "I'm sure his weekly poker games with the Duke of York had nothing to do with the honour. Evan, we need to go."

Jasper politely steps aside to let me pass, though I refuse to budge. "I want to stay."

Tibby glares at me, and the weight of her silence speaks volumes. I should go with her – I *know* I should go with her. But I'm terrified that if I walk away from Jasper now, I'll never see him again.

"It's all right," says Jasper at last. "I ought to find my father and congratulate him, anyway." He faces me and takes my hand in his. "I hope we meet again, Evan."

The way he says my name is suddenly my favourite sound. "I – I hope so, too," I say faintly. And before I grasp what he's doing, he bends down, his eyes once again locked on mine as he brushes his lips against my knuckles.

"Until next time," he murmurs. And as I watch in mild shock, he opens the door again and ducks into the Waterloo Chamber, disappearing from sight.

"Holy shit," I whisper, my entire body about as solid as jelly. "*Please* tell me we're not related."

"You're not related," says Tibby flatly, steering me in the opposite direction. "The Cunninghams are close friends of the royal family, though Maisie isn't particularly fond of Jasper."

"You say that like it's a bad thing," I say, still dazed. I glance over my shoulder, half hoping Jasper will reappear, but he's long gone.

"She's not without her reasons," says Tibby. "His father, Robert Cunningham, owns half the print media in Britain. Tabloids, newspapers, magazines – you name it, they can put your face on the cover. Jasper might be unnervingly attractive, but he's not worth it."

"I'm pretty sure I'm allowed to decide who my friends are," I say as we exit the throne room, and Tibby sniffs.

"As if *friendship* has anything to do with the way you were looking at him."

I don't dignify that with a reply. Instead, I let her lead me back to my suite, though as we walk through the infuriating finery and extravagance of Windsor Castle, all I can think about is Jasper's stunning smile. And despite Helene's and Constance's vicious insults, despite Alexander's *greatest mistake*, despite every miserable thing that's happened since I arrived, I decide England might not be so bad after all.

Chapter Ten

Maisie:
I can't go out tonight.

Rosie:
WHAT?? you have to!! xx

Maisie:
Daddy says You-Know-Who has to come with us, and that certainly isn't happening.

Gia:
Evangeline? Why not? xx

Maisie:
You are joking, right?

Gia:
Bring her along and ignore her. I want to see you. xx

Rosie:
you know, if she comes out with us, we can make sure she never wants to again. problem solved xx

Gia:
As much as it kills me to say this, Rosie's right. Bring her with you, M. We'll take care of the rest. xx

—Text message exchange between Her Royal Highness the Princess Mary, Lady Primrose Chesterfield-Bishop and Lady Georgiana Greyville, 8 June 2023

I spend the rest of the afternoon glued to my laptop, listening to music and scouring the internet for every morsel of information I can find about Jasper Cunningham.

He has no public social media accounts, which makes my search more difficult than I'd like, but his name does pop up in articles about high-society events and profiles of his famous father. I discover that he's a year older than me – a totally acceptable age difference – and that he attended Eton, which is apparently one of the most prestigious boarding schools in the country. I even find a photo of Jasper, Ben and a third boy with their arms slung around each other, all laughing and dressed in identical school uniforms. It takes a bit of squinting, but I realize that their companion is the dark-haired boy I saw briefly last night – the sombre one who was with Maisie and Ben when they found me eavesdropping. Jasper really is close with the royal family, I realize, and I have no idea whether that's a good thing or the excuse Jasper will use to eventually ignore my existence.

When I change tactics and include Ben in my search, I stumble across a gossip blog called the *Regal Record*. Unlike other royal gossip sites, which all seem to have hot pink backgrounds and logos featuring tiaras, this one is black on white, with simple text posts peppered with pictures. Most of them are of Helene and her outfits and Nicholas and his girlfriend of the week, but the latest features Maisie from the night before.

PRINCESS MARY SPOTTED CLUBBING
AFTER A LEVELS

In her first public appearance since reportedly sitting her A levels, Princess Mary was spotted leaving a private nightclub in Covent Garden Wednesday evening. Gawkers inside the club report the heir to the throne spent the outing with her cousin, Prince Benedict and their entourage in the VIP section, sipping drinks of indeterminable content before bolting early after receiving what seemed like a very important text. Is there trouble at Windsor?

I click on the gallery. There are twenty different photos of Maisie leaving the club, and though she doesn't look drunk or disheveled, she does look harried. In one picture, I spot Ben over her shoulder, and in another, Maisie stands between a pair of girls who look close to our age. I search the image, trying to see if one of the faces in the background belongs to Jasper, when someone else catches my eye.

There, lurking at the edge of the photo, is the dark-haired boy. I glance at the caption. *Princess Mary and friends leaving nightclub Villagarde on Wednesday, 7 June (from left: Lady Primrose Chesterfield-Bishop, Princess Mary, Lady Georgiana Greyville, Prince Benedict and the former Lord Christopher Abbott-Montgomery, now Earl of Clarence).*

My head is swimming from all the titles and hyphenates, but I recognize Abbott-Montgomery. Helene's maiden name. And a quick Google search confirms my suspicions: the boy with dark hair is Helene's nephew.

"Evan?"

My head snaps up. Standing in the doorway to my bedroom, wearing black pants and a plain grey button-down shirt that looks more expensive than anything I've ever owned, is Ben.

I hastily close my laptop, praying he didn't see what was onscreen. "What are you doing here?"

"I knocked," he says apologetically, gesturing to the sitting room. "But you must not have heard me over your music."

Shoving my computer aside, I climb off the bed and brush the wrinkles out of my T-shirt and leggings. Not exactly high fashion, but it's a step up from pyjamas. "I'm guessing the rest of the family isn't thrilled with me right now."

"That's putting it mildly. Grandmama is so furious that she's left for Balmoral two months early – after, of course, giving us all an impassioned hour-long lecture on *family loyalty* over tea."

I cringe. "At least you'll never have to deal with us in the same room again," I say, and one corner of his mouth twitches in amusement.

"There are worse things in the world. Like hiding in your bedroom when you're only a few miles from the best city in the world." Ben checks his watch. "Maisie and I are heading to a dinner party at Kensington Palace in half an hour, and she wanted to know if you'd like to join us."

I stare at him, not entirely sure I've heard him right. "What?"

His twitch stretches into a full-blown smirk. "Maisie," he says slowly, "wants me to invite you on a night out."

This has to be some kind of practical joke, I decide. Does she expect me to get dressed up, only for my driver to drop me off in some shady alley with no way back to Windsor? "Maisie has barely said a word to me, and I'm pretty sure neither of us would be heartbroken if it stayed that way."

"No doubt," agrees Ben. "But Uncle Alexander told Maisie that if we go out tonight, we have to bring you with us."

"Oh." I wilt a little, even though I have no idea why. "In that case, the answer's definitely no."

"Are you regretfully declining a royal invitation?" he says, his brows arched.

"Declining, yes. Regretfully, no."

"Evan." He steps towards me, his blue eyes wide and pleading. "You're miserable. I know it, you know it, and unless something changes, you're going to spend the whole month in your room, doing...whatever it is you're doing. Let me show you a good time – please. One night. If you hate it, I'll never ask you to come out with us again, all right?"

"Ben – thank you, but—"

"What if I told you Jasper Cunningham's going to be there?"

I blink, and my mind goes fuzzy again just from the sound of his name. "How—"

"He texted me," says Ben with a sly smile. "Don't worry, I didn't tell him who you are, but he does seem exceptionally keen to get to know you better."

"I—" I try to tell Ben that I really would prefer to stay in with Netflix and the ghost of Henry VIII, but suddenly all I can see are Jasper's sea-green eyes and that impossibly gorgeous smile. And that's why, exactly thirty minutes later, I'm climbing into a Range Rover with tinted windows, my insides in knots at the prospect of facing my half-sister again. Maisie's already buckled in behind the driver, and though I've braced myself for the onslaught of insults I'm sure is coming, she gives me a truly impressive cold shoulder instead, not even bothering to glance in my general direction.

That's one way to deal with the situation, I suppose. Rather than risking her ire, I slide into the back row with the dark-haired Christopher Abbott-Montgomery, leaving Ben to sit beside my pouting half-sister.

"We should have just left without her," says Maisie once the vehicle starts down the drive. "What's the worst Daddy could do? Ground me?"

She says this in a way that makes it clear she's never been grounded a day in her life. Then again, neither have I, so at least Alexander is consistent.

"You'll have Gia and Rosie to distract you," says Ben. "And Evan deserves to have a bit of fun, too, you know. I'm sure staying here is no picnic for her, either."

He shoots me an easy grin over the back of the seat, as if to reassure me he has everything under control. I force a wan smile, but I don't really care what Maisie thinks. I'm not here for her, after all.

"It's only three forks," says the boy sitting on the other end of the cushioned leather bench. His voice is so low that it takes me a moment to register what he's said, and in the intermittent light from the street lamps, I notice his dark eyes are fixed on me.

"What?" I say, confused.

"Ben told me about your, er, argument with Constance," he says. "And that you said you weren't interested in the kind of life that requires a dozen forks at dinner, but there are typically only three. Four when oysters are served."

I stare at him. "Who actually *needs* that many forks?"

"Picky eaters, I suppose," he says with a lift of his shoulder. "I thought you might like to know. For any scathing remarks you're planning for the future, I mean."

"Uh – thanks," I say. I can't tell if he's trying to be funny or simply making fun of me. Maybe a little of both. He's more reserved than Ben, though, and his words aren't cutting the way Maisie's are. And I don't know what to make of that.

The silence stretches uncomfortably between us, and he clears his throat. "Your bracelet is lovely," he says, and I glance down at my gift from Prisha, which is still fastened around my wrist. "Do you like music?"

"Everyone likes music, Kit," says Maisie. "Stop trying to make small talk. It's embarrassing."

Christopher – Kit – stiffens at her dressing-down, and my hackles rise. Maisie might be the heir to the throne, but she doesn't get to tell anyone to shut up.

"Yeah, I do," I say, louder than before. Loud enough so that Maisie can't even pretend to ignore me. "My favourite band is Reignwolf, but I'm also really into Banners, the Struts, MisterWives, Blackpink, Fleetwood Mac—"

"Maisie loves Harry Styles," says Ben. "And Taylor Swift."

"Harry has the soul of a poet, and Taylor saved me from a rather odious American actor at a film premiere last year," says Maisie defensively. "She has more wisdom in her little finger than most of Daddy's advisers put together."

"Her new album is fantastic," I say, even though I'm not feeling especially chummy towards Maisie right now. "I'm jealous you've met her."

"*I* didn't meet her," she says. "Taylor met *me*."

I raise an eyebrow, but mercifully manage to bite my tongue. As the Range Rover passes a street light, however, I catch Kit's curious gaze. For a moment he seems like he's about to say something, but instead he looks away.

Eventually Ben gets Her Royal Highness talking about some resort in Ibiza, and I spend the rest of the ride gazing out the window. London *looks* like a city that's been around for a thousand years. The architecture varies from street to street, and towering statues mingle with flashing neon signs. The traffic is thick even though it's getting late, and it only grows worse as we near Central London.

At last we pass Piccadilly Circus and turn down a narrow street in the West End, where dazzling advertisements for musicals and plays light up the night sky. But the sidewalks get darker and less crowded the farther we go, and for a moment I wonder if they really are going to abandon me in the middle of the city.

But when we finally stop behind what looks like a normal brick building, albeit with a pair of bouncers guarding the back door, the others unbuckle their seat belts. I, however, stay put.

"I thought we were going to Kensington Palace," I say. While I don't know where that is, exactly, I *am* sure a royal residence wouldn't be wedged between a Thai restaurant and an adult bookshop.

"No, this is a club opening in Soho," says Kit, with one foot out of the vehicle. "Who told you we were going to Kensington?"

"Daddy wouldn't let us leave without her," says Maisie unapologetically as she waits for the driver to open her door.

"And since Benny was sure she wouldn't want to go out in public with us, we decided that a little white lie was better than ruining everyone's night."

My mouth drops open, and Ben gives me a guilty look. "I'm sorry. It's perfectly safe here, I promise. Several of our protection officers are already inside – and so is Jasper," he adds, his voice rising a hopeful half octave. "He's an investor in the club, and he knows you're coming."

I glare at Ben. He was right – I would've never agreed to go to a nightclub in the most crowded part of London, where anyone can see me walk in with members of the royal family. But the sound of Jasper's name is like catnip to my brain, and suddenly my heart is beating a little faster. Dazzling, kind, thoughtful Jasper, who kissed my hand and hoped to see me again, is inside the building, and this might be my only chance to talk to him.

It's one night. I'm already here, and no one knows who I am.

And with Maisie and Ben in the room, no one will care. "Fine," I say through gritted teeth. "But you owe me, Ben."

Maisie scoffs. "None of us owes you a bloody thing," she says as the chauffeur finally opens her door, and she slips out with infuriating grace.

As soon as my feet hit the pavement, I register a faint thrumming coming from what must be the club. Before I can get my bearings, however, a squeal echoes through the alleyway, so high-pitched that I have to resist the urge to cover my ears.

"You made it!" A petite girl with a round face framed by blonde curls bounds towards Maisie, and after a quick curtsy, she catches her in a hug. This is Rosie, I think, judging by the pictures I saw of the girls on the *Regal Record*. And lingering near the door is a tall girl with dark skin, razor-sharp features and a scowl. Gia.

"Took you long enough," she says, kissing Maisie on both cheeks.

"*Someone* took her sweet time getting ready," says Maisie, glaring at me before turning back to her friends. The three of them link arms and disappear through the back door, trailed by two of Maisie's protection officers.

"Come on," says Ben, touching my shoulder. "I promise it'll be better than it looks from the outside."

I'm not so sure about that, but I follow him anyway. When we step through the narrow entrance, the thrumming turns into a teeth-chattering bass, and we all head into a dimly lit hall that curls downward. While most of it is empty, a few people linger, and I don't miss their curious stares as Ben and I pass.

Before I can process what those looks mean, however, Kit appears and offers me his elbow. "So no one assumes you're Ben's latest conquest," he explains, and a knot of dread forms in my chest.

"You think they'd…?" I say, and he nods.

"Every time he's photographed with a girl, it's front-page news. But no one bothers with what I do."

The only thing worse than being part of this family is having the entire world think I'm dating my cousin, and so I take Kit's arm. "Thanks," I say, the word heavy on my tongue.

"You're welcome," he says kindly. And as he sets his hand over mine, we fall into step with each other and descend into the depths of the building.

Ben is waiting for us beside another door, this one so dark that I don't see it until he pushes it open. I tighten my grip on Kit's elbow, and as the three of us walk inside, the bass becomes a wall of sound so thick it's almost tangible. Not far ahead of us, Gia wraps her arm around Rosie's waist, and they dance their way through the crowd. Though the main floor dominates the club, a second level hovers over a busy bar, and Maisie makes a beeline for the stairs, with Ben following at a more leisurely pace. A stocky man in a suit stands in front of the velvet rope that blocks their way, but the moment he sees them coming, he unhooks it. The four of them walk up the steps like they own the place – not surprising, considering everyone in the club seems to have noticed their arrival – and Kit starts to lead me over when there's a familiar voice in my ear.

"You made it!"

I spin around, dropping Kit's arm like it's suddenly on fire. Jasper Cunningham stands beside me, drink in hand and blond hair just the right side of messy. "Uh – yeah," I shout, my heart beating faster. "Ben invited me."

"I was hoping he would," says Jasper, his smile irresistible. He's every bit as attractive as he was that afternoon – somehow even more so thanks to the faint sheen of sweat on his forehead. "You look lovely."

My face grows hot, and I glance down at my outfit – a lilac sundress meant for a dinner party, not a club opening. "Thanks," I manage, tongue-tied and wishing my brain would just *work* already. "You look…gorgeous."

Gorgeous? Six years in all-girls boarding schools have done me no favours, but he's grinning again.

"I like you, Evan," he says, a dimple appearing in his cheek. "You're refreshing."

"I'll be upstairs," calls Kit over the music, and his dark eyes linger on me. "Are you all right on your own?"

"I've got her, mate," says Jasper before I can reply, and his hand brushes my hip, sending a shiver through me. "Tell the others I'll be up soon."

Kit's expression is unreadable, but he disappears into the crowd without argument, leaving Jasper and me on our own. I cast around for something witty or charming or even remotely interesting to say, and instead I land on, "Ben said this is your club?"

"I wish I could take the credit, but I'm merely an investor," says Jasper with a chuckle. "Can I get you a drink?"

"Yeah," I say, relieved this is an easy question. "A water would be—"

"*There* you are." Ben appears beside me, and I wince as he yells into my ear. "Come upstairs – it's quieter."

I try my best not to glare at him, but his timing makes it enormously difficult. "I'm talking to Jasper," I protest.

"It's all right," says Jasper. "I should do rounds anyway. But I'll find you in a bit, yeah?" He smiles, and it feels like sunshine. "Maybe by then, Ben will have found someone else to keep him occupied."

Jasper's gaze lingers on me as he steps away, and once he's disappeared into the neon darkness, I whirl around to face Ben. "Are you serious?"

"You don't want to seem too eager, do you?" he says with a smirk. "Come on, we'll talk upstairs."

Deeply annoyed, I keep my distance as I follow him past the velvet rope and up into the VIP area, where I most definitely don't belong. Everyone here is beautiful – the polished, shining kind of beautiful that only comes from wealth and fame and endless hours at a spa. I recognize a few faces from magazine covers and social media, and to my shock, I spot a woman who looks startlingly like the lead in one of my favourite movies. How exclusive is this club?

Exclusive enough to attract royalty, clearly. Heads turn as Ben leads me between the tiered booths, all circular and able to seat a dozen, but while I'm not surprised people are staring at him – an unmarried prince who's third in line to the throne – they all seem to be paying me an unnerving amount of attention, too.

I fall back a few paces, putting even more distance between us. If there's a single headline tomorrow about Ben and me supposedly dating, I'm not leaving my bedroom until it's time to board a plane back to the States.

Ben slips into a booth with arguably the best view of the DJ and dance floor, and I follow his lead. He's right – it's much quieter up here, and I glance around, trying not to be too obvious about it. Four protection officers stand guard around the VIP area, and I suspect there are others hidden in the crowd. How much security does it take for Maisie and Ben to go out like this?

"...*beyond* boring."

Gia's voice catches my attention from the centre of the booth. She and Maisie are sitting shoulder to shoulder, with Rosie on Maisie's other side. Ben is a few feet away from Gia, typing on his phone, and Kit is missing. There's a bottle of champagne on the table already, but while the others have glasses in front of them, I notice Maisie doesn't.

"Give it a chance," says Rosie with an earnest dose of optimism. "Jasper knows how to throw a good party."

"This isn't a party," says Gia. "And the only reason he's ever thrown a good one is because of his daddy's deep pockets."

I snort, and all eyes turn towards me. "Did Gia say something funny?" says Maisie, the challenge in her voice clear.

"I'm willing to bet all of your fathers have deep pockets," I point out.

"Of course they do," says Gia, "but *we're* not crass enough to flaunt it."

"If you say so," I mumble under my breath. I don't think they hear me, but Maisie sits up straighter.

"We can't possibly expect Evangeline to recognize the difference between class and crass," she says. "After all, look at her mother."

I clench my jaw, and beside me, Ben sighs. "Maisie, we talked about this."

"Did we?" she says sweetly. "It must have slipped my mind." There are a million things I want to say to her, but not here – not when any one of the other Very Important People nearby might hear us. Instead, I scan the crowd for Jasper, wondering how long it'll take him to join us.

"Could you imagine, though?" says Maisie with feigned incredulity. "Being *illegitimate*. I would never show my face in public."

Gia and Rosie giggle like this is the most scandalous thing they've ever heard, and I scowl. "At least I'm not a heartless snob," I mutter.

"What was that?" snaps Gia.

"Oh, you didn't hear me?" I say, louder this time. "You might want to get your ears checked. I hear inbreeding can do strange things to your genes."

The girls gasp in unison, and Ben grimaces. "Let's go to the bar, Evan," he says, slipping his phone into his pocket.

"I don't want anything," I say, but he's already sliding towards me, and I have no choice but to stand and let him out. He starts to guide me away, but before we take more than two steps, I hear a low hiss in my sister's honeyed voice.

"Bastard."

Only in the English aristocracy is that a literal insult, as if my parents' choices are some kind of moral failing of my own.

Shaking off Ben's hand, I turn on my heel and flash Maisie a dazzling smile.

"Better a bastard than a raging bitch," I say before spinning back around and marching away, leaving her stunned in my wake.

As I storm towards the steps, I can feel the burning stares of countless onlookers, all undoubtedly wondering what kind of juicy royal drama they've just witnessed. Thankfully Ben doesn't try to follow me downstairs, and as the bouncer lifts the velvet rope, I spot several other clubgoers watching me, too. I ignore them and stride through the crowd. My throat is scratchy, like I've been in a shouting match, and I'm desperate for water. When did it get so *hot* in here?

As I reach the bar, I notice a pair of girls with long black ponytails holding their phones and staring openly at me. At first their heads are bent together, but after a moment, the taller girl straightens.

"Hey," she calls, her sparkling eyeshadow catching the light. "Are you her?"

"Who?" I say, but instead of answering, she shoves her phone an inch from my nose. It's open to a post on the *Regal Record*, and the very first thing I see is a headline in bold letters:

ROYAL SHOCKER:
THE KING'S SECRET DAUGHTER

And directly underneath, taken mere minutes ago in the dim Soho alleyway, is a fuzzy picture of me.

Chapter Eleven

King Alexander has a secret daughter.

Seventeen-year-old Evangeline Bright, pictured in Soho this evening, is the illegitimate child of His Majesty and an unknown mother, reported to be American. Thanks to multiple palace insiders with intimate knowledge of the delicate situation, the *Regal Record* can confirm that Evangeline is staying at Windsor Castle, where she's been given a chilly reception by several members of the royal family. This is allegedly her first trip to the UK, and so far, our sources say she isn't impressed.

More details to come. For the latest breaking royal news, follow us at @TheRegalRecord.

—*The Regal Record*, 8 June 2023

My entire body goes numb, and everything around me seems to narrow as I grip the counter to keep from swaying.

No. *No.* This can't be happening. How do they know? Who— Both girls are still staring at me, and they aren't the only ones.

It isn't because I came down from the VIP area, I realize.

This post – made eight minutes ago, according to the time stamp – is spreading like wildfire.

"N-no," I manage. "That's not me."

"Are you sure?" says the other girl, leaning in closer now – so close I can smell the alcohol on her breath. "You're wearing the same outfit, *and* we saw you come in with the princess's entourage."

"We're friends," I mumble, and bright spots flash in front of me as I struggle to take a breath. "Excuse me."

I shoulder my way past them and stumble back towards the staircase. My annoyance with Maisie and Ben is nothing more than a faint memory now, and I have to find them. I have to tell them about the post before the entire club sees it. But as I approach the rope, the bouncer doesn't budge. "VIPs only," he booms.

"I *just* came down from there," I argue. "Please, everyone I'm with—"

"VIPs only," he repeats, and as the club starts to spin around me, I know there's no chance of swaying him. But I have to get out of here.

I dart towards the entrance we used minutes earlier, though when I tug on the door handle, it doesn't budge. I try again, but my attempts are only drawing more attention. Dammit. I have no idea where the main exit is. On the other side of the club, I guess, but the number of people watching me is increasing, and I can't make myself move away from the wall.

What the hell am I supposed to do?

Suddenly a pair of hands grabs my shoulders, and before I can pull away, a familiar voice fills my ear. "Evan, it's only me," says Jasper, and I'm so relieved that my legs almost give out. "Are you all right?"

I shake my head, and horror washes over me. Several people have their phones pointed at us now, clearly recording, and I turn my back to them.

"There's a post about me on – on some gossip site," I admit. "Yes, I just saw it," says Jasper with a grimace. "Let's get you out of here."

He doesn't demand to know if it's true. Instead, he leads me along the perimeter of the club without saying a word, and my vision is so blurry that I don't see the door until he's ushering me into a dark hallway.

The music is muffled now, and we pass an office and a tiny bathroom. "I'm sorry," says Jasper, and he takes my hand, squeezing it comfortingly. I've never held a boy's hand before, and his warm touch sparks against my skin, sending an electric jolt down my spine. But even though this would have made me melt five minutes ago, I'm too consumed by fear and panic to enjoy it now. How did this get out? Who leaked my paternity to the press?

"It's not your fault," I say. We've made it to the sloping hallway that leads to the back exit, and our eyes meet for a split second before I look away. "I need – I need to find the driver. I need to get out of here."

"I've got a car waiting for you," he promises. "Have you ever dealt with the paparazzi before?"

"I – what? No, of course not," I say, my voice rising in alarm. "They're here? How did they even find me?"

"I've no idea," he says with a scowl. "Listen – when we go out

99

there, they're going to take your picture and yell your name. All you have to do is keep your head down and say nothing, all right? I'll make sure you're safe."

We reach the door, and I stop, shivering in the darkness. "Why are you being so nice?"

"Because you look like you could use a friend, and I know what that feels like." He tucks a stray lock of hair behind my ear. "If you ever need someone to talk to, I'm here."

"Thanks," I mumble, and he rubs my bare arm. My skin still tingles at his touch, and I hate that a stupid gossip site has ruined this moment for me.

"Come on," says Jasper. "We might as well get this over with before half of London joins them."

He gives me his jacket to hide my face, and once I've taken a deep breath, he opens the door. I'm not sure what I'm expecting – a handful of men with cameras, maybe, and some inane questions about if it's true, if I'm really the American bastard.

Instead, when the warm night air hits me, it comes with an explosion of flashes as a horde of paparazzi take my picture all at once. Frozen and disoriented, I want to run back inside, but Jasper wraps his arm around my shoulders and leads me forward. I stumble along with him, my vision obscured as I duck my head as low as possible, and I silently pray that no one rips his jacket from me.

"Evangeline!" My name is shouted in an endless echo, the voices so close and loud that my ears are ringing.

"Over here!"

"When did you find out?"

"Where have you been hiding, love?"

"What's your mother's name?"

"Are you really the King's daughter?"

The twenty seconds it takes for Jasper to push our way through the crowd are the longest twenty seconds of my life. I'm assaulted with question after question until my head starts to spin, but at last we reach the town car, and I scramble inside.

"It'll be okay," says Jasper over the din. "I promise, Evan, it will be okay."

And then he slams the door shut, leaving me in a dazed, muffled silence.

When I arrive back at Windsor, Jenkins is waiting for me. "Evan..." he murmurs as I stumble out of the car, and he envelops me in his arms.

"I'm sorry," I hiccup, burying my tear-stained, snot-covered face in his chest, no doubt ruining his suit. "I didn't say anything to anyone, I swear."

"I know," he says gently. "Whatever has happened, it isn't your fault, sweetheart. Let's get you inside."

Half an hour later, my hair is wet, my face is free of make-up, and I'm dressed in a pair of clean pyjamas as I sit at the foot of a long conference table surrounded by palace officials. At the other end is Alexander, his expression grim as he stares into a cup of tea.

"Do we have any idea how this happened?" says a ruddy man seated to his right – the royal press secretary, I think.

"The leak could have come from any number of sources, Doyle," says Jenkins as he places a steaming mug in front of me.

"We've no hope of narrowing it down based on the information released."

"Are we sure we have no leads?" says Doyle, and I catch his eye. The others in the room – a dozen or more men and women – all shift their gazes towards me, and I tense at the obvious implication.

"You really think I'd do this?" I say, appalled. "I don't even want to be here in the first place."

"It was not Evangeline," says the King quietly. "And if I hear a single word of accusation against her, the party responsible will be immediately dismissed from service."

Doyle falls silent, though he spares me one last glance before focusing on his notepad instead.

"Regardless of how the news leaked," continues Alexander, "the fact is that it has. And now we must decide what to do about it."

"Deny, of course," says a woman with short brown hair and an upturned nose. "If we confirm the story, public opinion will plummet."

"It would be foolish for us to respond at all, Yara," argues Doyle. "A single gossip site running a few pictures and making an outrageous claim—"

"Is exactly the kind of fodder the tabloids love," she says. "Ignoring the story will only make it grow tenfold."

"And issuing a denial won't?" says Doyle. "Our greatest chance of getting ahead of this is to send Miss Bright away from London. The sooner she's no longer in play, the less time the press will devote to her, and the better the optics of the entire sordid—"

"You're talking like she's a chess piece for you to move around at will," says another voice from the far end of the room. Nicholas, the Duke of York, leans against the door with his arms crossed. "I realize that's how you see all members of our family, but given she's sitting right here, surely you could at least try to remember she's human."

I've never said a word to my uncle, but in that moment, I'm more grateful for him than I can possibly say. Doyle squirms in his seat, and at the head of the table, my father sighs.

"I'm aware that my actions nearly two decades ago are indefensible. But that is entirely on me, and your job is not to hide the fact that Evangeline exists. Your job is to make sure that I am the only one taking the blame."

I stare at Alexander, not entirely sure I've heard him right, and Doyle sputters. "But – sir, you are the King. She—"

"Is my daughter," he finishes. "Not an inconvenience. Not a scandal. She is of royal blood, and she will be treated as such by everyone in this castle."

Now it's Yara's turn to look distinctly uncomfortable. "You are…certain, sir?"

The room goes strangely quiet, and it takes me a beat to realize what she's asking. "Are you calling my mom a liar?" I blurt. "It's a possibility the press will raise within the first twenty-four hours," says Yara. "If there is any chance your mother was mistaken, and you are not His Majesty's child…"

For a long moment, no one says anything, and when I look at Alexander, I realize he's gone red. Not with embarrassment, though – his expression has hardened, and there's a coldness to him that sends a chill through me.

"Evangeline is my daughter," he repeats, his voice crackling with fury. "I will not have that questioned again, either to my face or behind my back. Is that understood?"

A murmur of reluctant agreement ripples through the conference room. I don't know what to say – I don't know why he's so sure. Was there a DNA test? There had to be. But his anger doesn't make sense.

Jenkins clears his throat. "As admirable as it is that Your Majesty is willing to go public with your relationship to Miss Bright, I have to wonder what she thinks about all of this, given it is her life that is changing so drastically."

Suddenly everyone in the room is looking at me again, and I slide lower in my seat, wrapping my hands around my mug. "Evan?" says Alexander, his voice softer now. "Would you prefer we deny the story?"

He doesn't say it, but the underlying question is obvious. He's willing to acknowledge me as his daughter, but am I willing to acknowledge him as my father?

I could say no. It's what Helene and Maisie want. It's what everyone in that room wants, save for Alexander and Jenkins. It might even get me a one-way ticket home. I'm the King's greatest mistake, after all, and telling the world won't change that.

But as he watches me, something flickers across his face. Regret, I think, and a kind of sadness I can't name. And I suspect that if I say yes – if I ask him to deny it publicly – I'll never get another chance to be his daughter. Even if the press gets tired of the story, I'll probably never be allowed to see Alexander again, in fear of someone finding out and exposing the monarchy's lie.

And I know unquestionably that the monarchy cannot be caught in a lie.

"If a gossip blog can dig this up, then they'll inevitably find out about the arrest, too," I say quietly, because it's only fair to warn him that I won't just be his illegitimate daughter in the eyes of the public – I'll also be a felon.

"*Arrest?*" bursts Doyle, and another murmur ripples through the room, but Jenkins coughs.

"Your former headmistress has agreed to inform the police that it was, in truth, an accident," he says. "We expect any pending charges to never see the light of day, and for all records of your unjust detention to be expunged."

I exhale fully now, until my lungs are so empty that my chest hurts. No doubt that cost Alexander a pretty penny, but I'm grateful, especially since the whole incident probably earned Jenkins a few more grey hairs. Windsor may be a prison in its own right, but at least it has Wi-Fi.

Despite Jenkins's reassurances, Doyle looks like he's about to swallow his own tie, and several others seated around the table fidget uncomfortably, clearly unwilling to voice what they really think. But I ignore them and instead hold Alexander's gaze like we're the only two people in the room.

"I want my mom to be safe," I say, my voice as hard as steel. "I don't want the press to hunt her down. I don't want them to camp out in front of her house. I don't want them to find—" I stop. I don't want them to find out about her illness, especially when they'll only bully and demonize her for it. "No matter what happens, I don't want them to find out who she is. Can you promise me that?"

"I cannot pretend the press will not search for her," says Alexander, "but she is well hidden and well cared for. That will never change, regardless of your decision." He hesitates, as if choosing his next words carefully. "I would like the opportunity to be in your life. I deeply regret how I have treated you and made you feel over the years, and it is my sincerest wish to rectify that. But this decision…this monumental, life-changing decision is yours and yours alone. I will always be your father, Evan. The only question now is if you want to be my daughter."

I exhale. Do I? I don't even know what it's like to have a father. I don't know what it's like to be someone's kid, really.

But Alexander looks at me with such blatant hope, his hands clasped so tightly that there's a slight tremor to them, and I don't know how to say no. Not like this. Not to his face. Not when the consequences are permanent.

And part of me – a part I've buried so deep that I've almost forgotten it exists – doesn't want to. I don't want to be a princess. I don't want to be famous, or to live in a museum with virtually no privacy. But I want to know my father. And maybe, in time, it would be nice to have a real family.

"Helene and Maisie will be furious," I say, because someone needs to. There's no chance they won't take this personally.

"They'll adjust," says Alexander quietly, and I can tell from those two words that he isn't fooling himself. This won't be easy, and it'll never be simple. But he wants to try, and so do I.

"Then – okay," I all but whisper, feeling like I've detached from my body. Doyle and Yara simultaneously sigh, though Alexander smiles for the first time that evening.

"You're certain?" he says, and I nod.

"I know it's going to be a massive scandal, but I'm sick of being hidden away like something you're ashamed of."

His expression falls. "I am not ashamed of you. I love—"

He stops, clearing his throat and glancing around the table, as if remembering we're not alone. Several staff members avert their eyes, but despite the awkwardness, he presses on. "I love you, Evan. And I am eternally grateful for the opportunity to prove it to you."

I'm not sure I believe him. But whether he's telling the truth or not, I'll find out soon enough.

"Okay," I say. "Let's do this."

Chapter Twelve

BUCKINGHAM PALACE PRESS RELEASE
From His Majesty The King, 9 June 2023

It is with both pride and shame that I confirm the recent reports that I have a daughter outside of my marriage. Pride in having the opportunity to introduce Evangeline to this great nation I humbly serve, and shame in knowing the hurt my actions have inflicted upon those dearest to me, particularly my loving and devoted Queen.

Evangeline has been an important part of my life since her birth, and Queen Helene and Princess Mary were made aware of her existence a long time ago. Both have offered forgiveness I do not deserve, and we are united in welcoming Evangeline into our family.

Though we understand the interest the public may have in our new circumstances, we respectfully ask for privacy regarding this personal matter.

Alexander R

Almost immediately after the press release is issued the next morning, headlines began to appear. The BBC, *The Times* – the Soho pictures of me are even plastered on the home page of CNN, and I'm trending on every possible social media platform.

PALACE CONFIRMS AMERICAN LOVE CHILD, screams one headline.

ALEXANDER'S ILLEGITIMATE DAUGHTER EXPOSED, yells another.

KING REVEALS BELOVED SECRET DAUGHTER is the kindest of them all, and I notice it's from the *Daily Sun*, the biggest paper in the Cunningham media empire. Jasper must have exercised his influence, I figure, and I'm grateful for it. Or maybe the Cunninghams aren't nearly as bad as Tibby insists.

In the days following the announcement, Lady Tabitha Finch-Parker-Covington-Boyle is as prickly as ever, but there's a strange protectiveness about the way she treats me, almost as if she's acting as a human shield. The team of stylists, etiquette instructors, private tutors and media relations specialists that now swarm my every waking hour are ruthless, drilling into me things they seem to think I should have known from birth – my genealogy and an offensively sanitized history of the Commonwealth. How to handle the press and play nice with the paparazzi. The difference between a marquess and an earl, the trick to getting out of a car without flashing my underwear, how to fake a smile for hours without looking deranged – even the way they think I should address other members of the royal family in public. My rank within their already-complicated hierarchy is muddled at best, considering I'm the daughter of the reigning monarch, but also illegitimate. I'm both important and so very much *not*, and even the most senior of my instructors seems baffled as to how to handle it.

"Don't worry so much about protocol," says Tibby during an especially arduous lesson, when my brain is swimming with royal rules I'll inevitably break. "Address the King, Queen and Queen Mother with respect, and the Duke of York as well, if you'd like. Maisie if she's not being a little shit—"

This elicits a stifled gasp from my etiquette instructor. " – and Ben if he insists, though he won't. But anyone else expecting a curtsy can sod right off."

It's great in theory, but I have no real chance to practise. While Ben makes a habit of dropping by for lunch, and Alexander checks in daily, the other members of the royal family do an impressive job of avoiding me completely. I'm not even sure Helene and Maisie are still at Windsor until I accidentally run across my half-sister in the corridor four days after the news breaks.

We stare at each other for a long moment, both of us frozen in place ten feet apart. Despite Alexander's supposed desire for family unity, we haven't seen each other since that night at the club, and Maisie eyes my fresh dye job and the heels I'm now required to walk in until I get the hang of them. Though it takes enormous effort, I resist the urge to squirm under her scrutiny, refusing to give her the satisfaction.

"Louis wasn't a fan of the green," I say, tugging on a lock of my brunette hair. "I tried to talk him into purple, but—"

Without a word, Maisie strides past me, her chin raised imperiously as if I'm not worth her precious time. I watch her go in silence. I can't really blame her, especially in the wake of Alexander's official acknowledgment and the public humiliation that must come along with it. But I also can't pretend her continued rejection doesn't sting.

The press coverage grows exponentially in the week following the announcement. Stories from my old classmates – names and faces I don't even remember – are emerging, and most of them aren't exactly kind. Though my arrest miraculously seems to remain a secret, my nine expulsions are uncovered by the *Regal Record*, despite the palace's attempts to keep them under wraps, and my nicknames in the press are multiplying at an alarming rate. "The Royal Rebel" seems to be the favourite at the moment, mostly because the more legitimate publications can print it without overtly offending the royal family. "The AmerEvan Bastard," however, is a charming contender.

Though the various media outlets have only a few pictures of me, they take vicious glee in publishing them side by side with images of Maisie, comparing her best to my worst. Really, it isn't even a comparison at all. Seemingly from her very first public appearance on the steps of the hospital twelve days after her birth, my half-sister has exuded grace and composure. Even in the photographs of her riding horses and spilling out of clubs at two in the morning, she doesn't have a hair out of place, and she looks every inch the princess and heir to the throne that she is. I, on the other hand, am squinting or blinking or making faces in all the photographs the so-called journalists have dug up, all exclusively from my boarding school years. There are none from my time at St Edith's, though, and I feel oddly sentimental towards Headmistress Thompson. Maybe spending five months without technology wasn't the worst thing in the world after all.

But to my relief, despite the overwhelming amount of speculation on gossip blogs and social media, no one has found my mother yet. Alexander has kept his word, and in the end, that's all I really care about.

I call her daily now, in the minutes before I pass out each night. She answers every time, and she's always eager to show me the magazines and articles she's collected, all with my face in them. She asks about my day and the things I'm learning, but our conversations inevitably circle back to Alexander, just as they did before. Maybe her new medication isn't working, or maybe this is all feeding her delusions in a devasting way. But I have to trust that her doctors are taking care of her, and at least now I know my mom is thinking of me, too.

"Are you all right?" says Tibby one morning nearly a week after the press release. She pulls back the curtains, and sunlight floods my bedroom. "You've seemed out of sorts lately."

"Really? Wonder why," I say darkly, sitting up and rubbing the sleep from my eyes. "Is this how it's going to be for the rest of the month?"

"The rest of the month? Darling, legitimate or not, you're part of the royal family now. This is how it's going to be for the rest of your *life*."

My expression must make it clear how thrilled I am at that thought, because Tibby sighs and perches on the edge of the mattress. She's stiff and a bit awkward about it, but I appreciate her closeness. With Jenkins up to his eyeballs helping Alexander handle the maelstrom of scandal that is my existence, I don't really have anyone else who's wholly on my team right now.

"I know you must feel…trapped," she says slowly. "For those who marry into the royal family, they have months – sometimes years – to prepare for this seismic shift in their lives. You've had less than a week, and none of it has been fair to you. But this" – she gestures around the room vaguely – "is preparation. The real tests are still to come."

"Real tests?" I say. She hesitates for a split second, long enough for me to know it's bad.

"His Majesty has requested that you join the family for Trooping the Colour this Saturday."

Instead of the horror she seems to expect, I stare at her blankly. "Trooping the what?"

She pinches the bridge of her nose. "I keep forgetting how *American* you are," she says wearily, as if this single question has drained her entire life force. "Trooping the Colour is a ceremony where the various branches of our military present themselves to the King. It's also the traditional celebration of the monarch's birthday, even though His Majesty was born in February. *Surely* you've seen the famous balcony pictures of the royal family during the fly-past."

I shake my head. But that's a lie – I've definitely seen a few in my late-night Google searches, and stark realization sets in. "He wants me to go out in *public* with him?"

"You are of course allowed to turn him down," says Tibby. "The monarch does not order, but it *is* considered to be in bad taste to refuse when issued an invitation. And you'll be the talk of the town whether or not you're on that balcony come Saturday, so you might as well give everyone a peek at your new look. Perhaps the media might even start using a picture without those hideous green ends Louis vanquished."

I gape at her, baffled. "I can't go," I croak. "I'm not ready."

"You'll never feel ready," she says. "But you're as ready as

113

you're going to be at this stage. Trooping the Colour is extremely public, of course, but you won't have to interact with the crowd. It is, in many ways, the perfect introduction for you."

"But – doesn't Alexander want to wait until the uproar dies down?"

"The uproar will only die down once the country has seen you for themselves," she says. "This will be your chance to show them that you're not some serial killer in the making who burned down her last boarding school."

I cringe. The press may not know about my arrest, but clearly the reason I was expelled from St Edith's is making the rounds. "Are people really saying that?"

"They are saying all sorts of things," says Tibby frankly. "And they will *always* say all sorts of things. None of it matters, though, because their opinions cannot reverse your paternity and change who you are. Your job – your *only* job – is to be the best version of yourself, and to do everything you can to set a good example from here on out. Right now, you have an opportunity to start afresh. The old stories will follow you for a while, but eventually new ones – stronger ones, with photographic evidence – will take their place and overshadow any gossip. And you're the one who decides what kind of stories those will be."

"Okay," I mumble, not completely sure I buy Tibby's pep talk, but it's nice of her to try. "Thanks, by the way. For – this, and for sticking with me."

"Please. This will look *fabulous* on my résumé."

But there's a hint of a smile on her face, and I return it. My entire world might be falling apart, but at least Tibby isn't letting it bury me. "Is that it? Just an appearance at Trooping the Colour?" I say, barely daring to hope.

"Hardly," she says, standing and smoothing her pencil skirt. "His Majesty has also requested your presence at Royal Ascot, for one. It's a horse race," she adds as I open my mouth to ask. "Then of course there's Wimbledon, the Henley Royal Regatta, various polo and cricket matches—"

I groan. "He knows I'm going back to the States in less than three weeks, right?"

"Perhaps he's hoping you'll change your mind."

I flop back onto my pillows and sigh. I knew going through with this would throw some kind of monkey wrench into my plans, but no matter how hard Alexander tries to include me, it won't change anything.

"As it happens," says Tibby reluctantly, "I *may* have received a text this morning that might cheer you up."

"What kind of text?" I say with a frown.

"A text inviting you to a small get-together in Belgravia this evening," she says. "From one Mr Jasper Cunningham."

I sit up so quickly that spots appear in front of me. "Jasper invited me to a party?" I haven't heard from him all week – according to Ben, he's been keeping his distance to give me some breathing room. Sweet, but completely misguided, considering Windsor Castle grows more suffocating by the day.

Tibby rolls her eyes. "Yes, though try not to feel too special. He's invited Maisie, Ben, and their lot as well," she says.

I frown. If he's asked Maisie and the others to come, then maybe this is only a pity invite. But what if it isn't? What if he actually wants me there? "Do you think it's safe for me to go?"

115

She sniffs like I've mortally offended her. "If I thought there was any chance this would go badly for you, I would have deleted the text and forgotten all about it. Jasper might be a Cunningham and a world-class sycophant, but I've been to his private parties before, and they're small and never leaked to the press. The other guests will all be members of the peerage or old friends, so they know how to keep a secret. The last thing I want is to talk you into a night anywhere near Jasper, but you've been working your arse off, and you deserve a bit of fun. If this is the only opportunity that's going to present itself, then I suppose you could do worse."

High praise coming from Tibby, and I comb my fingers through my tangled hair. I haven't forgotten Jasper's kindness that night at the club, and even though the few moments we had alone were marred by my panic and that damn article, I really, *really* want to see him again.

"Okay," I say at last. After all, if Maisie's going, it can't be that bad. "But I don't have anything to wear."

Tibby's mouth settles into a self-satisfied smirk. "That," she says, "will make Louis's day."

Chapter Thirteen

HENRIETTA SMYTHE: It's all rather scandalous, isn't it? And certainly unprecedented. No other modern-day sitting monarch has publicly admitted to having a child out of wedlock, let alone fathering a baby with another woman while his queen was at home, pregnant with his heir.

ITV: And we have no idea who the mother is at this time?

HS: None. There's never even been a whisper of infidelity between the King and Queen. Given Evangeline grew up in America, we can only assume her mother must be American, too.

ITV: Do you think this unknown woman may have been blackmailing the King?

HS: It's a reasonable assumption. Why else would Buckingham Palace admit to this sort of indiscretion? For this to have stayed a secret for so long, an exorbitant amount of money must have changed hands.

ITV: Let's hope none of it was funded by taxpayers.

HS: Oh goodness, let us hope!

—Transcript of ITV News's interview with royal expert Henrietta Smythe, 15 June 2023

That evening, as my driver weaves down a street in the ritzy London neighbourhood of Belgravia, I wipe my sweaty palms on the skirt of the emerald-green cocktail dress Louis selected for me and try to ignore my pounding heart. The residences here are so close to Buckingham Palace that you can practically peek through the windows, and I'm yet again struck by the overwhelming realization that I don't belong. It doesn't help that Maisie, Ben and Kit took another Range Rover, after my darling sister threw a fit at the prospect of having to see me again. Admittedly the car ride is peaceful without her constant snipes and gripes, but not for the first time that week, I feel completely adrift in the chaos that has become my life.

At last, we pull up to a four-storey white townhouse with several wrought-iron balconies. My insides are in knots, but I take a deep breath and slide out of the vehicle with my knees tight together, the way Tibby taught me. It's just a small gathering, I remind myself. Everything will be fine.

"Miss Bright," says the doorman with an almost comically low bow of his head. "Mr Cunningham is waiting for you in the parlour."

"Great," I say, and a thrill runs down my spine. I have no idea where the parlour is, but Jasper is expecting me, and that's enough to dissolve the worst of my nerves.

The foyer looks like it belongs in an interior design magazine, with all of its black-and-white marble and gold furnishings, and I linger longer than I probably should. What would it be like to grow up in a place like this? Who would I be if Alexander had acknowledged me from the beginning?

"There you are!" Jasper appears as suddenly as he did in the club, though this time, despite the low music playing somewhere deep within the house, I can actually hear him. His blond hair curls into his eyes, and he looks genuinely happy to see me. "I didn't think you'd come."

"I almost didn't," I admit. "It's been a weird week."

"That's certainly an understatement," he says, his green eyes twinkling with amusement. He offers me his arm. "I'll make sure you have the chance to relax."

The heat of his skin against mine is electric, and Jasper leads me up the stairs to what must be the main living area, where dozens of people have gathered, drinking and dancing and talking in loose groups that seem to shift like schools of fish. None of them look familiar, and I hesitate in the doorway.

"Tibby said this was supposed to be a small gathering," I say, and Jasper gives me an apologetic smile.

"It was, but you know how these things are. Don't worry," he adds in a low murmur. "I trust everyone here."

He may, but I don't. Still, I plaster on a smile as he guides me through the crowd, introducing me to his friends. I try my best to remember names using the tricks Tibby and my etiquette instructor have taught me, but as we go from room to room, everything starts to blur together until my head is swimming and beads of sweat form on my forehead. Despite their luxurious townhouse, the Cunninghams don't seem to believe in air conditioning.

"Did you ever find out who leaked your identity?" says Jasper as we pause near a large marble fireplace in what I think might actually be the parlour. He stands so close to me that it's easy to ignore everyone else in the room, even though I know none of them are ignoring us.

"No," I say, trying to casually wipe the sweat from my damp brow and silently hoping none of my make-up comes with it. "The palace did an internal investigation, but they haven't been able to narrow down the possibilities."

"You mustn't have been much of a secret, then, if so many people knew who you were. Odd that they went to some second-rate gossip site, though, rather than a more reputable outlet."

I shrug. "*The Regal Record* was willing to run the story. I guess that's all that mattered. Is it just me, or is it really warm in here?"

Jasper chuckles and rubs my bare arm, leaving my skin hot in the wake of his touch. "I'll get you a drink. Wait here."

"Oh—" I begin, but he's gone before I can ask for something non-alcoholic. I have no intention of getting even remotely tipsy tonight, not when I risk making a fool of myself in front of Jasper and his high-society guests. Feeling about as awkward as I must look, I scan the crowd. Though no one meets my eye, I can feel their curious stares when I turn away, and despite the heat, I cross my arms, holding my ribs tight.

It's fine, I tell myself again. Maisie and Ben and Kit are supposed to be here, after all, and Tibby said it would be safe.

Except Tibby was wrong about how many people would be at the party. And as I search the crowd once more, I realize I haven't seen any sign of Maisie, either. Or Ben, or Kit, or anyone I know. Was Tibby wrong about that, too? Are they not coming after all?

A block of panic forms in the pit of my stomach, overwhelming and irrational. I shouldn't be here. Seeing Jasper isn't worth the risk of more scandal, and if Alexander and the palace's public relations team find out –

"Evangeline?"

A familiar mop of dark waves appears in the crowd, and Kit joins me, a glass of clear liquid in one hand and his suit jacket draped over his arm. He's in a crisp button-down shirt and navy pants, but his sleeves are rolled up, giving him the air of someone at the end of a very long day.

"Kit!" I'm so relieved to see him that I don't even try to hide it. "I didn't think anyone else was here."

"We're all wandering about," he says with a lift of his shoulder. He studies me, his gaze dark and inscrutable. "Are you all right? I saw you come in with Jasper."

"I'm fine," I insist, even though it's a lie. "Jasper's getting me a drink."

Something in Kit's expression flickers. "You shouldn't be drinking tonight," he says. "These people treat Maisie well because she's their future monarch, and they want to get on her good side, but you're fair game to them."

I clench my jaw at the way he so casually mentions my sister's superiority. "Thanks for the warning, but I can take care of myself."

Kit frowns. "I don't doubt it. But Jasper—"

"Jasper's been nothing but nice to me," I retort. "And since that's pretty damn rare these days, forgive me for not caring what you think of him."

His lips thin, and it's the first time I've seen so much as a spark of anger from him. "Everyone here wants something," he says at last. "Mostly from Maisie and Ben, but you're still the King's daughter, and you *must* be careful who you let in. Jasper—"

"Talking about me, are you?" says Jasper, appearing beside me once more. "Only good things, I hope." He smiles warmly and hands me a glass. "Water."

"Oh – thanks," I say, relieved it isn't alcohol. "Kit was just leaving."

I half expect him to stay out of hereditary spite, but Kit doesn't argue. "I'll be in the kitchen with Ben," he says, which sounds more like a threat than a promise, and with a terse nod to Jasper, he melts back into the crowd.

As soon as he's out of sight, Jasper sighs. "You couldn't tell by his surliness, but we used to be best mates. We went to Eton together and were practically inseparable growing up."

"Really? What happened?" I ask, remembering the photo of them in their school uniforms. Jasper leans in towards me, his lips so close to my ear that I can feel his warm breath.

"His older brother died last summer," he admits. "It was all very sudden."

I blink, stunned. In the week I've spent at Windsor, no one has mentioned Kit losing a brother. "That's *horrible*."

"It is," agrees Jasper. "The Queen's family went into lockdown when it happened – nothing official appeared in the press, not even an obituary. Something about it must be fishy, and unfortunately the editor at one of my father's less reputable papers ran a story about it once the death certificate was filed. And – well, Kit hasn't trusted me since. Not that I blame him," he adds, scratching his head sheepishly. "But I certainly had nothing to do with the article, and he's refused to accept that."

"Grief does weird things to people," I say softly. But while I may not be Kit's biggest fan right now, talking about him like this doesn't feel right, and I seize the opportunity to change the subject. "Did you ask your father to be nice to me? When – the news broke?"

Our eyes meet. "I told him you were a friend," says Jasper. "As brutal as some of the media coverage has been, we always try to be respectful of the royal—"

"Is it true your mum's a prostitute?" slurs someone behind me, cutting him off.

I whirl around. Several girls in designer dresses, all with drinks in their hands, are clustered a few feet away. "What did you say?" I manage, the words catching in my throat.

"I heard her mum and the King had an affair for months, *and* that her mum gave him an STI," pipes up another girl, who doesn't seem nearly as drunk as the first. Her gaze slides to me. "It's all tragic, isn't it? Poor Helene, having to endure all of this. How can you even live with yourself for breaking up their family?"

"I—" I have no idea what to say to that. I didn't do anything, but I can't exactly throw my mother to the wolves. Or even Alexander.

Jasper wraps his arm protectively around my shoulders. "How dare you," he snaps at the girls. "If you can't hold it together in front of royalty, I'll have to ask you to leave."

"She's not royalty," says the second girl, wrinkling her nose. "She's *illegitimate*. And her mother is a home-wrecking—"

"I would be very, very careful what I say next if I were you," says Jasper, his expression hardening. My mouth hangs open as a dozen comebacks flash through my mind, each more vicious than the last, but he gently turns me away from the group. "I'm going to take care of this," he says quietly. "Go up two flights of stairs and wait in the first room on the left. I'll be up in a minute."

I almost tell him no. These girls aren't the only ones thinking those horrible things, and I won't be able to hide from most of the country. But I know that if I stay, I'm going to blurt out something I regret – something that, despite Tibby's reassurances, might reach the media. And this is how it's going to be for the rest of my life, no matter what I say or do tonight. Losing my temper isn't worth it.

And so I turn my back on the girls and stride towards the stairs with as much dignity as I can muster. When I reach the fourth floor, the hallway is dark, and all I hear are the soft strains of music from below. My feet are already throbbing, and I take my heels off, tucking them under my arm as I approach the first room on the left. I don't knock – there's no one else up here, after all – but when I step into the dimly lit room, I hear a gasp and the hasty shuffle of two people separating.

I stop cold, my apology stuck in my throat. Gia stares at me from her spot on the king-sized bed, her top missing and her lips swollen. And half-hidden behind her is –

Maisie.

Chapter Fourteen

Jasper Cunningham may not be famous yet, but if he has his way, soon everyone in England will know his name.

The son of notorious media mogul Robert Cunningham, who owns nearly half of the printed media in the UK, Jasper has been paving his own way in London high society since his graduation from Eton last year. A close friend of both Princess Mary and Prince Benedict, he prides himself on his discretion.

"I appreciate your interest, but their friendship means more to me than selling papers ever will," he says when I enquire about their relationship. "I'm here to forge my own path, not ride anyone's coat-tails."

A lofty statement indeed for someone born with countless connections, but he isn't fazed by the insinuation.

"Some people are born to exceptional circumstances," he allows. "But underneath the glamour and privilege, we're all only human, and even the thickest coating of gilded gold wears off eventually. I could, of course, coast on the empire my father has built, but where's the contribution in that? I want to change the world someday. I don't have time to be passive."

—*Tatler* magazine, April 2023

"Do they not teach you how to knock in America?" snaps Gia, shifting on the bed as she tries to block my half-sister from view. I turn away, but it's too late. There's no taking this one back, or pretending I have no idea what's going on.

"I'm sorry," I say, stepping towards the door. But before I can make a hasty retreat, Maisie stands, her expression like thunder.

"*You.*" Her gold dress is wrinkled and unzipped, but somehow she's managed to pull it back on in seconds. "Is it not enough that you've ruined my mother's life? Are you dead set on ruining mine, too?"

"I'm *sorry*," I repeat, my temper fraying. "I didn't know anyone would be up here, all right? And if you're so desperate for privacy, maybe you should've locked the door."

Maisie storms around the bed and plants herself between me and the only exit. "If you tell anyone—"

"If I tell anyone what?" I say. "That you have a girlfriend? What *century* do you people live in?"

"Maisie has a right to her privacy," says Gia, her voice far more even than my half-sister's, though her dark eyes glint with a silent threat I can't miss.

"I don't care who you make out with," I say, crossing my arms. "I wasn't born in the Dark Ages."

Maisie takes another step towards me, her lips curled into a sneer of hatred so fierce that I realize it might be the only real emotion I've seen from her. "One word of this," she breathes, "and I will burn you to the ground."

"I thought that's what you were already trying to do," I say.

"Or is this the part where you tell me I have no idea what you're really capable of?"

She opens her mouth to retort, but Gia touches her arm. "She isn't worth it, Maisie," she says in an oddly gentle voice. "If she says anything, we'll deny it, all right? And make her look like a sociopath in the process."

My half-sister glares at me with sheer unadulterated loathing, but she doesn't utter another word. Gia zips up Maisie's dress and pulls on her own top, and with one last look of warning, she ushers Maisie out of the room, leaving me alone.

I take a few deep breaths, trying to calm myself down. I'm not going to blackmail them – I'm not stupid, for one, but I would also never use something like this against anyone, let alone Maisie. I'm not a monster, no matter what they seem to think of me. I know instinctively that I'm going to pay for this somehow, though.

Sipping my water nervously, I glance around the sky-blue room accented with creams and golds. A pair of floor-to-ceiling glass doors are cracked open to let in the warm summer breeze, and they lead out onto a narrow balcony overlooking the street. Beside the fluttering curtains is a drink cart filled with crystal decanters, most half-filled with varying shades of amber liquid, and across from the bed is an antique desk with an open laptop on it. The screen is dark and the power is off, but I notice that Jasper has decorated the keyboard with swirling purple and green stickers that look like a galaxy. It's the only thing in the room that has any sort of personal touch.

"...no need for threats. I've got it handled," says someone quietly on the other side of the door. Jasper. There's a note of aggravation in his voice, as if I've caught the tail end of an argument. "Yes, I'm certain. Stick to your bloody job, all right? And let me handle mine."

A moment later, the door creaks open, and Jasper appears, silhouetted by the light pouring in from the hallway. He smiles as he tucks his phone into his pocket, but I see the irritation that lingers on his face.

"I kicked them out," he says. "They won't receive any invitations from me again."

It takes me a moment to realize he means the drunk girls downstairs, not the person on the other end of the call. "I'm sorry," I say. "I didn't mean to—"

"You did nothing wrong." He steps into the room and closes the door behind him. "Are you all right?"

I hesitate. I can't tell him about what I walked in on between Maisie and Gia, but even beyond that, I'm not okay. "I should probably go," I say. "I'm only causing problems."

"You're never a problem," he assures me, switching on a lamp, and I can see his smile in the golden glow. "Would you like something stronger?"

I look down at my glass. It's nearly empty now. "Pretty sure I've been humiliated enough lately without stumbling around drunk at a party full of strangers."

"One drink will not get you drunk, but I'll pour you another water. With ice, as you Americans seem to prefer," he adds, gently taking my glass and moving towards the drink cart.

I rub one sore foot against my shin. Today has not been my day, and although I desperately want to talk to someone about it, there's nothing I can really tell Jasper. As kind as he's been to me,

I suddenly understand why Kit pulled away. One wrong word, and I can imagine what the headline of tomorrow's *Daily Sun* might read.

As soon as I think it, I silently berate myself. We can't help who our parents are, and after all Jasper's done for me, I refuse to let anyone poison the well against him. No matter what Maisie and her circle seem to think of Jasper, he's shown me who he is since the day we met at Windsor, and I choose to believe him.

"Are you sure you're all right?" he says, handing me the refilled glass. He grabs his own drink – something the colour of dark caramel – and sits on the foot of the bed, patting the space beside him. I hesitate, but my feet really do hurt, and I'm starting to feel dizzy from the effort it's taking to hold myself together.

I ease down beside him, perched on the very edge of the mattress. "I never wanted any of this," I admit, toying with the charm on my bracelet. "Even when I was a kid, I never wanted to be a princess. Not that I am now, but – it's been a lot to deal with all at once."

"Did you always know who your father was?" says Jasper quietly.

I shake my head. "My grandmother told me when I was eleven, right before she died. At first I was thrilled. Not because he was a king, but – because I finally knew who he was, you know?" I manage a small, pained smile. "But then she said that no matter what I did, and no matter how many nice gifts he sent, I could never really be part of his life."

"It seems she was wrong," says Jasper. I shrug and sip my water.

"I don't know. Even now, it still feels pretty impossible to me."

He wraps his arm around me. "The country will adjust,"

he promises. "And when it does, you'll be as much of a shining star as Maisie."

I try to stifle my snort of disbelief, but I can't help myself. "People will always whisper behind my back, and his family will always hate me. Time won't change either of those things." I pause, leaning into his embrace. It's a little awkward, but he's warm, and I need that warmth right now. "I remember the exact moment I found out I had a sister – a half-sister," I correct myself. "I Googled Alexander, and one of the first pictures that popped up was of him and Maisie. She was three, maybe, or four, and I remember being so...*jealous*. Not because she was a princess, but because she had our dad."

Jasper rubs my back, and I take a deep, steadying breath, my head starting to ache as I struggle to hold back tears. "You have him now," he says. "Time is what you make of it. And as for what everyone else thinks of you..." He touches my chin, his green eyes locking onto mine. "The only people who matter are those who care about you. And I do," he whispers. "From the moment I saw you, before I knew who you were, I thought you were incredible. And getting to know you better...getting to talk to you...it's only confirmed my suspicion that you're someone very, very special."

He leans towards me, closing the distance between us, and before I know it, his lips are soft against mine. The nerves in my body ignite, and time seems to slow as he kisses me, gentle at first before he begins to build to something deeper. Something I can taste.

I've never kissed anyone before, and the heat between us intensifies until it's an intoxicating fire. The room begins to spin as Jasper moves his hand to my waist, pulling me to him, and I wrap my arms around his shoulders, anxious to be as close to him as possible.

I grow more and more muffled as I lose myself in him, relishing the warmth of his body against mine. At some point, seconds or minutes later, I realize my back is pressed to the mattress, and he hovers over me, his mouth working its way down my neck to my collarbone.

"Jasper," I say raggedly. "I – I haven't – I can't—"

"Trust me," he murmurs between kisses. "You're safe."

I try to lift my head, but another wave of dizziness washes over me. My thoughts are sluggish, and when I try to move my arms, they feel strangely heavy.

"Jasper?" His name comes out like a question, and I hear my voice – small and thin – as if I'm at the other end of a tunnel. My heart thuds slowly against my ribs, like it's taking up more space than usual, but it's only when I feel him tug at the zipper running down my side that I start to panic.

"Wait," I say, the word slurred, but Jasper is already pulling off my dress. I try to roll away, but he's there to catch me, his mouth capturing mine again.

"Relax, Evangeline," he murmurs. "I promise everything's all right."

My body is achingly heavy now, and I stare at him, dazed, as he smiles down at me. It's the same warm smile as before, and the rational part of my brain can't reconcile that gentleness with what I think he's doing.

Maybe I'm wrong. Maybe I don't understand. Maybe I'm just…confused.

But when he starts to undress, undoing each button on his

shirt with the kind of languid motions of someone who's in no rush, cold terror washes over me, and I know I'm not confused. "I like you, Evan," he says, his voice distant and distorted. "And I know you like me, too."

He pulls off his shirt, revealing a muscular torso. Mustering every ounce of strength I have, I squirm towards the edge of the bed, sure that if I can get to my feet, he'll stop.

But he's there again, his body solid over mine and his touch searingly tender as he traces the edge of my bra. "Relax," he repeats. "You're okay."

I'm not okay, though. I'm not even close to okay, but when I open my mouth to scream, a soft whimper escapes instead. I feel his body against mine, and –

"No." The word is more of a squeak, but I still say it. Jasper lifts himself off me for a moment, and I can see his jaunty smile in the golden lamplight.

"Evan, you want this," he says with a chuckle. "You said so yourself."

Did I? I don't remember, but it doesn't matter. I don't want to any more. "No," I repeat, firmer this time. My thoughts are slow and muddled, and the edges of my vision are growing darker, but I know that if I don't do anything now, while I'm still conscious and able to move, I won't stand a chance.

"You'll enjoy it more if you relax," he croons, his voice sickeningly gentle. "Can you do that for me, Evangeline? Can you relax?"

He leans in to kiss me again, and without any thought or plan, I bite his lip as hard as I can, the tang of his blood vile on my tongue.

His cry of pain is sharp – sharper than his voice or anything else around me, and he sits up, rubbing his mouth. "What the hell was that for?" he demands, a streak of red smeared across his chin.

"I said *no*," I snarl. And although my muscles tremble and a wave of vertigo threatens to overtake me, I force myself to sit up.

"And I said yes," he growls, leaning towards me again.

This time I'm ready. With a jerking motion, I knee him in the groin, and as he cries out again, I roll off the bed and fall heavily to the floor. My entire body feels numb, but I breathe through it as I grip the duvet and pull myself up, lurching until I've found purchase.

Jasper stands beside the bed now, his face reddening as he hunches over, clutching his groin. "You *bitch*."

The door is only a few feet away. I grab the nightstand and stagger forward, willing myself to stay upright. But he lunges after me, and I feel his fingers digging into my shoulder, his nails so sharp that I think they're drawing blood. Desperate, I whirl around, and in a stroke of enormous luck, my elbow slams into his nose with a sickening crunch.

"Get *away* from me," I gasp. My heart is pounding, and the lamplight seems to flicker as everything slowly darkens. His hands are on me again, and I flail clumsily with my too-heavy limbs, dull pain throbbing in my knuckles as I feel the skin split. Somewhere in the back of my mind, I think I hear glass breaking, and my knees burn as I fall onto the carpet again. But the air seems different now, and muffled music fills my head as I crawl forward unseeingly.

The next thing I feel is a pair of warm arms wrapping around me. I hear a voice that isn't Jasper's – low and murmuring, but

133

not in the way his was. Not sickening. Not threatening. Not angry. But not safe, either. No one is safe.

I lose time again, and then there's concrete beneath my bare feet before someone lifts me into a vehicle. A door slams, and as I slump against the cool leather seat, I grow vaguely aware of someone sitting to my left.

"You're all right," says the same gentle voice. And the last thing I see before my vision goes black is dark, wavy hair.

Chapter Fifteen

Rosie:
OMG did you see that?? xx

Gia:
See what? xx

Rosie:
kit and evangeline! I just saw them leaving. his jacket was over her shoulders, and I think she was in her knickers?? half the party's talking about it xx

Gia:
She certainly works quickly. xx

Maisie:
Wait, didn't Jasper go upstairs after her?

Gia:
Yes, why? xx

Rosie:
lmao what a slag xx

—Text message exchange between Her Royal Highness the Princess Mary, Lady Primrose Chesterfield-Bishop, and Lady Georgiana Greyville, 15 June 2023

Sunlight streams into my bedroom through a crack in the heavy curtains, and I groan.

My head feels as if there's an axe embedded between the lobes of my brain, and the sheets cling to me like I've been sweating all night. When I try to sit up, the pain increases tenfold, and I mutter a curse.

"Evan?" It isn't Tibby's voice, like I expect – it's Jenkins's, and the mattress gives slightly as he sits down beside me. "How are you feeling?"

"Awful," I croak, opening my eyes. Despite how bright the day seems already, it can't be more than a few minutes after dawn. "What are you doing here? Where's Tibby?"

"I'm right here," she says from the window. She's wearing the same outfit she had on the day before, but it's the look on her face that tells me something is wrong. Really, really wrong.

"What happened?" I say. My mouth is painfully dry, and I can't imagine what I must smell like, but Jenkins doesn't seem to care.

"You don't remember?" says another voice – a deeper, masculine voice coming from the chaise beside my desk.

Kit. For a moment I stare at him, wondering what the hell he's doing here, but then the memories of the night before hit me, fast and unyielding.

The party.

Maisie and Gia.

Kit's dark, wavy hair. Jasper touching me. Jasper kissing me.

Jasper grabbing me.

Jasper.

Everything's fuzzy around the edges, and there are whole

136

parts I don't remember – how I escaped the bedroom. How I made it down the stairs and out of the townhouse. How I arrived back at Windsor without an army of paparazzi storming the castle for pictures of me in my underwear.

But I remember Kit's voice and the sensation of him holding me upright. And as I look down, I realize I'm still wrapped in his suit jacket, wrinkled and sweaty now. There's gauze on my arm, too, half an inch beneath my elbow, and my knuckles are bruised and bandaged.

"Jasper," I whisper, barely able to say his name. "He – he—"

"The doctor drew some blood when Kit brought you back last night," says Tibby. "The drugs should be completely out of your system in another few hours."

"Drugs?" I stare at her stupidly before looking at Jenkins. "But – I didn't take anything. I swear, I didn't even drink."

"I know, sweetheart," he says, and he glances at Kit. "We think Jasper Cunningham drugged you. Ketamine, maybe, or GHB. Possibly Rohypnol."

"They're date rape drugs," says Tibby plainly, but with a softness that doesn't seem natural to her.

"He – what?" Horror and nausea wash over me at the same time, equally relentless. "But I only had water."

"Scotland Yard is testing the glasses," says Jenkins. "We should know more soon enough."

My heart skips a beat, and not in a good way. "The police are involved?"

"I had to report it," says Kit, but there's no apology in his voice. He leans forward, his hands clasped and hair falling into his eyes, and I notice he's also still in the clothes he wore to the party.

Has he been here all night? Did they all stay?

"Does Alexander know?" I say in a small voice, almost too afraid to ask. The shame of it weighs on me, making me wish I could crawl under the covers and never come out. How did I mess up so badly? How did I let this happen?

"His Majesty has been informed," says Jenkins, and he takes my uninjured hand. "Evan…"

"I have to talk to him," I say thickly. "He has to know I didn't mean—"

"He already does," he reassures me. "It's not your fault. None of this is. He would be here now if he could, but…"

As he trails off, Tibby presses her lips together, and Kit stares resolutely at the carpet. I look back and forth between them, confused.

"What?" I say. "What's going on? Does the press know? Are there pictures or—"

"The press doesn't know what happened to you," says Jenkins. "But Jasper Cunningham…"

"Did they arrest him?" My heart pounds so hard I can hear it. "Is he trying to claim I'm lying? Because I'm not. I swear I said no. He wouldn't – he wouldn't *listen*."

No one says anything for several seconds, and the tension builds until I can't take it any more. At last it's Kit who clears his throat, and he looks at me with bloodshot eyes. The eyes of someone who hasn't slept. Who can't sleep no matter how badly he needs to.

"Something else happened last night," he says quietly. "After we left, a pedestrian found a body in the street."

I feel the blood drain from my face, and suddenly a wave of

dizziness hits me, so powerful that for a split second, I can't breathe. "Is Maisie okay?"

"Her Royal Highness is fine," says Jenkins hastily. "She came home last night without a scratch on her."

I exhale, more relieved than I want to admit. "Then – who?" I say. "Is Ben all right? Gia? Rosie?"

"It's Jasper," says Kit, his voice like brittle glass. "He's dead."

Chapter Sixteen

JASPER CUNNINGHAM DEAD –
FOUL PLAY SUSPECTED

Jasper Cunningham, son of media mogul Sir Robert Cunningham, died last night at his family's townhouse in Belgravia.

The former Eton student and club financer was pronounced dead on the scene at a house party reportedly attended by multiple members of the royal family. Scotland Yard has launched an official investigation into the matter, and no further details are available at this time.

Cunningham was nineteen.

—Breaking news alert from the BBC, 16 June 2023

No one seems to know exactly how it happened.

When a detective named Erika Farrows interviews me later that morning, she tells me Jasper was found face down on the sidewalk. The glass doors to his balcony were wide open, and one of the curtains was torn, leading them to suspect he had lost his balance and fallen while drunk.

"But there's also blood present in the bedroom," she says, glancing at my bandaged knuckles. "Blood that we don't believe is Jasper's."

"Miss Bright has already informed you of how she came to be injured," says Wiggs, the palace lawyer with greying hair and sagging jowls who sits beside me at my dining table. "She was acting in self-defence and is in no way connected to Mr Cunningham's death."

"What time did you leave the party?" says Farrows. I shake my head.

"I don't—"

"As has already been established, Miss Bright was drugged by Mr Cunningham and does not remember," says Wiggs. "She was escorted out of the party by Lord Clarence, whom I believe you have already interviewed."

It's only then that I realize where these questions are leading, and my insides go cold. "You think I had something to do with Jasper's death?" I say, stunned. Wiggs pats my hand, a silent request for me to keep my mouth shut, and as he continues to argue my innocence, I obey.

I didn't kill Jasper. How could I? I could barely walk.

But as I close my eyes, I remember the crunch of bone as my elbow connected with Jasper's nose and the distant sound of shattering glass. And I begin to doubt.

After another hour, Detective Farrows finally leaves, and I crawl onto the couch in my sitting room and wrap myself in a soft quilt Tibby managed to dig up. My lessons have been cancelled for the afternoon – supposedly due to an unspecified illness, though with how queasy I feel, that's not entirely a lie –

and all I want to do is shut out the world.

I didn't kill him. I couldn't have killed him. Maybe Jasper really was drunker than I thought he was. Maybe that's why –

I cut off that thought before my mind can even formulate it. Some of my memories may be fuzzy, but that one isn't, and I understand exactly what almost happened. What *did* happen. I pull the blanket tighter around myself and bite the inside of my cheek. I can still feel every blistering kiss, every burning caress, and I desperately wish I could shed my skin like a snake, leaving behind every inch that Jasper touched until I belong to myself again.

"Do you need anything?" says Tibby from the dining table.

I shake my head.

"I just want to sleep," I mumble.

"You should at least try to eat something," she insists. "I'll order up sandwiches."

The thought of food is enough to make bile rise in my throat, but I don't have the energy to fight her. Instead, I lie still and pretend to nap, hoping that'll quell any desire she has for conversation.

It works, and I'm almost asleep when lunch arrives twenty minutes later. But the footman isn't alone, and as the tray gently clatters against the table, a familiar voice drifts over from the opposite side of the room.

"I can sit with her for a while," says Kit quietly.

"You're sure?" whispers Tibby. "I only need to shower and change."

"I'll stay until you're back," he promises, and Tibby murmurs her thanks before slipping out the door.

Kit doesn't greet me, and I'm grateful for his silence. Once the footman leaves, however, he picks up a plate and pads over to the armchair beside the sofa, and I can't resist cracking open an eye.

"That smells like peanut butter and jelly," I mumble.

"A sinister concoction if ever there was one," says Kit with a slight shudder. He offers me the plate of sandwiches, which have all been cut into quarters and arranged with an artistic flourish. "I believe Tibby ordered them especially for you."

I eye him and reluctantly take a quarter. I'm still vaguely nauseated, but the smell doesn't turn my stomach. "Do you not have peanut butter and jelly sandwiches here?"

"We have peanut butter," he says, "and we have jam, which is a combination I admit I've never tried. But our jelly is what Americans might call Jell-O. And no one in their right mind would put those two things together in a sandwich."

I nibble the corner of mine. The bread is warm from the oven, and the smooth peanut butter pairs perfectly with the tang of strawberry jam. I haven't had a peanut butter and jelly sandwich since my grandmother used to make me lunch in elementary school, and a strange wave of sadness washes over me. I'm not especially nostalgic about the years I spent with her, but right now, all I want is for her to wrap her arms around me and tell me everything will be okay.

"Good?" says Kit, and I nod.

"You should try one," I say. He wrinkles his nose, and I manage a faint smile. "Please. It'll make me feel better."

"Ah, so you thrive on seeing others suffer," he teases, but he picks up one of the triangles and gamely takes a bite. I half expect

143

him to spit it out, but instead he chews slowly, his face a mask of neutrality.

"Well?" I say. "Not bad, right?"

"I've had worse," he allows once he's swallowed. "I can see how it might be…enjoyable, once you've acquired a taste for it."

Somehow the thought of peanut butter and jelly being an *acquired taste* makes me snort. "I'm sorry, which of us thinks spotted dick and mushy peas are edible?"

"I'll have you know that both of those are delicious," says Kit, setting down the remainder of his sandwich. "And don't even get me started on toad-in-the-hole. It will change your life." I'm grinning now, and it's easy, even after the hell that has been today. But as I meet Kit's dark eyes, my smile fades. "Thanks, by the way," I say, tearing off a piece of crust. "For – what you did last night. After what I said to you, I didn't deserve your help, and…I really appreciate it."

"The only thing you didn't deserve is how Jasper treated you," he says quietly, but there's strength behind his words. Conviction I need to hear right now. "I'm sorry it took me so long to come find you. Are you feeling any better?"

I nod. "I'm still tired, and my hand hurts a little, but that's all."

"Good," says Kit, though I'm sure he knows I'm lying. An uncomfortable silence settles between us, and I stare at my sandwich, watching the strawberry jam ooze out from between the slices of bread. My nausea returns full force, and I set my half-eaten quarter down beside his.

"Did you see what happened?" I say. My voice is thin, and I can't stand how fragile I sound. "I don't remember all of it, but

– I remember hitting Jasper. And I remember hearing glass break."

Kit takes my hand. His skin is smooth and warm, but I automatically twitch away, and he hastily lets go. "I never even looked inside the room," he admits. "I saw you stumble into the hallway, and – well, it was fairly obvious what Jasper had tried to do, and making sure you were safe was my priority."

My face falls. "Oh."

"But," he adds, "whatever happened, however Jasper fell off that balcony…it wasn't your fault. You were protecting yourself. He's the only one who committed a crime."

I shift awkwardly underneath my quilt. I hate the thought of being a victim. I hate the way Kit is looking at me, with pity in his eyes. And I hate how I know that for the rest of my life, any time I'm in a room alone with a guy, I'm going to wonder – however fleetingly – if he'll try the same thing.

Maybe Jasper didn't deserve to die, but I didn't deserve this, either.

"What if the police don't see it that way?" I mumble. "Wiggs kept saying I was in no condition to push Jasper that hard, but – what if I did? And what if it still counts as – as manslaughter or something?" I don't even know if they have manslaughter in the UK, but the thought chills me to the bone. "What if it counts as murder?"

Kit studies me. "Those are a lot of what-ifs."

"I don't know how it works here, but in the US, you can be convicted of murder by driving the getaway car," I say. "And even though Jasper drugged me, if I'm still the one who pushed him…"

"Then I suppose we'll just have to prove it wasn't you," says Kit. "Or, if we can't, then offer them a more viable suspect."

I narrow my eyes. "What do you mean?"

"There were plenty of people at that party," he says. "Surely at least a few weren't all that fond of him."

"But – how am I supposed to know who didn't like him? And how is Wiggs—"

"Wiggs won't," says Kit. "But I've spent nearly a decade running in the same circles as Jasper. I can help, if you'd like."

I'm not sure what to say to that. Kit has done more for me in the past sixteen hours than most of my family has in my entire life, and asking even more from him – especially when I know he'll face the wrath of Maisie for it – seems like too much. But he watches me, steadily and unwaveringly, and I feel a little better at the prospect of having him on my side.

"I'd like that. Thank you," I say. The wheels in my mind are already turning, and I sit up, trying to recall the foggy names and blurry faces of the dozens of people I met last night. "We should start by making a list of everyone who was at the—"

"Evan." Kit leans towards me – not enough to cross the invisible boundary that now exists between us, but enough so I know he's serious. "Right now, the best possible thing you can do for yourself is rest. I promise we'll make that list as soon as—"

An urgent knock from the hallway startles us both. Kit leaps to his feet, and before I can tell whoever it is to go away, Maisie flings open the door.

"Your Royal Highness," says Kit, dipping his chin in a hasty bow. I don't stand, though. And I definitely don't curtsy.

"What are you doing here?" I say, immediately on guard.

Maisie is the last person I expected to visit me today, and judging by the stiff set of her shoulders, she's as uncomfortable in my presence as I am in hers. Or maybe she always looks like she has a tree trunk up her arse. Both are equally possible.

"My security team found your dress right before the police arrived, and I thought I'd drop it off," she says, but while she's speaking to me, she's focused on Kit. Her irritated stare lingers long enough for him to comprehend whatever silent message she's trying to send, and he clears his throat.

"If I might use your loo?" he says, and it takes me a moment to realize he means my bathroom.

"Uh, yeah – it's through the bedroom," I say, frantically trying to remember how much of a mess I made while getting ready for the party, but I'm drawing a blank. Last night feels like a lifetime ago.

Kit politely excuses himself, leaving Maisie and me alone together for the first time in our lives. Thankfully she doesn't bother with small talk – instead, she reaches into her large black handbag and produces the emerald-green dress I abandoned on the floor of Jasper's bedroom.

"Half the side seam has come undone. You shouldn't be so careless with couture." Maisie drapes the dress haphazardly over the back of the nearest armchair and glances around, taking in the paintings that hang on my walls. "Daddy gave you one of the nicest guest suites. Usually this is reserved for foreign royalty or world leaders."

"Well, we both know I'm not either," I say, eyeing the dress. It feels cursed now, and I wonder if Louis would object to me burning it to ashes. "Why are you really here, Maisie? We both know it isn't to check on me."

She sniffs imperiously at my use of her nickname, or maybe she isn't used to direct questions. "Do you have any…memory lapses from last night?"

I let out a choked laugh, though there's no real humour in it.

"Yes," I say, and at the flicker of hope that crosses her face, I add, "but not the thing you're hoping I forgot."

Her expression sours. "Oh."

I lower my head onto the armrest of the sofa. "I don't care, you know."

"I don't give a fig whether you care," says Maisie. "I care about who you're going to tell, and how long you're going to hold this over me."

Right. So she thinks just as badly of me as I do of her. "*Why* are you so convinced I'm a terrible person?"

She waves dismissively, as if the answer is obvious. "What will it be, then? Would you like me to say kind things about you to the press? Acknowledge your presence in public? Do you want money? Jewels? A title when I'm queen?"

All I want is to go home to my mother and forget this nightmare ever happened, but Maisie can't give me that. No one can. And even if she could, the thought of blackmailing her – of blackmailing my half-sister and the future monarch of the United Kingdom, no matter how much of a spoiled brat she is – makes my insides curdle.

"I want you to believe me when I say I'm not going to tell anyone," I snap. "I know how to keep my mouth shut."

"Do you?" Her words drip with sarcasm, but I hold Maisie's stare, and after several long seconds, the nastiness in her eyes

148

fades. "You don't understand what'll happen if it comes out that I'm—" She stops herself and sucks in a breath. "I'm the only direct heir, and I'll be the first queen regnant since Victoria. There are…expectations I must meet, and if I give the people any reason to believe the line of succession is at risk…"

I blink. "Are you seriously worried about how you're going to have kids with Gia? You're *seventeen*."

Her lips curl into a sneer. "I wouldn't expect someone like you to understand. Nothing is a problem to you, is it? You careen through life without the weight of responsibility and ruin everything in your path."

I clutch the quilt so hard I feel a thread snap. "I'm not going to out you, Maisie. It's none of my business, and yet again, *I don't care who you're screwing*. Just stop trying to screw me over, and we'll be good."

This seems to bring her up short, and my half-sister studies me with the intensity of an art critic trying to find a flaw in a piece. After an agonizingly long moment, she squares her shoulders. "Very well. Do make sure to hang that dress up. You wouldn't want it to wrinkle."

Maisie walks to the door, her heels muffled by the thick carpet. But once she reaches the threshold, she stops and peers back at me.

"You *are* all right, yes? Jasper didn't…" She trails off, but she doesn't need to finish.

"No, he didn't get that far," I mutter, my face burning.

Maisie nods, seemingly satisfied with this answer. "He had it coming," she says quietly. And without another word, she leaves.

* * *

149

I don't tell Kit about my conversation with Maisie, and he doesn't ask. Instead, once he reiterates that we can begin our investigation as soon as I've rested, I give in and eat half a sandwich while we settle on a Netflix movie to watch. After an hour or so, Tibby joins us, and while she doesn't seem thrilled about my cinematic tastes, she mostly keeps her disapproving tsks to herself.

They both stay until I fall asleep, and Tibby is back at dawn, drawing open my curtains and shoving me into the bathroom so I'm sparkling clean for Trooping the Colour. I pretend not to be surprised, but in truth, I completely forgot about the ceremony in the chaos of the day before, and I spend the entire shower trying to convince myself that I don't feel sick to my stomach. Fortunately, while the real members of the royal family are all participating in the parade – either on horseback, like Alexander and Nicholas, or in a carriage, like Helene and Maisie – I've only been invited to the balcony appearance that afternoon. Unfortunately, Louis still sends one of his assistants to make sure I'm presentable, as if I'm not entirely capable of grooming myself. In his defence, my hair, make-up, wardrobe – everything needs to be perfect today, and the tension in the air is palpable.

"Please stop pacing," I say to Tibby as she crosses in front of me for the hundredth time. "You're making me nervous, and I can't afford to have sweat stains."

"A little Botox will take care of that," she says, her eyes glued to her phone. A wrinkle appears between her brows, and suddenly Tibby swears so spectacularly that the stylist drops the curling iron.

"What?" I say, but she holds up a finger to shush me, turning away so I can't see the glow of her screen. "Tibby, *what?*"

She opens and shuts her mouth. "This cannot be happening," she mutters, her eyes huge. "How—"

I'm on my feet in an instant, and I ignore the stylist's objections as I storm over and snatch Tibby's phone from her hand. She tries to steal it back, but I whirl around, buying myself a few precious seconds to read what's on the screen.

And my heart drops to the floor.

Chapter Seventeen

KING'S LOVE CHILD KEY WITNESS IN MURDER INVESTIGATION – BLOOD FOUND AT SCENE

Evangeline Bright, illegitimate daughter of the King, was the last person to see Jasper Cunningham alive, according to a well-placed source connected to the case.

Seventeen-year-old Bright was allegedly attending a party at Cunningham's Belgravia residence the night he died, and multiple witnesses reported seeing her go upstairs with the son of media mogul Sir Robert Cunningham only minutes before he tragically fell to his death.

"This was no accident," insists one partygoer, who spoke on the condition of anonymity. "She couldn't keep her hands off him, and he didn't seem nearly as keen on her. When they went upstairs together, she looked furious with him."

Drops of the American teenager's blood were also allegedly found in the bedroom, mere feet from the balcony off which Cunningham fell. While the autopsy is pending, another source within the palace has revealed that Bright has injuries consistent with a physical altercation.

Scotland Yard has refused to confirm any details of the case, and a spokesperson for the royal household declined to comment.

—*The Daily Sun*, 17 June 2023

In the half hour since the *Daily Sun* article first appeared, the story has spread to every major news outlet in England.

According to whispered intel from my stylist, who surreptitiously checks Twitter while claiming to look for more bobby pins, #JusticeforJasper is the number five trending topic in the UK and rising by the minute. Tibby won't let me anywhere near her phone, but I can hear the incessant buzzing as she gets a constant stream of texts. I don't know who they're from, but her curses grow louder and more consistent, and I know this is only getting worse.

Finally, once I've been primped within an inch of my life and am wearing the pale blue dress Louis selected for my public debut, Tibby and I head out to meet the Range Rovers that will take me and the royal family to Buckingham Palace. Before we make it halfway down the corridor, however, I stop dead in my tracks beside a marble bust of a man with a squashed nose.

"I can't do this," I gasp. My chest feels so tight that I can barely take a breath. "Everyone thinks I killed him."

"Anyone who does is a pillock," says Tibby, and I'm fairly sure this is meant to be a cutting insult. "The lawyers will sort it out—"

"Sort what out?"

The door to my left opens, and Nicholas, the Duke of York, appears, wearing a red-and-blue military uniform heavy with medals and ribbons. Despite all the regalia, there's something oddly boyish about him, like he's younger than his thirty-nine years, and he studies me with an amused look.

"I—" I don't know what to say. How do you tell your newfound uncle that the whole country thinks you're the main suspect in a murder investigation?

"This wouldn't have anything to do with the tizzy everyone seems to be in over a particular dead Cunningham, would it?" he says, offering me his arm, and I reluctantly slip my hand into the crook of his elbow. Terrific. Not only has everyone on social media seen the article, but apparently the royal family has, too.

"*The Daily Sun* is heavily implying that I…did it," I say, trying to sound as if I don't care, but my voice catches, and I know I'm not fooling anyone.

Nicholas takes it all in stride as we walk down the hall. "I've met Jasper a number of times over the years. He and Ben have been friends for ages, and Robert and I play cards upon occasion. His death is a terrible tragedy," he muses, and I tense, bracing myself for the judgment that's about to come. "And yet, from the sound of it, so very well deserved."

He looks at me with his solemn blue eyes, and suddenly I'm sure he knows the full story – or at least as much of the full story as anyone knows right now. It feels crass to agree, and I press my lips together.

"It's going to be a media onslaught, with you at the very centre," he says. "Robert will make sure of it. But from a legal standpoint, all that matters is what Scotland Yard believes, and they're not basing their inquiry on gossip or speculation. And even if the facts of the case get muddled along the way, I promise you, Evangeline, we protect our own. If one member of the royal family falls, the rest of us will go down with them, and we certainly can't have that."

"I'm not a member of the royal family," I point out, and he arches an eyebrow.

"Then why are you joining us on the balcony today?"

"Because Alexander got caught with his pants down, and now he has to pretend to make the best of it."

Nicholas bursts out laughing. "We're going to get along famously, you and I," he says. "I wasn't sure at first, but I certainly am now."

The three of us make our way to the exit and step out into the crisp morning air. It's still absurdly early, and I shiver against the chill, but the sky is bright blue, promising a gorgeous day ahead. Four black Range Rovers are idling in the drive, and Ben leans casually against the hood of the closest one as he types something into his phone.

"I take it the ladies are running late, as per usual," says Nicholas drily to his son. "Think you'll be able to survive without your mobile today? I doubt Alexander will be thrilled if you've got your nose buried while the rest of us are staring at the sky."

"I'll find a way to cope." Ben tucks his phone into the pocket of his suit jacket and fixes his gaze on me. "I'm so bloody sorry about everything, Evan. If I'd imagined for even a moment that Jasper was capable of – of such a horrific thing…I thought he was harmless. We all did." He scowls, and a muscle in his jaw twitches. As angry as I am about what Jasper did to me, it's oddly comforting to know that Ben – and Nicholas, and even Maisie – are, too. "How are you holding up?"

"I'm fine," I say, even though that's definitely not true. "I'm just…"

Ben grimaces. "I'm sorry," he says again. "I suppose we all should have listened to Maisie from the beginning, though please don't tell her I said so. I'll never hear the bloody end of it. I'm sure the extended family will have questions today, nosy

155

sods, but stick with me, and I'll make sure they all know to piss off."

"Thanks," I say, and I mean it. I haven't even thought about how the rest of the royal family might react to me, let alone what they'll say about today's headlines, and a knot forms in my stomach. "How many people are supposed to be at this thing, anyway?"

"This *thing* is one of our most cherished traditions," says Nicholas, but there isn't any malice in his voice. "And while there will only be twenty-eight of us on the balcony, thousands of people are expected to attend. Not to mention it'll be broadcast live around the world and watched by millions more before the day is done."

"Millions?" I choke, and my uncle smirks, clearly amused by my horror.

"If it's any comfort, you'll only be on the balcony for fifteen minutes or so."

"Fifteen minutes is plenty of time for everyone to judge me," I mutter as I yank open the back door of the Range Rover, not bothering to wait for the chauffeur.

"You could always hide behind Cousin Albert," says Tibby smoothly. "He's terribly tall and as wide as a—"

"Miss Bright!"

I'm halfway into the vehicle when a ruddy man in a navy suit hurries out of Windsor Castle. It takes me a moment to place him, but once I do, I groan inwardly. Doyle, one of the palace officials who tried to stop Alexander from acknowledging me.

"Miss Bright!" he calls again, and I ease back onto the gravel, wishing I'd insisted on wearing my sneakers to Buckingham

Palace. He's panting when he reaches us, but he manages to bow to Nicholas and Ben with perfect form. "Your Royal Highnesses. I'm afraid there's been a change of plans."

Beside me, Tibby grows very still. "What do you mean, a change of plans?" she says in an unmistakable challenge. "Why wasn't I informed directly?"

"I've only just heard myself, ma'am. Given the...*optics* of the situation and recent reports in the media—"

"You mean that rubbish the *Daily Sun* is spouting?" says Ben.

Doyle hesitates, and that split second is enough to confirm it. "Given these unexpected developments, His Majesty has decided it would be best if Miss Bright abstained from participating in Trooping the Colour and His Majesty's birthday parade today." Doyle's voice quavers, but the message is as solid as stone.

Tibby lets out a sound like a whistling teakettle, and I clench my hands so tightly that my manicured nails dig into my palms. "Why?" I demand. "Because some biased article is quoting an anonymous source with bad information?"

"Because His Majesty doesn't want anything to divert attention from the military and its accomplishments today," says Doyle.

Nicholas scoffs. "The press will be preoccupied with Evangeline whether or not she's there. It'll probably be worse if she isn't."

"I'm deeply sorry to be the bearer of bad news, sir, but this comes directly from the King," says Doyle. "If you disagree, His Majesty is the one you ought to speak with."

Nicholas holds out his hand in front of Ben, clearly demanding

157

his phone so he can call Alexander, but I shake my head. "It's okay," I say around the lump forming in my throat. "I didn't want to go anyway."

"Evan—" says Ben, but I cut him off.

"Really. I'm exhausted," I insist. "Alexander's doing me a favour. I could use another few hours of sleep."

Ben starts to protest, but I walk away, kicking a few stray pebbles as I stride back to the castle. Dimly I hear Nicholas berating Doyle, and Tibby joins in, letting more than a few impressive curses slip, but I don't stick around to listen.

So that's it, then. Alexander only wants me around when the optics are good, and if some random reporter doesn't like me that day, then neither does he.

I know there's more to it – that this is unprecedented, and Alexander has the entire country to think about, not just me. But even though I know it's selfish, I want to matter. I want him to care as much about having me there as he does what the public thinks of him. And right now, it's painfully clear that he doesn't.

I come face to face with Helene and Maisie in the corridor, and although Maisie casts me a curious look, the Queen sneers as if she's stepped in dog shit. Briefly I think about what her adoring public would say if that image of her was on the cover of *People* or *Vogue*, but of course they would take her side. They already do.

Rather than start a fight, I avert my gaze and hurry past them, refusing to give them the satisfaction of seeing me cry. As soon as they're behind me, however, my eyes well up and my vision blurs. I shouldn't care this much. It's just a pointless appearance, and if Alexander is really so ashamed of me, then –

"Oh!"

As I turn another corner, I run straight into something solid. No, not something – *someone*, and I yelp in pain as hot liquid spills down the front of my dress.

"Oh, bugger." Kit sets his mug of tea down on a side table and pulls out a handkerchief to mop at my sopping front. But a split second before his hand touches my chest, he snatches it back, his eyes wild as if he doesn't know what to do. "Evan, I'm so sorry—"

"It's okay. I wasn't paying attention." I take his offered handkerchief and dab helplessly at the stain. My dress is ruined. That's two in a row now, and after all the hard work Louis put into my wardrobe, I'm sure he won't be thrilled.

Somehow this is the thought that breaks me, and before I know it, I dissolve into loud, ugly sobs. My shoulders heave as I gasp for air, and tears stream down my face, undoubtedly taking my mascara with them.

I feel Kit's delicate touch on my elbow, and I'm ready to pull away at the slightest sign of discomfort; then he guides me into a sitting room that smells vaguely like cleaning solution. While I bawl uncontrollably, he helps me into an armchair before disappearing for a few moments and returning with a bottle of water. I don't know how long we stay like this, me crying harder than I have since my grandmother's death, and him kneeling beside the chair, silent and worried. But finally the tears stop, and I'm left with hiccups that make my chest hurt.

"Drink," says Kit, and I take the bottle of water. The cap is sealed shut and clearly hasn't been tampered with, but I hesitate anyway before twisting it off. I'll never be able to accept a drink again from anyone I don't completely trust, I realize, and my red-hot hatred of Jasper grows.

I take a sip, and the cold water fizzes unexpectedly on my tongue. "Thanks," I croak. "I'm sorry, I—"

"You still don't have a single bloody thing to apologize for," says Kit, and to his credit, he doesn't ask me to explain my sudden meltdown. He doesn't demand anything of me the way everyone else seems to, in one way or another.

He's also set a box of tissues on the side table, and I blow my nose, taken aback when it honks like an angry goose. Kit doesn't laugh or mock me, though. Instead, he waits patiently while I wipe my tear-stained face with a clean tissue, removing half my make-up in the process. It doesn't matter. It's not like anyone's going to be taking my picture today.

"Why aren't you going to Buckingham Palace with everyone else?" I say at last, and to my relief, I sound mostly normal now. A little stuffy, but there's no way I'm risking another honk in front of him.

"I'm not a member of the royal family," says Kit. "The King may be my uncle, but we don't share any DNA. Only his blood relatives and their spouses are invited onto the balcony for Trooping the Colour."

I frown. "That doesn't bother you?"

"Not at all. I get a day to myself – can't beat that." Kit studies me. "The real question is, why are you still here? Maisie spent three solid hours screaming about your invitation earlier this week, so I know you received one."

"Haven't you heard? I'm too much of a *distraction*." I manage a rueful smile, but it fades quickly, and I toy with one of the tissues in my lap. "There's an article about me in the *Daily Sun* today – about how I was the last one to see Jasper alive, and how my blood was found in his bedroom. Alexander..." I swallow hard. "He decided he doesn't want me on the balcony after all." Kit's brow furrows, but his steady brown eyes are still on me.

"I suppose that settles it, then."

"Settles what?" I say, and he stands, offering me his hand.

"You need to get changed," he says, "because we're going on an adventure."

Chapter Eighteen

The Fit Prince is at it again. Nicholas, the Duke of York and the deliciously gorgeous younger brother of the King, was seen in Covent Garden last night with his arm around opera singer Natalia Sokolova. The two are rumoured to have met after the Russian star's performance in *Madama Butterfly* earlier this month, and they've reportedly been inseparable ever since.

This isn't the first romantic entanglement Prince Nicholas has found himself in this year – or even this season. Well known for his whirlwind romances that inevitably end as soon as they've begun, Nicholas has recently been spotted with model Trixie Hartwell, actress Vaani Patel, and even – gasp! – an unknown commoner, environmental lawyer Samantha Shaw.

Despite his string of conquests, none of them has matched the scandal of his sudden elopement with socialite Venetia Carmichael at age twenty, followed by the birth of their son, Prince Benedict of York, eight months later. Though the marriage lasted less than two years, the Duchess has made a career of being the prince's ex-wife, with three tell-all books, countless talk show appearances, and a skin care line.

Will Natalia become lucky wife number two? Time will tell, but we certainly wouldn't bet on it.

—*The London Mirror*, 17 June 2023

"Are you sure we should be doing this?" I ask, pulling my Union Jack baseball cap low against the wind. Most of the other passengers on the bright red double-decker bus crossing Westminster Bridge are focused on Big Ben and the Palace of Westminster, but I can't quell the creeping anxiety that one of them will recognize me any second now.

"The public hasn't seen you with your new hair," says Kit patiently, holding on to the brim of his matching cap. "And no one will expect you to be out and about today, not with Trooping the Colour going on."

Those may be excellent points, but they don't do much to soothe my frayed nerves. I glance over my shoulder at the two protection officers sitting behind us, both dressed in polos and khakis – their best "blending in" clothes, I suppose, even though they stick out like sore thumbs to me. "But why are we on a bus?" I say.

"Because you're new in town, and this is the best way to see London," says Kit. "Other than perhaps the Eye."

He nods to a massive white Ferris wheel across the river, and I lower my sunglasses to get a good look. "If that's the best way to see London, then why aren't we on it?"

"Because—" Kit flushes. "I'm not very good with heights."

This surprises me. Somehow, with all his calm reserve, I have a hard time imagining Kit being phobic of anything. "Then I guess the bus isn't so bad," I say, eyeing the murky and deeply uninviting waters of the Thames. "As long as it doesn't tip over."

"Statistically speaking, that's rather unlikely," says Kit. "It does, however, stop at a number of fascinating tourist traps. And while you're taking in all the overpriced sights, I thought we might discuss that list we spoke about yesterday."

163

My gaze snaps back to him like a magnet. "You made a list of the people who were at the party?"

"I did." He holds up his phone. "I can't guarantee that it's complete, but I spoke to Ben and Maisie – don't worry, I didn't tell them what we're doing – and between the three of us, I'm fairly sure we didn't miss many names."

I exhale, both exhilarated and overwhelmed. "All we need is one person who might have done it. There has to be someone at that party who didn't like him, right?"

"The more I learn about Jasper," says Kit grimly, "the more convinced I am that no one actually liked him at all."

"Then this should be simple," I say. Except as the bus sways closer to the muddy water and I grip the metal railing, I'm sure that even from beyond the grave, Jasper won't make it easy.

Kit and I spend the rest of the day dissecting the social lives of every single one of the thirty-six names on his list, all while hopping on and off the tour buses that weave through central London. Each of our stops – Hyde Park, Marble Arch, Baker Street, Madame Tussauds, the West End and Chinatown, St Paul's Cathedral – is punctuated by another discussion about who knew Jasper well, who was there as a plus-one, who may have had a grudge against him, and who went missing from the party for any period of time. Kit seems to know an enormous amount about nearly every single person on the list, from their dating history to their drinking preferences and, most important, how they felt about Jasper Cunningham. And while we're able to cross a few names off – people who either left the party early or who had too much to gain from Jasper's investments and business ventures to justify pushing him – for the most part, nearly everyone is a potential suspect.

"This is a good thing, right?" I say as we linger in a gift shop outside the Tower of London. I refuse to go inside the looming castle walls on principle, but Kit convinces me to duck into the store for a little relief from the sun. "If there are multiple viable suspects, then Scotland Yard will have to at least consider the possibility that it wasn't me."

"In theory," says Kit as he holds up a commemorative plate with my father's face on it. I roll my eyes, and he exchanges it for a tea towel featuring a cartoon raven. "But the more concrete the means and motive, the better. Was anyone else upstairs while you were there?"

I avert my eyes, pretending to examine a plastic tiara. "I don't think anyone else was around when Jasper came up," I say. Not technically a lie, but I still feel guilty. "You know, this is the closest I'll ever get to wearing one of these."

"Tiaras are rather heavy," says Kit as he turns to a rack full of key chains and jewellery. "My aunt always complains of a headache after state functions."

I set down the tiara and brush my fingers against the soft fur of a teddy bear dressed in a guard's uniform, complete with a bearskin hat. Which seems a little twisted, all things considered. "How long have you lived at Windsor?"

Kit purses his lips, and I immediately know I've overstepped. "A year," he says, before I can backtrack. "Since I graduated from Eton."

"You don't have to talk about it," I say, still stroking the teddy bear's fur. "I didn't mean to pry."

Kit chuckles and finally looks at me again. "You aren't prying.

You're asking questions, and I'm answering them. I grew up on my family's country estate in Somerset – in the south-west of England," he explains. "My older brother and I both went to Eton, which is near Windsor Castle, and after I graduated, I wanted to stay close to London, and so..."

He trails off, his brow furrowed, and I clear my throat. "You really don't have to explain," I say again. "We should probably focus on narrowing down the list anyway."

Kit pulls a small item off the rack and, to my surprise, grabs the teddy bear. "Do you like ice cream?"

I blink. "Doesn't everyone?"

"Come on," he says, heading towards the register. "I know a place."

Thirty minutes later, we're sitting on a kerb in front of a pink ice cream shop in a quiet part of London, both of us licking our cones. Kit opted for plain vanilla, while I have a double scoop of mint chocolate chip and fudge, and it's a race against time as it starts to drip down my fingers.

"I think this might be the best ice cream I've ever had," I say, catching a rivulet of sugary goodness before it can stain my jeans. A plastic shopping bag containing my new teddy bear sits between us, and Kit hands me a napkin.

"My parents used to bring me and my brother here whenever we visited Aunt Helene and her family," he says. "Has Tibby told you about him?"

I shake my head. "But...Jasper did," I admit, his name heavy on my tongue. "He mentioned that your brother..."

I trail off. Kit is quiet for a long moment, fixated on his cone, and at last he sighs.

"My brother, Liam, was three years older than me. I know it's a cliché, but he was the golden boy of our family. He had countless friends. Everyone loved him, and he was *good*," says Kit. "He genuinely wanted to make the world a better place. He *did* make the world a better place, simply by being part of it. And he was my favourite person."

Kit still isn't looking at me, so I also focus on my ice cream. It tastes like nothing now, and the pit of my stomach is hollow.

"He died by suicide," says Kit, barely audible, but his words pierce me like a hot stake. "I go over the moments I remember from that last year again and again, and I keep wondering if there was anything I could've done – any signs I missed, any cries for help. If a single conversation might have changed his mind, and I was simply too busy to have it. But I never come up with an answer, and I still have no idea why he did it. None of us does."

"I'm so sorry," I say, turning to him as my ice cream drips onto the street. "Whatever happened…it wasn't your fault."

"Maybe not, but I'll never stop wondering." He clears his throat. "Jasper didn't know that last part – how Liam died, I mean. No one outside of the immediate family does. Our father sees it as something shameful, a stigma he doesn't want tainting our family's legacy." Kit says this bitterly, and I don't blame him. "He copes by pretending Liam never existed. All of the family pictures are gone now, and nearly all of his things have been thrown away or donated. Our mother self-medicates – I don't think she's been sober since Liam died. That's why Aunt Helene took me in. She knew how bad it was at home, and I didn't want to go back, so…she offered me a room at Windsor. And I've been there ever since."

There's a note of finality in the way he says this, as if he's accepted that the life he had in Somerset will never be the same, and he doesn't want anything to do with the new version. I reach for his hand, and my fingers brush his.

"I'm sorry," I say again, feeling like a useless broken record. No combination of words will make it any better for him, though, and I take a deep breath. "Thank you for telling me. For… trusting me."

Kit hooks his pinky with mine, and at last he meets my eye. A shiver runs through me that has nothing to do with the ice cream. "I figured it might help if you knew you aren't the only one with a complicated family." He smiles slightly. "And seeing you go through this…it's comforting to know I'm no longer the biggest sob story at Windsor."

I snort in spite of myself. "You have no idea," I mutter, and though he doesn't ask, I can feel his curiosity.

The mess of melted sugar dripping down my hand is nearly a lost cause, but I take a moment to valiantly try to save it. Everything around us – the city sounds, the passing cars, the light ding of the bell as someone enters the shop behind us – is oddly muffled, as if Kit and I are in some kind of bubble, insulated from the rest of London. My pinky is still hooked with his, and neither of us pulls away.

"I haven't been home in almost seven years," I say. "Since my grandmother died when I was eleven and Alexander got full custody of me."

Kit frowns. "Not even for holidays?"

"Not for anything. I stayed at school over Thanksgiving and Christmas and Easter, and Jenkins took me to these fancy camps every summer. I got to ride plenty of horses and tie-dye a lot of shirts, but going home was never part of the itinerary."

Now that I've let my guard down, the story pours out of me with terrifying ease. My voice sounds detached from my body, as if I don't exist any more, but Kit feels warm and solid beside me, the only thing that's real as we sit on the kerb together.

"My mom has schizophrenia." I've never actually said those words out loud before, and they're oddly difficult to form. "That's why Alexander won't let me see her. She was diagnosed when I was four, and afterward I went to live with my grandmother. Her illness is manageable most of the time," I add quickly. "She always listens to her doctors and takes her medication, and when I was allowed to have a laptop at school, I called her a lot. She's – she's wonderful. Happy and funny and smart, and she's an artist and paints these amazing abstract landscapes. But...I miss her," I admit. Video calls are never enough.

Kit takes my hand fully now, lacing his fingers between mine. "You haven't seen your mum since you were eleven?" he says, and I nod. "Evan..."

"Don't," I say, but it comes out as more of a plea than a demand. I can't take two breakdowns in one day. "Really, I'm okay. As soon as I turn eighteen next month, I'm going to go stay with her. Alexander can't stop me any more."

Kit's eyes are locked on mine, his face so close I can count the freckles on his nose. But as I hold his stare, I realize that one of us – maybe both – is leaning in closer, and suddenly the tightness in my chest returns, every bit as painful as it was this morning in the hallway with Tibby. Swallowing hard, I let go of his hand and turn back to my messy cone, my heart thudding against my ribs.

"What about the drunk girls Jasper kicked out of the party?" I say thickly. "Do you think maybe one of them did it?"

Kit is silent for a moment, and I'm too afraid to look at him. "Chrissy has always fancied Jasper," he says at last, with the kind of ease I definitely can't muster right now. "I can see her being the supposed anonymous source who ran to the *Daily Sun* and made up that rubbish about you. But I saw her and Polly walking down the street together on our way back to Windsor. It's unlikely either of them pushed him, I'm afraid."

"Damn," I mumble, watching my ice cream dribble into a puddle on the asphalt. I think through the night again, retracing my steps, the conversations I had, the things that happened once I was upstairs, and I shiver. "What about the phone call?"

"Phone call?" says Kit. "What phone call?"

"Before Jasper came into the room, he was arguing with someone on the phone," I say, frowning. "It sounded like a business deal."

"Did you tell your lawyer about it?" says Kit, and I shake my head, finally mustering up the courage to look at him again. Whatever sparked between us is gone, and the invisible barrier is back. I don't know whether to be relieved or gutted.

"I didn't think it was relevant at the time," I admit. "But if we find out who was on the other end, maybe it'll lead us to a stronger sus—"

With an ear-piercing screech of tyres, a black Range Rover

whips around the corner, barrelling straight for us. I scramble backward onto the sun-warmed sidewalk, relinquishing the rest of my ice cream cone to the street, and the vehicle squeals to a stop beside the kerb, inches from where my feet were a split second ago.

"What the *hell* was that?" I shout at the driver. But when the window rolls down, a woman with a pixie cut pokes her head out, her face pinched with annoyance.

"I see you're determined to give the tabloids enough fodder to keep them going all summer," she says with a sniff.

"Tibby?" I say, shocked. "How did you—"

I stop and twist around, searching for the protection officers who have been trailing us all day. Sure enough, they're lingering nearby, looking completely out of place against the pink storefront of the ice cream shop.

"Get in," says Tibby impatiently. "Not you, Kit – another car will be here shortly."

I cross my arms. "He can come with us."

"Not this time," she says. "You've been summoned by His Majesty. We're going to Buckingham Palace."

Chapter Nineteen

ITV: Trooping the Colour was spectacular this year, was it not? But I have to ask, Henrietta – where was Evangeline, the King's illegitimate daughter?

HENRIETTA SMYTHE: I can't say for sure, John. All of my sources indicated that she was due to make her first public appearance today with the royal family on the balcony, and her absence was conspicuous.

ITV: Is it possible the King has changed his mind about parading her around in public?

HS: Possible, but unlikely. There's no putting that genie back in the bottle, I'm afraid – it will undoubtedly be considered the scandal of the twenty-first century, and the royal family and their advisers will be working overtime to do what they can to mitigate the damage this has caused. Which will require casting Evangeline in the best possible light. Holding her back from the balcony today only gives credence to the nasty rumours currently being circulated in the tabloids.

ITV: Regarding her involvement in the death of Jasper Cunningham?

HS: Yes. It's all speculation, of course – if Evangeline was at the party the night Mr Cunningham died, the palace will be keeping the facts of the matter hushed up, especially as the investigation is ongoing.

ITV: And if there is any truth to the rumours?

HS: Well, John, I suppose we'll see what the King is willing to risk in the name of family, won't we?

—Transcript of ITV News's interview with royal expert Henrietta Smythe, 17 June 2023

If Windsor Castle is a nauseating display of wealth, then Buckingham Palace is mind-bogglingly obscene.

The palace sits in the centre of London near Hyde Park, surrounded by a tall gate to keep out anyone with the audacity to be born a commoner. Once Tibby and I are inside, we're greeted by a young footman, and every room he guides us through is more opulent than the last. The huge entrance hall full of red velvet, white marble, and priceless works of art. The grand staircase that leads to the state rooms on the second floor. An enormous portrait gallery, a music room dripping with crystal and gold, and a throne room that would have been breathtaking if I weren't so furious at being summoned like a damn dog.

We head into a private wing of the palace – one the average tourist will never get to see – and the footman stops in front of a pair of double doors. Two uniformed men stand on either side, and they simultaneously reach for the handles like they're part of a choreographed dance, revealing a large space that's surprisingly sparse.

The King's office.

There's plenty of protocol for how to greet a monarch – all of which my etiquette instructor has drilled into me – but as soon as I spot Alexander behind his mahogany desk, I storm past the poor footman who's in the middle of announcing us and head straight for him. Jenkins lingers nearby, and I can tell from the look on his face that he wants to say something, but this is between me and my father.

"I get it. I'm an embarrassment to you and your whole family," I snap at Alexander, all of my hurt from that morning mutating into fury at the sight of him. "But you didn't have to rub my nose in it and humiliate me in front of the entire country. If you didn't want me at Trooping the Colour, then you shouldn't have bothered inviting me in the first place. Kicking me out at the last minute—"

"Was callous and unforgivable," says Alexander tiredly. "And I am very sorry for the lack of warning, but I thought it was for the best, and I stand by my decision."

"For the *best?*" I say, my voice catching. "You really think publicly ignoring me is going to help anything? You haven't even—" I stop. I haven't seen him since before the party. He hasn't called or dropped by, and while I didn't expect him to, his absence suddenly feels like a sucker punch to the gut.

Alexander watches me, his hands folded over a clutter of important-looking documents. "My advisers made it clear that it would be detrimental to your image and any future court case if you were to be seen smiling and waving less than forty-eight hours after the...ordeal you went through. Especially now that it seems Robert Cunningham has made it his mission to turn public opinion against you. I'm sorry," he says again, and to his credit, he sounds sincere. "The last thing I wanted was to hurt you."

But he did. "You could have called me yourself and explained, you know. I would have listened," I say. "Instead, you sent *Doyle*, of all people—"

Jenkins clears his throat. "That was my fault," he says apologetically. "I thought it would be easier if we broke the news before you left Windsor. I tried to ring Tibby myself, but I couldn't get through."

I remember the constant buzzing of Tibby's phone that morning, and I glance at her over my shoulder. She frowns and jabs at her screen, as if it's somehow personally betrayed her. "Three missed calls," she confirms. "I'm sorry, Evan."

My anger deflates, leaving a tender bruise in its wake. Maybe Alexander's decision wasn't malicious, but that doesn't make it okay. I struggle to find the words to articulate this, though, and in the temporary lull, my father leans forward on his elbows, his gaze locked with mine.

"How are you?" he says. "Has your recovery been going well?"

I ease down into a velvet chair in front of his desk as what little fight I have left drains out of me. Nothing I say would win that battle anyway. "I'm okay," I mumble, touching the bandaged stitches on my knuckles. "Barely hurts. And the rest of it—" I hesitate, my skin crawling at the memory of Jasper's touch. "I'll be fine."

"Good," he murmurs. "I'm pleased to hear it. Tibby mentioned you spent the day in the city?"

I'm not sure what he's expecting to gain from small talk, but I nod. "Kit wanted to show me some of the sights. We went to—" I fall silent as something catches my eye. The painting hanging above Alexander's desk is an abstract landscape, with bright splashes of colour against a background so muted it's almost grey. I don't recognize the image, but I do recognize the style.

"What is that doing here?" I blurt. Confused, Alexander follows my stare, and as he takes in the artwork like he's seeing it for the first time, I glance around the room. While he doesn't have much furniture – only the desk, a few chairs, and two velvet benches on either side of an antique bookcase – there have to be nearly a dozen paintings hanging on the walls. All abstract landscapes done in the same signature style.

My mother's style.

"Ah." Alexander turns back to me, and I notice his cheeks are pink. "I'm a great admirer of your mother's work."

"Apparently," I say, bemused. "Is that how you two met? Did you buy some of her art or—"

A knock cuts me off, and the double doors open again to admit a man with wiry grey hair – Wiggs, the lawyer who sat with me during my first round of questioning. He bows fluidly, as if it's as natural as breathing, and focuses on Alexander.

"Your Majesty," he says. "Detective Erika Farrows from Scotland Yard has arrived. She's on her way up now."

I go rigid, but Alexander doesn't seem at all surprised. "Very well," he says. "I suppose you both better make yourselves comfortable, then. On my side of the desk, if you please."

As Jenkins fetches Wiggs a chair, I gape at my father. "Is that why you called me here? To make me talk to the police again?"

"It is my sincerest hope that you will not say a word," says Alexander. "But yes, the detective wished to speak with you again, and I insisted on being present."

"But – why?" I'm not sure if I'm asking why the detective wants to speak to me or why Alexander wants to be there. He clearly assumes the latter, however, and his expression softens.

"Because you are my daughter," he says, "and I want to support you throughout this farce of an investigation. After a lifetime of poor behaviour, I owe you that much."

At least he doesn't think I had anything to do with Jasper's death, and the edges of my ire melt at this small gesture of compassion. It doesn't touch the white-hot fear that cuts through me, however, when there's another knock on the door less than a minute later, and Detective Farrows walks into the office.

She stops, clearly taken aback when she sees the three of us sitting in a row on one side of the sizable desk, but she quickly regains her composure and greets her monarch with a curtsy. Once she's seated in the lone chair Jenkins has arranged directly across from my father, she pulls a file from her briefcase and balances it on her knees instead of the polished wood. Alexander, for his part, seems completely unwilling to accommodate her further, and suddenly I'm glad he's here.

I hug my arms around my chest while the lawyer fields Farrows's questions. They're mostly follow-ups from the day before, with a few clarifications, and I mumble short answers when Wiggs indicates I should. She does at least confirm that the glass I drank from, the one with Jasper's fingerprints all over it, held traces of GHB – the same drug that showed up in my blood test. And even though it isn't a surprise, I sigh inwardly at this small piece of validation. I wasn't making things up. My mind wasn't playing tricks on me. Jasper knew exactly what he was doing.

"Miss Bright," says Farrows, after an especially riveting

tangent about the layout of the room, "if I may, in your initial account of the incident, you mentioned there was a laptop present at the time of the assault, yes?"

Wiggs nods towards me, and I sit up a little straighter. "Yeah, on the desk," I confirm. "It had purple-and-green galaxy stickers on the keyboard, but I was never close enough to get a good look."

Before Farrows can continue, Wiggs says shortly, "What does the computer have to do with the investigation?"

She barely glances at him. "No laptop was recovered from the scene," she says, "and Jasper Cunningham's family is unable to confirm which of his electronics may be missing."

Alexander, who's been quiet so far, clears his throat. "Are you exploring the possibility that he was killed for his laptop?"

"We're considering every angle, Your Majesty," says Farrows, and she turns back to me. "Do you have any idea where the laptop might currently be, Miss Bright?"

Yet again, my lawyer tries to interject, but I shake my head. "No idea. I never touched it."

Farrows shuffles a few papers from the file. "You've spent time at a number of boarding schools over the past seven years, yes? Including the Darrowood Institute, Clearwater Academy, and St Catherine's?"

"Miss Bright attended nine boarding schools from ages eleven to seventeen," says Wiggs. "What does this have to do with the case?"

Farrows doesn't acknowledge his question. "You were expelled from all three, were you not? For hacking into the school networks."

178

The temperature in the room seems to drop, and I say nothing.

"Again," says Wiggs, more insistently, "what does this have to do with the case?"

"By your own account, you were alone in Mr Cunningham's bedroom for some time before he joined you, correct?" says Farrows, her dark eyes still on me. "Do you consider yourself proficient with computers, Miss Bright?"

I stare at her, bewildered. "You think – you think I hacked into his laptop?" I blurt. "And – what, pushed him out the window when he caught me?"

"*Evangeline.*" I've never heard Alexander use that tone before, but even this doesn't snap me out of the sudden fog of panic that's swallowed me whole. Farrows doesn't believe Jasper attacked me. She thinks I'm a suspect. Maybe the *only* suspect.

All that matters is what Scotland Yard believes.

Nicholas's words cut through me like lightning, and suddenly I can taste my own fear.

"Unless you have any evidence to support this line of questioning, we're done here," says Wiggs.

The detective doesn't speak right away. I can feel her gaze burning into me, but I stare resolutely at my pale pink nails, trying to ignore the fact that I'm trembling.

At last Farrows agrees, and the interview is over. The footman escorts her out, and I only look back up when the door to Alexander's office closes behind her, my vision blurry with unshed tears.

"She thinks I did it," I say, stunned. "She thinks – she thinks I killed Jasper. *On purpose.*" It's one thing for a single article to accuse me, but for Farrows, who knows the full story, to sit there and imply I somehow hacked into Jasper's laptop in five minutes flat and then...

"The detective is only doing her job," says Jenkins, and I feel his presence beside me, warm and solid. "And right now, her job is to ask questions. If she had any evidence against you, she would be doing more than that."

I gulp. "You mean she'd arrest me."

"No one will arrest you," says Alexander firmly, but I shake my head.

"My blood's in the room and my DNA's all over him." I can't draw a full breath, and everything around me starts to spin. "I don't remember what happened. What if I did do it? What if—" Alexander starts to reach for me, but it's Jenkins who kneels beside my chair, his hands covering mine.

"Evan," he says softly. "Look at me, darling. You didn't do this. You didn't have the strength. In all likelihood, Jasper was intoxicated and simply tripped."

"But – but what if I did? Or what if they find enough evidence and—"

"A member of the royal family cannot be arrested in the monarch's presence," says Jenkins gently. "Nor on the grounds of a royal palace."

"So – what?" I manage, my voice thick and crackling. "I'm just supposed to stay in Windsor Castle for the rest of my life?"

Jenkins tucks a lock of hair behind my ear. "You did nothing wrong, Evan. I promise no one is going to arrest you."

"The police in Vermont did," I say tightly. "Detective Farrows could, too." Except this time, it wouldn't be for setting fire to a grade book. It would be for murder.

"We have the best lawyers in the United Kingdom," says Alexander. His hand twitches, and I think he might try to touch me, but he forms a fist instead. "They *will* see you through this safely."

I know he's probably right – he's the King, after all, and everyone who works for him is at the top of their game. But I don't feel safe. I feel like I've been tossed into shark-infested waters, and Alexander and Jenkins are debating whether to throw me a life jacket or let Robert Cunningham and his media empire eat me alive.

"You need to find another suspect," I say suddenly, looking at Wiggs. He's gathering papers into his briefcase, seemingly trying to be as unobtrusive as possible, and he meets my eye with an owlish blink. "There were people at that party who hated Jasper. People he hurt, people who could have pushed him. And the phone call – he had a phone call before he came into the room—"

"We can discuss all of this when you've calmed down, Miss Bright," says Wiggs, and I gape at him.

"You want me to *calm down?* Scotland Yard thinks I killed the boy who drugged me and tried to – to – and *you* think I need to calm down?"

"Evan," says Jenkins softly. "It's been a long day. Why don't I escort you back to Windsor Castle and—"

"Do you even know who else was at that party?" I say, laser focused on Wiggs. "Do you have *any* other suspects?"

"My team is diligently investigating the matter," says Wiggs, and a faint sheen appears on his forehead. "As I've said, we will discuss everything on Monday, once you've recovered from your ordeal—"

"That should be plenty of time for whoever's leaking information to the tabloids to let the entire world know I killed Jasper for his shitty laptop," I say bitterly. "Let me guess. Your team's looking into that, too."

Alexander clears his throat again. "Yes, we're also working to find the source of the leaks from within the royal household," he confirms. "For now, Jenkins and Tibby will accompany you back to Windsor, and—"

"At least get his phone records," I plead. "Whoever called Jasper, it sounded like a fight, or at least a disagreement. That could be something."

Alexander and Wiggs exchange a look. "Very well, sir," says Wiggs with a bow of his head. "I will look into it immediately."

"Thank you, Wiggs," says Alexander before turning his attention back to me. "I know you're frightened, Evan, but investigations aren't completed overnight. We're going to do this right, and that will take some time. You have every reason not to trust that I have your best interests in mind, but I swear to you, I do. We *will* get you through this. You have my word."

I clench my jaw and stare at the closest of my mother's paintings – a violet-and-emerald number that sends an unexpected ache through my chest. At least Alexander knows how little his word is worth to me, but in that moment, I want nothing more than to believe him. To believe that somehow this really will all be okay.

But no matter how much money and power he has and no matter how many royal titles he holds, that's not a promise he can make.

Chapter Twenty

In case you chose today of all days to start your social media cleanse, the *Daily Sun* has confirmed reports that Evangeline Bright had illegal drugs in her system the night Jasper Cunningham mysteriously fell off a balcony while the pair were alone in his bedroom.

#JusticeforJasper has been trending worldwide since the bombshell article was posted, and though neither Scotland Yard nor the palace has chosen to comment on the leak, we at the *Regal Record* can exclusively reveal that this isn't the first time the disgraced royal love child has been caught having a pharmaceutically enhanced good time.

According to former roommate Cassandra Drake, who lived with Evangeline for eight months in 2021, our half-blood princess has a penchant for the white stuff.

"She used to tell everyone her father was an international drug lord," claims Drake. "No one believed her, of course, but she always said she could get us drugs if we wanted."

With reports that cocaine was found in Cunningham's Belgravia residence the night of his death, an anonymous witness has come forward to confirm the palace's worst nightmare.

"She was high. There's no doubt about it. I saw her doing lines in the bathroom with two other girls, and they were already so wasted they could hardly walk straight. I think that's why Jasper told her to go upstairs – because she was acting like a lunatic, and he was trying to sober her up."

Drake confirms Evangeline's affinity for nose candy. "We went to a party together at the beginning of the school year, and another girl brought some. Not a lot – just enough for a few people – but Evangeline was all over it. She snorted so much that her nose started bleeding, and I had to take her back to our room."

With the case against Evangeline heating up, how long will the palace continue to hide her before justice is finally served?

—*The Regal Record*, 18 June 2023

When the knock sounds on my bedroom door the next morning, I'm already two hours deep into the comments section of the *Daily Sun*.

The vitriol is so bad that it's almost inspiring. Strangers who have never met me – who will never meet me, who don't even know enough about me to call me Evan instead of Evangeline – have dedicated their Sunday morning to tearing me apart. They cite friends of friends, blind gossip tweets, and gut feelings they have after seeing the few pictures of me that the press has managed to find. Everyone loves a villain, and everyone suddenly *loves* to hate me.

"Evan?" Kit's muffled voice startles me back into reality. Tibby takes Sundays off, and without her here to order me out of bed, I'm still in my pyjamas. My hair is a mess, my nails are bitten to the quick, and I haven't even brushed my teeth yet, but none of that seems to matter in the face of the country's seething hatred.

"Come in," I croak, tearing my eyes away from the screen for the first time all morning.

Kit opens the door slowly, like he's not sure what he'll find on the other side. "Did I wake you?" he says, and while my entire body feels heavy and numb, my heart does an odd little skip.

"I've been up for hours," I say, my voice thick with disuse. "There's…an article about me in the *Daily Sun*, with thousands of comments. I don't know why I started reading them, but… once I did, I couldn't stop."

After a moment's hesitation, Kit moves towards me with tentative steps, as if he's somewhere he knows he shouldn't be. Once he's close enough to see what's on my screen, he stops and frowns. "Evan…"

I open my mouth again to insist I'm fine, that I don't care what a bunch of strangers think of me, but the lie dies on my tongue. I'm not okay. The comments, the vitriol, everything Farrows said to me yesterday – none of it's okay.

"Someone leaked the results of my blood test to the *Daily Sun* – that's what the article is about," I mumble, averting my eyes. "But instead of mentioning I had GHB in my system, they're saying it was cocaine. And – and yesterday, the detective insinuated that I hacked into Jasper's laptop and killed him when he caught me." I swallow hard. "Everyone thinks I did it, Kit. *Everyone*. And I can't even say for sure that I didn't."

Kit is quiet for a moment. "I can," he says at last.

"You weren't in the room," I say, raking my fingers through my hair. "You don't know what happened."

"I know you were drugged. I know you were acting in self-defence."

185

"But – I don't want the whole world to know what Jasper tried to do to me." The very thought of the *Daily Sun* and the *Regal Record* and thousands upon thousands of commenters dissecting one of the worst nights of my life makes a lump form in my throat. "Even if I tell everyone what happened, they won't believe me. Or they'll say I deserved it, or I was asking for it, or that I secretly wanted him to, or they'll say *boys will be boys* and it was my fault for going into the bedroom alone with him in the first place, even though I – even though I trusted him."

I press the heels of my hands to my eyes and take a deep, shaky breath. Part of me expects Kit to insist that the public will understand, that as soon as they know the truth, they'll take my side. But instead I hear the rustling of papers, and I lower my hands.

"What's that?" I say, eyeing the folded packet he's holding.

"The list of names we discussed yesterday," says Kit. "Along with all the relevant information I could think of."

He hands me the packet, and I flip through it, stunned. It must have taken him hours – maybe even all night, with how many details some pages have. "Kit…thank you," I say. "You didn't have to do this."

"Some of the profiles are sparser than others, but this should give Wiggs a few leads," he says, and I snort in spite of myself.

"I tried to talk to Wiggs about our list yesterday, and about the phone call," I say. "But he told me I had to *calm down* and that we'd discuss it all on Monday. Alexander at least got him to agree to look into Jasper's call log, but Wiggs wouldn't listen to anything I said."

Kit considers this. "Then we'll just have to make him, won't we?"

"And how are we supposed to do that?"

"Well, it is Sunday," he says. "With all that's going on, however, I expect there's a good chance Wiggs will at least drop by his office today. If we leave this right in the middle of his desk, he can't miss it."

"Don't underestimate him," I mutter. But it's not the worst plan in the world, even though I can still imagine Wiggs throwing it in the trash. "I'm not really in the mood to venture out in public today. Possibly ever again."

"What about upstairs?" says Kit. "Would that be too far?"

I study him and the boyish smile that's tugging at the corners of his mouth, and his hope is almost contagious. "No," I say. "I think I can manage that."

The upper floors of Windsor are, as far as I can tell, mostly devoted to office space. Kit and I pass the conference room where I sat across from Alexander the night the news of my existence broke, and as we head down a particularly long stretch of hallway, I recognize Louis's office. We stop twenty feet away, in front of a door that doesn't look any different from the rest, and when Kit tries the handle, it doesn't budge.

"Locked," he says with a sigh. "We'll have to slide the packet under the door and hope for the – what are those?"

I pull my lockpicks from my pocket and nudge him aside. I've done this twice now, after all, and surely the locks in the UK aren't so different from the ones in the States. The tension wrench is easy enough to manoeuvre, and as I hold my breath, the tiny springs inside the lock give way until I hear a soft *click*.

Kit stares at me. "Is that part of the standard curriculum at American boarding schools?"

"If it was," I say as I open the door, "I might've actually paid attention once in a while."

I turn on the light, revealing an office crammed with a tiny desk, chair and filing cabinet. It's small – too small for the King's private lawyer, I think, until I see the nameplate on the desk: ASSISTANT TO R. WIGGS.

Kit, at least, seems to know where he's going, and he strides across the room and tries another doorknob. This one turns with ease, and I follow him as we step into a larger office with a life-sized portrait of my father hanging on the wall.

"Wow," I say, eyeing the painting. "Not sure I'd want my boss staring at me all day while I'm trying to work."

"He's unavoidable, I'm afraid," says Kit as he tries to smooth the crease in the packet. "His face *is* on our money."

I circle the office, which is really just a few chairs and a wide desk that overlooks a curtained window. Wiggs has a handful of photos arranged beside his monitor, and I bend down to peer at the cherubic faces of the children I assume are his grandkids.

"All right," says Kit as he places the list in the middle of the desk. "Now that that's done, Wiggs will have no excuse—"

"Wait." I spot a yellow sticky note attached to one of the picture frames. "This better not be what I think it is."

"What?" says Kit, and he joins me. I grope around for the power button on Wiggs's ancient monitor, and as it wheezes to life, I pluck the note from the frame and examine it.

"What are you doing?" says Kit cautiously, and from that single question I know he's never broken a real rule in his life. It's sweet, and my gaze lingers on him a moment longer than it should before I turn back to the computer.

"Testing my lawyer's competency," I say. When the password prompt appears, I quickly type in the same nonsensical series of characters that Wiggs – or maybe his assistant – has so carefully copied down and stuck beside his screen. Sure enough, a welcome chime sounds, and his inbox appears on the monitor.

Kit lets out a low whistle. "I suppose the rumours of your insubordination weren't exaggerated, then."

"You wouldn't believe how many people don't bother to memorize their passwords." I reach for the power button again, annoyed at how easy this was and determined to find a way to report it that doesn't include self-incrimination. Before I turn the monitor off, however, I catch sight of Jasper's name in one of the unopened emails' subject lines.

J. CUNNINGHAM – PHONE LOG

I suck in a breath. I shouldn't do it. No matter what my former principals and headmistresses assumed, I've never gone looking for anything personal on the various computers I've commandeered. Or anything that wasn't a vital part of whatever system I wanted to throw into chaos. But this is a clue about what really happened that night, and given my confidence in Wiggs has now been shattered, I'm moving the mouse before I can really consider the ethics of my actions.

Mr Wiggs,

I've attached the information you requested regarding the calls made to Jasper Cunningham's mobile on 15 June. Most have been identified, but the one he received shortly before his death came from a prepaid mobile number.

Regards,
E. Farrows

"Jasper got a call from a burner phone right before he died," I say. "That's weird, right?"

"Very," says Kit, taking a tentative step closer to the monitor, clearly not comfortable with my delinquent activities. "You're sure that's what it says?"

I read the entire email aloud for him. "Who did Jasper know that would use a burner phone?"

"Someone who was likely up to no good. Are you certain you don't remember his conversation with the caller?"

I press my lips together. Dwelling on that night isn't exactly my favourite thing in the world, and my mind shies away from the details of Jasper's call, though whether it's due to anxiety or because the drug in my drink erased that memory permanently, I don't know. "I think – maybe he mentioned a threat?"

Kit sighs. "You'll want to make sure Wiggs knows that, then, and doesn't dismiss – wait, what's that?"

I'm about to hit the power button again when Kit points to another unread subject line.

"Rhiannon Adams," says Kit. "She was at the party. Scroll down." I'm perfectly happy to let him take the ethical hit for this one, and I do as he says, scrolling slowly enough so we can both skim the subject lines. And while I try my best to ignore the ones that aren't relevant, the notifications of signed NDAs appear again and again over the past two days, each with the name of a partygoer attached.

"Guess Wiggs has been busier than I thought," I mumble. "He really managed to convince this many guests at the party to sign NDAs?"

"The crown can be quite intimidating when it wants to be," says Kit. "I expect he'll net them all, if he hasn't already."

I find this oddly comforting, and I scroll back up to the top of Wiggs's inbox before putting the computer to sleep and carefully replacing the sticky note. "That still doesn't change the fact that someone's spreading lies about what happened," I say. "Who do you think might—"

"*Ahem.*"

We turn towards the door at the same time, both of us frozen as we gape at the figure standing there.

Louis.

"I thought you both might like to know that Wiggs is due back soon," he says casually, as if we're discussing the weather instead of breaking and entering.

"Thanks," I manage, even though it comes out as more of a squeak. "We were just…dropping off some documents."

"Of course," he says. "I didn't see a thing."

Kit and I slink guiltily out of Wiggs's office, and as we pass Louis, I stand on my tiptoes and give him a kiss on the cheek. "You're the best," I whisper.

"And you need to work on your espionage skills," he says, but there's an unmistakable glimmer of amusement in his eyes. At least one of us is enjoying this.

Confident that Louis won't tell anyone – or, at the very least, that Jenkins won't once he finds out – I follow Kit back to the staircase, barely daring to breathe until the door is closed behind us.

"Thanks," I say as we hurry down the steps in an unspoken agreement to get as far from Wiggs's office as possible. "I'm not sure anyone else would have risked that for me. Or – made that list, or any of the amazing things you've done in the past few days."

Kit is still a little wild-eyed from our escapade, but he manages a smile. "It's my pleasure," he says. "That's what friends are for, or so I've heard."

I'm taken aback by how much my heart sinks at *friends*, but I don't have the right to be disappointed, not after I pulled away from him yesterday. "At least Louis was the one to find us," I say, trying to rally.

"Ah, yes," says Kit. "Wiggs can be rather frightening, particularly when he's forgotten to comb his hair."

"Oh, he would've been easy to deal with," I say with forced nonchalance. "I was thinking more along the lines of Henry VIII. I'm pretty sure his ghost has been spying on me."

"Is that so?" says Kit, as if this is a perfectly normal topic of conversation. "I think he followed me around for a while, too, when I first arrived."

"Really? You don't seem like his type."

"What, you don't think I could attract a lecherous dead king?" he says. "I'll have you know that the over–five hundred crowd *adores* me."

I snort. "Really, though," I say seriously as we slow our descent down the stairs. "I'm not good at this. At – friendship. Or any kind of relationship." I hesitate. "After my grandma died, I wanted to live with my mom so badly, and I thought if I was expelled enough times, eventually Alexander would run out of schools. So I never really let myself have friends, even when the other students tried. Why bother when I'd be gone soon anyway, you know?"

"That sounds like a very lonely life," says Kit quietly, and I shrug, a strange sense of embarrassment creeping over me.

"It wasn't so bad. And – my point is, I'm not good at this. Because…well, everyone leaves eventually, one way or the other. People aren't permanent."

We reach the ground floor and step out into the long hallway, but before we head back to my suite, Kit touches my shoulder. It's feather-light and somehow even more startling than it would be if he'd grabbed me, and I stop, unable to look him in the eye.

"Evan," he says softly, "you *are* good at this. Better than good, really – you're brilliant. And I hope you know that you don't owe me or anyone else your trust. I'm going to earn it, all right? Every single day, as long as you'll let me. Because I very much want to be in your life." He shakes his head. "I know how trite it must sound, but you're the first good thing to come my way in over a year, and I've every intention of doing all I can to make sure this doesn't turn into another missed connection I'll always regret."

I finally look at him, not entirely sure what to say, or if I'm even capable of speech at the moment. I don't deserve his kindness, or his loyalty, or anything he's offering despite barely knowing who I am. But as I stare at him for far too long, I'm absolutely sure that he would disagree.

"Kit," I manage, my voice cracking. "I—"

A muffled cry sounds from somewhere nearby, and I spin around, my heart pounding. The hallway behind us is empty.

"Did you—" I start to say, but a loud gasp cuts me off, and this time I'm sure it's coming from a room only a few yards away. "Is someone hurt?"

We tiptoe down the corridor and I press my ear against the door. Whimpers seep through the ancient wood, and I frown. Someone is definitely inside.

"I'm not sure that's a good idea," whispers Kit, but I'm already turning the knob. I nudge the door open, grateful the hinges don't squeak, and glance around. It's a sitting room with a layout similar to mine, though the furniture is all forest green and dark wood, with golden furnishings that glimmer in the sunlight. The whimpering is louder now, and it's followed by a moan.

Oh. *Oh.* I understand what I'm hearing a split second before I spot the pair tangled together on a velvet sofa. To my enormous relief, the back of the couch is blocking their bodies from my view, but their profiles are visible, and my blood turns to ice when I realize who I'm looking at.

Nicholas, the Duke of York. And Queen Helene.

Chapter Twenty-one

BRIGHT UNDER HOUSE ARREST

Evangeline Bright, the now-infamous illegitimate daughter of the King and an unknown American woman, is reportedly under house arrest.

According to a palace insider, Miss Bright was scheduled to be at Trooping the Colour before the media onslaught accusing her of being a key suspect in the death of Jasper Cunningham, son of media mogul Sir Robert Cunningham, owner of the *London Independent Standard*. We can now confirm that seventeen-year-old Evangeline has been disinvited from all future royal events, including the Royal Processions and appearances in the Royal Enclosure at this week's Royal Ascot.

Evangeline has allegedly not left Windsor Castle since the night of the party in Belgravia, and insiders are speculating that the King is keeping his daughter on royal property to prevent Scotland Yard from taking her into custody. Buckingham Palace has declined to comment.

—*The London Independent Standard*, 18 June 2023

Kit and I sprint the entire length of the corridor, and we don't stop until we're in my sitting room. I'm out of breath, and my head is spinning as I try to simultaneously absorb what I saw and block it out entirely.

"Did you—" I can barely get the words out. "Did you *see* that?"

Kit nods, but there's a strange look on his face as he closes the door softly behind him. "They didn't spot you, did they?"

"I don't think so. They seemed – otherwise occupied."

Numbly I note that this is the second time I've walked in on a member of my new family in a compromising position. I can't tell Kit about Maisie and Gia – I don't know how much of a secret that is, and I have no intention of outing my half-sister to anyone – but this *is* something we can talk about.

"How long has it been going on?" I say, my mind whirling as I pace in front of the fireplace. "Do you think it's new? Have you ever seen them flirting or—"

Kit is still leaning against the door, his arms crossed and his expression strained. I stop a few feet away and stare at him as the truth dawns on me.

"You already knew."

"I…strongly suspected," he admits. "They're very affectionate with each other when they think no one else is paying attention, and they do spend an inordinate amount of time together. But I've never stumbled across proof before."

I force myself to breathe at a measured pace as the room seems to tilt around me. This is big. The kind of big that could put a nail in the coffin of the monarchy. The country is angry enough that Alexander had an affair that produced me, a drug-addicted murderer, but for their sweet, perfect Queen to be sleeping with the King's playboy brother…

"Do you think Alexander knows?" I say. "If he doesn't, he should, right? It's his wife and his *brother*."

Kit pushes off against the door and takes a step closer to me. "I have no idea if he knows, but it isn't your place to tell him, nor is it mine. Your situation is precarious enough as it is," he adds, cutting off my protest. "The last thing you want is to be the bearer of this particular brand of bad news."

"But she's cheating," I say, baffled.

"And your father cheated on her," says Kit gently. "I'm not saying two wrongs make a right. But the King is not a pillar of morality, either, and it isn't our place to insert ourselves into their marriage. We have no idea what they're going through now or what they've gone through in the past, or whatever private arrangements they may have made—"

Someone raps loudly on the door, and both Kit and I nearly jump out of our skin. We glance at each other, and I see my own fear reflected on his face. What if Nicholas and Helene saw me after all? Or what if Wiggs somehow found out that we went through his inbox?

I'm not sure which would be worse, and when a second knock sounds, I automatically take a step back, too chicken to answer. My heel bangs into the leg of the sofa, but the pain is nothing compared to the anxiety coursing through me.

Kit, however, is apparently infinitely braver than I am, and he sucks in a breath and reaches for the knob. I want to tell him to stop, that whoever it is will go away eventually if we pretend we're not here, but he pulls open the door before I can say a word.

"There you are." Ben stands in the hallway, wearing a crisp blue button-down shirt and a wide smile. "I've been looking all over for you."

"I was showing Evan around the castle," says Kit easily, doing an admirable job of acting like everything's normal. I, on the other hand, have to lean against the sofa to stop my legs from giving out.

"Maisie and I are selecting our outfits for Royal Ascot in the white drawing room," says Ben. "Gia and Rosie are here, too, and I thought it'd be fun if we all spent the afternoon together. We haven't done that in ages."

"No, I suppose we haven't," says Kit, and even his glance my way is shockingly casual.

I force myself to smile, painfully aware that I'm not nearly as convincing. "You should go," I say. "I need to call my mom anyway."

Ben casts a strange look between us. "Evan, do you really think I'd invite Kit and not you?"

I blink. "Yes. I mean – not because you're a jerk, but Maisie can't stand me, Gia and Rosie think I'm some kind of joke—"

"I rather enjoy your company," says Ben. "And I think it's fairly obvious Kit does, too."

Kit scratches his neck, and I swear his cheeks turn pink. "Maisie's coming around," he assures me. "And while Gia's enormously protective and Rosie doesn't have an ounce of good sense, they mostly follow her lead. In the meantime, we'll make sure they don't eat you alive."

I snort. "They're not nearly as deadly as they think they are. But all right," I add cautiously. "As long as they aren't rude."

"Can't promise that," says Ben cheerfully. "But insults are Maisie's love language, so try not to be too offended."

He leads the way out of my room and around the corner, heading straight for the private apartments. Kit and I linger a few steps behind, and as our eyes meet, I mouth, *Does he know?* Kit shakes his head minutely, and even though I'm not sure I'll ever be able to erase the memory of Nicholas and Helene on that forest-green sofa, I let the subject drop as we follow Ben into the first drawing room. Oil paintings cover the vaulted white walls, which are decorated with gilded moulding that gleams despite its age, but the grandeur is obscured by the rows upon rows of dresses and suits shoved into every nook and cranny.

Louis riffles through the racks, pulling outfits to hand to a pair of assistants who hover nearby, and he doesn't look up as we enter. The far corner has been sectioned into a pair of curtained-off changing areas, and Gia and Rosie are curled up on one of several sofas that face the centre of the room. Rosie's pouting at her phone as she takes selfies, but the moment she spots us, she leaps to her feet.

"Kit!" she squeals, running over to hug him. He goes still as she kisses his cheeks, and though he's warm, he's not nearly as affectionate as she is. "I was hoping you'd be here. My followers have been *begging* me to post another picture of you—"

"I'd rather you didn't," says Kit kindly. "And you know the rules, Rose. No photos or selfies in the royal residences."

Rosie blushes to the roots of her curly blond hair. "I was just checking my make-up, I swear. I teared up a bit when I saw the last dress Maisie had on. It was *stunning.*"

"But far too fancy for Royal Ascot," says Gia, and she tilts her face so Kit can kiss her cheek in greeting. As he leans towards her, her dark eyes meet mine, and they harden.

So that's how it's going to be. Fine. I flop onto a chaise longue several yards away, stretching my legs out across the white velvet. Though part of me expects Kit to remain with the others, he strides over to join me, and I shift to make room for him, more pleased than I want to admit.

Gia raises an eyebrow. "Don't tell me you two are a thing," she says, and Rosie whips around to face us.

"You are?" she says, her tone souring, and it's not difficult to read into that. My insides squirm with something I don't want to name, and before I have to, Kit interjects.

"We're friends," he says easily. "Surely you've heard of such a thing."

"Apparently not everyone in this country hates me after all," I say, trying to match his casualness, but all I can think about is how easily he lied to Ben only minutes ago. Is this another lie? Or am I hearing things that aren't really there?

I chance a glance at Kit, only to find him watching me, too. But before either of us can say anything, Maisie pushes aside the curtain of her dressing area. She's wearing a beautiful baby pink sundress with long silk sleeves that flutter as she moves, and a third assistant helps her into a pair of nude heels.

"What do you think of this one?" she says, and once her shoes are on, she twirls with expert skill. As the billowing fabric catches the light, I realize there's gold thread sewn into the bodice and the skirt, making the dress glitter.

"Wow," says Rosie, her eyes round as she clutches her phone to her chest. "That's *gorgeous*."

"You look like a princess," says Gia cheekily, and for the first time I see a flicker of humour from her. "You have to wear it for the Gold Cup."

"Do you think?" Maisie stops in front of a three-panelled mirror and admires herself from several angles. "It would go well with Thimble's coat, if we make it to the winner's circle."

"Thimble is Maisie's favourite horse," says Kit quietly to me. "He's running in the Gold Cup, which is the biggest race at Royal Ascot."

"Got it," I whisper gratefully. They may all be fluent in high-society events and etiquette rules so complicated they make a calculus textbook look simple, but my tutors have made it clear that I don't know a diadem from a digestive. And now, seeing it all in action, I know they're right.

As Maisie disappears to change into another dress, I catch Rosie casting furtive looks at us. Kit's doing a good job of ignoring her, but I stare right back. "Can I help you?" I say.

Rosie squirms in her seat. "Aren't you two, like...related?"

I bristle at the insinuation, but Kit chuckles. "I'm Maisie's cousin," he reminds her. "Not Evan's."

"And they're only friends, Rosie," calls Ben from behind a curtain. "You can retract your claws at any time."

He steps out of his own dressing room in a grey morning suit and mint-green tie. After checking his appearance in the mirror, he says to one of Louis's fussy assistants, "The fit is excellent, thank you. Evan, will you be joining us at Royal Ascot?"

The tension in the air is thick, and while I appreciate that Ben is changing the subject, this is yet another minefield. "No," I say. "Horses aren't really my thing."

"Horses *aren't really your thing*?" mocks Maisie from behind her curtain. "Honestly, how Daddy expects any of us to put up with you is beyond me."

These are the first words Maisie has said to me in days, and after all that's happened this morning, I'm already at the end of my rope. Like she's really the one putting up with *me*. "I should probably go," I mutter, biting back a rude retort. "I need to make a call."

Before I can stand, however, Rosie peers at me again. "Are you not going to Royal Ascot because of all the stories about you in the press?"

"Obviously," says Gia. "You don't think the King would actually let her show her face right now, do you?"

"What really happened with Jasper, anyway?" says Rosie, still focused on me. "Maisie said he didn't shag you, but it must've been bad."

"Does Maisie tell you everything?" I say waspishly as I get to my feet, nauseated at the thought of going into detail in front of them. Or calling what Jasper tried to do to me a *shag*. "I really do need to go—"

"Kit, the girls said you're the one who found her," says Ben as he pulls off his jacket. "Of course Evan doesn't remember much, given the, er, drugs, but you—"

"It's an active investigation," says Kit smoothly, and he stands with me. "Neither of us can talk about it."

That isn't technically true – or if it is, no one's told me. Neither of us has signed one of Wiggs's non-disclosure agreements, after all. But I don't contradict him.

As we start towards the door, Maisie steps out of the dressing room once more, and this time she's wearing a stunning floor-length gold gown that looks like it was made for her. For all I know, it was.

"Wow," says Gia as Rosie's jaw drops. "Maisie, that's killer."

"I thought so, too," says my half-sister, and she spins on the spot. "Obviously it's far too fancy for Royal Ascot, but I was thinking it might be a contender for my birthday ball."

At the words *birthday ball*, my insides constrict, and I notice Louis goes very still as he examines a chic lilac number. Right. So Maisie's going to have a party on our birthday, and no doubt my name isn't anywhere near the guest list.

Ben must see the look on my face, because he takes a step towards me, upsetting the seamstress who's slipping a pin into the cuff of his sleeve. "Evan, you won't be here, right? That's what we all assumed, but if things have changed because of the investigation—"

"Nothing's changed," I say tightly. "I'm going home."

It's not a lie, or at least I desperately hope it isn't. I can't bring myself to look at Kit, though, and if he's at all dismayed, I don't let myself see it. Maybe he really did mean what he said on the staircase, but the pessimistic side of me – the *realistic* side of me – doubts it. Even if he did, I have a lifetime of evidence that proves I'm easy to forget.

"Have you decided what tiara you'll wear, Maisie?" says Rosie after a beat, her voice unnaturally high and cheerful.

"I've been considering the Lover's Knot," she muses. "I'd prefer Queen Alexandra's Kokoshnik tiara, but Mummy thinks it's too ostentatious. I suppose Queen Mary's Fringe tiara wouldn't be a terrible compromise, but I'm also keeping the

Girls of Great Britain and Ireland tiara on the list, depending on which dress I choose."

I can't listen to her any more. Moving on silent feet, I head back into the corridor, willing myself to keep it together. I'm not jealous of my half-sister, exactly. But I also can't deny how much it hurts to think about what Maisie will always take for granted and I'll never have. Not tiaras, but the respect and legitimacy that come with them. That come with having two parents who are married, even if it's clear they no longer love each other.

Footsteps echo behind me, but I wait until I'm standing in front of my door before I turn to face Kit. His mouth is twisted with concern, and even though I'm fairly sure I know what he's about to ask, I can't bring myself to offer him any reassurances. "Did you notice if Gia or Rosie signed an NDA?" I say before Kit can get a word in. He blinks, clearly taken aback.

"It's standard procedure for close friends of the royals to sign non-disclosure agreements. Even I had to sign one when I moved here," he says. "Why?"

"The leaks have been coming from someone inside Windsor," I say. "No one else knew I was here in the first place, and it only took the media twenty-four hours to find out about me. It could be a member of the staff, but the information that's come out about the case…" I shake my head. "It's personal. *Really* personal. And whoever it is wants to destroy me."

Kit considers this for a moment. "You believe it's someone in the royal family, then?"

"I don't know who else it could be. Unless…" I glance down the hall that leads to the white drawing room. "How long have they all known each other? Maisie, Gia and Rosie, I mean."

"Er – since they were toddlers, I expect," he says. "Their mothers are close friends. Maisie's always been privately tutored, and her trusted social circle is rather small."

"And how much does she tell them?"

Kit hesitates. "Loads," he admits. "Most things, really. You don't think…?"

"Yeah," I say, clenching my fists. "I do."

Chapter Twenty-two

ITV: Henrietta, what do you think about the report that Evangeline Bright is allegedly planning to flee the country on her eighteenth birthday?

HENRIETTA SMYTHE: Well, I can't say I blame her. The poor girl's being ripped to shreds in the media. She's seventeen, she's been thrown head first into an active murder investigation, and her entire life is being dissected in the press. If I were her, I would've been on a plane a week ago.

ITV: Do you believe there's any credibility to the rumours that she is Scotland Yard's top suspect in the death of Jasper Cunningham?

HS: While we've received no official word from either Buckingham Palace or Scotland Yard confirming she was even there the night of the party, I think that certainly might explain why the King has kept her under wraps. We've all been hoping for a glimpse of her during the Royal Procession at Royal Ascot, but four days in, it doesn't seem like we'll be so lucky.

ITV: Is it unusual, would you say, for a member of the royal family to stay out of the spotlight like this?

HS: The entire situation is unprecedented, and the King is no doubt making up the rules as he goes. While his advisers are almost certainly telling him that this is the best way forward, the longer Evangeline is kept from the public eye, the more frenzied the furore around her grows.

ITV: And how do you think this will all end?

HS: Well, it's difficult to say, isn't it? But for the sake of the monarchy's future, I very much hope this is all resolved as quickly and cleanly as possible.

—Transcript of ITV News's interview with royal expert Henrietta Smythe, 20 June 2023

With every day that passes, the articles grow more and more vicious.

It isn't just the *Daily Sun* now. Other newspapers and tabloids are joining in, and even CNN runs a story noting the timeline of the party and the supposed evidence against me. I pore over social media and online columns every morning, until the second day of Royal Ascot, when Tibby threatens to steal my laptop while I sleep. I start setting an alarm after that, and my morning reading is finished before she arrives.

I'm not surprised when the story of me supposedly fleeing the country surfaces, and though Kit tries to find another logical explanation, I spend hours tracing Rosie and Gia online in hopes of finding a clue about which one might be the leak. Rosie's easy – she has an Instagram page with nearly half a million followers, and she posts everything from her meals to her outfit of the day to videos of her adorable cocker spaniel. But Gia, as far as Google's concerned, is a complete mystery. The only time she shows up in a search is when her name's attached to Maisie's, and she doesn't have any public social media handles. Eventually, after scrolling through well over a thousand pictures on Rosie's Instagram account, I find a single black-and-white photo of Gia in an airy tutu standing en pointe. There's no context, though, and Rosie's only caption is *#proud*.

Even if they are feeding stories about me to the press, I'm painfully aware of the fact that they aren't the real culprits. It's Maisie who wants me gone, and they're only doing her bidding. It's no coincidence, I'm sure, that there's never a single mention in the media that the heir to the throne was at the party, too. And no matter how many enemies Jasper may have had, no matter how many people on Kit's list could have done it, my name is the only one the papers ever print.

It doesn't help that as the stories get worse, Wiggs refuses to do much more than assure me again and again that his team is taking care of it. They may be, legally speaking, but the public doesn't seem to care about the facts any more – only about the most salacious rumours that no one who was at the party can dispute, now that the palace has silenced them all. Whatever Wiggs is or isn't doing, the hole I'm in gets a little deeper with every new article and post, until it might as well be my grave.

On Friday night, after a week crammed with etiquette and history lessons that all feel meaningless now, I open my laptop to check Rosie's Instagram stories. Before I can click on the browser, however, VidChat pops up with a request from my mother.

Stunned, I accept it without hesitation. I've spoken to her

every night over the past week, but I can't remember the last time she initiated a call. "Mom?" I say, instantly worried. "Is everything okay?"

"Evie?" The feed is blurry at first, but once the video comes into focus, my heart sinks. Her eyes are red, and her fingers are tangled in her frizzy curls as she stares down at something I can't see.

"Mom, it's me," I say urgently. "Are you okay?"

"I don't understand." She shakes her head and finally looks at the screen. "Why is everyone saying you killed a boy?"

All the air leaves my lungs. "What? Who told you that?" I wheeze.

Rather than answer, she holds up a tabloid with my face on the cover. It's a grainy black-and-white class photo from when I was thirteen or fourteen, and it's arranged next to a much more recent picture of Jasper, looking happy and practically angelic in a clean suit and perfect lighting. The headline is out of frame, but I know what it must read.

"It's all a misunderstanding," I force myself to say as icy fear trickles through me. "Alexander's handling it, don't worry. It's... it's a mistake."

"It is?" The hope in my mother's voice kills me, and she looks at the cover again. Setting the tabloid aside, she picks up the front page of the *Washington Herald*. There I am again, in another one of the few pictures the press has managed to find of me, except this time I look wasted at a freshman dorm party. I wasn't, but my bloodshot eyes and goofy expression make it easy to believe.

She's collected half a dozen American magazines and

newspapers that outline the story, and by the time she's shown me the last, I feel like I'm about to throw up. "We know, Mom," I say haltingly. "It's all a bunch of lies, I promise. The lawyers – they're taking care of it."

The worry lines in her forehead are deeper now, and she doesn't seem to be listening as she flips through the pages. "This isn't real?"

I dig my nails into my thighs. "Those papers and magazines are real. But they're telling lies—"

"Then they're all wrong? You had nothing to do with his death?"

"I—" What am I supposed to say to that? "We don't know what happened. He – he tried to hurt me, and I don't remember—"

"Hurt you?" she says, her voice growing strained with distress. "Why isn't Alex protecting you? He's your father. He *swore* you'd be okay – he swore you'd be safe. He swore."

"He's doing everything he can, Mom," I say as my throat tightens. "Everyone is. And I—"

The feed goes black, and I curse. I try to call her back, but the ringing echoes through my bedroom on an endless loop before I finally give up and bury my face in my hands. I've never seen my mother this upset before, and I can't possibly explain the whole story to her, not when she's like this. But I also can't exist in a world where my own mother thinks I killed Jasper.

I refuse to get out of bed the next morning, despite Tibby's Herculean efforts. But not even the threat of having a bucket of ice water dumped on my head convinces me to rise and shine, and eventually, like she did on my first day at Windsor, she leaves me alone.

210

As the hours pass, I hear footmen coming and going in my sitting room, but no one shows up to tell me I need to eat. I don't know whether I'm happy they're all letting me be, or whether I'm miserable that nobody seems to care if I starve to death. Maybe a shamefully angsty combination of both. But there's no point to this charade now that the palace has lost all control of the narrative, and even if Wiggs does miraculously uncover evidence that someone else pushed Jasper, my name will never be completely cleared. Not when the public has already decided I'm guilty. No matter what I do or who I become, to the rest of the world, those awful minutes alone with Jasper Cunningham will always define me.

Around five o'clock, after I spend the afternoon trying to get ahold of my mother again, there's a soft knock on my bedroom door. I close my laptop and pull a pillow over my head, willing whoever it is to go away, but of course the hinges creak.

"Evan?"

Kit's voice is oddly soothing, and I hear the clink of porcelain against my nightstand. Reluctantly I push aside the pillow and breathe in the cool air. Kit's in the process of stepping back, and there's a plate next to the book I'm reading.

"There you are." He smiles, and even though my life is a complete disaster, I manage a small smile in return. "I brought you a peanut butter and jam sandwich."

My muscles protest as I sit up, and I run my fingers through my hair, trying to comb out the knots. After a full twenty hours in bed, it's futile. "Thanks," I say hoarsely. Between my puffy eyes and chapped lips, I must look like death warmed over, but Kit doesn't even blink.

"You don't have to say a word if you'd rather not," he says, "but I need to ask…are you all right?"

I don't know how to answer that. Instinctively I want to say yes, that I'm fine, and there's no need to worry, but obviously that isn't true. And I need to talk to someone about this.

"No," I admit, reaching for the plate and setting it in my lap. "My mom found out about everything that's going on."

"Oh." Kit studies me. "I take it she isn't handling the news well."

I shake my head. "She's a really good mom – the best mom. But sometimes her illness gives her delusions. Like how she thinks the three of us are all one big happy family, even though I'd never even met Alexander before I came here. When it gets really bad, she can't tell what's real, and I think – I think this is confusing her and making her doubt her own mind. And now she won't even answer my calls."

"I'm sorry," he says softly. "That must be incredibly difficult." He takes a half step towards the bed, as if he wants to comfort me, but he falters and moves back instead.

Immediately I understand. An invisible wall still looms between us, and yet again, it's because of Jasper. All of this is because of Jasper. I want to be furious – I *should* be furious – but all I feel is a bone-deep exhaustion I'm sure will never disappear.

"I just want life to go back to normal," I mumble, rubbing my swollen eyes. "Even if it's only for a little while, you know?"

Maybe Kit understands my frustration, or maybe he's been working up the nerve all this time. But eventually he takes a full step towards me, and though he doesn't get too close, he crouches beside the bed. "As it happens," he says, "that's the reason I'm here. I have a surprise for you – one I think might cheer you up. It would, however, require you to leave your bed and get dressed."

I eye him suspiciously. "Did you find out something new about the case?" I say. Even though Wiggs has all but gone radio silent on me, I'm not entirely sure I'd welcome more information right now. Not unless it includes a full confession that exonerates me completely.

"No," says Kit. "This is solely for you."

I bite my lip. Whatever he has planned, it probably won't make things worse, at least not on purpose. But every time I leave my suite, trouble seems to have a knack for finding me. "I'm not really sure I should go anywhere," I admit.

"It's up to you," he says. "But I promise I'm taking every precaution. And you deserve to feel like yourself again, if only for a few hours."

I'm not even sure who I am any more, or who I ever was in the first place. But as Kit's brown eyes lock on mine, suddenly I want nothing more than to find out who he sees when he looks at me like I'm the only person in the world.

"Okay," I say at last. "I trust you."

He smiles, and for the first time all day, I do, too. "Brilliant," he says as he rises. "Now brush your teeth and change into your favourite outfit. We're going out."

Two hours later, after Kit and I gorge ourselves on takeaway from a Pizza Express, our driver pulls up to an old building with

213

a crumbling exterior only partially masked by black and silver paint. A neon marquee flashes above the entrance, but we're too close for me to see what's playing.

"I haven't been to the movies since I was a kid," I say, tugging nervously on a lock of my ginger wig as the driver hops out and opens the door for us. A dozen or so people in their teens and twenties lean against the building, checking their phones and talking excitedly among themselves, and as I climb out, I crane my neck to read the name of the film.

But it isn't a movie theatre. It's a music venue, and the marquee displays the name REIGNWOLF in bold letters.

My mouth drops open, and I whirl around as Kit climbs out of the vehicle. "You're *joking*. A Reignwolf concert?"

"I thought you might be interested," he says cheekily. "I looked up their concert schedule a couple of weeks ago and got tickets. I realize the timing could be better, but..."

I throw my arms around him and hug him so fiercely that my sunglasses nearly fall off. Two weeks ago, we barely knew each other. "The timing is perfect. *Thank you*."

Kit freezes at first, almost as if he doesn't know what to do, and for a moment I think I've broken him. But he finally wraps his arms around me in return, and heat rushes through me, warming me from the inside out. "You're very welcome," he says quietly, and I allow myself a few more seconds before I reluctantly let him go.

Two protection officers follow us inside – Kit even had the foresight to snag them tickets, too – and I eye a table full of merchandise as we pass. "I've never been to a concert before," I admit.

"Really?" he says. "Then let's hope this is a good one."

I can't imagine any scenario where tonight would be anything short of exceptional, and I eagerly lead the way through the crowd and towards the stage. It's a small venue – standing room only – that can fit a couple hundred people at most, and it's already dangerously close to capacity. The floor is concrete, the walls are papered in faded flyers advertising old gigs, and there isn't a single frill anywhere. It's the opposite of Windsor Castle and Buckingham Palace, and I want to stay here for ever.

The opening band finishes their set as we find a spot off to the left. Our security lingers nearby, close enough to protect us but far enough to offer us some semblance of privacy, and I take off my sunglasses, satisfied that no one will recognize me from my old school photos in the low light. Part of me is irrationally afraid that a detective from Scotland Yard will jump out of the shadows and arrest me on the spot, but standing here with Kit in the cool darkness of the venue, I feel oddly safe. Anonymous. As if I'm just another face in the crowd, and that's exactly how I like it.

At last, everything goes black, and smoke appears in the air as the first chords explode from amps, a thunderous sound that rattles my teeth and surrounds me on all sides. As bright lights illuminate the stage and the band appears, I'm instantly riveted.

Kit stays by my side throughout it all – the singing, the jumping, the shouts of delight as I recognize song after song. Those shouts turn into giddy shrieks at my favourites, and more than once I clutch his arm and tell him this is the best night of my life.

But halfway through the show, he checks his texts. At first I think nothing of it, but then another message comes, and another, and another. And before long, Kit doesn't bother to put his phone back in his pocket as it lights up almost as often as Tibby's did the morning of Trooping the Colour.

"Is everything okay?" I shout in his ear. There's a deep furrow between his brows, and even in the shadows, he can't hide his worry.

"Perfectly fine," he calls back, barely audible over the wail of an electric guitar. He flashes me a smile, but I can tell it isn't real and a sense of foreboding slowly chases away the intoxicating euphoria that's settled over me.

I cast a surreptitious glance at our protection officers. Neither of them seems at all bothered, so whatever's going on, it can't be that bad. But then Kit's phone goes off again, and when I see the look on his face, my stomach drops. It *is* that bad. I just don't know why yet.

Kit must notice the shift in my enthusiasm, because he finally slips his phone back into his pocket and focuses on the show instead. I can't tell if this is a good sign or not – if the crisis is over, or if he's only trying to help me forget for a little longer, before the night is ruined. I take his elbow and lean into him, desperately hoping it's the former.

Finally the show ends with a deafening roar from the crowd, and I put my sunglasses on again before waiting in the long bathroom line. When the protection officers and I find Kit near the door, he's bought me every piece of available merchandise, and I know something is really, truly wrong.

"What is it?" I say once we're back in the Range Rover. My ears are ringing, and my buzz has worn off completely, leaving me hollow and terrified.

216

He exhales. "We should wait until we return to Windsor. It won't be long—"

"Kit, please," I say, my voice cracking. "Whatever it is, I need to know."

Reluctantly he pulls his phone out of his pocket. It's silent now, but he unlocks it and hands it to me. "It's a video," he admits. "Of Jasper's bedroom in Belgravia. Evan..." He swallows hard. "It shows you pushing him off the balcony."

Chapter Twenty-three

It is with heavy hearts that we announce we have received exclusive video from the night of Jasper Cunningham's death. We have passed it on to Scotland Yard to aid in their investigation, and now we are sharing it with you so that there can be no cover-up of the truth. Our thoughts are with Jasper's family and loved ones.

Warning: the following footage may be disturbing to some viewers.

—*The Regal Record*, 24 June 2023

I'm hunched over the foot of the same conference table I sat at two weeks ago, on the night the news of my paternity leaked. Frantic palace officials argue among themselves on either side of me, and at the head of the table, Alexander solemnly stares into a mug of hot tea.

My own mug sits beside me, untouched. I'm staring at Kit's phone, watching the silent video for the umpteenth time while he stands a few feet away, not technically invited to this meeting but refusing to leave my side. Jenkins hovers protectively near me, and having them here is as much of a comfort as I'm going to get right now.

The recording is from Jasper's missing laptop – that's obvious from the very first frame. He made it look like his computer was powered off, but the camera was positioned to capture the bed and the balcony beyond, and there's only one feasible reason why this footage exists.

Jasper wanted to film himself raping me.

Why? Bragging rights? Blackmail? Good old-fashioned profit? Or did he derive some sick pleasure from humiliating and degrading others? I don't know, and he's too dead to ask. For now, my skin crawls as I drag the cursor back to the start, and the clip plays again.

It's only a minute and a half long, and most of that shows me lying on the bed as Jasper undresses me. From this distance, my attempts to squirm away from him make me look like I'm into it instead, and thanks to the lack of sound, no one can hear me say no. Jasper pushes my dress off the bed, and it puddles onto the floor, all but disappearing into a shadow as he continues to paw at me.

It's surreal seeing myself in this position. Even though I know how it ends, my gut twists every time he settles over me, trying to hold me down with his weight. I can see now how much he was enjoying it. I can see now how close I was to being raped. But a surge of pride runs through me as I watch myself knee him in the groin and roll off the bed, struggling to get away.

He comes after me again, his face twisted with fury, and there's no question that I elbow him. My lips move, but I have no memory of what I said, and as he makes another grab for me,

I lurch towards the doorway and out of the frame completely. Jasper follows me, and that's when it happens.

One moment neither of us is on-screen, and the next Jasper staggers backward, clutching his nose. He crashes into the drink cart, and a glass falls to the floor. It must break, because he trips over his own feet trying to avoid the shards, and in doing so, he stumbles through the open window and onto the sliver of a balcony. Then, already wildly off-balance, he hits the low railing and falls.

The video ends there, and without so much as blinking, I move the cursor back to the starting position and play it again.

"It won't hold up in court," says the woman whose name I think is Yara. "Not with proof of GHB in her system."

"That's for the lawyers to sort," snaps Doyle, and out of the corner of my eye, I notice he's beet red and sweating more than any man in an air-conditioned room should be. "Can we force the site to remove the footage?"

"We can try, but it's already been duplicated and uploaded in multiple other places," says a thin man I don't recognize. "I suspect our efforts will be put to better use focusing on what we can control."

"Which is what, precisely?" says Doyle furiously, spittle flying from his mouth. "Robert Cunningham's already demanding her arrest, and he won't be the only one. No doubt the most damaging stills from the footage will be on the front page of every paper in the country tomorrow."

"We have our side of the story," says Yara pointedly. "The GHB, Miss Bright's account of events—"

"You're not suggesting we go public with a sexual assault on a member of the royal family?" says Doyle with such indignation that Yara might as well be suggesting he tell the press his own sordid secrets.

"The clip already makes it clear there was an…encounter," says Yara, and I stare at the screen as Jasper pushes my dress off the bed again. "We certainly can't deny that. We could claim that the girl isn't Miss Bright, but—"

"It's obviously her," says Alexander quietly. They're the first words he's spoken since the meeting began, but I don't look up from the video. It should bother me that he's seen it, and somewhere deep down, I'm definitely nauseated. But I'm too focused on Kit's phone to react. "I will not be intimidated by Robert Cunningham," my father continues. "Scotland Yard has the footage and the facts, and they can judge the matter for themselves."

"Sir," says Doyle, "if we say nothing, the media will eat us alive—"

"My primary concern right now is my daughter," says Alexander. "Not the media."

Yara clears her throat. "Sir, if we allow Evangeline – Miss Bright – to issue a statement explaining her side of the story, that may earn us some support in the press. The longer we remain silent, the more vulnerable she and the truth will be to public outrage and manipulation."

Several seconds pass as Alexander contemplates this. "Evan?" he says at last. "What do you think?"

I'm rewatching the same three seconds of the video now, again and again and again. And while I'm vaguely aware everyone is staring at me, I say nothing, fixated on the screen instead.

"Sir," says Jenkins delicately from his spot behind me. "To ask a seventeen-year-old to make a public statement recounting her trauma for the sake of earning positive press...it's unconscionable."

"What's unconscionable," bursts Doyle, "is allowing the entire monarchy to fall because of the actions of a teenage girl!"

The room devolves into a shouting match again. I ignore it and watch those three seconds one more time before finally standing, leaving my tea untouched.

"Evan?" Alexander's voice rises above the fray, but I don't answer. Instead, as Kit trails after me, I walk out of the room without a word, leaving them to their bickering.

Kit keeps up with me easily despite my determined strides, and he only speaks once we've reached the ground floor. "Alexander won't let them do it. He won't let them leak the details of what Jasper did to you."

I don't know how I feel about that, and I don't have the energy for any soul-searching right now. The whole incident is already out there, after all. Anyone who's curious can see what he did to me with their own eyes.

Except it isn't the whole incident. It isn't even close to the whole incident, and I stop suddenly in the middle of the corridor and hold up Kit's phone. "Look," I say as those same three seconds of footage repeat. "Do you see it?"

Kit studies the video with every bit of intensity I could hope for. "See what?" he says. "You and Jasper aren't on-screen."

"No, we aren't," I agree, and I rewind so he can watch it again. "Look. On the floor by the bed."

He frowns and takes the phone, and even though it's his, I'm reluctant to give it up. "I'm sorry, Evan, I don't see anything."

I stand beside him and go back three seconds one more time. "*Look*," I say yet again, pointing at the dark corner. The screen brightness is already all the way up, and I don't know how else to make him notice. "That flash of green."

Kit's eyes widen, and he finally looks at me. "Is that…?"

"My dress," I say. It's at the very edge of the frame, and in the shadows, it's almost impossible to see. "It's there for the first two seconds."

"And then it disappears," says Kit, stunned. This time he's the one who repeats the clip, and he shakes his head. "Evan…"

"The video was edited," I say. "I wasn't the last person to see Jasper alive."

And I turn towards Maisie's door and knock.

Chapter Twenty-four

Oh my god. Oh my GOD. Why isn't Evangeline locked up??
Has Scotland Yard seen this?? It's definitely her, right??? WHY
ISN'T SHE UNDER ARREST???? #JusticeforJasper #SHEDIDIT

—Twitter user @dutchessdame172,
24 June 2023, 11:04 p.m., London, UK

Maisie answers the door in a pink silk dressing gown, her strawberry-blond hair wavy and damp. For the first time I see her without any make-up on, and I'm struck by how young she looks without eyeliner and fake lashes. How innocent and vulnerable she seems.

"It's late," she says coldly, her voice no less barbed than usual. "Can I help you?"

"The green dress I was wearing the night of the party," I say without preamble. "Your security team found it after Jasper died, and before the police arrived?"

Maisie narrows her eyes. "Yes. Why? You didn't lose it again, did you?"

"You're sure about the timing?" I press, ignoring her jab.

"Positive," she says stiffly, and she focuses on Kit. "Do you know what this is about? Or has she finally gone mad?"

"Can I see your phone again?" I say to Kit, and he wordlessly hands it over. The video is already queued up, and I hold it out for Maisie to watch from the beginning.

After only a few seconds, her expression twists in horror. "Is this—"

"The night Jasper died," I say numbly.

She gapes at the phone. "He was recording? In that room?"

The rising fear in her voice isn't surprising. She and Gia were in that bed before me and Jasper, and judging by the state I found them in, they'd been there for a while. "From his laptop. Keep watching," I say tersely.

"I don't want to see this," she insists, trying to turn away, but I follow her into her sitting room, which is twice the size of mine and has a white piano artfully arranged near the window.

"Keep watching," I demand. "It's important."

I expect her to refuse, but her blue eyes snap back to the screen, and she pales as the seconds tick by. Only when Jasper falls does she finally look away, and I lower the phone.

"The Regal Record posted this two hours ago," I say. "It's all over social media, and there's a good chance it's playing on the news. And it makes it look like I'm the one who pushed him."

A wrinkle forms between her immaculate brows. "Were you?"

"I don't remember what happened, and I've spent the past week terrified it was me. But it wasn't," I add. "And now I'm sure."

I click back to those three seconds where Jasper is beyond the edge of the frame, and Maisie doesn't try to move away as I join her. Angling the screen so both of us can watch, I point to the shadow.

"That's my dress," I say. "And that's my dress disappearing into thin air moments before Jasper dies."

Maisie takes the phone with trembling hands. She rewinds and watches those few seconds again and again, squinting like she isn't sure what she's seeing, but we both know she is.

After another long moment, she lowers the phone and hands it back to me. "Leave," she orders, and I start to argue before I realize she doesn't mean me. She's speaking to Kit, who still stands in the doorway.

"Try not to destroy my mobile, Maisie," he says as he steps back into the corridor. "Evan, I'll meet you in your suite, yeah?"

"Okay," I say, my throat tight with apprehension. He closes the door softly behind him, and resounding silence fills the room as I look at my half-sister expectantly.

She avoids my stare, her gaze glued to the wall instead. "Who else knows about the edit?" she says at last.

"Just Kit," I say. "I wanted to talk to you first."

A muscle in her jaw twitches. "I have no idea why the dress isn't there," she says. "Perhaps Jasper moved it, or maybe my protection officer was in there earlier than I thought."

"Maybe," I agree casually. "I guess we'll find out when whoever has Jasper's laptop releases the whole video."

A hint of panic flashes across her face, and she focuses on me again. "Do you think they will?" she says, and I shrug.

"I don't know. Whoever edited this clip wanted to make it seem like I was the one who killed him – they even removed the

226

audio so no one could hear me say no. So unless Jasper managed to record something even more shocking than his own death, I doubt it'll surface anytime soon. Are you worried about the footage of you and Gia? Because if you are—"

"It's not that," says Maisie tightly. She takes a deep breath and exhales in a rush, averting her gaze once more. "I mean, it is that, but…"

Knowing it's a risk, I take a step closer. "Maisie," I say quietly, and though her nickname still feels too personal coming out of my mouth, she doesn't tell me off. "The full video is out there somewhere, and we have no idea who has it. If there's something you aren't telling me…"

She waves her hand dismissively, but it's half-hearted at best. "You can drop the act, Evangeline. I won't be manipulated by anyone, least of all you."

"I'm not trying to manipulate you," I say. "I just want to know what really happened."

Maisie begins to pace, crossing the length of her sitting room and coming perilously close to stubbing her toe on the piano bench. At first she says nothing, and I'm not sure she will. But finally, with her fists clenched at her sides, she begins to speak.

"Rosie's the one who saw you leave with Kit. She said you weren't wearing your dress any more, and I thought – well, I didn't know Jasper had drugged you, of course. But I thought perhaps he'd tried something. So I went upstairs to confront him. It couldn't have been more than two minutes after you'd left, if that, and he was still shirtless. He insisted it was consensual, that you'd changed your mind and had a panic attack, and he wouldn't stand for any false accusations. I saw your dress and took it, and when I was heading out—"

She cuts herself off and continues pacing. There's something slightly feral about the way she's moving now, like a wild animal that's been cornered, and I stand near the door, waiting for her to speak. Or to not speak. Because she doesn't need to say it for me to understand.

But the urge to defend herself must be stronger than the knowledge that staying silent is her best option, and she blurts, "I threatened to tell my security detail what he'd done. I was sure he'd forced you, or – tried to, anyway, and I started to leave. That's when he grabbed me." She pulls up the sleeve of her dressing gown to reveal a yellowing bruise above her elbow. It's starting to fade, but it's unmistakably in the shape of a handprint.

I gasp. "Maisie…did you show anyone? Did you take pictures or—"

"Of course not," she says witheringly. "I've been hiding it with make-up all week. And I certainly didn't mean to hurt him. I was only trying to get away, after all. I've no idea how much he had to drink, but he seemed rather tipsy, and I suspect that's why he – why he fell."

I replay the video in my mind. The way he staggers back. The drink cart in his way. The glass he must have stepped on. "No, it wasn't your fault," I say. "It wasn't anyone's fault except his. Maisie…you went back upstairs to defend me?"

She scowls. "Don't look so doe-eyed about the whole thing. Our family has a reputation to uphold, and no one – especially not *Jasper Cunningham* – can get away with treating royal blood that way. Even if it is illegitimate and" – she shudders – "*American.*"

I'm so touched that I barely register the insult. "You can't keep this to yourself, especially with the full video out there. If you tell the lawyers what happened—"

"And give Robert Cunningham reason to spend the rest of his life destroying me in the press?" Maisie sniffs imperiously, but her eyes are shining with unshed tears. "You'd certainly like that, wouldn't you? It'd get your *name* out of the papers."

"That's not what I—"

"Some of us have real secrets, Evangeline," she snaps. "We can't afford to be dragged through the mud because of a misunderstanding."

"And you think *I* can?" I say furiously. "Is that why you're having Gia and Rosie leak information about me to the press? To cover your own ass?"

Her mouth drops open. "How *dare* you. They've done no such thing, and I won't allow you to level such a heinous accusation against my friends." She shakes her head, her cheeks an angry red now. "You're a nobody who has nothing to lose. I'm going to be queen someday, and I cannot afford to have a scandal of this magnitude casting a shadow over my reign. People will always wonder – there will always be supposed witnesses coming forward saying it was more than it was. And the monarchy – the *family* – will not survive that kind of doubt. You've already caused us enough grief," she adds. "Surely you can do this small thing to help mitigate the damage."

I try to choke out a response, but I'm speechless. She wants me to fall on this sword for her. She wants me to take the blame for Jasper's death so she can keep her nose clean and uphold a pristine image that's nothing but smoke and mirrors.

She stares at me, clearly expecting some sort of reply. A meek agreement, a fiery refusal to be her punching bag – I can tell from the way she squares her shoulders that she's ready for anything I could possibly say to her. Ready to deflect, to twist, to tell me why my life and reputation aren't nearly as important as hers. Why she matters more than I ever will.

And so I do the only thing she doesn't seem prepared for – I turn on my heel and walk away.

"Evangeline?" she says. "Evangeline, don't you dare leave. I'm not done with you—"

I'm done with her, though, and I slip out of her apartment without saying a word, closing the door behind me.

Chapter Twenty-five

NNbonza: Has Evangeline been arrested yet?? #JusticeforJasper

0TrixBix0: She's lying there like a dead fish. Are we sure she's okay?

UFurMeMeMe: lmao wicked right hook. must be the coke.

RylRmncer: she's ugly

milamason5297: omg HE'S HOLDING HER DOWN wtffff

BeeeJannsen: jasper cunningham was PACKING #rip

LondonLvir: arrest her

ashlyen04: ARREST EVANGELINE. #justiceforjasper

XxPOMGRLxX: #RIP #JUSTICEFORJASPER #SHEDIDIT

—From the *Daily Sun* comments section, 25 June 2023

I toss and turn for most of the night, and the few hours of rest I do manage are filled with dreams of green dresses and shattering glass. I can't get Maisie's words out of my head, and at last, in the predawn light, I give up on sleep entirely and open my laptop.

The video is everywhere. Social media, gossip sites, CNN, the

BBC – my name and #JusticeforJasper are the top two worldwide trends, and the comments section on the *Daily Sun*'s article is bursting with vitriol. Thousands of strangers have an opinion about the clip, and while some of them realize I'm not reciprocating Jasper's *affections*, most seem to chalk it up to whatever drug they think I'm on. Those who are on my side – the ones who point out that Jasper's holding me down and not letting me go – are drowned out by the sheer loathing towards me.

And no one notices the editing.

For the first time since Robert Cunningham set his sights on destroying my life, I find the comment box and start typing. I hit each letter with purpose, the clack of the keys loud in the eerie quiet of my bedroom, and once I'm done, I stare at what I've written:

The video is edited. Look at the shadow in the bottom right corner at 1:24. The dress disappears.

Eighteen words – that's all it would take to exonerate myself. My finger hovers over the submit button. I know my comment will probably get lost among the countless others, and if anyone does see it, they'll think I'm a conspiracy theorist. But the need to post it – to do *something* to gain control over my own life – is overwhelming.

I have a right to defend myself. I have a right to point out the truth. I owe Maisie nothing, and if our positions were reversed, she would never take the blame for me. I know all of this, but I still hesitate, and I have no idea why.

Suddenly there's a knock on my door, and without waiting for me to respond, Tibby steps inside. "I see you're already awake," she says as she heads towards the window. "No mystery as to why."

I quickly shut my laptop, my face growing hot like she's caught me looking at something dirty. "No mystery," I agree a bit too quickly. Tibby raises an eyebrow.

"I haven't watched it, if that's what you're afraid of," she says as she pulls back the curtains. "I've no interest in it, and frankly anyone decent ought to be appalled with themselves for even clicking the link."

"By now I think we both know that the world isn't full of decent people," I say, squinting in the flood of sunlight. In truth, I'm relieved that at least one person in my life hasn't seen it. "Wait – isn't it Sunday? Why are you here?"

"Because even though you've only been in England for a fortnight, you've managed to become the biggest scandal this country has seen in more than a century, and *someone* needs to make sure you keep to your schedule. Speaking of, His Majesty has requested your presence in an hour, if you think you can wash the stink off by then. Where on earth did you go last night? A pub?"

"A concert," I say, smelling the ends of my hair. "And a Pizza Express."

"That certainly explains the garlic." Tibby opens my wardrobe. "I'll run a bath. Extra bubbles, I think."

"I prefer showers, and I can turn the knob on my own. Thanks, though," I add after a beat, because no matter how prickly she is, I really am grateful she's here.

Tibby nods curtly, and she's quiet for a moment as she selects a blouse. "Whatever His Majesty and his team of pompous advisers try to tell you, do remember that what happened wasn't your fault. If anyone dares to insinuate that you were asking for it—"

"I wasn't. I know I wasn't," I mumble, and she gives a soft hmph of what I think is approval. But as worried as Tibby seems to be, I'm not surprised there's another meeting, especially after I walked out of the one last night without explanation. Now that I know what really happened, though, I don't know how I'm supposed to face Alexander and lie.

I debate what I'm going to tell him while I dry my hair, and as soon as I'm dressed, Tibby escorts me to the same conference room from the night before. I expect to see Alexander and his entire senior staff sitting around the table once more, all undoubtedly miffed that I ignored them. Instead, the only people present are Alexander, Maisie, Helene and Wiggs.

I freeze in the doorway, taking in the sight of them. Yet again, Alexander sits at the head of the table and stares into a mug of tea, not bothering to look up at my arrival. Maisie is to his right, her face red and splotchy, and Helene hugs her with a fierce protectiveness I don't understand.

"Your Majesties," says Tibby politely. "Your Royal Highness." She curtsies, her eyes down and her form perfect. Before I can grab her elbow, however, she excuses herself and closes the door behind her, leaving me to face whatever this mess is on my own.

"What's going on?" I say warily, fighting the urge to turn tail and run.

My half-sister glares at me. "I told them," she says, the accusation in her voice impossible to miss. "You've got nothing to hold over me now."

I scowl. "I'm not holding anything over you."

"It certainly didn't seem that way last night," she says spitefully as she dabs her eyes with a tissue, and Helene murmurs soothing words I can't make out.

"Miss Bright, if you would take a seat," says Wiggs, nodding to the empty chair beside my stepmother. I would rather gnaw off my right arm than sit anywhere near Helene, but my feet are sore from the concert, and so I head to my usual spot at the foot of the table instead. A digital camera rests near my elbow, and I notice Maisie is wearing short sleeves, the handprint-shaped bruise on her arm fully visible.

Wiggs frowns, but Alexander is still staring into his tea and doesn't seem to notice where I'm sitting, let alone care. Clearing his throat, Wiggs begins to search through a manila folder in front of him. "Miss Bright, it has come to my attention that you believe the, er, video posted online of you last night is edited."

"It *is* edited," I say evenly. "If Maisie's told you the whole story, then you already know that."

"Yes, yes." Wiggs clears his throat again – a nervous tic, I suspect, and I can't blame him. The tension in the room is unbearable, and it isn't lost on me that this is the first time I've had to face all three members of my father's family since the night I arrived at Windsor. Judging by the look on Helene's face, she'd like nothing more than for it to be the last.

With a jolt, I remember the sounds she made in the guest room with Nicholas. My cheeks grow hot, and I stare at my nails, willing someone to speak. But as Wiggs shuffles through several sheets of paper, the others seem content to ignore me, and so it's up to me to break the silence.

"Did you call me here for a reason?" I finally say. "Because it sounds like Maisie has it handled."

"Wiggs has something for you to sign," says Helene with a sniff. "As we all know, Maisie is not present in the footage, and any accusation that she is involved—"

"I know how to keep my mouth shut." Now it's my turn to glare at her and her snivelling daughter. "You're wrong about her not being in the video, though. Maybe not the clip that was posted, but *someone* edited it, and that same someone has the whole thing. Including the full timeline."

Maisie pales at that, and Helene's arm tightens around her shoulders. Before either of them can speak, however, Wiggs finds the paper he's looking for and slides it across the table. He has to stretch to get it anywhere near my vicinity, and I don't finish the job for him. Even from a distance, I can read the words NON-DISCLOSURE AGREEMENT in bold letters, and while I know I should have expected it, I feel like I've been slapped in the face.

"The potential content of the full video is another matter we wish to discuss," he says, settling back into his seat, and for one wild moment I wonder if Maisie told her parents about Gia, too. "It is my belief that the best defence for both of you, should the footage surface, is to get ahead of any rumours that might start circulating."

"You mean other than the ones that are already out there?" I say bitterly, glaring at the NDA. At the bottom of the page, beside the empty signature line, someone has already scrawled a date in black ink: 1 July 2023.

My eighteenth birthday.

"Rumours specifically regarding Her Royal Highness's

involvement," clarifies Wiggs. "We have ample evidence that she acted in self-defence, but should Robert Cunningham press the matter, the situation could get tricky."

"And what does that have to do with me?" I say, crossing my arms and leaning back in my chair.

Wiggs purses his lips, and I immediately know it isn't good. "With the footage of the…assault now readily available for public consumption, we believe we have a golden opportunity to both defend your innocence and to deflect any potential future accusations away from Her Royal Highness. If you are willing to address the events of that evening, we believe the public will be receptive and sympathetic to your experience—"

"I'm not willing," I say, glaring at Alexander, but he doesn't look up. "You said you wouldn't let Robert Cunningham intimidate you. You said you cared about me, your *daughter*, not the media—"

"*Maisie* is his daughter, and the future queen regnant," snaps Helene. "You are not and never will be his priority."

My ears begin to ring, and it has nothing to do with the concert. "That's why I'm here? You want me to lie and say I killed Jasper so no one suspects your precious heir to the damn throne?"

"No court in England would convict you with such a…*specific* sedative in your system," says Wiggs in a tone clearly meant to try to calm me down. "All of the evidence is on our side—"

"Except for the full video that could show everyone who really did it."

"Her Royal Highness isn't visible when Jasper Cunningham falls," says Wiggs. "If there's already a confession in place, and if the courts have dismissed the case—"

"I'm not confessing to a damn thing, because *I didn't do anything wrong*," I snarl, standing and pushing my chair aside. "Aren't you supposed to be *my* lawyer? Why are you trying to protect her at my expense?"

Maisie's face grows even redder now. "I was trying to protect *you*, you ungrateful—"

"You pushed him because he grabbed you," I say viciously. "And he fell because he ran into the drink cart and stepped on broken glass. You're not guilty, I'm not guilty, and I'll take my chances with Scotland Yard, thanks."

I storm around the table towards the exit, but as I pass her, Helene seizes my wrist. Her grip is so tight that the sharp edge of her wedding ring digs into my skin, and I yelp in pain.

"Should you decide not to do this, then we'll be left with no choice but to take whatever steps we must to protect our daughter," she says, her voice icy with rage. "If you sign the agreement and confess, we can offer you legal protection and the privilege that comes with being a member of the royal family."

"Because nothing says *family* like an NDA," I growl. "Are you making Maisie sign one, too? Or am I the only person no one trusts, even though I've been telling the truth the whole time?"

Helene's eyes narrow, and her pupils are black pinpricks in an ocean of blue. "If you choose not to support your future queen, then you will lose any and all of our support permanently."

I yank my arm back. "Good," I say coldly. "I don't want it."

When I finally reach the door, Tibby is waiting for me on the other side, and she jumps at my sudden appearance, nearly dropping her phone. "Is the meeting over already?" she says, and I nod.

"I'm starving," I mutter. "Let's get breakfast."

Before I walk away, however, I glance into the room one more time. Helene cradles her daughter, who's crying openly now, while Wiggs reaches for the non-disclosure agreement I refused to touch. But even though Alexander didn't say a word, he's watching me now, and our eyes meet. Instead of anger or frustration, however, all I see is anguish and a silent apology.

I don't care. I pull the door shut, and the click echoes down the corridor. He had his chance, and at least now I know better than to ever give him another.

Tibby must have texted Kit about the mood I'm in, because when we return to my suite, he's waiting for me with a fresh pot of my favourite tea. She excuses herself under the pretence of ordering from the kitchen, and as soon as the door closes behind her, I let out a string of curses so elaborate that Kit's eyebrows nearly reach his hairline.

"Tough morning?" he says once I've paused to catch my breath.

"The worst," I mutter, sitting down heavily beside him at the table. "You wouldn't believe what—"

I falter mid-sentence as realization sets in. I can't tell him about the meeting. Even though I didn't sign the NDA, if I turn right around and shoot my mouth off like Maisie and Helene expect me to, then I'll only prove them right in not trusting me. And no matter how badly I want to tell Kit what's going on, I refuse to justify their heinous demands.

But while I can't tell him the details that include Maisie,

I can at least tell him the rest. "Wiggs asked me to make a statement about what really happened," I admit. "He thinks now that the video is out there, it'll be better for me if I do. And—" I hesitate. This might be a step too far, but after all he's done to help me, Kit deserves to know. "He wants me to confess."

"*Confess?*" Kit nearly spits out his tea, and anger flashes across his face, so foreign on him that I don't recognize it at first. "But you didn't do anything wrong. Does Wiggs know the video is edited?"

I nod. "It's a long story, and I can't tell you everything, but… he thinks it's my best chance."

Kit's jaw tightens, and he grips his teacup so tightly that I'm worried the handle might break. At last, with exaggerated care, he sets it down and faces me, his expression stormy.

"Whatever's going on," he says, "whatever details you can't share with me…you shouldn't do this, Evan. The press will die down eventually, but there's no reason in the world for you to confess to a crime you didn't commit."

He's right, and I know he's right, but I can't forget the look in Helene's eyes when she threatened me, or the way her ring cut into my skin. The mark is still there, a tiny purple bruise now, and I rub it gingerly. "I don't know what else to do," I admit. "No matter what happens, people are always going to think I'm a murderer."

"But you're not." His fingers flex, and for a split second I think he's going to touch me, but he doesn't. "I don't understand why Wiggs won't use the video to exonerate you. The edited footage *proves* it wasn't you, and there's no reason for him to—"

Kit stops suddenly, his eyes widening, and my heart sinks as

I watch him put the pieces together. I've told him too much, or maybe he's just that smart. He's been there for nearly every moment, after all – from the night of the party to my confrontation with Maisie barely twelve hours ago. And while I may be illegitimate, there are only a handful of people Wiggs would prioritize over me. Over my real innocence and tattered reputation.

"Oh," says Kit softly.

"Oh," I echo, staring at my hands. I don't ask him not to say anything. He knows that better than I do, more than likely. But I still feel like I've somehow betrayed Maisie, like some part of me knew he would figure it out – like some part of me *wanted* him to figure it out. And I hate myself a little for it.

We're quiet for a long moment as Kit absorbs his realization. He toys with his teacup, his brow knitted and attention diverted, while I sit beside him, hollowed out and weary. At least now we both know why there's no point in arguing my innocence – not when I'm perfectly positioned as a scapegoat for the real star of the show.

"What if we're going about this all wrong?" he says at last, his voice rough as he breaks the silence between us. "We know you're innocent, and – well, we can assume that Jasper's fall was…an accident. But there is one malicious party in all of this."

"You mean the person who took his laptop?" I say, and Kit nods.

"That's why Wiggs is worried, isn't it? Because no matter what sort of argument he presents to Scotland Yard, someone out there – someone who was at that party – has the real story all on video."

I stare at him. "You're really damn smart, aren't you?"

241

Kit turns a sweet shade of pink. "There are only so many things that make sense in all of this," he says, scratching the back of his neck. "And if someone at the party did steal the laptop..."

"Hacking into someone's computer without their password isn't easy," I say, my mind racing after this new thread. "Unless Jasper was using something embarrassingly generic, whoever edited and released the video almost definitely knew his, which means they were probably close with him."

"Most likely an ex or a business partner," muses Kit, drumming his fingers on my dining table. "And if there was something on that computer the thief didn't want the police to see, that would be reason enough to risk being caught in Jasper's bedroom moments after his death. Maybe they simply got lucky, stumbling across the recording."

"Or maybe they knew all along," I say quietly. "A sex tape featuring the King's feral love child would be worth the risk."

Kit frowns, and I know he agrees. "But instead of using it as blackmail against the Crown, whoever it is chose to edit the video and directly target you. Why?"

It's an excellent question, and I don't have any answers. But I do know that all this time, we've been focused on people who wanted Jasper dead, or at least those who wouldn't mourn his passing. But someone close to him – someone who had nothing to do with his fall, but could still profit off the recording...that has to be a much smaller pool.

"Do you still have that list of names?" I say. And as Kit reaches into his pocket for his phone, I scooch closer to him, ready to get to work.

*   *   *

242

"Evan? Are you awake?"

Grey morning light filters through my room as Tibby opens the curtains, and I cringe away like a vampire afraid of being burned. It's early – much earlier than she usually arrives – and my head still aches after a long day spent researching Jasper's inner circle. After focusing on the most tech savvy of his close friends and business associates, Kit and I managed to narrow our list down to four, and I have at least as many hours of sleep left before he's due in my sitting room with breakfast.

"Go away," I mutter, pulling my knees to my chest. Tibby's muffled footsteps grow closer, however, and I groan into my pillow.

"I'm very sorry to disturb you," says Tibby. "But I'm afraid this is important."

Her apology catches me off guard. We may have only known each other for a few weeks, but I'm pretty sure *sorry* isn't the kind of word that comes naturally to her, especially when I'm involved. Reluctantly I open my eyes, and as she swims into focus, I instantly know something's wrong.

She's wearing leggings. And a sweatshirt. And *sneakers*.

"What's going on?" I mumble. "Is everything okay?"

She hesitates before perching on the edge of the bed, a tablet in her hands, and a spike of adrenaline chases away my exhaustion. One look at her face, and I'm positive it's bad.

"I know you check the news when you first get up," she says, "and I wanted to be here when you did."

"What are you talking about?" I say, my heart pounding. She was acting like this the morning after the party in Belgravia, too, when she was about to tell me Jasper was dead. "Is everyone okay? Is Kit—"

"He's all right," she assures me. "Everyone is. But…"

She presses her lips together and, after a split second of indecision, she offers me the tablet. I turn it on, and as the screen lights up with the Monday edition of the *Daily Sun*, I understand why she's here at five-thirty in the morning. I understand why she didn't want me to be alone when I saw it. And as I read, I understand, with the striking clarity of someone watching the scene unfold from a distance, that my life has burned to the ground while I slept, and nothing will ever be the same.

Chapter Twenty-six

HIS MAJESTY'S MISTRESS REVEALED

American artist Laura Bright has been identified as the former mistress of the King and the mother of his illegitimate daughter, Evangeline.

Bright, 43, of Arlington, Virginia, is alleged to have had an affair with His Majesty during the autumn of 2004. According to an anonymous family friend, Alexander broke it off when he discovered his wife, Queen Helene, was pregnant with the couple's daughter, Princess Mary. By then Bright was also expecting Alexander's child, and the months that followed were allegedly filled with legal battles revolving around their unexpected souvenir.

"He wanted her to get an abortion," recalls Jackie Merton, a former schoolmate of Bright's who kept in touch after the pair graduated from Three Oaks Academy in Arlington. "She refused, of course. We didn't know at the time who the father was, but it all makes sense now, her determination to keep it. To keep the King of England's baby."

In a twist of fate, the two half-sisters were born within hours of each other on 1 July 2005, Princess Mary in London and Evangeline an ocean away in Arlington. Soon after the births, the King relinquished all custody of Evangeline and focused on patching up his marriage, and Bright reportedly walked away with a seven-figure settlement in return for her silence. The ex-lovers never saw each other again.

Unbeknownst to the King, in the years that followed, his former flame began to show signs of mental illness. "She was acting paranoid," claims Merton, who often visited Bright and her young daughter. "She thought people were following her and tapping her phone. She began to withdraw from me and our group of friends, and when she did show up, she'd burst into tears over nothing. We all thought she was depressed. I encouraged her to get help, but she insisted she was fine."

Bright's mental state continued to deteriorate until the night of 17 November 2009, when Arlington police received a frantic phone call from Bright's mother, the late Betty Bright, who believed her granddaughter was in imminent danger. When the police arrived at the Bright residence, they discovered Laura had barricaded herself in a bathroom with four-year-old Evangeline.

"We had to break down the door," recounts retired officer Gerald Way, who was present at the scene nearly fourteen years ago. "And when we did, we found the suspect holding her daughter down in a bathtub filled with water."

Bright was arrested and charged with attempted murder, while Evangeline was treated at Arlington Children's Hospital, where she remained in intensive care for several days. Betty Bright was granted sole legal and physical custody of her granddaughter, and though His Majesty was made aware of the incident, he allegedly declined to visit his estranged offspring.

In the weeks and months that followed, Laura Bright was diagnosed with schizophrenia, a lifelong mental illness that often has a genetic component. Her doctors testified that she had suffered a psychotic break that led to the attempted drowning, and the charges against her were dropped in favour of inpatient mental health treatment. Two years after the incident, she was released.

Though Bright's current whereabouts are unknown, an anonymous family friend claims Evangeline hasn't seen her mother since Betty Bright's death in 2016. Evangeline, who was expelled from no fewer than nine North American boarding schools in a six-year period, often for criminal behaviour, is currently a suspect in the murder of Jasper Cunningham.

—*The Daily Sun*, 26 June 2023

When I was little, I used to have the same dream almost every night. I'd be wading into the ocean, bobbing up and down with the gentle waves while the sun beat down on me under a wide blue sky. My mom and grandmother would be unpacking a picnic or reading books on the shore, and I would dig my toes into the sand, as happy as I've ever been.

I would spot a colourful fish nearby, or maybe a shell – whatever it was, it was always pretty and caught my attention, and I would chase after it until the water grew so deep that I had to go back. But the shore always vanished. Even if I'd only taken my eyes off my mom and grandmother for a split second, I would look up and find myself alone in the middle of the ocean. And the waves weren't gentle any more.

The water would close in around me until I couldn't breathe, and I would sink, suspended in the ever-darkening sea and unable to move. Sometimes I would call for help. Sometimes I would try to swim, even though I didn't know how. But the dream always ended the same way: right as I was blacking out, I would scream myself awake, and my grandmother would come running into the room to comfort me as I sobbed.

I never understood why I had those dreams. She and my mother never took me to the beach or the local pool. I didn't even learn how to swim until I was eleven, at the very first boarding school Alexander sent me to after my grandmother died. But that nightmare has haunted me for years, and now I finally know why.

"It's utter rubbish." Tibby sits beside me on the bed, her hand hovering over my shoulder even though she doesn't actually touch me. I've never heard that tone of voice from her before – almost gentle and reassuring, but too full of anxious concern to pull off either. "Records like that would have been sealed, and half of it comes from an unreliable source who was undoubtedly paid to make her story juicy—"

"Where's Alexander?" I manage. There's a hole in my chest, like I've been ripped open and every vulnerable part of me is exposed, and I don't know how to staunch the bleeding. "Is he awake?"

I climb to my feet, and even though I'm wearing a ratty tank top and shorts, I move with single-minded focus towards the bedroom door. Tibby scrambles after me, her sneakers thumping on the carpet.

"He may still be sleeping," she says, but she falls into step beside me. "I'll wake him if he is."

I'm too numb and adrift to fully appreciate her loyalty in this moment, but some part of me recognizes how lucky I am to have her. She stops me only long enough to make sure I put on a robe and slippers, and then we're off, heading down the brightly lit corridor that connects the royal family's private apartments.

The palace is eerie this early in the morning, with fog rolling through the courtyard, but we aren't completely alone. We cross paths with two cleaners on the short journey, and as we round the corner towards the door that leads into Alexander's private quarters, I nearly run straight into a tall figure dressed in sweatpants and a T-shirt.

Kit.

"Evan, you're awake." Without asking, he catches me in an

unexpected hug, breaching that invisible wall between us like it doesn't even exist any more. "I'm so sorry. I was just on my way to find you—"

"Have you seen the article, then?" says Tibby in a hushed voice.

"I have, yeah." Kit grows still, and finally he seems to notice I'm not hugging back. Immediately he drops his arms and steps away from me. "Evan? Are you all right?"

His warm brown eyes are full of concern, and his dark hair, still tangled from sleep, frames his face. Both are familiar – everything about him is familiar – but all I feel when I look at him is betrayal.

"You're the only person I ever told," I whisper, the words catching as I force them out. Kit stares at me, and realization slowly dawns on him.

"I didn't say a word," he says, lowering his voice to match mine. "I would never—"

"No one else. Not anyone from school, not Ben, not Maisie, not even Tibby – no one else knew about my mom," I say tightly. No one but Jenkins, and I trust him more than anyone else in the world. He wouldn't do this.

Kit swallows, and his Adam's apple bobs. "You didn't tell me her name," he says. "Or about…about what your mum did to you."

"All Robert Cunningham needed was a tip-off. He could have found the rest on his own." Every word I say sounds alien to my own ears, like I'm not the one who's really speaking any more. "I thought Maisie and Rosie and Gia were the leak, but – you're the only one who knew it all, Kit. You were right there the whole time."

I expect him to get angry – to shout, to deny it, to tell me how wrong I am and that I'm being completely irrational. Instead, he takes a deep breath and rakes his fingers through his hair, only succeeding in making his waves stand up more than they already are.

"I swear to you, I didn't breathe a word to anyone," he says in a shockingly calm tone. He's upset – I can tell from the slight shake of his voice and the deep grimace on his face. But he isn't taking it out on me. "I understand why you think I might have. I know trust doesn't come easy for you—"

"*Don't.*"

A muscle in his jaw twitches, and he clenches his fists. "I want to be in your life, Evan. Badly. And I would never do anything to jeopardize that, I swear."

"You told them about my *mom*."

"It wasn't me." He says this with such gentle reassurance that for a split second, I almost believe him. "Feel whatever it is you need to feel right now. Be as angry and upset with me as you want. And when this is over and we know who really did it, I'll still be here. I promise. You won't lose me, and I would never do anything to risk losing you."

Kit steps aside, giving me and Tibby ample room to pass. I stare at him for a long moment, doubt and fury and a dozen other emotions I can't name warring inside me, but I don't know what to say to that. I don't know what to say to any of it. And when I finally walk past him, the urge to break down washes over me, and I shove it away. One terrible thing at a time, I tell myself. That's all I can take right now.

As Tibby and I approach Alexander's suite, the walls start to spin with the effort it takes for me to hold myself together. Despite the early hour, Tibby knocks loudly, an urgent rap that echoes down the hallway. After a few seconds pass, she knocks again, harder this time.

"Maybe he's in his office," she says. "Or maybe he's not in residence, though I could have sworn the flag was up—"

The door bursts open, and Alexander stands on the other side. He's dressed in a plush blue bathrobe, and there's stubble on his jaw that makes it clear he hasn't been awake for long. At first his expression is thunderous, but as soon as he sees me, his anger seems to melt away.

"Evangeline? Is everything all right?"

"You said they would never find her," I say, my mouth bone dry. "You *promised*."

"What are you talking about?" he says, but his voice catches with the same fear that's already coursing through me.

"I take it you haven't seen this, Your Majesty," says Tibby, offering Alexander the tablet. When he unlocks it, the front page of the *Daily Sun* appears, and he's silent as he scrolls through the article, skimming the text with such efficiency that I'm not sure he's even reading it.

"Is it true?" I demand, my throat tightening. "Did my mother have a psychotic break and try to drown me? Is that the reason you haven't let me see her all this time? Not because her medication's being tweaked, but because *you* think she's some kind of monster who would ever willingly hurt me?"

Alexander's mouth hangs open, and he seems torn between answering me and reading the rest of the article. "Evan, I—"

"*Yes or no?*"

He exhales sharply, and that's all I need to know the truth. "Your mother was very ill—"

251

"You had *no right* to keep me from her," I snarl, the words exploding from me in a burst of rage and pain. "Once she was being treated and taking the right medication, she was *fine*. My grandma let me see her – she didn't send me to boarding school because she thought my mom was one bad day away from having another break—"

"Boarding school was your mother's idea, not mine."

I stop abruptly and stare at him. "That's not true. She loves me—"

"She loves you very much," he agrees, "but after your grandmother died, Laura made it clear she had no desire to take custody of you or be responsible for your well-being. She's lived in fear that she might hurt you again—"

"But she wouldn't," I say, angrily wiping my cheeks.

"She wouldn't, no, but her illness did once, and you nearly died because of it." Alexander grimaces. "I'm very sorry, Evan, but she was the one who insisted on sending you away."

His words are spiked and jagged, and they cut me into ribbons as I stand there, speechless and feeling like everything I've ever known has been a lie.

"Sweetheart…" He reaches for me, but I jerk away, nearly colliding with a vase.

"You're lying," I say. "She didn't. She *wouldn't*."

"Evan—" he begins, but I turn on my heel and hurry back towards my apartment, breathless and half-blinded by tears. It can't be true. All I've wanted for nearly seven years is to see my mom, even if it was only for a little while. But if she never wanted to see me…if she's the one who made sure I could never go home…

Then I really am alone.

Chapter Twenty-seven

GIA: You did what?

MAISIE: It's surely not that unreasonable, all things considered.

GIA: Maisie, darling, I know you're used to getting your way, but asking her to take the blame for you is cruel.

MAISIE: But the lawyer said—

GIA: The lawyer is paid to protect you and your parents, and that means throwing everyone else under the bus if need be, Evangeline included.

MAISIE: Yes, well, I will be queen someday.

GIA: Oh? I hadn't heard. [pause]

MAISIE: You're angry with me, aren't you?

GIA: Yes, I am. She's your sister. Half-sister, whatever you want to call her, she's your blood. And she's in a foreign country surrounded by strangers, most of whom deeply dislike her, and she's already had to endure a horrifically traumatic experience that's now on display for anyone with an internet connection. And you think it's all right to ask her to take the blame for a death she didn't cause?

MAISIE: Well, she's already up to her neck in it. I don't see what one more scandal—

GIA: Maisie. Listen to yourself. Don't you have an ounce of compassion for her?

MAISIE: Do you think she has an ounce of compassion for me?

GIA: Considering the truth of what happened that night isn't on the cover of every tabloid in the country, yes, I think she does. She could take the heat off herself simply by pointing out the video was edited, but she hasn't. That speaks volumes.

MAISIE: She still could, you know. Benny said she's gone mad after all that rubbish about her mother in the papers today, so really, it's only a matter of time before she decides to burn us all to the ground.

GIA: After all you and your mother and the bloody Cunninghams have put her through, I certainly wouldn't blame her. I might even help her light the match.

MAISIE: Gia!

GIA: I mean it. If this is the person you're growing into... [pause]

MAISIE: I'm sorry. You know how difficult this has all been for me.

GIA: If it's been difficult for you, then just imagine how difficult it's been for her.

MAISIE: Do I really have to?

GIA: Only if you want to be a decent person. But if this isn't who you are any more, do me a favour and tell me now, before you break my bloody heart.

—Phone call between Her Royal Highness the Princess Mary
and Lady Georgiana Greyville, 9:41 a.m., 26 June 2023

254

Tibby refuses to leave me.

While I curl up on the sofa in my sitting room, buried yet again under a quilt, she plants herself on the love seat across from me and talks about a million things I don't care about. Gossip about a viscount gambling away his family fortune in Monte Carlo. Which of her relatives have scored prime tickets to Wimbledon. A Welsh movie star who's reportedly pregnant with her boyfriend's baby despite announcing her divorce from her husband only a week ago.

I appreciate Tibby's efforts and her company, but it's static to my ears. All I can think about is that article, and all I can hear are the words Alexander said to me.

My mom was the one who sent me away. She's kept me at arm's length on purpose. This whole time I've blamed Alexander for boarding school, for all those years of having no one, but she was the one who decided she didn't want me any more. She was the one who made me fend for myself, leaving me without a family and without a home.

I squeeze my eyes shut. It doesn't matter. She's sick – she doesn't know how much she's hurting me. But even as I tell myself that, I know it's also a lie. She may have bad days, but her illness is mostly under control. This was her choice. This was what she wanted.

Shortly before lunchtime, there's a knock on my door. While Tibby rises to see who it is, I burrow even deeper into my quilt. There's no one in the world I want to talk to right now, and definitely no one who lives in Windsor Castle.

"Your Royal Highness," says Tibby tartly, and I feel another surge of affection towards her. "I'm afraid Evangeline isn't feeling well."

"Obviously." My half-sister's voice is cutting, and I wince inwardly. "No one would in her position, but I need to speak to her anyway."

From my spot on the sofa, I can't tell if Maisie pushes her way into the room, but I'd like to think Tibby at least pretends to put up a fight. Maisie's footsteps are muffled by the carpet, but I hear her circle around and take a seat in the armchair near my head.

"Will you at least look at me?" she says stiffly, and I mutter a few curses as I pull the blanket from my face.

"What do you want? To rub my nose in it? The media is doing a great job of that already, thanks."

If she's offended by my distinct lack of respect, she doesn't let it show. "I...wanted to see how you're doing," she says slowly, as if every word is a battle.

"Everything's fantastic," I mutter. "What's not to love?"

Maisie laces her fingers together, and I think I see a flicker of unease in the way she frowns. "I had no idea your mother was... ill. You have my sympathy."

"I don't want your sympathy, or your pity, or anything else you have to offer," I snap, sitting up and wrestling with the quilt until my arms are free. "Being diagnosed with schizophrenia isn't a death sentence. It's treatable and manageable, and my mom hasn't been putting in the work for years just so you can offer your *sympathy*."

Maisie flinches, and her knuckles turn white. "Yes, well. I'm afraid I don't know much about it."

"Then educate yourself," I say shortly. "That's not my job."
Silence settles between us. She fidgets, clearly uncomfortable, and a nasty part of me hopes this is enough to make her leave. Maisie stays where she is, though, and at last she draws in a deep breath and squares her shoulders.

"I also want to apologize for what happened yesterday," she says. "When I told Gia, she was utterly furious, and of course she was right to be. You've been through enough of an ordeal without anyone asking you to do…such a thing."

Her gaze darts over to Tibby, who watches us from a spot beside the window, her arms crossed and her eyes narrowed. I sigh. The last thing I want is to be alone in a room with Her Royal Highness, but I'm too exhausted and emotionally drained to speak in riddles and allusions.

"Tibby, could we have a minute?" I say, slipping my hands back into the folds of the quilt.

"Are you certain?" she says, and I nod. "Don't go far, though. Please."

She sniffs at my request, but heads into the corridor without arguing and closes the door behind her. The sitting room feels oddly empty now, and I turn back to Maisie, determined not to let my nerves show.

"Are you trying to apologize for asking me to confess to Jasper's murder?" I say bluntly.

"Was that not clear?" she says, and I resist the urge to roll my eyes. "Truly, it was a despicable thing to ask of anyone. But after your assault and the release of that video, and of course the revelation of what your mother did to you—"

"We're not talking about that," I cut in, and she must hear

257

how deadly serious I am, because she nods once and presses her lips together.

"My point is, you've been through enough, and I'm deeply sorry for asking you to take on a burden that should be mine. It wasn't fair to you, and it certainly wasn't sisterly of me."

Sisterly? I gape at her for the better part of ten seconds. "We're not sisters. You've made that crystal clear."

"Well – no, we're not," she agrees. "We're half-sisters, though. And in this family, we protect one another, no matter how much we may otherwise disagree. It's the only way to keep the hounds at bay, isn't it? To close ranks and watch out for each other."

None of them seemed terribly interested in closing ranks around me twenty-four hours ago. "What about the full recording? Aren't you worried that'll leak, too?"

Maisie blushes and averts her eyes. "I can't pretend it isn't at the forefront of my mind. I keep thinking about how it all unfolded – how angry I was, how I confronted Jasper, what that must have looked like on camera. *I* know what my motives were, but of course I'm concerned about how a viewer might interpret my actions. And the ripple effect that may have on my reign. A queen hasn't ruled in over a century, after all, and far too many will see it as proof that I am…unstable."

I'm quiet as I consider this. I don't have the insight to reassure her, though, despite the annoying urge to do so. "Have you talked to anyone else about what happened at the party?"

She sighs. "Gia, naturally. And I also spoke to Benny and Kit this morning." Maisie pauses, her painted pink lips tugging down in a frown. "They both knew something was wrong, of course – I spent all of yesterday in tears. But I told them everything at breakfast. I had to, didn't I? They were both at the party, and I'll need their support if the full recording ever comes out. Thankfully we're all in agreement that it was entirely Jasper's fault."

"It was," I echo hollowly, and part of me wonders what Kit thought of the full story. "Thank you again for confronting him. For defending me."

She gazes past me for a moment, her blue eyes unfocused. "We may not be on the best of terms, but as I said, our family protects our own. And after what he did to you…he deserved to fall off that balcony. I don't regret what happened to him in the least."

Her fierce protectiveness isn't the most surprising thing about today, but it's close, and the ice inside me begins to thaw. Not much, admittedly, but enough that I want to believe this olive branch is real.

"He was my first kiss," I admit, picking at a ragged nail I must have chewed off. "My first – anything. But all people see when they look at that video is some slut who changed her mind."

Maisie scowls. "Even if you were a – a *that* who changed your mind, Jasper should have left you alone the moment you said no. Your level of experience doesn't void your right to withdraw consent."

"I know," I say. "But he didn't listen."

"And that isn't your fault."

I don't know what to say to that, and we sit in silence for a full minute. I want to ask why she's being so nice to me, especially after the way we left things yesterday morning. But even though I don't trust this newfound peace between us, I don't want to be the one to break it, either. Too many parts of my life have already crumbled to the ground today, and even if this is a trick, it would be all too easy to let myself believe it.

At last Maisie stands. "Daddy and I have a meeting with his advisers in a few minutes. You'll be all right, yes?"

I nod. "I don't think Tibby's going anywhere."

Maisie hesitates. "Perhaps you and I could have dinner tonight. If you're feeling up to it, that is."

I stare at her. "Seriously?"

She looks me up and down with a critical gaze. "*If* you brush your hair and put on some clean clothes," she amends. "Pyjamas are strictly prohibited."

With that, she strides towards the door, and I watch her go, letting her have the last word. Outside the walls of Windsor Castle, the media storm is raging, but it's strangely comforting to know that Hurricane Maisie may not be so lethal after all.

Much to Tibby's relief, I order a fruit salad and some toast for lunch. She doesn't ask any questions about my conversation with Maisie, but more than once I catch her watching me out of the corner of her eye. I've left my laptop in my bedroom, positive I'm not strong enough to resist the temptation to see what the world is saying about my mother, and I'm halfway through a chapter of a novel I've been meaning to read when there's another knock on the door.

"Finally. I'm *starving*," says Tibby. She's still in her sweatshirt and leggings, and I make a mental note to tell her to go home after lunch. She doesn't need to babysit me, and besides, I'm exhausted. As soon as I have something to eat, I fully intend on napping until it's time for dinner.

When she opens the door, however, it isn't a footman holding a tray – it's Jenkins. He looks about as weary and wrung out as I feel, but when our eyes meet, he musters up a smile. I pretend I don't see the hint of pity behind it.

"Evan, darling," he murmurs, and I untangle myself from the quilt and hurry towards him. By the time we reach each other, his arms are outstretched, and I bury my face in his suit jacket.

Jenkins holds me as the seconds tick by, neither of us saying a word. I'm not crying any more, but I need this – I need his comfort and his silent reassurance, and he seems to sense it. And when I pull away, to Jenkins's credit, he doesn't even smooth out the wrinkles I've made in his lapel.

"How are you feeling?" he says, tucking a wayward lock of hair behind my ear.

"I don't know. Numb, I guess," I mumble. "Is my mom okay? Has anyone checked on her? I tried calling earlier, but she wasn't picking up."

"She's perfectly fine," says Jenkins. "Far more worried about you, I suspect. His Majesty has hired extra security for her as a precaution, but no one will find her, Evan. She's as hidden as hidden can be."

I wish I found this reassuring, but Alexander made similar promises the night this whole farce began. "This is bad, isn't it?" I say as guilt surges through me. Why did I trust Kit? *Why* did I tell him about my mom?

"It's not ideal," concedes Jenkins. "Are you too tired to pack a bag?"

"A bag?" I say, confused. "I'm pretty sure I'm not allowed to leave town."

"Scotland Yard has reviewed the footage posted online, and they've come to the same conclusion you so cleverly deduced," says Jenkins. He smiles again, but it doesn't reach his eyes. "We expect the investigation against you to be officially dropped this afternoon. In the meantime, His Majesty and I have spoken, and we're in agreement. Evan..." He hesitates. "It's time for you to go home."

Chapter Twenty-eight

EDWARD IX DIES UNEXPECTEDLY AT BUCKINGHAM PALACE; ALEXANDER, 22, NOW KING

Edward IX has died at age 49. The King reportedly suffered a stroke in his sleep and passed peacefully during the night at Buckingham Palace. While details are scarce, a palace aide alleges that the King felt ill before retiring early, though the nature of his complaints are not yet known.

His son, Alexander Edward George Henry, is now King. On holiday in the United States, the new sovereign is scheduled to return to London later today.

At 22 years, 2 months, and 27 days old, he becomes the youngest monarch to be crowned since Queen Victoria, who ascended the throne in 1837.

—From the archives of *The London Independent Standard*,

14 May 2001

I only say goodbye to Tibby.

No one else seems to know I'm leaving, and I prefer to keep it that way. After she and I share an awkward hug, I ask her to tell Maisie I'm sorry for missing dinner, but I'm fairly sure my half-sister will recover from the crushing disappointment. Tibby fusses over me and insists on giving me her phone number, email address, social media handles, and physical address to both her London townhouse and her family's country estate, in case I get the urge to write her a letter. I accept them without arguing. I'd like to think we'll stay in touch, but I know myself, and I'm sure that within a month or two, Lady Tabitha Finch-Parker-Covington-Boyle will be yet another name on a long list of people who aren't permanent.

Neither of us tears up as she escorts me to the Range Rover. And when the vehicle drives away, I wave to her through the window, but as soon as we turn the corner and out of sight, I drop my hand and sigh.

Jenkins doesn't ask, and I don't volunteer. Instead, we ride to the airport in silence, and I try not to think about the fact that my mom doesn't want me. I've imagined what it would be like to turn up on her doorstep so many times that it almost feels like a memory. But now I know there will be no happy cry of surprise, no hugs, no tears of joy. Just confusion and hurt and pain.

I'll stay for one night, I tell myself. Just one night, and then I'll find a hotel. And from there...I don't know. I don't want to force her to remember what must have been one of the worst times of her life. I don't want to make her feel unsafe in her own home. But the thought of walking away from her – from the only place I've wanted to be for almost seven years – breaks my heart.

With my carry-on slung over my shoulder, I climb the boarding staircase to the royal jet. Once I've reached the top, I turn around and take in the sight of London for the last time. The sky is bright blue, the clouds are puffy as they float in the summer breeze, and I ache with the certainty that I'll miss this place more than I think I will. For all the hell I've been through here, there were good moments, too. Really good ones.

When I step inside the plane, I'm exhausted and ready for a long nap over the Atlantic. I automatically start down the aisle towards my favourite seat, but when I look up, I realize someone's already in it. Someone with thinning hair and ears I was unfortunate enough to inherit.

Alexander.

"No," I say instantly, whirling around, but Jenkins is blocking my escape route. "I'm not doing this."

"You don't have to speak to him," he says gently. "It's a large plane, Evan. There's plenty of room for you both."

I start to protest, but the flight attendant is already shutting the door, locking us all inside. I've never felt claustrophobic before, but suddenly the narrow metal tube seems to be closing in on itself.

"What is he even doing here?" I say tightly, not bothering to keep my voice down. "Does he think I'll try to parachute back onto English soil if he isn't there to stop me?"

Out of the corner of my eye, I notice Alexander turn his head towards us, and Jenkins clears his throat, also apparently aware that his boss is listening. "His Majesty intends on seeing you safely to your mother's house, that's all."

I snort humourlessly. "Great, so now he's going to show up

and confuse her even more. I'm sure her doctors will love that."

Jenkins doesn't reply, and I storm down the aisle, ignoring Alexander as I head to the very back of the plane. Flopping onto a cushioned bench seat, I pull out the book I've been reading and prop my elbows up on the table in front of me, hoping Jenkins gets the picture and leaves me alone. I'm not in the mood to be placated.

As I expect, he sits down across from Alexander instead, and they speak in hushed voices as the plane takes off. Still holding my book in front of my face to block their view, I stare out the window and watch as London grows smaller and smaller beneath us, until we're over patchwork green countryside. Maybe it's because I'm so tired, but a lump forms in my throat, and I finally look away.

The armchairs towards the front are much easier to sleep in, but as soon as we're at cruising altitude, I stretch out across the bench seat and use my sweater as a pillow. Normally I have no problem sleeping on planes, but as the minutes tick by, I can't relax. Why is Alexander *here?* Why can't he leave me and my mom alone?

I must doze off eventually, because I jolt awake some time later. Sunlight streams in through the window nearest me, and I rub my eyes and sit up. According to the clock above the cockpit door, we've been in the air for three hours, and all I see when I glance outside is the steel-blue ocean.

"Tea?"

I jerk around. Alexander stands in the aisle, a sheepish look on his unshaven face. He's holding two steaming mugs of tea, and while I want nothing more than to tell him to go screw himself, my mouth is as dry as cotton and tastes about as appetizing as an old shoe.

I nod tersely, and he sets one of the mugs in front of me. Wrapping my hands around the warm porcelain, I wait for him to leave, but instead he slips onto the bench seat across from me. I clench my jaw and stare into the milky depths of my tea, wishing I could disappear into thin air.

"You have every reason to be upset with me, and I don't blame you in the least," says Alexander. "But I'd like to tell you the whole story of what happened between your mother and me, if that's all right."

Rather than answer immediately, I sip my tea. It's the perfect temperature, and I hate him a little for it. "I know the story. You two had a fling. Nine months later, I was born, and you've regretted it ever since."

"Your mother and I didn't have a fling," says Alexander. "I met her during our first year at university."

This is the last thing in the world I expect him to say, and I finally look at him, stunned. "You – what?"

"We studied together at Oxford," he says patiently. "She tutored me in art history when I fell behind thanks to my royal obligations."

I had no idea my mom even went to college. I'm not surprised – she's smart, after all. But she's never talked about her life before me. "You – you were friends?"

The corners of Alexander's eyes crinkle like I've cracked a joke. "No, we were never friends. From the moment I saw her, I was completely and irrevocably in love with her."

I clutch my mug as if it's the only thing keeping me upright.

In love. The words echo through my mind like I'm hollow, and right now, I might as well be. I open and shut my mouth, grasping for something to say that isn't gibberish. "But – you were twenty-six when I was born," I croak.

"I'm getting there," he says with a tiny smile. "Your mum and I were together for almost four years – all throughout university and the year that followed. It only takes three years to get a degree in Britain," he explains when he notices my confusion. "We spent that fourth year travelling, and I stayed with her in the States for several months."

"You lived in Virginia?" My voice doesn't sound like mine any more, and part of me feels like I'm floating outside my body. "But – you're the King."

"I wasn't then," he says. "I was the Prince of Wales, yes, but my father was young. He'd only been on the throne for a decade, and by all accounts, he would rule for another thirty years. I had no interest in being king," admits Alexander, staring into his tea. "I wanted to live my life on my own terms – I didn't want the shackles of the throne. My parents were furious that I spent so much time away and neglected my duties, but Nicholas was seventeen, and he was everything they could want in an heir. And so, during those months in Virginia, I decided to give up my position in the line of succession, and I proposed to your mother."

I'm gaping at him now, too shocked to think of anything to say. Not a one-night stand. Not a fling. A relationship. An *engagement.*

He chuckles at the look on my face. "That was very much my parents' reaction, too," he says. "In truth, I've always wondered what role my decision played in my father's untimely death.

A stroke," he adds, correctly assuming I have no idea how Edward IX died. "He was only forty-nine. I was with your mother when I got the news, and of course, when one monarch dies, there is never a vacancy. From the moment my father took his last breath, I was king."

I'm silent for a long moment as I try to absorb this. "So you had to go back to London, and...you dumped my mom?"

Alexander's expression crumples. "No. I wanted your mother to come with me. I still wanted to marry her. It would have been...unorthodox for a king to marry a commoner, and an American commoner at that. But I refused to let anyone tell us no." He studies me. "Have you ever heard of Wallis Simpson?"

"Who?" I say faintly, and he shakes his head.

"No, of course you haven't. She's infamous in our family, but I suppose she's little more than a footnote in history now. Wallis Simpson was the mistress of Edward VIII, my great-grandfather. He wanted to marry her long before he ascended the throne, but he would've had to give up his place in the line of succession. She was an American divorcée, you see, and nobody in the family or Parliament approved. But in the end, he chose country over love, and he married an aristocratic woman who later became Queen Catherine. My grandfather, Alexander I, was born less than a year later, and the rest, as they say, is history."

He sighs, a full-body motion that seems to wring out the last of his energy. Leaning towards me, he clasps his hands, as if silently begging me to understand.

"I wanted to marry your mother more than anything in the world. I would have walked away from the throne for her – I would have given up everything to spend my life with her. But my brother was only seventeen at the time, and far too young and immature to be king. *I* was far too young and immature to be king, but my family needed me, and the very last thing your mother wanted was to be queen. She was the one who broke things off. I didn't have a say in the matter – she simply told me that's how it would be. That she loved me, but it could never work. Looking back on it, perhaps she was right. But I was utterly heartbroken. In many ways, I still am."

"Oh." My head is spinning, and I'm still trying to process the fact that I'm not the product of a one-night stand. "And then… you married Helene instead?"

Alexander nods. "A year after I ascended the throne, my mother presented me with a list of suitable brides, and I chose Helene. We'd known each other since childhood, and I could certainly see our friendship turning into something more in time – though in all honesty, I couldn't imagine ever truly loving anyone like I'd loved your mother. Like I still loved her." He shakes his head. "Helene was willing to take on the burden of being queen, and so we agreed to marry."

This is, I think, the most pathetic proposal story I've ever heard, and a pang of sympathy hits me. Not just for Alexander, but for Helene, too. "Sounds like you were both thrilled," I say, and he manages a faint smile.

"It was a convenient arrangement, and of course the public loved Helene the moment she was announced as my future bride."

Somehow I'm not surprised. "So, what – you marry her, and then decide you miss my mom?"

Alexander yet again averts his eyes. "I tried to remain faithful to Helene. She was my wife, after all, and I did love her, though I was never in love with her. I suspect she was never in love with me, either, and – I suppose, in the end, that's how I justified returning to your mother. She wouldn't have me at first, but I visited her over Christmas, and we rekindled our relationship. I'm not proud of it," he adds softly. "But I was weak and lonely and young, and I felt like my life had no meaning without her in it, dramatic as it all may sound."

"You don't have to justify it to me," I say quietly into my rapidly cooling tea.

"I think I'm justifying it more to myself," he admits. "I felt horrendously guilty the entire time. I still do. But the year and a half that followed…it was one of the happiest moments of my life. Your mother visited London, and I would visit Virginia as often as I could. We would spend hours on the telephone talking nearly every night, and it felt like old times again. We didn't intend to get pregnant," he says, lowering his voice. "But I was over the moon when I heard."

I frown. "That article said you wanted her to get an abortion."

"That article," he says firmly, "is a load of bollocks. Or at least that part of it is. I loved you from the moment your mother told me. I began to consider abdication again – by then Nicholas was married, and he and his wife were parents to a healthy baby boy. I thought perhaps…"

He trails off, and I wait a beat before I fill in the next part of the story for him. "But Helene was pregnant, too."

Alexander's grip tightens on his mug, and he nods. "I informed her that I wanted a divorce, that I would be abdicating – that I was in love with someone else, and she was having my

271

child. And that was when Helene told me."

We're both quiet for several seconds. I can picture that conversation, and I can picture my mother's heartbreak when Alexander undoubtedly told her he couldn't leave. Walking away from a wife he didn't love was one thing, but walking away from his legitimate child and the heir to the throne was another.

"Was it a coincidence that Maisie and I were born on the same day?" I say at last. I don't know why I care, but it's always bothered me. It doesn't feel right.

Alexander looks up, and to my surprise, he's smiling. "You're as clever as your mother," he says, but his humour quickly fades. "I don't know if it was a coincidence, in truth. I got on a plane to Virginia the moment I heard your mother was in labour. Helene wasn't due for another four weeks, but of course she knew about Laura. I'd told her, hadn't I? According to her medical team, she developed excruciating pain in her abdomen, and she gave them no choice but to perform a C-section. I don't want to believe Helene would have ever jeopardized Maisie's health and safety," he adds quietly, like he regrets saying the words out loud. "But I can't deny the possibility."

I don't know Helene, not really, but I have no problem imagining her desire to guarantee that her daughter – the *rightful* heir to the throne – was born first. "Is that it, then? You stayed with Helene and Maisie, and my mom and I stayed in Virginia?"

"I visited you as often as I could," he says. "Your mum and I – we had to make some tough choices. I tried to convince her to move to London, but of course she wanted to be close to her mother. I can't blame her. I couldn't offer her the support she needed, and Betty was there to fill the gaps." He hesitates. "Do you remember me at all during that time?"

I shake my head, my stomach in knots. I know what's coming, and I'm not sure I'm ready to hear it. "I had no idea you ever visited at all."

He looks suitably dismayed by this, like he expected me to cherish some snippet of memory from when I was a toddler. "Your mother and I were still together for a few years after you were born, but eventually the strains on our relationship became too much. When you were three, we decided to end things. I still visited you both, of course, but your mother behaved differently towards me. Hostile. She accused me of trying to take you away once, and after that...I didn't want to upset her."

"But that had to be her illness," I say, and Alexander nods.

"I didn't know it at the time, but she was unwell. If I'd had any idea..." He clears his throat, and his wet eyes reflect the sunlight streaming in through the window. "Your mum rang me the night it happened. She insisted that Helene had found you both – that she'd sent some kind of threatening note through the post and was going to kidnap and torture you to get back at us for the affair. Laura was absolutely convinced my wife wanted to kill you, and nothing I said could change her mind. They were delusions, of course," he adds. "I won't pretend Helene has ever liked the thought of you, but she would never..." He trails off again and shakes his head. "I knew then that something was very wrong. I rang Betty, and she's the one who contacted the police."

I stare at the polished tabletop without really seeing it. "That part of the article was true, then?"

"Yes," he says, so quietly I can barely hear him. "Your mother was suffering from undiagnosed schizophrenia with paranoia, and – in the midst of her break with reality, she thought the only way to protect you was…"

"To drown me in a damn bathtub," I mumble.

He doesn't flinch at my language. Instead, he reaches across the table and touches my fingers. His skin is warm, and I let him take my hand. "She was deeply unwell," he says, his blue eyes bearing into mine. "But she loves you more than anything in the world, and as soon as she came back to us…she's never forgiven herself. Even after she was diagnosed and put on the proper medications, she's always feared one day she might break again."

"And that's why you both sent me to boarding school after my grandma died," I say thickly. "Because Mom didn't trust herself and you didn't want me."

Alexander squeezes my hand. "I regret sending you away more than I can possibly express. I should have never made you feel like you weren't part of my family. You *are* my family, you and your mother. You always have been."

Tears prickle my eyes, and I blink furiously. "Then why did you stop visiting me? Why did you pretend I didn't exist?"

"Because—" The corners of his mouth tug downward in something even deeper than a frown. "Your grandmother asked me to stay away. She thought my presence was the reason your mother became so ill, and – when I visited you in hospital, she insisted it would be best if I kept my distance. I don't know if she was right," he says. "But I was terrified for both of you, and – I didn't want to make your life more tumultuous than it already was."

Tumultuous. He thinks my life is tumultuous. I open my

mouth to tell him how much I've hated him over the years, to tell him how lonely I've been and how desperately I've wanted everything he held out of my reach. To tell him how badly he messed up, and that I'm the one who's had to pay the price, not him. But instead, to my horror, all my anger dissolves into tears.

Alexander is at my side in an instant, hugging me like he's done it a thousand times before. At first I stiffen – I don't want his sympathy or his comfort, but the tears quickly turn into sobs, and I need someone to lean on. I bury my face in his chest, and even though I'm getting snot all over his button-down shirt, he doesn't seem to care.

"I never should have left you," he whispers into my hair. "I'm so sorry, Evie. I am so very, very sorry."

The sound of my nickname – the nickname my mother uses – sends a muted jolt through me, but I don't react. Maybe he called me Evie, too, when he was still in my life. And I find that I strangely don't mind.

As my sobs turn into sniffles, I finally slip my arms around him in return, pressing my cheek to a dry patch on his shoulder. "Everyone—" My voice is hoarse from all the crying, and I clear my throat, but I don't pull away. "Everyone knows now. They'll think she's – she's unstable, or that she's violent or—"

"I will make sure there are mental health experts on every news show in the country, educating the public about what schizophrenia really is and what it means to live with a diagnosis," he says. "I refuse to allow the press to use misinformation and fear against your mother, or against you."

Even he doesn't have the power to muzzle the media, though, and besides, Robert Cunningham already has a head start. But I sniff again and wipe my eyes with my sleeve. "They're going to go after her."

"They won't find her," he assures me. "The house isn't in her name, her records are protected, and her medical team has signed ironclad non-disclosure agreements. And if the press does manage the impossible, I'll immediately move her to a new location. You and your mother *are* my top priority, Evan, and I'm going to take care of you both like I should have all along. I swear."

His arms tighten around me like he doesn't want to let go, and neither do I. After everything that's happened and everything that's coming, I know I've lost all control. And now there's nothing I can do but trust him.

Chapter Twenty-nine

BBC: Dr Schafer, you're considered one of Great Britain's foremost experts in the diagnosis and treatment of schizophrenia. In your opinion, is Laura Bright's alleged behaviour typical?

DR RUTH SCHAFER: I must begin by saying I've never met Ms Bright, let alone treated her or been privy to her medical records, so I'll be speaking in generalities. Schizophrenia affects roughly one out of every hundred people in the United Kingdom, and it presents differently in each person with the diagnosis. There are a variety of positive, negative, and cognitive symptoms—

BBC: Positive and negative symptoms?

RS: Positive in the sense that they gain symptoms – hallucinations and delusions, for instance, which are both extremely common in those diagnosed with schizophrenia. Negative symptoms are the absence of certain important behaviours, including difficulty talking, withdrawing from others, apathy, or the inability to convey emotions. Cognitive symptoms may involve poor memory or concentration, struggling to express thoughts, disorganized thinking, or trouble understanding the information being presented, though of course these are only a sample of the symptoms patients with schizophrenia may experience.

BBC: And what of Laura Bright's reported symptoms, including her alleged attempt to drown her daughter?

RS: Again, I am not her doctor, so I can only speak in generalities. There are several different types of schizophrenia, and should a case similar to Ms Bright's be presented to me in a clinical setting, I would likely explore a potential diagnosis of paranoid schizophrenia. This is marked by the aforementioned hallucinations and delusions, particularly that an entity may be out to get them or their loved ones.

BBC: You believe this is why she allegedly tried to drown Evangeline?

RS: It's impossible for me or any other doctor to say without knowing the facts of Ms Bright's case. Given the circumstances we're aware of – her relationship with His Majesty and the likely fear that she and her daughter would be exposed in the press – it would be feasible that someone suffering from paranoia and acute psychosis might believe they are acting to protect a loved one from a worse fate.

BBC: Is violent behaviour common in patients such as Laura Bright?

RS: Perhaps the most prevalent and enduring misconception about what it means to be diagnosed with schizophrenia is the strong association with violence. People living with schizophrenia are by and large nonviolent towards others. The real danger is self-violence, and it's estimated that ten per cent of people living with schizophrenia die by suicide. Less than a quarter of all individuals who experience acute psychosis – which can be brought on by many different factors, including thyroid issues, brain tumours, and the use of illegal drugs – exhibit violent tendencies. And to equate being diagnosed with schizophrenia with being dangerous and deranged is enormously harmful to the hundreds of thousands of people in the United Kingdom living with and managing this mental illness.

BBC: Will Laura Bright ever be able to live a normal life? Is it likely she's living a normal life now, wherever she is?

RS: Again, I cannot speak to Ms Bright's case specifically, but I have seen marvellous improvements in patients. With the help of proper ongoing treatment, which may include medication and therapy, an individual living with schizophrenia can lead a very normal, very healthy life.

—Transcript of BBC News's interview with mental health expert Dr Ruth Schafer, 26 June 2023

Alexander and I stand side by side on my mother's porch as the sound of the doorbell echoes through the house.

I grip an apple pie from a bakery my mom loved when I was a kid, and he holds a bouquet of irises and forget-me-nots – her favourites, according to him. My heart is pounding so hard I think it's going to crack a rib, but when I glance at Alexander, there's a small smile on his face, and he's more relaxed than I've ever seen him. Almost as if I'm not the only one who's finally home.

Suddenly, before I can fully prepare myself, the front door opens. And for the first time in almost seven years, I come face-to-face with my mom.

She's still a few inches taller than me, and her frizzy auburn hair is pulled back in a loose bun with spiral curls framing her face. Instead of the paint-splattered apron she's always wearing when we VidChat, she's in jeans and a cream cashmere sweater, and her grin is so wide that every beautiful laugh line on her face is visible.

"Evie!" She pushes past the screen door with such speed that I'm sure she's going to hug me. Before she can close the distance between us, however, she stops abruptly, and uncertainty flickers across her face.

Does she think I'm afraid of her? Does she think I'm upset? Both possibilities feel like a knife to my heart, and even though I'm all but frozen in place, I clumsily shove the pie into Alexander's free hand and wrap my arms around my mother as tightly as I dare. She's startlingly angular and bony underneath her sweater, but I can feel her strength as she hugs me back fiercely. "I've missed you so much," she says in a choked voice, and those five words vanquish every worry I had about coming here.

"Are you okay?"

I can tell from her tone that this isn't just a polite question, and my stomach twists into knots. "I will be," I say. It's the closest I can get to the truth without Robert Cunningham stealing this moment from both of us. "What about you? Are you all right?"

She hesitates, and in that split second, I know she's aware of every single word the media is saying about her. The knots turn into nausea, and I feel an overwhelming urge to fight every so-called journalist who seems to think telling the world about the most difficult time in her life counts as news – or worse, entertainment. "As long as you're okay, so am I," she says at last, offering me a smile I almost believe. "How was the flight? Have you had anything to eat today?"

"The flight was fine," I say, my tongue heavy with the things I want to say, but can't. Not yet. Maybe not ever. "I had lunch earlier."

"That was back in London, though," says Alexander quietly, seemingly reluctant to intrude on our conversation, but I don't mind. And judging by the way my mom squeezes his forearm like there's no barrier between them at all, neither does she.

"It's nearly midnight there," she says. "You must be starving. Come on – I've made lasagne." But as she reaches for the door again, she falters. "Do you like lasagne, Evie?"

"I love lasagne," I say. "It's one of my favourites."

My mom visibly relaxes and leads the way inside. The house is smaller than I expect, probably because I've spent more than a third of my life in sprawling boarding schools and, up until this afternoon, lived in an actual castle. The furniture is shockingly neutral, but her paintings hang unframed on the walls, their abstract designs and bold colours adding liveliness to the otherwise tidy decor.

When we walk into the warm kitchen, with its red walls and gold accents, a flood of impressions and snippets of memories suddenly overwhelm me. "Whoa," I say, stunned into reverie. "I think I remember this place."

"You do?" She sets the pie down on the counter and grabs oven mitts to extract the lasagne. "You used to stand on a stool and help me bake."

I look at the pattern in the countertop, and an image of yellow frosting flashes through my mind. "I remember that, too," I say, even though I'm not sure I do. But the way my mom beams makes up for any uncertainty on my part, and she insists Alexander and I take a seat at the table while she serves us.

As he and I sit down across from each other, he catches my eye. "All right?" he says so softly that I read his lips more than I hear him, and I nod. I'm not entirely okay – I feel like I've walked straight into a dream, and there's a faint buzzing in my ears. But there's nowhere else in the world I'd rather be.

My mom carries out plates of lasagne and garlic bread, and as she joins us at the table, there's a moment when we're all silent and glancing at one another. A surreal sensation washes over me, as if I'm watching this scene unfold in a cheesy movie, but I can feel the cool wood of the table beneath my hands. I can smell the plate of food in front of me, and my mouth is watering. This is as real as it gets, and the fact that I'm sitting at a dinner table with my parents – it's everything I've ever wanted and never thought I could actually have.

The conversation focuses entirely on me. My mom asks about my time in London, about the shows and movies I've been watching and the book I'm reading. She asks about the staff – several of whom she names specifically, including Jenkins and Louis – and what my favourite part of my trip was.

This last question gives me pause. I think about all the horrible days I spent in Windsor Castle, under the tutelage of strict etiquette instructors or holed up in my room, with only my laptop and the opinions of strangers for company. I think about all the articles the tabloids and gossip blogs have written about me, and I think about all the nasty things my father's family has said to my face. It's hard to see the good beyond those bleak moments, but as I swallow my bite of lasagne, I know my answer.

"There's this little ice cream shop in London," I say. "Kit – this boy I met – he took me there. And it was the best ice cream I've ever had."

"You met a boy?" says my mom with an odd mixture of protectiveness and delight.

"Kit is Christopher Abbott-Montgomery," says Alexander. "He's Helene's nephew. Her brother's younger son."

He says his wife's name easily, like he's used to discussing her with my mom, and I can't help but watch for her reaction. I expect – I don't know. Hurt, maybe. A flicker of bewilderment and distress, like I've seen so many times on VidChat. And when my mom frowns, my insides clench.

"Is his older brother the one who passed?" she says, and I exhale. How does she know about that?

Alexander nods, oblivious to my surprise. "Kit is staying at Windsor for now. Evan, Tibby mentioned you two have been spending a great deal of time together."

My face grows hot. As much as I'm enjoying having a normal family experience, being grilled about my social life is more than I bargained for. Especially considering all the grief Kit caused. "Yeah," I mumble, stabbing my lasagne. "How did you know about his brother, Mom?"

She blinks. "Alex told me," she says, glancing at him for

confirmation. "Sometime last year, I think. I remember we spoke right after the funeral."

I look between them. "You two still talk?" I say, trying to mask my astonishment with mild interest. It doesn't work.

"Of course," says my mom, and she smiles at Alexander like they share an entire lifetime of secrets. "I've mentioned that before, haven't I, Evie?"

I nod, my appetite gone. Not because I'm upset with them, but because I'm furious with myself. I've spent years dismissing my mother's preoccupation with Alexander as a sign of her illness – yet another tangled delusion that separated her world from ours. But I'm the one who's been so caught up in my own reality that I can't tell truth from fiction.

"Tell me more about Kit," says my mom with such warmth that I can't refuse. I press my lips together and stare down at my plate, hoping my face isn't as red as I think it is.

"He took me to a concert a couple days ago," I say. "And we've hung out a bunch. But – I don't think it's going to work out."

"Oh?" She sounds disappointed. "Why not?"

I bite the inside of my cheek. After years of keeping our family's secrets, I can't admit that the leak about her illness came from me. "It's a long story. And I'm still not really sure what happened."

"If he isn't worth your time, then walk away and don't look back," she says, reaching across the table and taking my hand. Flecks of green and purple paint stain her short nails, and I squeeze her fingers gently. "But if he's one of the good ones, then you owe it to yourself to try. You deserve wonderful things, Evie. And you deserve to be surrounded by worthwhile and supportive people."

I try to smile, but I can feel it come out as more of a grimace. "I am," I promise. "I have you and Alexander and Jenkins."

"You need more than just us, as much as we all love you. Did you meet Maisie while you were there?"

At the casual mention of his legitimate daughter, the corners of Alexander's mouth turn downward, and he's suddenly fascinated by the crusty remains of his garlic bread. No doubt he's thinking about the meeting yesterday morning, and what Helene and Maisie tried to make me do.

"I did," I say. "It was a rocky start, but – she stopped by before I left, and we had a nice talk."

"Did you?" says my mom eagerly. "I always hoped you two would meet one day. What's she like?"

"Very much a princess," I say wryly, and when I glance at Alexander, I think I see a faint smirk. "But once you get past the layers of pride and snobbery, she seems like a good person."

The topic flits to the others I've met – Ben, Nicholas, Tibby, even Helene, although when my mom asks what I think of her, Alexander hastily changes the subject to the painting hanging on the wall. While she enthusiastically describes the nearby park that's become her most recent inspiration, I excuse myself.

It takes me a minute to find a half bath with lilac walls and gold furnishings, and after I've done my business and washed my hands, I pause. This wasn't the bathroom where it happened – where my mother tried to drown me in the throes of a psychotic break. And while every part of me cringes away from that painful thought, I suddenly have a burning need to see it for myself. To see the four walls where the course of my entire life changed.

I slip out into the living room. The floorboards creak as I

walk, but there's no pause in the conversation filtering in from the dining room, and I hurry towards the staircase.

The upstairs hallway is dark, and I consider turning on the light, but I don't want to alert my mom or Alexander to the fact that I'm snooping. I shouldn't be so scared of getting caught – this is my home, after all. But even though that's technically true, I'm now certain that while I may have lived here when I was little, this is no more my home now than St Edith's ever was.

I grope around until I find a door to my left. Twisting the knob, I slowly ease it open and reach for the switch that has to be there. And while I'm not entirely sure what I expect to see, as soon as I turn on the light, I freeze.

Pink curtains, a neatly made bed covered in teddy bears and a purple quilt, a cushioned window seat that looks out over the backyard – I don't remember this room, but I'm sure it was once mine. There's a beautiful pastel mural of a garden on one wall, hand-painted in my mother's distinctive style. I look around, taking in the rows of picture books and the collection of finger paintings framed on the dresser. Almost fourteen years after I last slept here, it's a time capsule more than anything, and I can't help wondering why my mom keeps it like this. Is she afraid she'll forget if this room ever changes? Or does she simply miss me, and this makes her feel closer to the family we once were?

I should be nostalgic for this childhood I barely remember, but while there's a pang inside me for the life I could have lived, I easily push it aside. This room belongs to a little girl I haven't been in a long time. These aren't my memories – they're my mom's, and I leave them undisturbed as I step into the hall again and softly shut the door.

I almost go back downstairs. This feels like a bad idea – like I'm dragging the tip of a knife across a long-healed scar, practically begging for it to reopen. But I'm here now, and I need to know, and so I open the door across the hall and flip the switch.

Light fills the room, and instantly I know this is it. There's an incongruous modern feel to the bathroom, like it's been remodelled within the past decade even though the rest of the house has stayed the same. The granite countertop is clear of any clutter. The tile floor is pristine, and pearl-grey hand towels hang neatly on their hooks. And opposite the toilet, where I'd expect a bathtub to sit, is a shower stall with stone walls.

I stand there, my entire body numb as I take it all in – the gleaming fixtures, the small window with a gauzy grey curtain, the fluffy bath mats that look like they've never seen a drop of water. A long moment passes, but at last I understand why this room feels so wrong.

She's never used it.

My mother must have a suite, because this bathroom, expensive and luxurious as it is, has never been touched. There isn't even a toothbrush on the counter or a single long hair on the floor. Alexander may have had it remodelled for her, but just like my old bedroom, this place is also frozen in time.

Yet again I step back into the hall and close the door. This isn't my life any more, and it feels wrong to breach the threshold of my mother's inner world. These rooms – these memories – are none of my business, and the only version of me that has a place in this house is four years old. I don't need to be here to find forgiveness, because there's nothing to forgive. It wasn't her fault. She did the best she could, and she shows me she loves me every day by taking her medication and taking care of herself. That's all I can ask for, and that's all I'll ever need.

I head back downstairs, careful not to make a sound. The conversation in the dining room has gone silent now, and my heart skips a beat. Do they realize I'm missing? Will my mom take one look at me and know where I've been?

But when I turn the corner, I stop cold. Soft music plays from a stereo by the foot of the table – some old nineties song that sounds vaguely familiar – and Alexander's arms are wrapped around my mom as they sway in place. His nose is buried in her hair, her head rests on his shoulder, and their eyes are closed as if they're in their own world.

The love between them is obvious, and even though I've never seen them together before, I don't know how I could have missed it. They're two puzzle pieces that form a single perfect image – two stars that have been orbiting each other since before time began, and it makes me ache for something I'm sure I'll never be lucky enough to find. I'm glad they did, though. And suddenly I grieve every single day they've had to spend apart.

I watch them for another few seconds before turning away. I might be the product of their love, but I have no place in this moment, and I exit on silent feet, leaving them to their song.

Chapter Thirty

@dutchessdame172: is schizophrenia genetic? lmao
27 June 2023, 12:19 a.m. UTC – Twitter for iPhone, London, UK

@btswhisktang: @dutchessdame172 it's not okay to mock someone for having a mental illness. she's getting treatment and that's what matters.
27 June 2023, 12:21 a.m. UTC – Twitter for Android, Sydney, Australia

@dutchessdame172: @btswhisktang I wasn't mocking anyone. it was a question. #JusticeforJasper #shedidit
27 June 2023, 12:53 a.m. UTC – Twitter for iPhone, London, UK

—Twitter exchange between users @dutchessdame172
and @btswhisktang, 27 June 2023

Balancing two plates on my arm, I carefully open the door to the SUV and slide onto the cool leather seat beside Jenkins. He's talking to someone on his phone, but as soon as I appear, he cuts the conversation short.

"You didn't have to hang up," I say as I offer him a slice of pie.

"I was merely saying goodnight to Louis," he says as he accepts the plate. "It's chaos at Windsor right now. Apparently, His Majesty didn't inform the rest of the family that you were both leaving."

"Doubt any of them really care that I'm gone," I say darkly, turning my attention to my own slice. I can feel Jenkins's gaze on me, but he lets me eat a few bites in silence before clearing his throat.

"I owe you an apology," he says. "Regardless of the circumstances behind my decision, I should have never brought you to England without your consent. What I did was selfish and arrogant, and no matter what my intentions were, I caused both you and His Majesty a great deal of pain. For that I will never forgive myself."

My fork falls onto my plate with a clatter. "Are you serious?" I say, scowling at him. "You've been there for me whenever I needed you for years. You cared about me – and you made sure I *knew* you cared about me – when it felt like no one else in the world did. You didn't bring me to England because you wanted to prove you knew better than me or Alexander. You brought me to England because you wanted to protect me – you wanted to protect us both from our own serious errors in judgment. You knew how much we were hurting, and you were willing to risk your job and your entire livelihood to give us a chance at a real relationship." I shake my head. "I'm not going to pretend it's been a cakewalk, but you were right. I needed to know this side of my family. I needed to find something to hold on to."

Jenkins clears his throat, and for one horrifying moment,

I think he might actually tear up. Instead, he toys with his fork, inspecting the decoration on the handle with distracted interest. "Your understanding means more to me than I can possibly put into words," he says quietly. "Please forgive my overfamiliarity, but…through the years, I've come to think of you as family, and it's been a privilege to watch you grow up."

A warm and fuzzy feeling runs through me, and I have to bite my lip to stop myself from grinning. "You're not too bad yourself, you know," I say. "Half the time I got kicked out of boarding school, it was only because I wanted to see you again."

He chuckles and finally looks at me. "All you ever had to do was ask. But speaking of…" He pulls a manila envelope from his briefcase and hands it to me. "It's not your birthday yet, but I believe I owe you this."

It's heavier than I expect, and I undo the metal clasp. "What is it?"

"Your passports," he says. "Along with a credit card linked to a bank account His Majesty has arranged for you. There will always be funds for you to access, and you may have whatever you want or need, no strings attached."

I pull out two dark blue passports – one for the US, one for the UK – and a black credit card with my name on it. I should be elated. This is the freedom I've always wanted, and I'll be able to live my own life and make my own choices for the first time. But all I feel is emptiness and dread.

There's something else in the envelope, too, and I pull out a plane ticket. It's blank, but it has my name on it and first class stamped in the corner.

"As promised," says Jenkins, "this will get you a seat on any

Virgin Atlantic flight in the world."

I stare at the ticket. A month ago, I would have done damn near anything for the contents of this envelope, and here it all is, mine for the taking. "I can go wherever I want?"

"New Zealand, Malaysia – wherever you would like," he confirms, and though he's doing a valiant job of maintaining his composure, I think I hear a catch in his voice.

I'm quiet for a long moment as I run my finger across the bold type. "What about England?"

"England?" he says, unable to hide his surprise.

"Some of the food's a little iffy," I say, "but I've heard good things."

"Yes," says Jenkins slowly. "The food can be questionable. But I suppose I could pull a few strings, if you're sure that's what you want."

"It is," I say, and I tuck the ticket back in the envelope. "Eat your pie before it gets cold. It's the best in the city, and I won't let you waste it."

A flicker of a smile passes over his face. "Yes, Your Royal Highness," he says, and he hastily dodges the sharp end of my elbow before digging in.

I expect confusion when I tell my mother I'm returning to Windsor with Alexander, but instead she acts as if this is a given. Maybe to her, it is – or maybe we both know that me staying with her was never really an option.

Before we all say our goodbyes, however, she hurries to her studio and returns with a wrapped canvas roughly the size of a poster. There's a card attached with my name on it, and she hands me the gift with some hesitancy. "Wait until your birthday to open it," she requests. "It's nothing special, but I thought of you while I worked on it." She pauses. "I think of you every time I paint."

I carefully hand the present to Alexander before catching my mom in another hug. "I love you," I mumble into her shoulder, and she kisses my hair.

"I love you too, Evie. And I'm so glad you two have gotten to know each other. I've wanted nothing more for a very long time."

Alexander clears his throat, and I think I see his eyes shining in the warm lamplight. "I'll take good care of her," he promises. "And we'll come and visit you as often as we can."

"I know you will," says my mother, and she reaches for his hand and squeezes it fondly. "I'm already looking forward to it." She stands on the lit porch as the SUV drives away, and both Alexander and I crane our necks to keep her in view for as long as possible. Once we turn the corner and she disappears, he and I let out simultaneous sighs, and I notice Jenkins press his lips together to keep from smiling.

"Are you sure about this?" says Alexander from the front seat. "We can always find a hotel for the night if you'd like some time to think it over."

"I'm sure," I say. "And I want to schedule a meeting with Doyle and Yara and the rest of your royal goons."

"To discuss what, exactly?" he says warily.

"The TV interview I'm going to give about what happened the night Jasper died," I say. He gapes at me like he hasn't heard right, and I press on. "Everyone already thinks I did it. Dragging

Maisie into this mess isn't going to help, and Jasper's caused enough pain already. There's no point in making it worse."

"Evie…" Alexander grimaces. "You don't have to take the blame. The lawyers and I will find another way to keep this contained."

"I know you'll try," I say, "but I want to do this. And I've thought it through – I just have to admit the clip was edited and reveal someone helped me escape. I won't say who, but I'll make it clear I was still the one who pushed Jasper when he came after me again. The footage doesn't show who really did it, after all, and no one will ever know the truth." I shrug. "And if the full video *is* released, most people will see Maisie as a hero who risked her safety to protect a half-sister she barely knew. And anyone who tries to claim I'm covering for her will be labelled a conspiracy theorist. Problem solved."

Alexander spends the rest of the ride to the airport trying to talk me out of it, but at last, after we've boarded, he personally makes the call to Doyle to schedule a meeting for tomorrow. Or later today, I guess, given what time it is in London.

Once Jenkins and I are settled in across from each other at our usual table, I pull out my laptop and connect to the plane's Wi-Fi. I have every intention of going straight to Netflix and falling asleep to an episode of my favourite show, but almost as soon as I sign on, a video call pops up. Hope surges through me, but it isn't from my mom – instead it's from a UK number I don't recognize.

Did the press find my email address? Is this some reporter trying to get a scoop? I almost reject the call, but something – morbid curiosity, maybe, or my propensity to go for the worst possible choice every single time – makes me accept it instead.

"Evan!" Immediately my half-sister's face fills the screen. She has no make-up on, her hair is done up in rollers, and her blue eyes are huge as she leans in towards the camera. "I've been trying to call you all day. Where *are* you?"

Jenkins looks up from his crossword, an eyebrow raised at the volume, and I quickly connect my headphones. "We just left Virginia," I say. "We, uh – we went to see my mom."

"How is she?" Ben's face appears beside Maisie's, and I catch sight of his silk pyjama top.

"She's good," I say, bracing myself for the familiar defensiveness that rises within me whenever someone brings my mom up. But she's healthier than I've seen her in a long time, and even though she'll always have to deal with her illness in one way or another, she doesn't need me to fight her battles for her. "Maisie, I wanted to talk to you about something—"

I stop suddenly when I catch a glimpse of wavy dark hair behind them, and my stomach flip-flops. Kit.

"About what?" says my half-sister. "Is this about dinner? There's no need to apologize, of course – Benny joined me instead, and we had a rousing debate on who's likely to make the finals of Wimbledon."

"No, it's not about dinner, but I am sorry for leaving you hanging," I say, and I hesitate. "I'm going to do the interview – the one we talked about earlier. I'm going to tell everyone I pushed Jasper." Maisie's mouth falls open, and there's stunned silence on the other end of the video call. "But – Evan, you don't have to do that," she says, sounding jarringly like Alexander.

"I know," I say. "I want to, though. We're family, right?"

Maisie stares at me through the screen, her eyes rapidly filling with tears. "We're family," she echoes softly. "Evan...I wasn't trying to manipulate you earlier, if that's what you think—"

"It's not," I promise. "This is entirely my decision. No one talked me into it."

"Then allow us to try to talk you out of it," says Ben from his spot beside her. "There's no reason for you to go public with what happened to you. You should be discussing this with a therapist, not a BBC reporter."

"Benny's right," says Maisie, and I can hear the dismay in her voice. But as she continues, it's drowned out by that same fierce protectiveness she showed in my sitting room that morning. "You don't owe anyone an explanation, especially about something so...*traumatic*."

"I don't," I agree, "but they're going to be circling like vultures until they get one. And if the full video ever comes out..." Silence crackles between us, and Ben's scowl deepens. "I know you think you're doing the right thing, but if it ever *does* come out, your confession won't protect Maisie."

"It will," I say firmly. "I've thought it through, and I'm going to tell them—"

There's a sudden movement in the background, and both Maisie and Ben turn around, giving me a quick view of Kit standing and walking off-screen. "You're leaving?" says Maisie.

"I'm going to bed," he says gruffly, and I hear the sound of a door close. Maisie sighs and turns back to the camera.

"You really ought to forgive him for whatever he's done," she says. "Surely it wasn't *that* egregious, and he's been in a wretched mood all day."

"Good," I mutter. But before I can tell her that he deserves every ounce of that misery, Ben cuts in.

"Evan, perhaps you'd be better off staying with your mother for a while instead of coming back," he says. "When you decide to return, no doubt the press will have found bigger stories—"

"Alexander's already scheduled the meeting," I say. "I appreciate that you both care, but I've made my decision. I'm not backing out of this."

We speak for a few more minutes before Maisie's giant yawn ends the conversation. After we all say goodnight, I close my laptop and head to the kitchenette in the back of the plane to get something to drink. Jenkins is already sipping a large cup of coffee, and so I carry two mugs of tea to the table where Alexander sits, his laptop open and a video call playing on his screen. I expect to see Doyle's ruddy face, but instead Nicholas is on the other end, his hair mussed and dark shadows prominent underneath his eyes.

" – swear to you, I have no idea how they found out," he says, his hands clasped like he's pleading with my father.

"All of the court records were sealed, and I moved mountains to ensure no one could find her," says Alexander, so quietly that I can barely hear him over the hum of the jet. "Robert Cunningham didn't simply stumble across this story. Someone gave it to him. And you're the only person I ever told about Laura's illness and arrest." A wave of dizziness washes over me, and I go completely still.

Vaguely I realize I'm in danger of dropping the tea, but I don't care. Nicholas says nothing for several agonizingly long seconds, and a strange expression flickers across his features before he buries his face in his hands.

"I don't know, Alex. I don't *know*. Maybe it was her doctor or a disgruntled caregiver."

My father shakes his head. "They had no idea she was connected to me in any way. Try again."

Nicholas digs his fingers into his hair and tugs. "I – I suppose it's possible I accidentally let it slip to Robert while drunk," he admits. "Some of our poker games get rowdy, and—"

Alexander shuts his laptop with such force that I'm surprised he doesn't break it. He inhales deeply, as if he's trying to calm himself, and I don't know what to do. I can't stay silent, though, and before I can even begin to sort through my jumbled thoughts, I hear myself speak.

"It was Nicholas?"

My voice is thin and strained, and Alexander twists around. "Evie? What are you—" He notices the drinks I'm holding. "Is one of those for me?"

I hand him a mug. "Nicholas is the one who leaked the story about my mom to the press?" I say, more insistent this time. Alexander sighs.

"He's the only other person who knew, and the details were far too accurate to have come from anyone who didn't have the full story. I'm so sorry, my darling," he says. "I thought…well, I thought I could trust my own brother."

I nod tightly, and after mumbling an excuse, I head back to my seat across from Jenkins. He looks at me curiously, but I turn away, unable to force a smile.

If Nicholas really was the source of the leak, then I've made a massive, massive mistake.

Chapter Thirty-one

Has the Killer Princess been exiled to the United States?

Palace insiders claim that Evangeline Bright was whisked away by her father, the philandering King Alexander, on a private jet heading across the Atlantic this afternoon. While details are scarce, we at the *Regal Record* have confirmed that no one in the royal family was informed of this decision beforehand.

With the news of Laura Bright's mental illness and violent history breaking only hours earlier, did her daughter finally see the writing on the wall and decide to flee the country? Considering the evidence Scotland Yard has accrued in its active investigation against the seventeen-year-old for the murder of Jasper Cunningham, this may be the first smart decision Evangeline has made since landing in the UK.

—*The Regal Record*, 27 June 2023

As soon as we arrive at Windsor the next morning, I head straight for Kit's suite.

Though I barely slept on the red-eye flight back to London, too consumed by my own gut-wrenching mistake, my heart is pounding and every muscle in my body propels me through the royal family's private wing at a near-superhuman pace. I have to find him. I have to apologize, to tell him what a horrible, broken human being I am, and in the meantime, everything else can wait.

I bang on his door, my hands shaking and my nerves fraying more and more with each passing second, but there's no answer. Eventually Jenkins finds me, and with his usual gentleness, he guides me back down the corridor.

"Kit will turn up," he promises, even though he has no idea what's going on. "Let's get some food and caffeine in you, shall we?"

Tibby's waiting in my sitting room, and she barely glances up from her phone when we arrive. "I see she decided to return. I believe you owe me a tenner," she says to Jenkins, and without a word, he pulls a colourful ten-pound note from his pocket. She snatches it up and finally focuses on me. "Have you had any rest at all since I last saw you? You look positively feral."

"She didn't sleep much on the plane," says Jenkins. "She and His Majesty have a meeting upstairs in an hour and a half, but do try to make her eat and drink something before then, will you? I've ordered a full English from the kitchens."

Tibby nods, and once Jenkins slips out of the room, she eyes me up and down. "Coffee, I think," she says. "Espresso, if you can stomach it."

"Have you seen Kit?" I say, the adrenaline slowly seeping out of me. "I need to talk to him."

"I'm afraid I only arrived at Windsor twenty minutes ago," she says in a clipped voice. "Next time you decide to leave royal life behind, do be certain to stick to the plan. I was in the middle of a job interview at Christie's."

"Sorry," I say wearily, combing my fingers through my messy hair. "I'll try to be more considerate next time the press targets my mom and calls me a murderer."

"Please do." But even as Tibby says it, I spot a faint quirk of her lips. "Now, what's behind your sudden change of heart with Kit—"

A soft knock on the door echoes through the room, interrupting her. I perk up, my pulse racing again in anticipation of Kit being on the other side, but Tibby frowns. "Surely the chef isn't that quick today," she says, striding over to open it. "Can I help—"

"Hello, Tabitha," says a soft voice that turns my hope to ash. "Might I have a moment alone with Evangeline?"

Tibby immediately sinks into a curtsy. "Er – I'm sorry, Your Majesty, but I'm afraid she's had a long night—"

"I'll be brief," says Helene with a note of finality. As the Queen steps into the suite, Tibby catches my eye and mouths an apology before disappearing into the corridor, leaving my stepmother and me alone together for the first time.

"What do you want?" I say, too tired to feign politeness. After what she pulled at the meeting yesterday – or the day before, I realize – she doesn't deserve it.

Helene takes a deep breath, her judgmental gaze sweeping over my sitting room like I've decorated it myself. "I'd like to apologize," she says. "For my behaviour since you've arrived. I fear I have been far too harsh with you."

"No shit," I mutter, not caring if she hears me. "I guess Maisie told you about the interview I'm doing, then."

"She did," says Helene, and she finally looks at me, her perfect

301

eyebrows knitted together in a frown. "And I cannot tell you how grateful I am, Evangeline."

"I'm not doing it for you," I say shortly, and she seems to shrink a little under my glare.

"I know, but it still means a great deal to me. And in truth, I was hoping we might be able to start over. Wipe the slate clean, so to speak."

I stare at her, my exhausted brain beyond confused now. Two days ago, she threatened to destroy my life if I didn't do exactly what she wanted, and now she's *apologizing*. It doesn't make sense.

"Why do you suddenly care?" I say coldly, and guilt flickers across her delicate features before she averts her eyes.

"You have enough going on at the moment, what with the press obsessing over you and the news about that – that horrible incident with your mother. I thought I might extend an olive branch and try to make your life a little easier, that's all."

There's no way that's all. I'm doing exactly what Helene wants, and she's held the same cards from the beginning. Her hand hasn't changed, unless –

The blurry picture in my mind focuses, and everything snaps into place. The threats, the NDA, her determination to protect Maisie at all costs – and the look on Nicholas's face during his video call with Alexander. Helene wanted to turn me into a scapegoat from the beginning, and she did, I realize. But not by targeting me directly. By going after my mother and trying to make us both look dangerously unstable in the process.

"Nicholas told you about my mom, didn't he?" I say. "About why she lost custody. And you're the one who tipped off the press."

Helene's every bit as smart as she wants the world to think

she is, but the shock on her face makes it clear she wasn't expecting me to know this puzzle existed, let alone put the pieces together. "What—" she breathes, but I cut her off.

"Alexander said that Nicholas is the only other person who knew the details that were in the article." My hands are shaking – with fury or devastation or exhaustion, or maybe all three – and I take a step closer to her.

"And why would Nicholas tell me?" she says in an unconvincing attempt at innocence. "He loves his brother—"

"Because you're having an affair with him."

The silence in the room is instantaneous. Helene gapes at me, her fingers laced together so tightly that the tips are turning purple. "I – I am not—"

"Yes, you are," I say easily. This part, after all, isn't a guess. "I saw you together last weekend, in one of the unused rooms. I don't know why Nicholas told you about my mom, but he was surprised when Alexander accused him – he clearly had no idea he was the only other person who knew. He covered for you, by the way. Said he thought he might've slipped up and told Robert Cunningham when he was drunk. I really hope he loves you," I add quietly. "Because you might've just cost him his relationship with his brother."

All the colour drains from her cheeks. "What do you want?" she croaks.

"You're going to leave my mom alone," I say flatly. "If anything else about her life leaks to the press – and I mean *anything* – I'll have no choice but to give the media a story that'll run her out of the headlines."

Helene shudders. "You'll only be hurting Alexander, you know."

I think about the sight of my parents standing in my mom's dining room, holding each other as they sway to a song. "I don't think I will be," I say. "But I do know I'll be hurting you and your reputation. And I have a feeling that means more to you than your marriage."

Helene clenches her jaw, and I half expect her to take a swing at me. I wouldn't blame her. She's spent twenty years building up her image as the admirable and enviable queen, and a story like this – from inside the royal family to boot – would ruin her. But she exhales instead, seeming to calm herself, though her posture is painfully stiff. "No clean slate then, I take it," she says, and I shake my head.

"You have to live with the consequences of this one."

She opens her mouth like she wants to retort, but there's nothing she could possibly say that would change my mind. Helene seems to realize this, and with a small, barely discernible nod, she turns on her heel and departs the way she came, leaving me alone in my sitting room.

As soon as she's gone, my shoulders slump and what little energy I have left drains from my body. I sink into one of the antique chairs around the dining table and hold my head in my hands, trying to pull myself together. I don't regret a single word I said to her, but I also know that this time I really have drawn a line in the sand I can never erase, and the magnitude of threatening my stepmother – of threatening the *Queen* – settles over me like a crushing weight. Helene will never let this go, and if I ever have to release that story, I'll have nothing else to hold over her and no collateral to protect my mom.

As I'm running through the endless possible scenarios in

my mind, I catch sight of a small silver gift box beside a vase of fresh lilies on the table. The flowers aren't unusual – they change every few days, and they're always beautiful. But I've never seen the box before.

Frowning, I pick it up. It doesn't seem like something Tibby might have left here, and I turn the box over in my hands, inspecting it from all angles. It's definitely not professionally wrapped, but there's a certain sweetness to the lopsided purple bow.

Even though I'm not entirely sure it's for me, I untie the ribbon and remove the lid. Tucked inside is a folded note on heavy card stock, and as I read it, my insides twist with guilt.

Evan,

This may not be the real thing, but you are to me.

Yours,
Kit

Nestled in tissue paper is a tiny silver charm shaped like a tiara. I recognize the tag – the Tower gift shop where he bought me the teddy bear in the guard uniform – and a lump forms in my throat.

How long has this been sitting here? Days? A week? No – he must have left it recently, else Tibby, at the very least, would have spotted it. I attach the charm to my bracelet, my determination to find Kit rekindled. Before I can do anything more than stand, however, the door to my sitting room bursts open and Maisie rushes inside.

"You're back!" She all but tackles me in a hug, her thin arms far stronger than they look. Tibby slips into the suite after her, holding two travel mugs and rolling her eyes, and I smile into Maisie's shoulder.

"Couldn't stay away," I say, and at last my half-sister releases me from her iron grip. "Have you seen Kit?"

"I saw him at breakfast," she says, smoothing her yellow sundress before reaching out and arranging my tangled hair for me. "I believe he went to Mayfair – something about a meeting with his lawyer."

"Lawyer?" I say as Tibby hands me one of the mugs, and the scent of strong coffee assaults my nostrils. "Why?"

"Haven't a clue," says Maisie. "He's been rather tight-lipped since last night. I think he's upset you're giving the – you know." She side-eyes Tibby. "But I've no idea what he could possibly do about—"

She stops suddenly, at the exact same moment a light bulb goes off in my brain, and we lock eyes. "You're sure he's visiting his lawyer?" I say, my mouth dry, and she nods.

"Positive. You don't think…"

But I absolutely do, and I gulp. "He's going to tell Scotland Yard he's the one who killed Jasper."

Chapter Thirty-two

Maisie:

Kit, where are you?

Kit, don't you dare do this.

Kit, this won't erase anything the press has said about her, and it'll shine a spotlight on Liam and your parents that won't ever go away.

Kit, all this will do is make things worse for everyone. Do you really think going to prison will help her? Is that where you want this deeply misguided display of chivalry to end?

Christopher, I swear on all you hold holy, if you do this, I will never, ever, ever forgive you.

CHRISTOPHER, ANSWER ME.

—Text messages from Her Royal Highness the Princess Mary to Christopher Abbott-Montgomery, Earl of Clarence, 27 June 2023

I pace the length of my sitting room as Maisie and Ben huddle together on the sofa, trying Kit's number again and again with no success.

"Why isn't he answering?" says Maisie, her voice rising with frustration as she sends what must be her umpteenth text.

"Clearly he's switched off his mobile," says Ben, jabbing his screen harder than necessary. "Every call goes directly to voice mail."

"Do either of you know where his lawyer's office is?" I say as a potent combination of caffeine and fear chases away the worst of my fatigue. "Can we meet him there?"

The pair of them exchange a questioning glance, and both shake their heads. "I could ask my uncle," says Maisie doubtfully. "But he won't be happy to hear what Kit's up to."

I remember the way Kit talked about his father, and I immediately know that's not an option. "Do you think Kit and his lawyer would go to Scotland Yard? Would it be worth it to try to find them there?" I say.

"You have a meeting with His Majesty and the public relations team in forty minutes," says Tibby idly from the corner, where she's mostly ignoring the conversation as she scrolls through her phone. "And there is no bloody way I'm letting you anywhere near Scotland Yard right now."

Ben tries Kit's number again, and in the quiet of the room, I can hear an automated voice telling him to leave a message. He sighs and hangs up. "What I don't understand is why he's trying to take the fall in the first place. Evan has a solid story, video evidence of her assault, and a blood test to back it up. What does anyone gain if Kit confesses?"

"Isn't it obvious?" says Maisie as she begins yet another text. "He's trying to protect Evan."

"Protect her from *what?*" says Ben. "The clip of her and Jasper is already out there – millions of people have seen it. And if he's

308

worried about the full recording being released and the real story coming out, his confession won't fool the public, and it certainly won't protect anyone. Kit isn't even *in* the full video—"

"But if he takes the fall, she won't have to go on TV and tell the entire world about how that arsehole assaulted her," says Maisie pointedly. "Maybe *you* don't care how traumatic that might be for Evan, but I certainly do. And clearly so does Kit."

As they bicker, I stand perfectly still. If Maisie's right, then what would a confession mean for Kit? Would he be arrested? Thrown in prison? Or is the footage enough to prove that it was an accident, no matter who pushed Jasper into the drink cart and inadvertently sent him careening to his death?

But something else Ben says settles over me like a blanket and muffles their argument, which is growing increasingly heated in my silence. I turn his words over in my mind, studying them from multiple angles, and at last I refocus on the squabbling pair.

"We need a plan," I say, cutting off their debate. "Ben, I know it's a long shot, but could you try to find Kit's lawyer? Or even go to Scotland Yard to see if he's there? Please," I add when he opens his mouth to protest. "I have this meeting, and Maisie can't be seen wandering around in public."

"And I can?" says Ben, eyebrows arched, but his face falls under the weight of my stare. "Yes, all right. I'll make a few calls and see if I can figure out who represents his family."

"Thank you," I say, digging my fingertips into the cuffs of my sweatshirt. "When you track Kit down, can you have him call Maisie? I need to talk to him."

Ben releases an enormous sigh. "It's mad you don't have your own mobile," he says as he stands. "Why is that, anyway?"

"Because most of my boarding schools didn't allow them," I say. "And because my mom doesn't like talking on the phone, and I've never had anyone else to call."

He flinches at my bluntness. "I'll do my best to find him," he promises, and with that, he heads into the corridor, shoving his hands in his pockets as he goes.

As soon as the door closes behind him, I turn to my sister. "Did Kit ever talk to you about what happened the night Jasper died?"

"No," she says. "I mean – we all know he got you out of there, of course. But he isn't the sort to gossip. All of what I know is from you, the video and the papers."

I think back to the articles I've read that detail what the press claims went down that night. "Did you know that Kit never went into Jasper's bedroom?"

Maisie tilts her head. "He didn't?"

"No. I got out of there on my own. Kit found me in the hallway, but he never went inside," I say. "If he didn't tell you and Ben what happened, then how the hell does Ben know Kit isn't in the full video?"

She runs her fingers nervously through her styled waves. "I don't understand—"

"Just now," I press. "Ben said that even if the full video comes out, Kit isn't in it, so his confession won't protect anyone or—"

"*Oh.*" Comprehension dawns on her, and we stare at each other for a long moment. "But that would mean…"

"How else could he possibly know?" I say. "Unless you think Kit might have told Ben without telling you."

She hesitates. "No," she finally admits. "They were close at

Eton, when it was the three of them – Benny, Kit and Jasper – but after Liam…" She trails off and shakes her head. "Ben could just be guessing."

"Maybe," I allow. "But when you heard that Kit helped me get away from Jasper, *you* assumed he was in the room, right? And Ben knows the video was edited," I add. "The only way he could be absolutely sure about Kit is if he's seen the whole thing."

I'm not sure how strong my logic is, or if it even holds water, but Maisie bites her lower lip in thought. "Even if Benny *has* seen it, that doesn't mean he's done anything wrong."

"No," I agree. "But it does mean he's been lying through his teeth. And if he's lying about something as important as this, what else is he keeping from us?"

Maisie sucks in her cheeks and stares at her phone for a beat. "You don't think he has Jasper's laptop, do you?"

The fact that this has even occurred to her is enough to push all of my self-doubts aside. She knows Ben better than anyone. If she thinks there's a chance, then there's no question there might be.

I shrug. "Only one way to find out."

Tibby agrees to be our lookout only after I promise to take the blame if she's caught.

"His Majesty won't punish either of *you*," she says as we approach Ben's suite, completely visible to anyone else passing through the busy corridor. "I, however, will most definitely be fired."

"That's not going to happen, Tibby," I say as Maisie knocks on the door. "Just say I asked you to wait for him, all right? For news about Kit."

Tibby doesn't look convinced, but at that moment, Maisie pokes her head inside the apartment. "Benny?" she calls with all of the acting ability of a cheesy soap opera star. "Benny, are you in here?"

Silence. After several seconds, she waves for me to join her, and we slip into his sitting room and close the door behind us. As I look around, my blood is pumping so hard that I can feel my pulse.

Ben's suite is also much bigger than mine and decorated in blues and golds. A portrait of a man hangs above the fireplace, and I eye his impressive sideburns. "Relative?" I say, and Maisie barely glances up.

"Some great-great-great-uncle, I'm sure," she says. "Check the credenza. We might as well be thorough."

If that's Maisie's definition of *thorough*, then we're in trouble. While she searches the extensive bookcases on either side of the fireplace, I open the antique cabinet near the dining table, assuming that's what a credenza is. Inside are stacks of dishes and silverware, all neatly arranged and crammed alongside piles of even more books that Ben must have shoved in there when his shelves filled up. Paperback science fiction novels seem to be his drug of choice, and I'm vaguely intrigued that, considering how many books he owns, this has never come up in conversation.

Muffled footsteps in the hallway bring me back to the present, and Maisie and I both freeze as Tibby greets someone politely. Whoever it is keeps moving, however, and we both refocus on the task at hand.

While Maisie seems more concerned with searching the obvious spots – the bookcases, another cabinet, and even underneath the sofa – I start moving rugs to check for any sign of loose floorboards. Maisie stops, throw pillow in hand, and stares at me.

"What on earth are you doing?"

"What are *you* doing?" I counter. "Do you really think Ben would hide a key piece of evidence that places him at the scene of Jasper's death under a pillow? If he has it, it won't be in plain sight or anywhere a staff member could accidentally find it."

"Fair point," she allows, setting the pillow back on the couch and rearranging the tassels. "And in that case, I know where we should be looking."

Maisie heads straight for a door beside one of the bookcases. When she tries the knob, however, it doesn't budge.

"He's locked it," she says, astonished, as if this is an entirely new concept to her. "Why would he—"

"Why do you think?" I say, and I replace the rug before crossing the room to join her. "Hold on, I've got this."

My lockpicks are tucked into the hidden pocket of my jeans, and once I dig them out, I get to work. Between breaking into Mr Clark's classroom at St Edith's and Wiggs's office only days earlier, my confidence is at an all-time high.

Maisie watches me with wide eyes, her mouth hanging open. "Have you used those elsewhere in the castle?" she says, horrified. "Have you used those to break into *my* apartment?"

"Of course not," I say, ignoring her first question as I minutely adjust the pick while holding the lock taut with the tension wrench. The doorknob is old, and for a moment I'm afraid it might not be a pin tumbler lock. After thirty excruciating seconds, however, it opens, and I flash Maisie a grin. "But if I did, you'd never know."

She huffs, although there's also wary admiration in the way she looks at me. "You'll have to teach me," she says in an imperial voice that offers no choice in the matter, and I'm too pleased with myself to argue.

I follow her into Ben's matching blue-and-gold bedroom, complete with a huge canopy bed. The curtains are drawn, casting the room in ominous shadow, but Maisie doesn't seem bothered. Rather than search for a light, she pivots towards an imposing wardrobe and pulls the doors open.

"My mother doesn't like it when we eat sweets," she says, removing several pairs of shoes from the bottom and setting them aside. "Our nannies used to give them to us as treats behind her back, though – mostly because we were insufferable and those were the only things that would guarantee our good behaviour. Benny and I used to make a game of coming up with creative hiding places when we were in the nursery together. We'd stash them in the rocking horse or a stuffed toy with a loose seam – it was our version of hide-and-seek, I suppose."

As she speaks, she feels around the floor of the wardrobe, clearly looking for something. "I take it Ben usually won," I say, considering the throw pillow incident, but Maisie merely gives me a confused look and continues.

"We still hide sweets, even though we're both allowed them now – in moderation, of course," she says. "Benny, Kit and I were watching a movie a few nights before you arrived. I'd just finished my exams and was desperate for chocolate, so Benny raided one of his stashes. He's never explicitly told me about this spot, but I saw him kneeling next to the wardrobe and reaching inside, and I'm fairly sure he didn't notice – *aha!*"

She lifts the entire floor of the wardrobe, revealing a recessed compartment below. My mouth drops open. "Maisie, you're a genius."

"I know," she says, but even in the low light, I see her smirk. "Hold this for a moment while I turn on the torch."

"Are you going to light it on fire?" I say, kneeling down beside her and propping up the false floor. It's surprisingly heavy, and I can see how this would have made a convenient hiding spot for nefarious royals over the centuries.

Maisie gives me another strange look, but rather than fumble around for matches or a lighter, she pulls out her phone. With a few taps, bright light floods the bottom of the wardrobe, and we both fall silent.

The space is surprisingly clean, with only a hint of dust in the corners. A small tin box holds a handful of candy bars, and beside it sits a pile of upside-down Polaroids. More than a dozen dirty magazines haphazardly cover the rest of the compartment, and while Maisie cringes, I frown.

There's no laptop.

"Why does he bother with *magazines* when the internet exists?" says Maisie with a small shudder. "I suppose he must have other hiding spots. He did always like stuffing things into his mattress—"

"Wait. You're right," I say suddenly. "Why *does* he have all these magazines? They look like they're from twenty years ago."

She wrinkles her nose. "I've no idea, and frankly I'm not interested in whatever it is that tickles his fancy. Some secrets deserve a bit of privacy, you know – *what* are you doing?"

I pull a button-down shirt off a hanger and bury my hand inside, using it as a glove. "Look at how neatly stacked the Polaroids are," I say as I reach into the compartment. "Do you really think he'd leave the magazines so messed up? Unless…"

I push aside what I'm now sure is an intentional layer of media that no member of the royal household staff would ever try to organize, and Maisie gasps. "Is that—"

"Yeah," I say grimly as I unearth a laptop. Every cell in my body is buzzing with a combination of horror, excitement and dread, and still using the shirt as a barrier, I lift the screen.

The keyboard is covered in green and purple stickers that form an image of a galaxy.

"But – but how?" says Maisie in a choked voice as she peers into the compartment, moving the light of her phone around as if searching for some kind of explanation. "I don't understand. Why would he have it? Why wouldn't he have told me?"

"I don't know," I say as I turn on the laptop. I cross my fingers as the Welcome screen appears, but of course the log-in prompt quickly follows. "Damn. You don't see a sticky note with a password anywhere, do you?"

Although Maisie shakes her head, she gingerly reaches into the wardrobe and extracts a manila envelope that must have been beneath the laptop. "Aren't you supposed to be good with computers? Isn't that why you were expelled?"

"Breaking into school networks takes weeks of work, sometimes months, and I had to steal several passwords from teachers and administrators. Slow typers," I add at her baffled look. "All you have to do is follow their fingers. What's in the envelope?"

Maisie slowly unwinds the red string holding it together and peers inside. Though she doesn't remove anything, she turns ghostly pale, and for a moment she seems to stop breathing.

"What is it?" I say. But the magazines catch my eye again, and I make a face. "Do I even want to know?"

She shakes her head and hastily ties the envelope shut. "More dirty pictures," she says shakily. "Wait – I thought this was supposed to be Jasper's laptop."

"It is," I say. "It has the same stickers on the keyboard."

"But that's Benny's icon," she says, eyeing the small photo of a crooked crown. "He took it himself at a state dinner last year." I click around a bit, but there's no other user listed. Just Benny's icon. "Any chance you happen to know his password?"

"Of course I do," she says loftily. "He would never try to hide anything from me."

Despite Maisie's confidence, however, she stares at the screen for a long moment, and a bead of sweat trickles down the back of my neck. We don't exactly have an infinite amount of time – the meeting with Alexander and his advisers is starting soon, and more worryingly, there's no telling when Ben might reappear. But finally, with a strangely assertive crack of her knuckles, Maisie starts to type, her fingers flying across the keys.

Log-in failed.

She curses with such vehemence that I jump. "The little weasel changed his password."

"It's okay," I whisper, suddenly aware of Tibby's voice filtering

317

in from the hallway. "You have two more tries. Any more than that, and he might get an alert."

She grumbles to herself, but after another long moment of consideration, she starts typing again, slower this time. I follow her keystrokes: *threetothethrone*

"What the hell does that mean?" I say, and Maisie rolls her eyes.

"He's third in line to the throne," she points out. "Three people have to die before he's crowned."

"Charming," I say, and she hits Enter once more.

Log-in failed.

This time she swears so loudly that I'm sure Tibby and whoever she's talking to must hear. My heart pounds, and using the shirt again, I hastily spread out the magazines to cover the empty space. "We need to get out of here," I whisper as I replace the false floor. "Someone's outside—"

"You said I have one more try," insists Maisie.

"All right," I mutter, scooping up Ben's shoes and doing my best to arrange them neatly at the bottom of the wardrobe. No doubt he'll notice they've been moved, but if we're lucky, he'll blame the staff. Then again, depending on how often he checks his secret trove, we might have a matter of hours before he discovers the laptop is missing and –

"*Yes!*"

Maisie's shriek of delight makes me drop the last shoe, and it hits the floor with a dull thud. "What?" I gasp. "Did you—"

"I'm in," she says smugly, and she turns the laptop towards me. Sure enough, the desktop is visible, along with a picture of Ben inside the Buckingham Palace throne room. "The password's

318

kingbenedictthefirst. As if he has a chance of ever being crowned—"

Suddenly her phone buzzes, and we both look down at the screen.

It's Kit.

Chapter Thirty-three

As you've undoubtedly heard, given the constant bombardment of advertisements on every available form of media this past week, Evangeline Bright will make her official debut on BBC One this evening for an exclusive hour-long interview with Katharine O'Donnell.

This is her first appearance as a tangential member of the royal family, as well as the first public glimpse of her – if a drawing room in Windsor Castle counts as public – since Buckingham Palace admitted her existence over three weeks ago. And while we're all curious about what sort of questions the palace has agreed to – her paternity? Her mother's mental illness? – no one can ignore the real elephant in the room:

Will she finally admit to the murder of Jasper Cunningham? Tune in to BBC One at seven o'clock tonight to find out.

—*The Regal Record*, 30 June 2023

Fifteen minutes before the interview is supposed to begin, I stand in the middle of my sitting room as a make-up artist puts the finishing touches on my blush.

Everything about my appearance, from my loose waves to my natural-looking make-up to my pale pink dress, is designed to make me look as soft and innocent as possible. And while no one has directly said so, I know that this interview will determine how the public perceives me for the rest of my life and beyond. This is my trial by fire, and one wrong word – one wrong look or giggle or facial expression – and I'll be burned at the stake.

"You look stunning," says Louis, adjusting my lacy sleeves. "Angelic, even."

"That's the idea, isn't it?" says Tibby. She studies me with a critical eye, clearly trying to find any flaw the public and the media might use against me. "I suppose you'll do. Remember to keep your legs crossed at the ankle, not at the knee."

"I know," I promise. "I'll be careful."

The past few days have been a whirlwind of preparations. Doyle has taken perverse delight in pointing out all the ways I'm too American, from my posture to how I speak to the way I hold my hands in my lap, and he's spared no effort to correct each tiny issue. Any time not devoted to my appearance has been dedicated to the long list of questions the palace approved, and my head is spinning with the exact answers I'm supposed to give. It's all choreographed, from the way I greet Katharine O'Donnell to when and how I smile, or frown, or look pensive, or – if I can manage it – cry. I may be the one getting interviewed, but none of it's really me.

"Who else is going to be in the room?" I say as Louis makes one last adjustment to the dainty silver cross that hangs from my neck – supposedly a token of good luck from Maisie's personal collection, but it's as much a prop as everything else about me tonight. The only thing that's mine is the platinum bracelet around my wrist, though even with the tiny tiara dangling beside the music note, I still secretly think of it as Prisha's. Considering what I'm about to do, however, I need that reminder with me – a reminder of what I'm capable of. A reminder that not everyone outside of Windsor hates me. A reminder that no matter what I have to lose, sometimes the risk is worth it.

"I imagine there will be some production staff milling about, but the BBC has assured us that their presence will be minimal," says Louis. "And Jenkins and His Majesty will meet you in the green drawing room before the interview begins."

My stomach churns, threatening to make the few bites I had for dinner reappear. "They're going to watch?"

"They want to support you, that's all," he says kindly, and he holds out his elbow. "Would you like me to escort you?"

I shake my head. "I mean, yes," I add hastily. "But I've sort of already asked someone."

As if on cue, a knock sounds from the hallway, and Tibby opens the door. Silence settles over the room as a handsome boy in a button-down shirt and pressed trousers steps inside, and we lock eyes.

Ben.

"Wow," he breathes. "You look stunning."

I twirl for him in my kitten heels. "Think the country will like me?"

"They'll love you," he says, and he offers me his arm. "Ready?"

"No." But I take it anyway, and I flash Louis and Tibby a grateful smile before stepping into the corridor with the asshole who tried to frame me for murder.

We walk along in silence for several yards before Ben clears his throat. "How are you feeling?"

"Nervous," I say truthfully. "I feel like I'm heading to my own execution."

"Katharine O'Donnell is sympathetic to the family, and I suspect they've chosen her because she's spoken about being sexually assaulted in the past," says Ben. This is new information, and I turn it over in my mind before he adds, "Do you know what you're going to say?"

"Doyle and Yara had me memorize about a hundred canned statements they wrote for me," I say. "At this point, they might as well give the interview themselves."

Ben chuckles. "They would if they could, I'm sure," he says, and he hesitates before adding, "What did they decide to do about the Jasper situation?"

I shrug with as much nonchalance as I can muster. "Tell the truth, mostly. It's our best defence, after all." I glance at him, taking in his profile until he notices and meets my eye. "This must be hard for you."

"Hard for me?" He seems taken aback, and I nod.

"Given how close you and Jasper were, I mean. I've never lost a friend before. Throw in all the drama of the investigation, and – well, I can't imagine how much you must be hurting."

Ben looks oddly uncomfortable, and he refocuses on the long stretch of hallway ahead of us. I'm moving slowly, teetering in my low heels, and he doesn't urge me into a quicker pace. "Our fathers are friends. *Were* friends," he corrects himself. "I suppose they're not exactly bosom buddies now, are they? And Jasper, Kit and I ran in the same circles at Eton. But Jasper was an arse – even beyond what he did to you – and I would hardly call us friends, especially at the end."

I consider that. I don't know what to believe any more, but one thing I *am* sure of is that the first time Jasper and I met, he knew exactly who I was and where to find me. "I wonder if the full video will ever surface," I say quietly. "I hate that we might spend the rest of our lives waiting for the other shoe to drop. Whoever has it could blackmail Maisie, especially once she's queen."

"I can't imagine it'll ever see the light of day," he says in what I think is supposed to be a soothing voice. "If whoever has it wanted to target Maisie, they would have from the start. Clearly they've decided to target you instead."

"Why do you think that is?" I say as we make our way around the corner towards the drawing rooms. "Because I haven't been able to figure it out."

He tilts his head. "I've no idea. Maybe they don't like the thought of an outsider in the royal family, or an American. Maybe they wanted to humiliate you, and it all got out of hand."

"Framing me for murder counts as getting out of hand?" I say wryly. "It's not like I'll ever be queen, and I was planning on leaving as soon as I turned eighteen anyway."

"*Was* planning?" he says. "Have you changed your mind, then?"

I nod. "I like it here. I like having people who at least pretend to care. It's nice."

In my peripheral vision, I see his expression sour for a split second before his mask of concern returns. "What happens if the investigation goes to trial? Are you willing to risk imprisonment?"

"I'll take my chances," I say. "Right now I'm way more worried about Kit. You still haven't heard from him?"

Ben shakes his head. "I wish Scotland Yard would tell us if he's confessed. You shouldn't have to go through with this circus if it'll directly contradict his statement. The public has no right to demand that you put your trauma on display for their entertainment."

"I know. But if there's even a chance he didn't go to the police after all…" I trail off for a moment. "This way, I can protect them both."

Ben sighs. "I'm sorry, Evan, truly. It's a noble thing he's doing, but no doubt it's created any number of complications."

"It really has," I say softly, and I teeter for a few more steps. We're almost to the white drawing room now. "Can I ask you a question?"

"Of course," he says. "Anything."

"How did you know Kit wasn't in the full video?"

He looks at me, a spark of wariness in his eyes now. "What do you mean?"

"When we first found out that Kit went to his lawyer, you said that he wasn't even in the full video. How did you know?"

"I – I've no idea," says Ben, faltering. "I assumed, I suppose. We've no way of being certain, have we?"

"Guess not," I say. "The only way we'd know for sure is if we'd seen the whole thing."

"And I certainly haven't," he assures me. "Perhaps Scotland Yard will eventually be able to trace where the clip came from."

"Maybe." We step over the threshold into the magnificent white-and-gold drawing room. I stop and crane my neck, gazing at the paintings that decorate the walls. "Can I ask you another question?"

"Of course," he says again, though this time he doesn't follow up with *anything*.

"Did you and Jasper plan it together from the start?" I say. "Inviting me to the party. Spiking my drink. Recording the assault and releasing the video. Or was it all his idea, and you just got caught up in it?"

He gapes at me. "What?"

"Obviously you got lucky, accidentally recording his death – you must have been *thrilled*, especially when you realized you could make it look like I was the one who did it. But what were you even going to do with the video before he died? Blackmail me? Blackmail Alexander? Hope I didn't tell anyone what Jasper did to me and, once all the physical evidence was gone, release it and try to shame me into leaving the country?"

Ben drops my arm and turns towards me. "Evan, I never—"

"There's a lot about this I haven't figured out," I say, ignoring him. "And I can't even begin to guess your motives. But what I haven't understood from the start is why anyone at that party would risk getting caught in Jasper's bedroom minutes after his death just to steal a laptop."

"I—" Ben flexes his fingers like he wants to reach out for me. Or wrap his hands around my neck. "Evan—"

"The rewards had to outweigh the risks," I interrupt, not interested in his denials. "Which means if that laptop found its way to the police, you would have been implicated somehow."

"I didn't steal the laptop," he insists. "You have to believe me—"

"No, you didn't steal it," I agree. "It was always yours. The recording was under your account, and if the police found it –

well, that wouldn't have looked all that great. Maisie knows your secret hiding spots, by the way," I add casually. "And your passwords. King Benedict the First? Really?"

He clenches his jaw, and his expression goes from shock to twisted fury in seconds. "You had no right to break into my bedroom—"

"*You* had no right to record Jasper assaulting me," I snarl. "Or to release it to the public. Or to frame me for murder. I've seen the full video, Ben. It doesn't stop recording until *you* show up two minutes after Jasper dies. You don't even look upset. You look straight into the camera and—"

"You rotten *bitch*."

He lunges for me, but I'm expecting this, and I'm not nearly as inept in my low heels as I've made him believe. I dodge out of his path and sprint towards the tall double doors that lead into the green drawing room, but to my relief, they're already opening.

"Keep your bloody hands off my daughter."

Alexander strides forward, placing himself between me and a purple-faced Ben. My father may not be a physically intimidating man, but he is the King, and for the first time in my life, I'm enormously grateful for that fact.

Ben stumbles to a stop, his eyes huge. "Your – Your Majesty," he stammers. "I can explain—"

"Can you?" says Alexander drily, and two royal protection officers join us, neither looking especially pleased. "Does your explanation include what you were doing in possession of the recording of Jasper Cunningham assaulting my daughter?"

All the blood drains from Ben's purple face, giving him an

unappealing mottled appearance. "There – there's been a misunderstanding, sir—"

"Then I'm sure you're eager to sort it out," says Alexander, and through the other doors – the ones Ben and I just came through – enters Detective Farrows. She's with a slightly stooped Wiggs, who's carrying his briefcase, and another protection officer dressed in a black suit. Ben looks back and forth between us all, panicked.

"Your Royal Highness," says Farrows, and to my satisfaction, she doesn't bother curtsying to Ben. "My name is Detective Erika Farrows, and I'm leading the investigation into Jasper Cunningham's death. Would you mind joining me and my colleagues to answer a few questions?"

Ben's mouth drops open. "I – I didn't kill him. I didn't do anything wrong. He's the one who drugged Evan, and Maisie – Maisie's the one who pushed him. She's the one who killed him, not me—"

"Maisie was with me in the Range Rover," I say. "She rode with us back to Windsor to make sure I was okay."

"That – that's a lie," he says roughly. "Maisie pushed him – you can see it in the video—"

"You can ask Kit," I say. "Or our driver. Or half the people at the party. They all saw us leave together."

"You're a liar – you're a lying bitch," he sputters. "I can prove it. The laptop – it's on the laptop—"

"Which is precisely what I'd like to speak with you about," says Farrows, and the protection officer takes Ben by the arm.

It's not an arrest – Alexander is standing right in front of us, after all – but judging by the tightness of the guard's grip, Ben won't be having a good time. "My team is waiting at Scotland Yard. I hope you didn't have anything planned for this evening, Your Royal Highness."

"It wasn't me!" he wails. "It was Maisie, I swear. Your Majesty – Uncle Alexander, *please*."

Alexander blinks. "You expect me to support your preposterous claim that my daughter was involved in that boy's death?" He shakes his head and focuses on Wiggs instead. "Please keep me updated. I'll make sure the Duke is informed."

Wiggs bows his head. "Of course, Your Majesty. I'll check in before midnight, if I can."

Ben grows oddly mute at that, and at first, as Farrows starts to lead him away, I think he's going to go quietly. But after only a step or two, he whirls back towards me, his arm still in the guard's grip.

"*You*," he snarls, and instantly Alexander's protection officers are between us, but I can still see the rage in Ben's eyes. "I'm going to destroy you. Once I've finished, everyone in the world will know what a lying, rotten, evil crazy bitch you are. And Maisie—"

"Maisie's your future queen," I say. "And I'd be *really* careful about what I say right now, if I were you."

"Maisie has secrets, too." Ben looks at Alexander now, a twisted sneer on his lips. "And I know *all* of them."

With his voice still ringing off the gilded ceiling, Farrows and the protection officers usher him away, leaving Alexander and me standing on our own in the doorway between the white and green drawing rooms. I hold my breath until their footsteps have faded, and only then do I exhale.

"So…he snapped," I say, hoping some dry humour will distract from the slight shake of my hands. Alexander doesn't look fooled, however, and he gently touches my shoulder.

"Are you all right?" he says, his face creased with concern.

I nod.

"Could've been worse. I'm glad you were standing on the other side of the door," I admit. "Did you get everything?"

"Jenkins is reviewing the audio recording now," he says. "But really, are you okay?"

I think about this – really think about it for the space of several heartbeats. "I wish we knew why he did it," I admit. "What's the point? If he's after the crown, I'm definitely not standing in his way, so there's no reason to try to chase me out of the country. If it was blackmail, I have nothing to give him, and what could you possibly offer that would make all of this worth it?"

Alexander's face grows haggard, and though I might be imagining the flicker of unease in his eyes, he glances away from me for a split second. "I've no idea," he says. "Perhaps he'll admit it during interrogation, but if not, then I suppose some mysteries will always remain unsolved." He pulls me into a gentle hug. "Thank you for trusting me, Evie. I'm so sorry for everything he's put you through."

I wrap my arms around my father, careful not to mess up my hair or make-up. "I'm just glad we found the full video before he posted it somewhere," I mumble.

"Rather ingenious of both you and your sister," says Alexander with a chuckle. "You two make quite a team. You're sure he didn't create a backup copy?"

I hesitate. "It's possible – he could've used an external drive, but there's no evidence he backed it up digitally or sent it to anyone. And security will grab his phone, right?"

Alexander nods. "His mobile will be destroyed before your interview is over," he assures me, and he glances into the green drawing room. "Speaking of, I believe it's time."

Reluctantly I let go of him, and he offers me his elbow. I grin and take it. "I don't know what it is about this dress, but everyone seems to think I can't walk in it on my own."

"We English are nothing if not masters of chivalry," he says as we step inside. "Though I must admit, it certainly can't hurt to make sure the BBC knows you have my full support. Do you feel comfortable with the questions?"

"Doyle and Yara and I went over them about a million times, and I can recite the answers in my sleep. But some of the things I'm supposed to say…" I frown. "They don't feel like me."

Alexander places his hand over mine, the heat of his palm comforting. "I'd recommend you keep the spirit of the approved script in mind," he says, "but I would also encourage you to be yourself. This is your grand introduction, after all, and if their lines don't feel right, then say something that does."

"That's a surefire way to make headlines tomorrow," I say, and he laughs.

"You'll be making headlines one way or the other for the rest of your life, Evie. It might as well be on your terms."

We reach the doors to the crimson drawing room, and two footmen open them for us. Beyond the archway, I see that the velvet curtains have been closed, leaving most of the room in darkness, but there are two pools of bright spotlights above a pair of scarlet and gold love seats. A black-haired woman wearing a tailored grey dress stands beside a man with thinning red hair and square glasses, and they both turn towards us expectantly.

"Ready?" whispers Alexander, squeezing my fingers, and I nod.

"Ready," I say, and we enter the room together.

Chapter Thirty-four

KATHARINE O'DONNELL: Evangeline, you've had quite the month, haven't you?

EVANGELINE BRIGHT: That's one way to put it. It's definitely been eventful.

KOD: We all know what the press has been saying, of course, but we've never before had the chance to hear your story straight from you. Have you always known who your father is?

EB: I found out when I was eleven, right before my grandmother died.

KOD: And how did it feel, discovering you're a princess?

EB: That's a pretty romanticized way of looking at it. In truth, I'm not a princess. It's a huge job that requires a lifetime of training and dedication, and I'm in awe of everything Mary does. But finding out my father is an actual king…[low whistle] It felt like I was in some kind of teen rom-com where I was about to get a makeover, a cute boyfriend, and a tiara, all while learning a deep but painfully obvious truth about myself.

KOD: [laughter] And how was your relationship with His Majesty before you arrived in England?

EB: Distant. There's no sugar-coating that. He was around when I was young, but I have no memories of him then. And while he made sure I got into all of the best schools and had every opportunity to better myself, he and I never actually had a conversation until I came to the UK.

KOD: Never? That must have been difficult for you.

EB: It was difficult for both of us.

KOD: And how has life changed since you arrived?

EB: In every possible way, I suppose. But nothing compares to meeting my father and his family.

KOD: Do you and Princess Mary get on well?

EB: [laughter] I won't lie – it was dicey at first, but of course it would be for anyone. After my paternity was leaked to the press, though, she was there for me, and she's been my rock throughout this entire experience. I'd say she's the sister I've never had, but – well, she's the sister I've always had and never got to know until now.

KOD: Was she with you the night Jasper Cunningham died?

EB: [pause] Yes. We both went to that party.

KOD: It must be a very painful memory for you, and I'm sorry to ask, but given the intense scrutiny and misinformation out there about the details of that night, would you be comfortable walking me through what really happened?

EB: [longer pause] I don't want to sound rude, because I know it's not your fault, but...I'm not comfortable with any of this. What happened to me was – a violation, and anyone else would have been given privacy and space to heal. But the tabloid press has spent weeks twisting unsubstantiated rumours about me into supposed facts, and they've given me no choice but to relive one of the worst nights of my life in a very public way in order to set the record straight.

KOD: I'm very sorry, Evangeline. If you'd rather not talk about it, you don't have to.

EB: I do, though. That's the thing – wasn't it Winston Churchill who said that a lie gets halfway around the world before the truth has a chance to get its pants on?

KOD: Yes, it was.

EB: I know some people have already made up their minds about me and what happened that night, but this is the only chance I'll have to tell the truth.

KOD: Take your time, then. And you can stop whenever you'd like.

EB: Thank you. [pause] The party happened maybe a week after the news that I'm His Majesty's biological daughter was leaked to the press, and at first I didn't feel comfortable with the idea of going. But I'd met Jasper a couple of times already, and he was...really kind to me, or at least he seemed to be.

KOD: Did you fancy him?

EB: I – yeah, I guess I did. I attended all-girls boarding schools from the age of eleven on, so I haven't really had any experience with boys. Or – men. And Jasper flirted with me a lot. So when he personally invited me, I thought...it couldn't hurt, right? Especially if my sister and her cousins would be there.

KOD: Prince Benedict and the Queen's nephew, Christopher Abbott-Montgomery, Earl of Clarence, yes?

EB: Right. I thought I'd be safe.

KOD: Did Jasper greet you when you arrived at the party?

EB: Yes. He was waiting for me, and he introduced me to a bunch of people. It was crowded and hot, and he offered to get me a drink, and I accepted. He brought me water.

KOD: Earlier today, Scotland Yard released the results of a blood test revealing that there was GHB – commonly known as a date rape drug – in your system that night. Do you believe Jasper was the one to slip it into your drink?

EB: I'm positive. Scotland Yard also confirmed that our fingerprints were the only ones on the glass, and Jasper knew what he was doing. After a couple of partygoers started asking me intrusive questions and calling me names, he told me to meet him upstairs in his bedroom while he removed them from the party.

KOD: His bedroom?

EB: I didn't know it was his bedroom when I went up. I just wanted a break from all of those questions and insults, you know? And once I got there – I mean, like I said, I don't really have any experience with boys. I knew it was maybe a little strange, but...no one had ever taught me how to protect myself in those situations, or what red flags to look out for.

KOD: And when he joined you, what happened?

EB: We talked a bit, and he invited me to sit next to him on the edge of the bed. By then I was woozy, so – I accepted.

KOD: You don't need to describe the rest.

EB: I know I don't, but...a lot of people have seen the clip that was released online, so it's no secret. And I need to make sure everyone knows what really happened, not just – what they think they saw. [long pause] That video came from a laptop he'd positioned on his desk to film us. To film him assaulting me. It was completely premeditated. I had no idea the laptop was recording, and I didn't consent to anything Jasper did to me. I was numb for most of it and could barely move. I had to struggle to stay conscious, and once I figured out what he was trying to – to do to me, I told him no and did my best to push him away. I didn't want to be with him or – to sleep with him, but...he didn't listen.

KOD: I'm so very sorry that happened to you, Evangeline.

EB: Me too.

KOD: Why do you believe Jasper decided to record the sexual assault?

EB: I have no idea. Blackmail, I guess. Or maybe he was looking for a story to make him infamous. I'm sure he had plans. I just don't know what they were.

KOD: If you're comfortable speaking about it...may I ask how you got away?

EB: I don't really remember much. I kneed him in the groin, I know that. And I tried to run, like you see in the recording. Most of it's a blur, though. I just – I just remember being so scared of what he'd do to me if I stayed. You hear about those things happening in movies or to other people, and I never thought it'd be me. I just...I knew I had to try to get away while I still could.

KOD: And you did. You did an admirable job.

EB: I got lucky. Not everyone does, and that's not their fault.

KOD: Yes, of course. In the video, we see him follow you into what I presume is the doorway, which isn't visible from that angle.

EB: I was terrified. Jasper was so much bigger and stronger than me, and I knew he wouldn't have any problem dragging me back into that room. I was already on the verge of passing out, and if he caught me...

KOD: He did grab you, though, didn't he?

EB: [long pause] Yeah, he did. I remember that part.

And – I pushed him away. He stumbled – he was drinking hard liquor earlier, and I wouldn't be surprised if he'd started before I arrived. I don't know what happened next, though. I heard a crash, but I didn't look back.

KOD: According to the police report, it was Lord Clarence who found you, wasn't it?

EB: Yeah, at the top of the stairs. He got me out of there, and Maisie – my sister joined us on the ride back to Windsor Castle. Without them, I don't know what would've happened to me.

KOD: I think I speak for the whole country when I say how relieved I am that you're all right.

EB: [pause] Thanks. I'm not yet, but…I will be.

—Excerpt from the transcript of Katharine O'Donnell's interview with Evangeline Bright, 30 June 2023

On the morning of my eighteenth birthday, I wake to the sound of my laptop ringing.

At first I think I'm dreaming, but the noise grows more and more insistent, and finally I grope around for my computer. The curtains are still drawn, though a few thin beams of light manage to sneak past the heavy fabric, and I use them to locate my laptop underneath a pillow.

"Evie!" My mom's face fills the screen as I accept the call. "Did I wake you up?"

"Mom?" I rub the sleep from my eyes and try to tame my wild hair. "What are you doing? It's the middle of the night in Virginia."

She waves her hand dismissively. "I wanted to be the first to wish you a happy birthday. Have you opened your present yet?"

I sit up. With all that's happened over the past few days, I completely forgot about the wrapped canvas my mother gave me. "Not yet," I admit. "I think Alexander still has it."

"Oh. Well, there's plenty of time for that later," she says, but even though I expect her to be disappointed, she's smiling widely. "Why don't you go into your sitting room, sweetie? I can barely see you."

There's nothing subtle about that prod, but I'm too groggy to second-guess it, and I take her at face value as I gather up my laptop and pad into the other room. "Have you slept at all yet?" I say. "You know how important it is to keep a regular sleep sched—"

I stop mid-sentence, and my mouth hangs open. My sitting room is filled with the same gilded antique furniture as before, but instead of portraits of people I don't know and landscapes of places I've never been, every single painting has been replaced with vibrant abstracts.

My mother's vibrant abstracts.

"Mom…" I move to the middle of the room and turn around slowly, taking in each piece of art. Some I recognize from our VidChat sessions, and others are familiar because of the locations they depict. A few are completely new to me, but I can tell they're recent, and my heart swells at the thought of how long she must have worked on them.

And there, hanging above the mantel in pride of place, is the painting she showed me the day I arrived in England. Blues and greens with dots of pinks and violets scattered across the canvas – my grandmother's garden.

"Do you like them?" says my mom eagerly, leaning in so close to the camera that I can't see her forehead. "I wish I could be there with you, but Alex and I thought this might be the next best thing."

"I wish you were here, too," I say thickly, not even remotely embarrassed about how choked up I am. "And I love every single one."

"I thought of you while painting them," she says, echoing what she told me in Virginia. "I always think of you."

"Thank you, Mom," I say, wiping my wet cheeks. "This is the best gift I've ever gotten."

Her face glows with delight. "Well, you're the best gift I've ever gotten," she says. "Happy birthday, Evie. I'm so proud of you."

We talk for over an hour, and I ask her about each painting in turn. She tells me what inspired her, and to my surprise, they're all memories of me. The tree in her backyard that she and Alexander planted when I was born. The park we played in when I was a toddler. Her neighbour's flowers, which I used to steal and tuck into my braid. I have no memory of any of it, but her words paint mental images so vivid that by the end, they all feel real to me.

Eventually she can no longer keep her eyes open, and we say our goodbyes. Feeling lighter than I have in ages, I head to the bathroom for a long, hot shower, determined to make the most of my morning off. Tibby isn't set to arrive until after lunch, and I have several glorious hours all to myself.

But when I enter my sitting room thirty minutes later, novel in hand, Maisie is perched on my sofa, her nose buried in her phone. Though it's still early, she's wearing a baby pink sundress and a glittering headband that looks suspiciously like a diadem, and her hair and make-up are perfect.

"Good morning," she says cheerfully without bothering to look up. "Happy birthday to us."

"Happy birthday to us," I repeat, taken aback. "How long have you been here?"

"Long enough to realize how horribly uncomfortable this sofa is," she says, climbing to her feet and glaring reproachfully at the offending furniture. "We were due in the breakfast room ten minutes ago, and Mummy hates it when I'm late."

"We're having breakfast with Helene?" I say, but Maisie doesn't seem to register my alarm. She hooks her arm in mine, and I barely have time to set my book down before she whisks me into the hallway.

The breakfast room is tucked away in the sharp corner of the main corridor, across from the private royal apartments. It's much cosier than the glittering formal dining room, and Alexander and Helene sit at opposite ends of a table that could comfortably seat ten. He's wearing a suit, and she's in a blue dress similar to Maisie's, and I'm suddenly painfully aware of the fact that I'm barefoot and wearing an oversized Reignwolf T-shirt with fashionably ripped leggings. Not exactly the kind of attire one's supposed to wear while dining with the royal family.

"Happy birthday, Evan," says Alexander, and he stands,

catching me in a warm hug and kissing the top of my head. Out of the corner of my eye, I see Helene's mouth pucker like she's tasted something sour, but she doesn't speak. "Did your mother call?"

I nod. "Thank you – the paintings are perfect."

"Don't thank me. It was her idea," he says with a chuckle as he lets me go. "So, girls, how does it feel, finally being eighteen?"

"About the same as seventeen," says Maisie. "Except now you can't give me a curfew."

"Still my castle, still my rules," says Alexander, but he's chuckling, and there's a certain sparkle to him that I've never seen before. Maybe it's because this is the first time he, Maisie and I have hung out and not been at each other's throats. Or maybe he's always like this around his family.

Breakfast is a buffet of what I assume are all of Maisie's favourite foods, but when I spot a platter of chocolate chip pancakes with strawberries and whipped cream, I stop short. "Wait – those are exactly like the pancakes my grandma used to make me when I was a kid."

"They're also the pancakes your mother used to make you," says Alexander beside me. "And me, when I had the chance to visit."

"They're not bad," says Maisie from the table, a few bites already missing from her stack. "A bit American for my taste, but one could do worse."

I'm oddly touched, and while I take a little of everything, I fill a separate plate with pancakes, ignoring Helene's mildly disapproving look. I keep bracing myself for one of her acerbic comments, but to her credit, she seems determined to keep things civil.

"We watched your interview last night," she says as she daintily cuts into a poached egg. "You handled yourself very well, Evangeline."

"I can't believe she asked you all of those awful questions," says Maisie, shaking her strawberry-blond waves in disgust. "I thought Katharine O'Donnell would have some bloody compassion, not make you *relive* it. You didn't owe her answers. You didn't owe her any of it."

"I know," I say, my fork hovering over my pancakes. "It was my choice."

Maisie scowls, stabbing a sausage with her fork. "Still, it's not fair," she grumbles. "But at least Benedict won't be causing any more problems for a while. That reserve in Kenya doesn't have Wi-Fi, does it, Daddy?"

"It does not," says Alexander carefully. "And Nicholas and I have tentatively agreed on a plan that will keep him there for the foreseeable future."

"Good," says Maisie. "I hope he's eaten by a lion."

I snort into my tea, and though it might be my imagination, I think I see Alexander bite back a smirk before he busies himself with a scone.

"The headlines today are very favourable," says Helene with aggressive politeness. "It remains to be seen if the public will be swayed by Evangeline's interview, but for now, we have the press on our side."

"What about the *Daily Sun*?" I say, almost too afraid to ask. "Is Robert Cunningham still out for my blood?"

Alexander clears his throat. "I expect he'll never completely let it go," he says. "But for now, the real story of what his son did

344

has left him…*somewhat subdued.*"

I don't know what somewhat subdued means, and I'm not sure I want to. Instead of asking, I nod and take a bite of my pancakes, relieved that it wasn't all for nothing. Even if Ben did make a copy of the full video, and even if he does release it eventually, now that I've confessed – sort of – Maisie will always have some form of plausible deniability.

The rest of breakfast is oddly enjoyable, with easy conversation flowing between the three of us, and Helene occasionally chiming in with pleasantly neutral remarks. Maisie, who's scheduled a handful of charity appearances before her birthday ball, eventually excuses herself, and Helene hastily follows, leaving Alexander and me alone. He gazes out the wide windows that overlook the courtyard, and I toy with my napkin, trying not to think about how full of pancakes I am.

"Are you excited for tonight?" he says, and I raise an eyebrow.

"Does that mean I'm officially invited? Tibby scoffs every time I ask her."

"Of course you're invited," he says, taken aback. "It's your birthday ball, too."

Both my eyebrows shoot up now. "Does Maisie know that?"

"She was the one who suggested a joint event," he says, and he studies me for a long moment. I'm not sure what he sees that makes him so interested – the dark circles under my eyes from all the tossing and turning I did last night, or the freshly dried hair I barely brushed before Maisie dragged me out of my suite. Maybe my untamed eyebrows or the zit that's threatening to erupt on my chin.

I fidget in my seat, trying not to look as uncomfortable as

345

I feel, and he smiles apologetically and reaches out to cover my hand with his.

"I'm sorry," he says. "You look so much like your mother, that's all, and it never ceases to astonish me. I have a gift for you."

"A gift?" I say, secretly pleased at the comparison to my mom. I know we look alike, but hearing him say it feels special somehow. "What kind of gift?"

"One that I hope will make you feel more at home here, with me and the rest of our family."

At that moment, Jenkins steps into the dining room carrying a sizable velvet box. It's much bigger than any piece of jewellery I can think of, and as he sets it down on the table, it looks surprisingly heavy.

"I hope you'll forgive me for not wrapping it," continues Alexander. "It isn't a gift one ought to rip open."

"It's not?" I say suspiciously, eyeing the box. "What's in it?"

Without a word, he undoes the gold latch and slowly opens the lid, revealing a sparkling diamond tiara.

For the second time that morning, my mouth drops open. "You're *joking*."

"Queen Florence, my grandmother, had it made in the seventies," he says. "It was her favourite for years. She knew about you," he adds with a faint smile. "While my mother was busy having a coronary, Florence very much wanted to meet you. She died before she had the chance, I'm afraid, but in her will, she specifically left this to you."

"She did?" Somehow this is more shocking than the sight of the glittering tiara, with its delicate points and swirls and the smooth pearls dotted among the countless diamonds. It's beautiful, and I can't take my eyes off it. "What's it called?"

"The Queen Florence tiara," he says. "Simple, but it's yours now."

He lifts it out of its velvet case, and I hastily lean back. "Wait – my etiquette instructor told me that tiaras aren't supposed to be worn before your wedding day," I say. "I know Maisie wears them sometimes, but she's the heir to the throne."

Jenkins chuckles. "I told you she has a knack for learning the rules, sir, if only to figure out a clever way to break them."

Alexander grins widely, and he suddenly looks a decade younger. "You did warn me," he says, shaking his head with amusement. "And yes, Evan, in most cases, that's quite true. However, the family has always made an exception for the daughters of the monarch. Maisie will be wearing the Girls of Great Britain and Ireland tiara tonight, and it'll set tongues wagging if your head is bare. I won't have anyone thinking you aren't Maisie's equal in my eyes, because you are. You always have been."

This time I hold still as he gently sets the tiara on my head. It's heavier than I expect, but still light enough that I think it won't cause any headaches. Jenkins produces a hand mirror seemingly from thin air, and with more trepidation than I want to admit, I look at my reflection.

The dark circles under my eyes, the messy hair, the incoming zit – it all fades away in the splendour of the gorgeous tiara. I stare at myself for longer than I probably should, gently moving my head to test the jewels' weight. "Helene is going to hate this," I say, mostly to myself.

"Helene's opinion no longer matters," says Alexander. "As of tomorrow, she and I will be quietly separating."

I snap around so quickly that the tiara nearly falls off. "*What?*"

"I'll continue to divide my time between Buckingham and Windsor," says Alexander, gently adjusting my headpiece, "while Helene will move into one of the apartments in Kensington Palace. With Nicholas, I expect."

I stare at him. "You *knew?*"

"I've known for a very long time," he says. "I had no right to be upset or angry, of course, after I carried on with your mother, and I certainly don't hold it against Helene. Our marriage never turned into the love story both of us had hoped for, and we decided years ago to separate when Maisie turned eighteen. What surprises me," he adds, "is that *you* somehow found out about her and Nicholas in less than a month."

"It was an accident," I say, my face growing hot. "I didn't want to keep anything from you, I swear, but – I didn't know how to tell you."

"Understandable," he says kindly. "Helene did express her gratitude that you were willing to keep her secret, though I won't pretend she was thrilled you used it as leverage to protect your mother."

My heart sinks. "She told you about that, too?"

"I believe she feared you would do so first." He touches my cheek. "I am very, very sorry for all the trouble this family has caused you. But tonight is a fresh start, and I hope you'll make the most of it, Evie."

I glance into the mirror one more time, and when I see the person I never thought I could be – the person I never *dreamed* I could be – I know I won't waste it.

Chapter Thirty-five

Princess Mary will be celebrating her eighteenth birthday with a ball tonight at Buckingham Palace.

According to royal insiders, no fewer than two hundred of the princess's closest friends are expected to attend, along with members of the extended royal family. What isn't known, however, is if Princess Mary's half-sister, Evangeline Bright, who shares a birthday with the heir to the throne, will make an appearance at the glitzy affair.

Members of the public have jumped to Ms Bright's defence after her tell-all interview with Katharine O'Donnell aired on BBC One last night, during which Evangeline discussed her childhood and the fateful evening Jasper Cunningham fell to his death. #VengeanceforEvangeline has trended worldwide on Twitter and other platforms, and eagle-eyed viewers have spent the day dissecting the infamous clip of Cunningham's death and his alleged sexual assault of Ms Bright in support of her story.

During Princess Mary's annual birthday appearance at Great Ormond Street Hospital for Children in London, she reportedly spoke to several of the patients about how excited she is to have a sister.

"She was going on and on about how proud she was of Evangeline," says Kelly Altman, the mother of sixteen-year-old Jana Altman, who's battling leukaemia. "Most of the younger children aren't aware of what's going on, of course, but the older ones were keen to hear how Evangeline is doing, and Princess Mary was all too happy to talk about how close they are."

Though press isn't allowed inside the birthday gala tonight, pictures from the event are expected to be released on the royal family's social media accounts later this evening.

—The Daily Sun, 1 July 2023

The clock strikes seven thirty, and Maisie is still missing.

"Where *is* she?" I say, anxiously watching the door as I toy with the tiny crystals sewn into the bodice of my midnight-blue gown. I desperately want to pace across the unfamiliar drawing room in Buckingham Palace, but my heels are too high to waste a step. And I'm genuinely afraid that if I make one wrong move, the tiara sewn into my updo will come loose and slide off in front of all my half-sister's guests.

"Her private secretary texted me five minutes ago," says Tibby from the other end of the antique sofa we're sharing, her nose yet again buried in her phone. "They're on their way. Oh, *wow* – look at these."

Tibby shoves her phone in my face, and it takes me a moment to recognize myself in the poorly lit picture she's pulled up. I don't look like me – not after hours of styling and make-up – but the sleeves of my dress are visible through the rain-splattered window of the Range Rover, and diamonds in my tiara sparkle in the low light.

"I didn't know photographers could see us in the car," I say as another spike of anxiety shoots through me. "I should have smiled."

"No, these are brilliant," says Tibby, pulling her phone back and scrolling more. "People are loving it. No one's identified the tiara yet, but everyone's thrilled you're wearing one."

"Everyone?" I say disbelievingly, and she sniffs. "Everyone who matters."

I reach up to scratch the spot where a pin is digging into my scalp, but I hastily drop my hand before I can knock something out of place. "I really shouldn't be here," I say for the dozenth time that day. "It's Maisie's moment, not mine, and I barely know anyone—"

Suddenly a full-length mirror only a few feet from the couch swings open, and Maisie hurries inside. She's wearing the long gold gown she modelled two weeks ago, and somehow it looks even more stunning than before.

"What a day," she says in a rush, touching the base of the glittering tiara on her head. It's slightly bigger than mine – I wouldn't be surprised if that's why Maisie chose it – and it's strikingly regal and perfect for a future queen. "I decided to stay at the hospital longer than my schedule allowed, and naturally it threw everything off. Oh, Evan, you look *gorgeous*."

My irritation at her tardiness fades, and I fold my arms self-consciously. "Thanks. You do, too. Gold is your colour."

"Your Royal Highness." Tibby, now on her feet in her own sleek silver dress, curtsies deeply to my half-sister. In theory, I should follow suit, but as long as I still have my American passport, the rebellious colonial side of me refuses. "Evangeline was just telling me that she shouldn't be here, since it's your moment, not hers."

"Don't be ridiculous," says Maisie, striding towards me and

ignoring my glare as she loops her arm in mine. "It's your birthday, too, and I won't have you spending it alone watching one of those insipid vampire shows on Netflix."

"What if that's how I want to spend my birthday?" I say, only mostly joking. "I don't need a party, and I don't know anyone other than the family, anyway."

"You're coming with me, and that's a royal command," she says haughtily. "I'm never going to be able to repay you for what you've done for me, but I'd very much appreciate it if you'd let me try."

I open my mouth to argue, but at that moment, a tall young man with flaming-red hair rushes through the door. "There you are, Your Royal Highness," he says to Maisie in a chiding voice, even as he lowers his head in a bow. "We're late."

"Evan, this is Fitz, my private secretary," says Maisie airily. "Fitz, have you met my sister?"

"Er – I haven't had the pleasure," he says, bowing to me as well, and a blush creeps over my face.

"You really don't need to—" I begin, but Maisie is already sweeping me out into the red-carpeted corridor and towards the other side of the wing, where the guests await.

The double doors of the ballroom stand open, and as we walk down the gallery towards them, my heart is in my throat. Most of the people near the entrance look to be middle-aged, and I don't recognize a single one of them.

"Relax," murmurs Maisie, squeezing my arm. "They're going to love you."

That's a massive overstatement, and as we step up to the threshold, a man dressed in a fancy uniform announces us.

Or, rather, announces Maisie. My name feels like little more than an afterthought.

Still, a hush falls over the party as everyone turns towards us. Maisie's painfully tight grip on my arm is somehow comforting, and as we walk into the room, those around us all bow and curtsy in a dip that seems to ripple through the crowd. It has nothing to do with me, of course – they're all greeting their future monarch – but my stomach is still in knots, and I've never felt more out of place in my life.

"Your Royal Highness," says a man in a white-tie tuxedo, and he bows deeply to my sister. "Miss Bright. Allow me to wish you both the happiest of birthdays."

"Thank you, Prime Minister," says Maisie with all the warmth and grace of a born diplomat. "I was honoured to receive the bouquet you sent this morning. And allow me to offer a belated congratulations to you and Priscilla. It was a pleasure watching Galavant's Grit win the Gold Cup."

"Ah, yes, of course you were there," says the prime minister, clearly enormously pleased with himself and what I assume to be his horse. "I left Priscilla with Their Majesties a few minutes ago. She's still basking in the glory of Galavant's win, and she'll talk your ear off about it if you let her."

"I'd like nothing more," says Maisie. And as the prime minister steps back, another man I've never seen before approaches us and bows. Without missing a beat, my half-sister greets him by name and asks about his son.

Even though I can feel the crowd's stares and curious glances, no one offers me more than a brief "happy birthday". It's probably for the best, considering where their inevitable questions would lead, and if I hear the name *Jasper Cunningham* even once tonight, I might actually scream. Instead, I'm perfectly fine with watching in awe as Maisie addresses the guests by name and asks them specific questions. I don't know if she's been coached or if she really does remember all of these people and the details of their lives, but either way, it's the most impressive thing I've seen since arriving in London.

At last, after what must be forty minutes of this, Alexander steps into view. The crowd seems to orbit him like he's the sun, staying a respectful distance away without actually leaving his gravity. And while he still looks like my thin, unremarkable, slightly balding father, he radiates an invisible power that leaves no question he's the most important person in the room.

"Happy birthday, darlings," he says, and he leans forward to kiss both of my cheeks before doing the same to Maisie. "Are you enjoying yourselves?"

"Immensely," says Maisie cheerfully. "I think Evangeline could use a break from her heels, though. Would it be terribly rude if I asked you to excuse us?"

"My feet are fine," I insist, even though that is definitely a lie, but Alexander ignores my protest.

"Of course," he says to Maisie, and there's a strange glint in his eye. "Take all the time you need. One wouldn't want your poor feet to suffer."

With that, Maisie hooks her arm through mine again, as if I'm not allowed to be anywhere but at her side, and she makes a beeline for the nearest door. She's moving so fast that I really do stumble trying to keep up with her, but as soon as we pass into the magnificent gallery that connects the ballroom to the

354

rest of the second floor, she slows.

"Whew," she says, brushing an imaginary bead of sweat from her forehead. "I thought we'd never make it out of there."

"What was that about?" I say, glancing over my shoulder. The door is still open, and several of the guests in their white-tie finery are watching us, but we turn a corner and cut off their prying stares. "I'm not going to pretend I won't have a blister or two in the morning, but I really am okay—"

"You," says Maisie, "are *utterly* guileless."

I'm not sure if that's a compliment, an insult, or both, and I'm too puzzled to come up with a witty response anyway. Instead of stopping in one of the opulent drawing rooms, like I expect, Maisie leads me down the entire length of the gallery. In the distance, I hear the faint thrum of music that would make the hair on those middle-aged politicians' toupees stand up, and I frown. "Where are we going?"

"To the real party, of course," she says, flashing me a mischievous smile. "You didn't think I'd put up with that stuffy affair all evening, did you?"

Two footmen standing at attention reach for a set of double doors as we approach, opening them for us in perfect unison. The blast of a Kesha song and strobing rainbow lights greet us, and before I know what's happening, a wall of voices ring out.

"Surprise!"

Maisie's hand flies to her chest with the same dismal acting skills she displayed in Ben's suite, but even though she clearly knew what was happening, I'm floored. More than a hundred people in their teens and twenties gather in the throne room, which has been turned into a nightclub, complete with a disco ball and a DJ in a space helmet. As Gia and Rosie rush forward to hug Maisie, I take in the black-clad servers carrying trays of neon drinks, golden fountains of what I think might be chocolate, a long wall made entirely of pink and white roses, and the giant tiered cake that sits at the front of the room, only inches from the thrones. I've seen plenty of over-the-top parties before – mostly fictional, admittedly – but this blows them all out of the water.

"This is *wild*," I say, turning back to my sister, but Rosie is already sweeping her into the throng of tipsy blue bloods and celebrities. Gia trails a few steps behind, however, and when our eyes meet, she looks me up and down, not bothering to hide her judgmental gaze.

"You haven't got the poise to pull off that gown, and your make-up isn't doing you any favours," she says. "But…the tiara suits you."

"Thanks," I manage warily, not entirely sure how to respond. "You look nice, too. And, uh – thank you for talking to Maisie about the…you know. Whatever you said to her helped."

Gia shrugs. "Someone has to tell her when she's being an arse." Despite her dry tone, she offers me the barest hint of a smile. "I'll see you around. Try not to cause any international incidents tonight, yeah?"

"But that's half the fun," I joke. And although Gia follows Maisie onto the dance floor without another word, I swear I see her smirk.

On my own now, I linger near the doorway, hoping I don't look as awkward as I feel. I stand up a bit straighter and smooth the front of my dress, as if that'll somehow make me look like I belong, though of course it doesn't change a thing. Like the crowd in the ballroom, everyone here is a stranger to me, and other than a few shameless gawkers, none of them seem interested in changing that.

But then, almost as if he materializes out of thin air, I see the face I've been unconsciously searching for since I arrived at Buckingham Palace, and my heart skips a beat. His tux is perfectly tailored, his wavy dark hair perfectly dishevelled, and his chocolate-brown eyes are perfectly focused on me.

Kit.

"Happy birthday, Evan," he says over the music, and even though I'm not an official member of the royal family, he dips his head in a bow. "You look incredible."

"Thank you," I say, my throat tight. I haven't seen Kit in person since accusing him of selling my secrets to the press, and I ache in his presence. "Where…how have you been?"

"I've been all right," he says with a small smile and a familiar hint of amusement. "And as for where, I considered following Maisie's orders and lying low at a hotel for a few days, but I decided to visit my mother instead. She's doing better than I thought," he adds. "She's not entirely well, but she is trying."

"Good – I'm really glad to hear that," I say, excruciatingly aware of how trite I sound. Even though there's only a couple of feet between us, it feels like an ever-expanding gulf. "We missed you. I missed you."

"I missed you, too," he says with unmistakable sincerity, and I don't understand how I ever thought he was the one leaking my secrets to the press. His gaze flickers up to the diamonds sewn into my hair, and he raises his eyebrows. "Is that the Queen Florence tiara?"

I nod and touch it self-consciously, making sure I haven't knocked it askew somehow. "Alexander said she willed it to me. Which doesn't make sense, but—"

"It makes perfect sense," he says, cutting through my nerves with his calm steadfastness. "It's stunning. Though not as stunning as you."

My face grows hot, and I'm sure I'm blushing again. By now the other partygoers have migrated onto the dance floor in the middle of the room, giving Kit and me some semblance of privacy, but I still step away from the double doors. "It's nice," I agree, "but it's not my favourite tiara."

I hold out my wrist, showing him the new charm attached to my bracelet. Kit takes one look at it and laughs. "You have terrible taste."

"Probably, but that's nothing new." I glance down at the tiny crystals as they catch the rainbow lights. "It's my good luck charm."

"Oh?" he says curiously. "What sort of good luck are you hoping for tonight?"

I roll the minature tiara between my fingers, taking a deep breath as I gather my courage. "I have to apologize to someone," I admit. "Someone I really care about. I accused him of something horrible, and it was wrong of me – *completely* wrong of me – and I'm not sure it'll ever be the same between us. Which makes me sick to my stomach, because…" I hesitate. "He's the best thing that's happened to me in a really, really long time, and I can't stand the thought of losing him."

Kit gazes down at me, a faint frown tugging at his lips. "You didn't believe me, did you?"

"Believe you? About—"

"About still being here when it was over," he says, and a shiver runs down my spine. "As long as you let me stay, I'm not going anywhere."

I stare at him, bewildered. "I said some pretty awful things to you."

"You were hurting," he says. "We all say some pretty awful things when we're in pain."

"But – I accused you of—"

"Evan." He offers me his hands, and I only waver a moment before taking them. "If it helps, I will happily and wholeheartedly accept your apology. But from where I stand, there's no need for one in the first place. I'm so very sorry you've had to go through this. I know you don't need anyone to fight your battles for you, but I want to be there for it all. As a friend, as a supporter, as…a companion. In any capacity you'll have me. Though…" Now it's his turn to hesitate, and I swear my heart stops. "I will admit to hoping for the opportunity to be something more, if you're willing, once you've had time to heal."

I feel infinitely more unsteady in my heels than I did two minutes ago, and I tighten my grip on his hands, acutely aware of the eyes that are turning our way. I don't let go, though, and neither does Kit. "Do you really mean that?" I say, my voice low.

"Yes," he says, matching my tone. "Unequivocally, yes. But only if it's something you want, too."

I do want it. I want it more than practically anything else in the world. As I open my mouth to say so, however, I falter yet again. "My life here is never going to be easy," I say at last. "It's already chaotic and overwhelming and – and a giant mess, and there's a good chance it'll stay that way. I know you think I'm worth it, but I'm not. I'm really, *really* not. If the press finds out we're – whatever we are, they'll target you, and—"

"Let them," he says. "My parents know how to protect themselves, and they've already allowed my brother's battle to define their future. I refuse to let it define mine."

I don't know what to say to that. After everything the media has put me through, I can't in good conscience drag anyone else into it, especially someone like Kit. Someone good and kind and thoughtful, who doesn't deserve any of the hellfire the press would rain down on him if he dared to get publicly tangled up with me.

But I can't look away from him, either.

Before I know what I'm doing, I lean forward and brush my lips against his, not caring who might be watching. Part of me expects him to pull away. I wouldn't blame him, and no matter how sure he is, I don't think I'll ever be able to completely silence the niggling doubts in the back of my mind.

Kit knows exactly what he wants, though – he has this whole time. And as he kisses me in return, every bit as gentle as he always is, I think I might finally believe him.

Chapter Thirty-six

Evangeline Bright, illegitimate daughter of the King, has announced her first patronage.

While normally this privilege is reserved for actual members of the royal family, Evangeline seems to be taking a perverse amount of delight in flaunting her new spot on the social ladder. In addition to wearing the Queen Florence tiara to Princess Mary's birthday ball – which caused a very mixed reaction among fans and detractors alike – Buckingham Palace confirmed yesterday that she's been given a place at Oxford, no doubt stolen from another, far worthier student. The nine-time expellee will reportedly take a gap year to focus on what a palace insider has dubbed "necessary social training".

Her choice of patronage, for the few of you who may be curious, is the deeply predictable Open Arms Foundation, which supports children who've been affected by mental illness in their home life. Considering Evangeline reportedly refused to answer any questions about her mad mother, Laura Bright, during her interview with Katharine O'Donnell last week, royal watchers have called the move "tacky" and "attention-seeking", and one can only hope that she doesn't bring more harm to the children who rely on the foundation.

With Evangeline set to make her first public appearance at Wimbledon today alongside lifelong tennis fan Princess Mary, we can only wonder which blunder she'll commit next.

—*The Regal Record*, 6 July 2023

As the Range Rover pulls up to the side entrance of the All England Club, my head is spinning and my limbs are numb. Through tinted windows, I see the hundreds of people who've gathered behind the ropes that line the pathway into the stadium, and I can hear their cheers as we roll to a stop.

"Remember, selfies are strictly prohibited," says Tibby from the front seat, where she's clutching her ever-present tablet and a pair of designer sunglasses. "They'll beg and plead, but the answer is always no. Hugs are also discouraged, and absolutely *no* public displays of affection between the pair of you," she adds, glaring at Kit, who sits beside me on the leather bench. "And for God's sake, Evan, keep your knees together while getting out of the car. If you give the paparazzi a shot up your skirt, I will quit on the spot."

"Right," I say, my mouth dry as the driver hurries over to open my door. "Knees together, no selfies, and keep our hands to ourselves."

I manage the first part well enough as I climb out of the vehicle. A blinding series of flashes explode from the press pool, but I plaster a smile on my face and pretend I don't notice. Ahead of us, Maisie gracefully exits her Range Rover in a mint-green sundress, and she practically skips with excitement as she goes

362

to greet her fans. Fitz and Gia follow, but they keep their distance while Her Royal Highness works her magic.

Though the crowd is mostly focused on my sister, more than a few pairs of eyes are trained on me. I flex my trembling hands into fists, feeling like my heels are rooted to the pavement. I don't know who these strangers are. They could hate me, or think I'm a delinquent or a murderer or any of the other horrible things anonymous commenters are still saying about me and probably always will. But no matter what insults the public throws at me, I'm under strict orders to take it all with a smile.

"You can do this," says Kit in my ear. "Look at them – they're excited to meet you."

"They're excited to meet Maisie," I say quietly. "They just have to put up with me, too."

"Lucky them," he murmurs, and even though he's behind me, I can hear his smile.

I take a deep breath and will myself forward. Technically I don't have to talk to anyone if I don't want to, even though Tibby insists that'll get me labelled as uppity and unfriendly. So long as I smile and wave, I can walk past the crowd as quickly as possible and let my sister handle her well-wishers. I can't avoid the inevitable glares and jeers completely, but at least this way, they won't last long.

I've taken three steps when my name starts to echo in the crowd. "Evangeline!" shouts a female voice, and then another, younger this time – *"Evangeline!"*

Against my better judgment, I turn towards the rope, bracing myself for what's to come. But instead of sneers, all I see are eager smiles.

"Evangeline!" says a woman with a strong Scottish accent. "We came all the way down from Edinburgh to meet you, love."

"Really?" I say, genuinely stunned. "Thank you."

"We're from Cornwall," pipes a man with his arm around a thin grey-haired woman. "My mum and I watched every minute of your interview. Couldn't tear our eyes away."

"It was so brave," says the woman shakily. "So very, very brave. You remind me of my youngest, Angelica. She went through the same thing, you know, but no one believed her." I freeze, momentarily rendered speechless. Nothing in my endless hours of media training has prepared me for responding to something so personal. But I know what I'd want someone to say to me, and so I reach out and clasp her hand between mine. "I hope Angelica's doing better now," I reply. "And tell her I believe her."

The pavement stretches only thirty feet or so, but it might as well go on for ever. I inch my way down, saying hello, grasping hands, and smiling into cameras for selfies I'm not supposed to take. With Maisie working the opposite side of the crowd, we swap a few times, and I'm not completely immune to the disappointment on some faces when they're greeted by me instead. But even though I accept several small bouquets on Maisie's behalf, everyone is shockingly kind and polite. At last, when the doors to the stadium are no more than a few yards away, a little girl with her black hair in two buns ducks under the rope, clutching a handful of crimson daisies.

"Hi," I say warmly, kneeling down to look her in the eye. "Those are lovely. Are they for Mary?"

The little girl shakes her head shyly, and when she offers them to me, my heart feels like it's going to burst.

"Thank you so much," I say, taking them reverently. They really are beautiful, and I gaze at the soft petals. They're the first flowers anyone's ever given me. "What's your na—" I stop as I look up. The little girl is gone, and I climb to my feet once more, hoping to catch sight of her in the crowd. But she's disappeared without a trace.

Puzzled, I glance at the bouquet again. Nestled among the daisies is a card with *Evan* scrawled across the front in deep-red ink, stark against the creamy paper. Not Evangeline, I realize – not the name the media and the public know me by, but the nickname only the people in my life use. The nickname I insist on.

Even though there are still onlookers waiting to meet me, I step away from the barrier as I tentatively open the card. And as I read the spidery script inside, my blood runs cold.

No matter where I am in the world,
I still know your secrets. Enjoy this while it lasts.

There's no signature, but I don't need one. Even though I've never seen his handwriting before, there's only one person who would have dared to send this.

Ben.

I scan the crowd again, my smile long gone as I search for any sign of him or the little girl. All I can see is an ocean of strangers with their eyes on me, and my throat tightens with dread.

"Oh, daisies – how lovely," says Tibby from only a few inches

365

away, and I nearly jump out of my skin. "Would you like me to take those for you, Miss Bright?"

There's an edge to her voice that makes it clear this isn't a question, and once I pluck the note from its plastic holder, I fork over the bouquet. "Is it time to go inside?"

"If you can tear yourself away."

With feigned reluctance, I wave apologetically to the crowd and follow Tibby to the entrance, silently crumpling the note in my fist. Kit is waiting for me under the awning, and he must notice something is wrong, because he leans towards me until his lips nearly brush my ear.

"All right?" he whispers, and even though I nod, I can tell he isn't fooled. We lock eyes for a long moment, and as Maisie and Gia enter the stadium, he silently offers me his hand.

I hear the click of a dozen cameras and feel Tibby's hot glare on us both, but if we're going to break the rules, we might as well do it in spectacular fashion. And so I lace my fingers with his, more grateful for him than I've ever been before, and we walk through the doors together.

*More rumours
More secrets
More romance...*

Look out for

**ROYAL
SCANDAL**

For news follow

 @Usborne

 @UsborneYA

Acknowledgements

First and foremost, a huge thank-you to my agents, Rosemary Stimola and Allison Remcheck, for all you've both done to see this book – and me – to the finish line in one piece. None of this would have happened without you.

Thank you to the entire Stimola Literary Studio crew, especially Alli Hellegers and Stephen Moore, who both worked so hard to bring this book to new audiences. You're all rock stars.

Thank you to my editor, Kelsey Horton, for seeing the potential in this trilogy and for your unending enthusiasm along the way. You've been a guiding light.

Thank you to the team at Delacorte Press for taking a chance on me and this book, including Beverly Horowitz, Colleen Fellingham, Joey Ho, Jenn Inzetta, Kate Keating, Ray Shappell, and Dr Tasha M. Brown. I'm eternally grateful for your belief in this book and your hard work turning words into something real.

Thank you to my friends who not only put up with me talking endlessly about this book for three years straight, but who also took the time to read early drafts and help make it better than I ever could have on my own. Malcolm Freberg, Andrea Hannah, Sara Hodgkinson, Becca Mix, Karla Olson-Bellfi, Carli Segal, Caitlin Straw – this book exists because of your support, guidance, and ability to stay awake while I rambled on about crime scenes and tiaras and exactly how many forks the real British royal family uses at dinner.

Thank you to Lauren DeStefano, Ryan Hutchinson, Rosalina Joy, Kristin Lord, Veronica O'Neil, Meryl Wilsner, Diana Urban, and Ashley Zajac for the cheers and support along the way – I appreciate all of you so much.

Thank you to Jordan Cook for allowing me to use the very real and very excellent band Reignwolf in the book, and thank you to all of the musicians mentioned for creating the music I wrote to most days.

I'd be remiss not to acknowledge the fact that my cats and dog occasionally stayed off the keyboard long enough to let me work, so Fred, Murphy, Beau, and Pippa – maybe next time I'll keep your "edits". But probably not.

And as always, thank you to my wonderful dad for encouraging me to write from the moment I showed interest and never once asking if I could make a living off of it. Your belief is the reason I tried.